ABOUT THE AUTHOR

Emma Everitt-Story was born in London in 1988. She is an old soul who, at thirty-one years old, is already too set in her ways to learn about new technology, much to the frustration of her eleven-year-old son! She will always be socially awkward, and although life may have taught her to hide her anxieties beneath the veneer of a confident, approachable adult, deep down she is still reliving that time when she was twelve and she went to collect a creative writing award in a whole school assembly and tripped over on her way up to the stage.

Samantha Drury's Secret Diary: Emotional Ghost Train

Emma Everitt-Story

Samantha Drury's Secret Diary: Emotional Ghost Train

Vanguard Press

A CIP catalogue record for this title is
available from the British Library.

ISBN 978 1 78465 782 6
*Vanguard Press is an imprint of
Pegasus Elliot MacKenzie Publishers Ltd.*

www.pegasuspublishers.com

First Published in 2020

**Vanguard Press
Sheraton House Castle Park
Cambridge England**

Printed & Bound in Great Britain

Dedication

To Taylan, who always kept me on track.

Sunday 6th September 2020

WEATHER WARNING: STORM STEPHANIE IS HERE!

One family tries to keep its feet on the ground as the winds of change bring a sister twister their way. We hope that no homes are destroyed as Storm Stephanie rages, but only time will tell what level of destruction she will leave in her wake.

Today we had the shock of our lives. None of us saw it coming. She could have called ahead, at least! Maybe she thought Dad would do a runner if she gave him the chance. He wouldn't have because he's a good father. Yes, he's immature, but he's not irresponsible. Well, I suppose he is, a little bit, to have allowed this to happen. And I guess it was irresponsible of him to have the affair in the first place. Or am I confusing irresponsibility with dishonesty? He knew what he was doing, he didn't accidentally begin a relationship with Sophie. But he did accidentally have a baby with her.

So, Stephanie is my new half-sister, and it appears she's here to stay. Not stay with Dad but stay in our lives. I'm still getting my head round it; I can only imagine what's going through Dad's mind! After Sophie brought her round this morning and turned our lives upside down, she sat in the kitchen and had a long (private) talk with Dad while my brother, Frogsplash, and I sat watching Stephanie in the living room with Dad's flatmate Richard. Dad was supposed to take us home at midday but, given the circumstances, we decided not to remind him of it until after Sophie and Stephanie had left.

After their private talk, Dad and Sophie came in to chat with us. Stephanie is going to visit Dad every other weekend, just like Frogsplash and I do. They said we could make it so that we visited at the same time, so that we could get to know Stephanie, or we could alternate weekends if we didn't feel comfortable with that. They kind of put us on the spot a bit there, if I'm honest, because this was a huge decision that we'd had no time to think about, and yet it was set to affect us for the rest of our lives. It wasn't a hard decision though. I've got a sister now, and I want her in my life, no matter how many times she sucks on crisps and then puts them back in the sharing bowl (five times... I saw her do it five times).

She's two years old and I have to admit she's a little cutie. She has wisps of golden blonde hair and big blue eyes, and she has a wonderful glowing smile. It's really easy to make her laugh, and the only time she cried is when Sophie tried to strap her in the buggy to go home. She can walk and talk and by the end of her visit I'd taught her my name – "Samantha" was a bit of a mouthful, so she just calls me Sam. Likewise, "Frogsplash" proved a bit too tricky so she calls him Frog, although I think that confused her a little bit. I don't blame her, he's almost sixteen years old, he should probably go back to being Fred sometime soon!

Dad drove us home at around two p.m. and he couldn't stop apologising to us for being so late. His time-keeping is never great, and he usually doesn't even seem to notice, but I guess he was worried that we might think that this means he's going to start prioritising Stephanie over us. I'm not worried, though, Dad's been prioritising work over us for years. No, I've had all day to think this over now, and I'm quite sure this is happy news. It's certainly a shock, but change is good. If things never changed life would be so dull, wouldn't it? And anyway, it's nice to have new family members. Last year Mum started seeing Graham, and they're not married or anything, but I'm starting to think of him and his son Billy as family.

In fact, we had our usual family Sunday dinner earlier this evening, all five of us – seven if you include our dogs, Max and Trousers. Well, it wasn't quite the same as it normally is. Mum was rather shaken by the news about Stephanie, and when Mum's in a mood like that she goes into roast mode. She gets this inexorable urge to cook a roast. It's some kind of comfort thing, but who wants hearty comfort food in early September? We were meant to have a barbecue, but that's normally Graham's job. Mum throws together a salad and us kids get the sauces and burger buns out, then we chill in the garden while Graham cooks all the meat. But today Mum insisted on cooking everything. I'm starting to think that she might be the one person who's not happy about Stephanie coming into our lives.

Graham was clearly anxious about the situation, so he checked on Mum frequently under the pretence of topping up her glass of home-brewed wine. She accepted his beverage offerings but refused to accept any help with the barbecue, much to Graham's frustration. By the time dinner was served, thanks to Graham's incessant refills, Mum was well past tipsy, and we were all starving. We were so hungry, in fact, that we didn't stop to speak and ate in semi-silence for at least ten minutes, occasionally stopping to breathe or compliment Mum on her first attempt at cooking a barbecue for the whole family. We gave some chicken scraps to Max and Trousers, but I guess they didn't like the smell of the spicy marinade, because they didn't devour it like they usually do.

Once we had eaten almost everything we began to slow down, only picking at bits of food because they were on our plates. The meal was done and all of us had things to do because tomorrow is the first day back at school. But there was a sense that we shouldn't leave the table, because although Mum was becoming more loquacious, there was something that was not being said. She was talking almost constantly; the rest of us couldn't get a word in edgeways.

Oh god... she's gearing up for something big. All that home brew has been brewing inside her! She's a ticking time bomb. Graham and Billy have no idea what's about to go off!

"So how does it feel to have a new baby sister all of a sudden?" she asked.

Oh brother, we must tread carefully.

"Um… it's just… very strange. It's such a shock," I said delicately.

"Yeah," Frogsplash agreed when Mum locked her eyes on him expectantly, "it hasn't really sunk in yet. It's mad, isn't it? Must be even madder for Dad!"

Oh dear…

"Hmm," said Mum falsely, "Yes… one must empathise with your father during these difficult times. Although… do you *really* think he had no idea?"

"Trust me, Mum, he was in total shock," Froggo said.

"Right, sure…" Mum said disbelievingly, "and what's she like?"

"Oh, you know, a regular two-year-old: blonde hair, dribbles a lot…" I said.

"No, no, I meant Sophie. What's *she* like?"

(Here's where Graham and Billy started to look really uncomfortable.)

"Oh," I replied hesitantly when the silence became too heavy. "Well, we didn't really see much of her. Obviously she and Dad had a lot to talk about in private."

"But you must have been there when she first walked in... what was she *like?*"

"Um... she seemed... nice," I said out of a loss for anything else to say.

BIG MISTAKE!

"Oh... NICE! NICE? A woman who destroys a family and then keeps a baby a secret from its father for TWO YEARS seems NICE?!"

"Well... I mean, obviously she's done some really bad things..."

"Oh, I'm sorry, Sammy!" Mum said, "It's not your fault; I shouldn't be interrogating you! It's just such a shock. She's like this horrible ghost from my past that I thought would be gone forever. I was terrified that she and your dad would stay together, and she'd end up being your step-mum. I don't care about your dad any more, but knowing that woman is part of your lives now... it was my worst nightmare and it's come back to haunt me!"

"She's not though, Mum, honestly. It's just about Stephanie. Dad doesn't like Sophie any more and I don't think she likes him much either."

"I suppose you're right," she said, "I'm sorry for getting emotional – too much wine!"

"That's all right, Cassie," Graham cut in. "It's a huge shock. Suddenly your kids have got this new part of their lives that doesn't include you – and it's come from nowhere!"

"I just don't want anything to change between us lot," Mum said. "This is such a happy home now."

"It won't, Mum," said Frogsplash, "we promise."

Monday 7th September 2020

4am:
We are the house of the living dead. Barbecue. Chicken. Food poisoning. So much for the first day back at school.

4pm:
It has transpired that Mum is the only one who didn't touch the chicken. She was so worked up about all her emotional "ghosts from the past" that she barely ate anything. So now she's nursing the rest of us back to health (and nursing a pretty bad hangover) and apologising profusely. She's intermittently apologising for getting upset last night and apologising for nearly killing us slowly with chicken. Honestly, I just want to recover in peace, but her guilt seems to be insatiable and she keeps infringing rudely upon my convalescence just so that she can apologise again! If anything, she should be apologising for apologising, but if I tell her that these apologies are bothering me, she'll only bother me with more apologies!

I've slept for most of the day and only woke up half an hour ago to discover a string of worried texts from my best friends, Danny and Carla, asking why I wasn't in school. I feel weak right now, but I'm determined to go back in tomorrow – I have so much to tell them! Besides, I'd rather be at school with my friends than at home with Mum. The pain in my stomach is nothing compared to the irritation of an overbearing mother. It has been a dreadful first day of year eight. I hope that this is not a prelibation.

Tuesday 8th September 2020

NATURAL PHENOMENON:
PRE-TEENAGE NUISANCE PYGMY TURTLES!

Marine biologists are baffled by the sudden appearance of a vast quantity of young miniature turtles washed up on the playground of a local school. The strange creatures have small bodies with enormous shells on their backs which are, according to scientists, disproportionately heavy for the tiny terrapins. They flock in large, chaotic groups and seem confused by their new habitat, often moving in a disorderly manner which interferes with the native species, making it difficult for them to go about their regular routine.

The new year sevens seem to be everywhere, and they don't seem to have a clue where they're supposed to be or how to get there. They all look so tiny! I can't believe I was that small only a year ago. They all seem to be wearing these enormous backpacks – some of which are bigger than the child who's wearing it! I don't remember my bag ever being that big. The problem is, they don't seem to be *aware* that they're carrying these huge things on their backs, because every time one of them turns around their bag swings around behind them and whacks into you. I'm going to be covered in bruises tomorrow.

I had to pick up my timetable from the office because I missed them being handed out in form time yesterday. I noticed my Art teacher, Mack, was exiting the room just next to the office, which I know to belong to the school counsellor, Mr Donahue. Mack is not very good at remembering his students, at least not until they've produced a masterpiece, so he didn't say hello to me when we crossed paths. The woman at the school office looked at me disapprovingly when I explained that I had been absent yesterday, and I guessed she must have suspected that I'd been lying about the food poisoning and that I'd been returning from a late summer holiday, which is very much frowned upon.

I was pleased to see that my first lesson of the day was Biology. Year eight is the first year we get to do separate sciences, and I think I'm going to enjoy Biology more than Chemistry or Physics, mostly because it seems easier to understand. Little did I know, Biology was set to be my favourite lesson of the day.

"Sam, come sit with us!" I heard Carla's voice from somewhere in the middle row. "Can you believe it? We're all in the same class together!"

Sure enough, sat next to Carla was Danny, my other best friend. We've never had any lessons together before! I had to talk to them in short bursts, and only when the teacher wasn't looking. I told them all about the huge revelation at Dad's on Sunday, and about the wretched food poisoning courtesy of Mum, and they listened wide-eyed and attentive to my every word.

"Is there something you'd like to share with the rest of the class?" interrupted Mr Pinter, our Biology teacher.

"Oh no, we're fine thank you," Carla replied confidently.

"No, no, go ahead. It must be something really important if you're discussing it in the middle of my lesson. I think we'd all like to hear what it is."

"It is very important, sir," Carla said, "my friend here is in the middle of a family crisis. It's extremely personal. How would you feel if I asked you to share your personal family dramas with the entire class?"

The rest of the class laughed at Carla's audacity, and even Mr Pinter gave a little smile.

"A family crisis, you say. Well that does sound very interesting, but does it really have any relevance to my Biology class?"

"It might do," I said, spurred on by Carla's infectiously bold attitude, "my dad just found out he's the *biological* father of a two-year-old he never knew existed! It was a TOTAL shock. He had no idea!"

"A TOTAL shock?" Mr Pinter repeated playfully. "He had no idea. Well perhaps your dad should have paid more attention in Biology class too!"

The entire class, including me and the girls, let out a roar of laughter.

"All right, all right, settle down now. I know it's the start of term and we've all got juicy gossip that we're desperate to catch up on. What do you think we talk about in the teachers' lounge every day – our *darling* students?

Psh! We've all got our lives outside of school, but can we at least keep them outside of the classroom? Thank you."

"Samantha, can I have a word?" he said to me at the end of the lesson. Danny and Carla gave me an anxious look as they walked out behind everyone else.

"I'm sure you'd probably prefer to talk to your friends, but if you ever wanted an adult to talk to about your family worries – or anything else – you can always talk to me, or there's the school counsellor, Mr Donahue, he's very good."

Ugh. Just when I was beginning to like this teacher he has to go and make things awkward.

"Er, thanks," I said, feeling a lot less bold than when I had Carla and Danny by my side. "Can I go now?"

"Yes, go on," he said, and I was free to go and cringe all the way to the Maths department.

Most of the time, when something happens to me, the worst part is the fact that everyone thinks I want to talk about it, or that I *need* to talk about it. They want me to talk about my *feelings,* they say it's not good to keep it all "bottled up". It's painfully patronising. If that's the way they like to process things then that's fine, but why do they always think that their way is the best way for *everyone?* I know I'm perfectly capable of processing my own thoughts by myself. I have a practical mind, and I'm very good at thinking without saying things out loud. It's like reading a book – when you read out loud to an audience you don't take it in properly because part of you is concentrating on your audience and your performance. But when you read alone, in your head, you can completely absorb the content of the text. It's the same with thinking: it's best done in one's head.

I don't mind telling my friends because I think it's important to share with them the things that are going on in my life, and anyway, they don't try to force it out of me or look at me like I'm a sad case and they're my therapists! Danny and Carla are pretty much the only people who never annoy me. They're the only people I can sit in comfortable silence with, and the only people who seem to understand the difference between "alone" and "lonely". They know that when I say I want to be alone it doesn't mean I'm angry with them or that I'm sad or that there's anything wrong at all. I like being alone and they respect that.

Friday 11ᵗʰ September 2020

Wait. Just you wait until you hear about today. It was Geography and it was the last lesson before lunch. We were all a bit lackadaisical at the end of the first week back, and I don't know too many people who are enthusiastic about Geography even at the best of times. We all filed into the classroom, took our seats, and when there was still no sign of any teacher most of us began fidgeting. Some got out their pencil cases and homework diaries and started doodling, others (me) took out books to read, while others played on their phones or picked dirt out of their fingernails. Some time elapsed and the boredom gave way to suspicion.

People began to talk. Nobody volunteered to go to the office and get to the bottom of this clerical error; we all shared that one objective: to waste lesson time in whichever way we saw fit. But we all talked, because it would have been strange not to comment on the situation, and because it made it more exciting to acknowledge that we were in the mythical twilight zone, that miraculous and rare phenomenon: the unsupervised class. We began discussing the rules of the situation, for example: how much longer should we wait before we're all allowed to leave? Some were saying that if no teacher turns up within the first fifteen minutes then legally we're allowed to leave the classroom, but I can't imagine that's the sort of thing they're discussing in the House of Commons. Then we wondered what was going on: had our teacher called in sick at the last minute, and had the school not found a substitute in time?

"Who's the teacher?" someone asked.

"Mr Roberts, it says here," came the reply.

"He's new this year," said Tamara Sandy near the front of the class, "maybe he got lost or something."

"Screw this, I'm starving!" said Demetri Michael, sat right at the back, "I'm going to get lunch before the queues start."

"You idiot," said Ross Rillington two spaces from me, "they won't serve you before the lunch bell goes!"

"They will if they think I'm sixth form!"

"Sixth form don't wear uniform, numpty!"

Then suddenly, the door at the back of the classroom swung open and someone turned the light off. We were left in a dull, shadowy light and we couldn't see who was at the door. No one was at the door. The door was closed, and the mysterious figure was out of sight. Then there was shuffling. It was a man shuffling along the floor like a soldier in training, staying close to the ground whilst making his way towards the front of the room. We couldn't see his face, but the back of his head was bald, and he was dressed in beige shirt and shorts, more like a survival expert than an army soldier. He was neither stealthy nor swift, and seemed to inch his way along the dusty wood-panelled floor rather than slither or glide as I'm sure he was supposed to. He must have hoped to look like a snake or a dolphin in water, but he looked like a slug. It was worse than a slug, because it looked like he was putting a tremendous amount of effort into it. There was a painful, high-pitched screech as one of his bare knees pushed against the surface of the floor, trying to slide gracefully but instead catching and causing a nasty friction which must have been agonising.

"Did you feel that?" he gulped breathlessly, and at first I thought he was referring to the friction burn.

"Did you feel that tremor?" he said, at last reaching the front of the room, still committing himself to the hardwood floor. "That's an earthquake! There's a quake coming!"

I don't think anyone believed him. Whoever this slug man was, he had made such a poor first impression that none of us was going to take anything he said seriously, probably for the rest of the year. He was now tucked under the teacher's desk, apparently taking cover from the earthquake.

"When you feel a quake coming you must hide under your desk with your head tucked between your knees! *Come on*, everyone, get down!"

"That doesn't seem right," said Ross, who's a bit of a smart-arse. "The earthquake is coming from beneath you. Hiding under a desk won't help. In fact – you're more likely to get trapped that way. The rubble will pile on top of the desk and you'll suffocate."

"He's right," Tamara agreed, "you're thinking of bomb scares… maybe hurricanes."

Slug man didn't say anything. The silence rang out and again we all looked round at each other wondering what to do. After a solid minute someone in the front row got out of their chair, followed by a second, then a third, then a fourth person. Gradually we all got up and gathered around the front desk to look down upon the strange, cowering figure. The man was crouched on the floor with his head tucked between his knees, only by this point I don't think it was the earthquake he was hiding from. He must have made a snap decision. He jumped out. Well, not quite jumped, it was more of a clumsy clamber in which he tripped over a leg of the chair that he'd pushed out of the way to get under there. Eventually he was out and at last standing at full height.

"Surprise!" he said. "There *was* no earthquake! But you must always be prepared. And a special surprise to YOU, Samantha Drury!"

I knew why he had singled me out. My stomach did one huge somersault then leapt into my throat.

"Class let me introduce myself. I'm Mr Roberts, but you can call me Richard."

Yes. Richard. *That* Richard. I never knew his full name. Richard Roberts. The blokiest of bloke names. A bald, middle-aged, English-bloke-with-a-hairy-beer-belly sort of a name. I've seen my Geography teacher's hairy beer belly. I've seen him drunk. I've seen him cry. I've been on his shoulders at a rock concert. Richard, my dad's cringe-worthy flatmate, and now my Geography teacher.

"And we might as well get it out in the open now – I live with Samantha's dad! That's right, we're practically family! I sleep in Samantha's room. I sleep in her bed!"

There was a mixed response to that remark. Stifled sniggers, naturally, but also a lot of uncomfortable silence, like people were holding their breath, unsure how to react, whether to laugh, gasp or run screaming to a responsible adult. No one in that room considered Richard to be a responsible adult, with perhaps the exception of Richard himself.

"Of course, it's not her room any more," Richard clarified at long last, "Sam shares a room with her brother now, but sometimes I still find pairs of her knickers in my drawers!"

This is a nightmare. I must be dreaming. Nothing in real life can be this bad. Any minute now my teeth will all fall out or I'll fly out of the window and look down at the class laughing. This is all a horrible, horrible dream. It feels so real, but the worst ones always do, don't they? Why am I not waking up?

"So, we're starting the term by learning about earthquakes. Does anyone know what causes earthquakes?"

No one said anything. Some of them must have known the answer. *I* knew the answer, but no one was ready to dive straight into Geography after the entrance Richard had just made.

"I can't tell you how many times I've wanted to spill the beans," Richard said, looking at me again. Clearly he wasn't that bothered about getting into the lesson either. "When I found out I'd got the job here at Duke John Jameson I insisted upon teaching your class! How exciting is this?!"

Everyone was staring at me. How could this be happening? Didn't Dad try to stop him? I've never really liked Geography, but I never thought it could be this bad. I have a feeling this is going to be a difficult year.

Saturday 12th September 2020

Today began our first proper weekend at Dad's with Stephanie. Dad was surprisingly calm about the situation. It's been ten years since I was two, but he seems to think he remembers it all with crystal clarity.

"You were an easy child," he was saying as he lounged on the sofa while I cleared the coffee table of wine glasses, scissors, paracetamol tablets and other potential hazards. "You were always so calm and quiet, and you loved playing alone. You'd spend hours and hours perfectly happy in your own company. Sometimes you'd be so silent that I'd have a sudden fit of panic thinking that you'd fallen down the stairs or suffocated yourself with a plastic bag, then I'd go running up to your room and there you'd be, minding your own business, blissfully wrapped up in your own little world."

I don't know how old I was when Dad was leaving me completely unattended for these long stretches of time, but I'm glad I'm here now to supervise his care of Stephanie. When she arrived, it was a little bit awkward between him and Sophie, and I guessed that they must have argued a bit last time she was here, or perhaps over the phone during the week. I suppose I'd be angry if someone had waited two years to tell me I had a child, but she must have had her reasons. Anyway, she said an anxious goodbye to Stephanie, offloaded a huge amount of baby paraphernalia and was gone, leaving us alone with the tiny hurricane.

Dad and I led her towards the living room, where Frogsplash was watching one of those shows where ex-footballers sit around commenting on current football, usually with some celebrity guests and a bunch of daft challenges and sketches. It never ceases to amaze me how much time people can spend talking about football, and how many people enjoy watching them talking about football on TV. Dad and Froggo both love that sort of stuff and I rarely get a say in what programme we watch, and even when I do I have to listen to them complain or mock the shows that I like to the point where I can no longer enjoy watching them. So, when Stephanie picked up the remote and started pressing random buttons it occurred to me that she might just be the little angel I need to re-shift the balance of power in Dad's flat.

"Dad don't let her play with the remote! She'll change all the settings!" Frogsplash said.

"I think she just wants to watch something else," I said gleefully.

"But I was watching that! I'll let her put something else on after... hasn't she got some toys to play with?"

"Normally I'd be on your side, mate," Dad said apologetically, "but this is her first visit and I need her to enjoy it. If she doesn't have fun she might not want to come back!"

"Uh, fine!" Froggo said, and he huffed off to our room moodily.

"What would you like to watch?" I asked Stephanie, scrolling through the kids' channels and reading out the titles of the shows. "There's *Yoga Tots... Numbertumble... All Aboard the Rainbow Bus! The Pirates of Pickle Lane...* do you like that one? No, no, OK... there's *Dotty Dancing, Barry Bumble's Boat, Animals of the Forever Forest...*"

"Forever Forest!" she repeated excitedly. We have a winner. I changed the channel and settled down on the sofa with Stephanie, who was instantly transfixed by the TV. The Forever Forest appeared to be a verdant land with a few sparse trees. It must have been filmed on set, because the grass looked like it was made out of felt and the trees were clearly plastic. The animals were people dressed in full body suits who spoke in a sort of simplified semi-English. In this episode, Mr Fox was troubled by the falling of a single brown leaf from one of the plastic trees. Mr Fox seemed to think that the tree was broken.

"What's that, Mr Fox?" the narrator asked. "Oh, I see. The leaf has fallen from the tree."

(The narrator was very good at filling in the gaps whenever the narrative was unclear. And also, when it was very plainly obvious what was happening.)

Mr Fox went looking for his friends, Mr Badger, Mr Rabbit, Mrs Squirrel and Little Miss Mouse. He showed them the leaf and, with the help of the narrator, conveyed his distress to his fellow woodland creatures (he did not seem the least bit interested in hunting and eating any of them). They, too, began to feel concern, and then a gust of wind blew by and a whole shower of leaves fell from a nearby tree, and let me tell you, the Animals of the Forever Forest were not at all prepared for this turn of events. Little Miss Mouse was utterly disconsolate, Mrs Squirrel was apoplectic, Mr Rabbit was in a state of severe consternation and I could tell Mr Badger was contemplating suicide.

"What's the matter, Mr Fox?" the narrator asked when Mr Fox started chugging on a bottle of cheap whisky in the Forever Forest's only gutter, allowing the depression to spiral rapidly. "Are you worried that the Forever Forest might not last forever?"

Mr Fox nodded dolefully.

"Perhaps you should go and see the Wise Old Oak," said the narrator, "he might be able to help."

And, as I'm sure you can guess, the animals visited a talking tree which explained to them what autumn is and that was that. Stephanie was very keen to watch another episode, so I left her to it and went to help Dad unpack her things.

(I made up the bit about the cheap whisky, by the way.)

Dad was in his room trying to set up the travel cot, which we eventually figured out together, then we took her feeding bag to the kitchen to unpack that. There were beakers and plastic forks and carrot-flavoured snacks with zero added salt and, right at the bottom was a huge box of chocolates with a label addressing it to me and Frogsplash (sort of).

Dear Samantha and Frogspawn,

I'm terribly sorry for intruding on your weekend last Sunday, I hadn't expected you to be at the flat when I arrived. Thank -you for being so understanding and for accepting Stephanie into your lives. I hope you enjoy getting to know your sister, and I hope she doesn't cause too much trouble!

Love,
Sophie.

It was a very thoughtful surprise, and it made me wonder how Sophie was feeling. She probably feels really guilty. First she breaks up our family, then she deprives us of a sister for two precious years! But the truth is, I don't hate her. I can understand why Mum would hate her, and Dad has every right to be angry with her, but I just feel sort of neutral towards her.

I don't really know her, and I don't really know the motives behind her past actions. I don't see her as the woman who destroyed our family; for one thing that was Dad's choice, but also I don't feel like anything was destroyed. We are all still breathing, and we're all happy.

I walked through the living room, where Stephanie was watching Mrs Squirrel having trouble putting the three squirrel children to bed, walked down the hall and knocked on Frogsplash's door, which is technically our shared door, but we have a strict mutual knocking policy as part of the sibling code.

"Come in," he said in monotone.

"Sophie gave us these chocolates," I said. "They're to thank us for welcoming Stephanie into our lives. You should really come out and get to know her – she's family now."

I don't know whether it was me or the chocolates, but something drove him to get up off the bed and come into the living room and sit on the sofa with me and Stephanie.

"Look what your mummy left for us!" I said to Stephanie, and once her eyes had flickered over the chocolate box she lost all interest in *Animals of the Forever Forest.*

"Dad! Is she allowed chocolate?" I called to the kitchen.

"Ooh, chocolate!" Dad said, poking his head in the door. "Yeah, why not? She's old enough."

"What if they contain nuts?" I asked worriedly.

"Oh, she'll be fine! When you were her age your favourite food was mashed banana and peanut butter."

"Ugh! Gross! Still, we better make sure she chooses one that's not too chewy or full of coffee…"

"OK, you can have one, Stephanie, just bring the box over to me," Dad said as he sat down in the armchair. Stephanie slid off her seat carrying the box, then she took off the lid and walked towards Dad. Rather than give him the box, though, she held it in front of him and said:

"You can have one."

"Oh, OK," Dad said, "thank you," and he picked the coffee one.

She came back around to me. "You can have one," she said again, so I took the chewy toffee and thanked her.

Next she went to Frogsplash. "You can have one." He took the hazelnut cream and thanked her.

"Now I can have one," she said, and she took the vanilla fudge and ate it. Then she went back around. First to Dad, "You can have one," she said. He took one. Then to Froggo, "You can have one…"

"What a sweet, generous girl!" Dad said, in awe of the little cherub.

"You see what she's doing, don't you?" I said as I took the dark cherry swirl. "She knows she can always have one as long as everyone else does. She knows we can't say no to her if we've each had one ourselves."

"Don't be daft!" Dad said. "She's only two years old! She can't possibly have that level of forethought! Sophie must have told her about the box of chocolates and reminded her to hand them out politely. She just wanted Stephanie to make a good impression!"

"Now I can have one!" Stephanie said, and, ever so briefly, I saw the look of evil genius flash across her eyes.

Oh, Dad, this one's going to run rings around you.

Just then Richard returned from whatever overnight exploit had kept him out of the house since before our arrival.

"Well, if it isn't my star pupil!" he said when he saw me sat on the sofa. "Gave you quite the surprise yesterday, didn't I?"

Of course, by this point I had told Dad and Froggo all about that fateful Geography lesson. Dad found it particularly entertaining because he's been suffering through Richard's latest phase: survivalist training. Richard carries a compass and a penknife wherever he goes, and last night he went camping alone in a nearby wood.

"It was an adventure!" he told us proudly. "I was terrified, but I was determined to see it through. There were noises… horrifying, gut-churning noises… things that would make your skin crawl."

"Wow, really?" said Froggo. "Like what? Were there wolves? Foxes? Deer?"

"Teenagers," said Richard in all seriousness. "Out on a Friday night, drinking and smoking… there must have been seven of them, at least!"

"Wow – really?!" Dad asked sarcastically. "Did they approach you? What did you do to defend yourself?"

"Well, they didn't approach me per se," Richard replied. "But we did come to cross paths during one of my toilet breaks… there I was squatting by a tree when two young lovers should come my way. I was expertly camouflaged, so they couldn't see me…"

"Why were you squatting?" Frogsplash asked innocently. "You're a man, you can do it standing up!"

"Ah yes, well – it was more of a *solid* toilet break."

Ew.

"So, there I was, on one side of the tree, and they were approaching from the other side. It was very dark, and I was having some trouble finding enough leaves of a decent size, then I heard these two talking and giggling – a girl and a boy. I made an aural assessment to determine the threat level of the situation and, given their light spirits and the way in which they were too distracted with each other to notice me, I decided there was no need for me to instigate a display of self-defence, despite my extensive training in the martial arts. I was still searching for smooth, flat, large leaves, preferably with a high absorbency and soft, quilted texture, when I heard them leaning heavily on the other side of the tree, passionately kissing each other. I had given up my search for leaves and decided to rough it out nature-style, so I got to my feet and attempted to pull up my trousers…"

By this point we were all cringing so hard on Richard's behalf it was almost impossible to comprehend his willingness to share this story with us. But that's Richard for you.

"The young couple must have heard me rustling on the dry leaves underfoot, because they immediately exited their embrace and crept cautiously around the tree trunk to investigate the source of the disturbance. I attempted to circle the tree as swiftly as they did, cork-screwing around it like a squirrel under the watch of a dog, but my trousers were barely above my knees, and these young, agile creatures were quick to catch up with me. At last they caught me in plain sight, with both underwear and trousers pulled down. The only thing that was left in my power was to assume the threat stance, so as to scare off these younger, fitter opponents whilst in that vulnerable position. They ran screaming; my mastery of the threat stance had overcome the virility of their youth."

What a lovely woodland adventure. I wonder how the Animals of the Forever Forest would have coped with *that* chain of events. I can almost hear Mrs Squirrel's screams. Stephanie began to grow restless, probably from eating too much sugar, and she started to charge around the flat at an incredible speed for someone who's only just learnt to walk.

"Maybe we should take her out somewhere," I suggested.

"We can't," Dad said, "I've got no buggy, no car seat, and there's not a playground anywhere for miles around."

"There must be!" I said. "There's always a playground nearby."

"Trust me, the only ones around here are rusty old death traps where teenagers go when they want to escape their parents. Even I'd be scared to go near them," Dad said.

"There's no such thing as fear, Duncan," Richard said helpfully, "only weakness and failure. You don't have to be afraid if you're strong, and there's no need to fear anything unless you fail to prepare. You know what to do if you fail to prepare?"

"Prepare to fail?" Dad said irritably.

"Exactly!" said Richard. "If you go in there with a pocketknife and a mobile phone with 999 already typed into the keypad then you can handle any situation."

"There you go!" I said, "Richard can come with us!"

After hearing Richard's tale of blunders with the teenagers last night I was very keen to see how he handled the teenage gangs of the local area.

"Great," Richard said, a little half-heartedly, "I'll show you how it's done. Just give me a minute to fuel up on trail mix…"

So, Richard went squirreling in the kitchen cupboards while we got Stephanie ready. Under any normal circumstances I'm sure Frogsplash would have stayed behind and watched the Saturday game, but apparently he, too, couldn't resist the idea of seeing bald, middle-aged Richard confront a group of hormonally-charged teens in a public play area. It took some time to get Stephanie's shoes and jacket on, and we had to walk slowly because Dad and I were holding her hands and walking at her pace, but eventually we arrived at the playground. I have to admit I was a little disappointed to see that there were no teenagers loitering anywhere near, but at least that meant Stephanie could play in peace.

Dad was right about it being run-down and rusty, though. There was graffiti everywhere, and believe me, it's a good thing Stephanie can't read! We had to stay very close and attentive just in case she wandered near any broken glass or cigarette lighters on the floor, and the place was covered in

27

empty cans of beer, cigarette butts and fast food wrappers. There was only one swing that was still operational: one of them was missing a seat entirely, another looked like it had been chewed by a dog with a very strong jaw, and the third had been swung over the top bar so many times none of us could reach it. Stephanie didn't seem to mind any of this, though, and she giggled joyfully as Dad pushed her and I stood in front taking photos while Frogsplash sat on the bench staring at his phone and Richard stood in his "threat stance" assessing the area for danger.

He must have noticed the gang of teenagers approaching, but he didn't say anything. He looked scared. They were older than Frogsplash, some of them might have been eighteen, but they obviously still saw him as the biggest threat, because they ignored the rest of us and marched straight up to him. My stomach sank. This felt all wrong. They were too old, and this wasn't what I'd pictured at all. In my head they were just a group of loud-mouthed kids who hung around in the park to keep away from their parents, but these people weren't like that at all. They were very intimidating.

"Oi, this is our spot," one of them said to Frogsplash.

"Oh, sorry," he said, "I didn't realise… I'm just here with my family."

"He's with us," Dad cut in, sensing trouble.

"Well he needs to go," the boy/man said to Dad.

"We don't want any trouble," Dad said. "Look, we're just here with my daughter. This is a kid's playground. We won't be here long."

"No, you won't," the boy said, turning to Dad, "because you're going to leave now."

"No, we're not," Dad said firmly, "this is a public space meant for young children to enjoy. You don't own it and you have no right to go around being a menace to the community!"

The boy looked enraged and began to march over to Dad. He looked very threatening.

"You think it's wise to say no to us, old man? You're here with your kids, and you're going to step up to us? You better be ready to defend them before you go mouthing off like that!"

"Are you threatening me?" Dad said, "I'm not going to let you drive us out of our local play area! Go and loiter somewhere else if you have to, this spot is for children!"

28

"We are children, and we were here first," the man/boy said, "we grew up here. This is our territory. Now move, before I move you," and he squared up to Dad, proving that he was no smaller in stature than a fully-grown man.

"Oh no you don't!" Richard cut in, holding out his pocketknife with the blade sticking out.

"He's got a knife!" one of the other members of the gang called out.

"Richard, what are you doing? Put that away!" Dad said, but it was too late. The police were already on the scene.

"Sir put the knife on the ground!" said the first officer to approach.

"No, no, I wasn't… it's not a real knife…" Richard stammered.

"Put the knife on the ground!"

Richard put the knife on the ground in front of him. It all happened very quickly. The police searched the pockets of the boys in the gang, as well as Richard, Dad and even Frogsplash. I kept swinging Stephanie on the swing, hoping to distract her from the tense situation. Nobody was carrying anything illegal, apart from Richard.

"Can someone explain to me what happened here?" the second officer said, and Dad spoke to her, explaining everything, while the other officer took a statement from the gang of teens. I listened closely to Dad and the second officer.

"How did you get here so quickly?" he asked after the officer had got all she needed.

"We got a phone call… sounded like the phone was in someone's pocket. We tracked the location and as soon as we found out it was this place we came straight here. This area is a hotbed for gang crime; we're really trying to crack down on it."

Richard… he said he was going to type 999 into his phone! HE called the police by accident!

When both officers were done taking statements, they approached Richard.

"Richard Roberts, you are under arrest for carrying an offensive weapon. You have the right to remain silent. Anything you do say may be held against you in a court of law. Do you understand?"

And as we watched Richard being driven away in the back of a police car, I couldn't help but think that this whole thing had happened because of me.

Sunday 13th September 2020

FAMILY FEUDS, FOLLIES AND FELONIES: A DARK AND HARROWING INSIGHT INTO BRITAIN'S MOST DYSFUNCTIONAL FAMILY

*Following last year's piece on the highly functional Figueroa family, we bring you a brand new, deeply disturbing report from the opposite end of the spectrum. In the past week alone, this family has seen the revelation of one secret lovechild, the public arrest of one adult **in a children's playground,** and a deeply emotional, cage-rattling intervention which has dragged up some haunting ghosts of the past.*

After yesterday's incident we went straight back to Dad's flat and put more *Animals of the Forever Forest* on for Stephanie while we talked. Dad and Froggo both thought it was hilarious that Richard had not only managed to accidentally call the police with his phone in his pocket, but actually got himself arrested in the process. I still felt guilty for suggesting the idea and encouraging Richard to come with us, but I didn't tell him to bring a knife and I certainly didn't tell him to pull it out!

"Do you think he'll be in serious trouble, though?" I asked worriedly.

"I doubt it," said Dad, "if he's got any sense at all he'll explain to them that he still had the knife in his jacket from a camping trip last night. The coppers will see he's still wearing his ridiculous utility outfit and they'll be able to verify that he was indeed camping yesterday. As for pulling out the knife, he'll say he was protecting us. Those youths were threatening us, and we had young children."

"Hmm…" I pondered, *does Richard have any sense at all?*

My question was answered this morning when he came home around ten a.m. looking drained and very pale.

"What a night that was!" he announced as he entered the living room, "A night in a police cell – me!"

He told us what had happened, and to be honest it doesn't sound all that exciting. They kept him in overnight, probably just to scare him enough to make sure he doesn't do anything stupid like that again, and they let him go this morning with a caution. But the way he was talking about it, you could tell he felt like some sort of hard man rather than a Geography teacher. He was obviously very pleased to have such an exciting story to tell, and he seemed to have entirely forgotten the part in which he inadvertently called the police on himself. Ah well, all's well that ends well. The only slight worry we all had was that Stephanie might mention something about the incident to Sophie. I don't think it would sound too good if she found out that her two-year-old daughter was present when Dad's flatmate got arrested for wielding a dangerous weapon.

Sophie picked Stephanie up at eleven a.m. and she didn't mention anything, but kids often blurt things out when you least expect it, don't they? Anyway, Dad dropped us home at the usual time and everything seemed perfectly normal: Mum had just got back from the shops and was unpacking things into the fridge, Trousers was barking at a helicopter in the back garden, and Graham, Billy and Max were at The Mill on the Hill, the pub that Graham runs. I camped up in my room for the afternoon, only going downstairs briefly to make a sandwich, and finished the homework I hadn't yet done. Billy and Graham (and Max) always come over at five p.m. on Sundays for our family dinner, leaving Graham's adult son Arnie in charge of the pub. It's sort of a new family tradition.

Another new family tradition, it would seem, is for all the drama to lay dormant until the aforementioned Sunday family dinner, when it erupts climactically before getting brushed under the carpet again on Monday. We were just tucking into our dinner of baked aubergine and couscous (all of us have been off our meat since Monday) when once again Mum began to make her feelings known.

"I feel like you kids are drifting away from me," she said. "You've been at your dad's the past two weekends and you barely show your faces during the week!"

"Sorry, Mum," I said, "we'll be home next weekend. It was only a one-off so we could synchronise our weekends with Stephanie. Sophie wanted it to start as soon as possible."

Mum visibly bristled at the mention of her name.

"It's not just that," she went on, "I'm a little concerned that this is going to drag you away from Billy and Graham. It doesn't seem fair on Billy to be the odd one out in all of this."

"I don't mind, honestly," Billy said in his usual, laid-back manner, "I've got my own stuff to do. I can always take more shifts at the pub."

"Well, I'm glad to hear that… I do worry, you know, especially when I don't know what you lot are thinking. So often I fear the worst just because none of you ever really *talk!* So, I've decided to create an environment in which we can all talk openly and express our feelings…"

Right now, I feel like I want to run head-first into a brick wall.

"We know we can talk openly," Froggo said hurriedly. He must have suspected something, too. He knows what Mum's like with her random phases, most of which involve self-improvement… and not just for Mum, either… her idea of self-improvement is making everybody else improve themselves, like last year when her New Year's resolution was to make me and Frogsplash do more chores.

"But the problem is that you *don't* talk openly! I never know what's going on with you guys any more! I'm not asking you to tell me every single detail of your personal lives, but so many things are changing in all of our lives right now and I really think we need to talk about that!"

This is my worst nightmare. SURELY this time I must be dreaming!!!

"So, I've decided," Mum went on, "that every week after Sunday dinner we should all sit together in the living room and have at least one hour of 'Family Talk Time'. We'll all get a chance to say what's on our minds, ask questions, even confront each other about things that someone else in the family has done that may have annoyed us or upset us at some point during the week, and of course we can also spend that time showing appreciation for one another. It's an open field for communication."

"Mum, that sounds horrible," I said, sensing that now was the time to be honest. "Normal families don't do that sort of thing. And if someone does something that annoys us shouldn't we just say so at the time instead of bottling it all up until Sunday and letting it all out in one sudden outburst?"

"Actually," Mum said, "Doctor Marianne Duval says that it's better not to react to things instantly and instead to take some time to think them through before communicating those feelings to whoever upset you."

"Marianne Duval?" I asked sceptically. "You mean the woman who wrote that dog training book? Are you using dog training techniques on us?"

"She's a very wise woman," Mum said defensively.

"Just answer me this one question," I said. "When she says, 'whoever upset you' is she talking about a human being, or not?"

Mum hesitated.

"Oh, come on, she's not even a real doctor!" said Frogsplash.

"Not only that, she's a terrible dog trainer!" I added. "You have to react instantly when a dog misbehaves, otherwise they won't understand why they're being told off!"

"Well, there are different schools of thought..." Mum said.

"This is why Trousers still steals food from the kitchen counter," I said.

"Never mind that; we're getting far too off topic. In fact, this is precisely the sort of thing we should be talking about in Family Talk Time. It's going to be really beneficial for all of us, I promise."

"Mum, I really don't think it will be. I'm with Sam: I really, really don't want to do this," Frogsplash said desperately. "How about if we just agree to tell you if something's on our minds?"

"No, because then it'll just go back to the way it was before! We need to set aside a designated time for real, honest conversation."

"But what if we don't have anything to say?" I asked, "I'm not keeping anything from you, I'm just not much of a talker."

"Samantha, you keep a diary! There must be loads of stuff in there that you don't tell me!"

"Mum! How do you know about my diary? Have you been sneaking around my room? Have you read it?!"

"No of course I haven't! I just found it when I was cleaning."

Yeah right. Oldest excuse in the book. I'm going to have to find a new hiding place for it now.

"Well anyway," I continued, "it's my choice and my right if I want to keep things private."

"Of course, it is," Mum said, "I'm not saying you have to share *everything*. I just want us to have more open discussions."

"What if we don't want to?" asked Frogsplash.

"It's not open for discussion," Mum said without any hint of irony, "this is happening."

"Wait, does this count as part of it?" I asked. "Is this part of our hour of talk time?"

"No, this is dinner table conversation. The hour starts after dinner once we've all sat down together in the living room."

"Oh what?!" said Frogsplash. "Well in that case I'm not saying another word. If we *have* to talk for a full hour I might as well save what I've got to say until then!"

"Me too!" I said stubbornly. As annoyed... no, *outraged* as I was, I do like it when me and Froggo are on the same side.

"Well, I think it's a great idea," said Graham, "communication is always a positive thing. And being able to talk frankly is an important life skill and it will prepare you for adulthood."

Ugh, he is so straight-laced sometimes! How about I communicate a few rude words, Graham, would that be a positive thing?!

"I don't mind talking for an hour," said Billy, probably in an attempt to defuse the tension, "but you know with me it's just going to be football chat and anecdotes from the pub!"

Mum looked somewhat displeased with this, but she will always hold her tongue with Billy. He's been in our lives as Frogsplash's friend for a long time, but he's only been her sort-of stepson for about six months. Normally he doesn't need any encouragement to talk; he's grown up helping his dad out at the pub, so he's used to making small talk with the customers and he's learnt from them how to tell funny stories in just the right way so as to hold an audience. But we all know that he's bottling things up because he never, *ever* talks about his mum. Fourteen months ago, she walked out on Billy and Graham completely out of the blue, and neither of them have heard anything at all from her since.

The rest of dinner went by in awkward silence. Mum glanced around the table furtively, looking for further signs of dissent within the group. Billy cleared his throat as if to speak, but words failed him, and he fell back in line with the rest of us. The sound of knives screeching against plates rang out sharply. You could hear Graham gulp his beer and then desperately try to swallow down a belch that was rising in his throat. "Pfft," the gas escaped his mouth slowly after he failed to stifle it. "Pardon me," he muttered almost imperceptibly. Even the dogs seemed subdued, though perhaps that was because there were no scraps of meat to be had.

Everyone refused dessert, even though the aubergine main course had hardly been filling. We all wanted this thing over with. Mum led the way to the living room as though she was leading us to the gallows. We all took our places on the sofa, and I picked up Trousers and put him on my lap as a sort of buffer for conversation. Maybe I would be forgotten behind a cute blonde puppy. Mum set the stopwatch on her phone and pressed start. "Right," she said a little nervously, "where shall we begin?" And for the next hour we argued about why this whole thing was such a stupid idea, then we all went to bed feeling irritable and resentful towards each other.

Friday 18th September 2020

The household has been awfully tense since "Family Talk Time" and we've all been keeping ourselves to ourselves much more than usual. Graham and Billy, who live in the flat above Graham's pub, only came over once on Tuesday, and they didn't even stay the night. Basically, the whole thing backfired magnificently, but it would be very optimistic to assume that Mum will give up just because of that minor setback. If anything, it's only going to strengthen her resolve: she'll say that this awkward communication breakdown only proves her point that we need to talk more, but the real reason she'll want to keep trying is because she just hates to be proven wrong, especially by her children.

Now we're even more cautious to say what we're really thinking; all of us are retaining all of our feelings, but that only serves to make them more palpable. Around every corner is some lurking emotion or unspoken accusation. Things were dragged up on Sunday, but they were never laid to rest. They're floating in the air and taunting us: personal poltergeists for the irritated mind. People talk about things being an "emotional roller coaster" when there are highs and lows, but this is not like that. There are no highs or lows, and it's not fun or thrilling in any way. It's less like a roller coaster and more like one of those low-budget fairground ghost trains. An emotional ghost train, and no one ever gets off.

School has been the only antidote and laughing and joking with Danny and Carla has never been more essential to my psychological wellbeing. Biology is fast becoming my favourite lesson, not just because my two best friends are in my class but also because Mr Pinter is a good laugh and a great teacher. The only thing is there's this new kid who moved here from another school and he's an absolute nightmare. His name is Elliot and, rumour has it, he got expelled from his old school for "aggressive behaviour". He's incredibly disruptive and he constantly tries to push Pinter's buttons. I don't mean to sound like a goody-two-shoes; I like a bit of fun in class, but what he does isn't fun and it's kind of mean to the teacher. He's just rude and no one enjoys it. He's obnoxious.

He's in my Art class, too, although I didn't notice him straight away. He doesn't bother trying to pick on our Art teacher, Mack, because he's so laid back it would have no effect whatsoever. This kid Elliot obviously preys on the weak. I really like Mack, but it's very clear that he doesn't really care how well we do in class. He was my teacher last year, too. There are only four Art teachers in the whole school and the other three are designated to the older years, the ones who are closer to their proper exams. Basically, they're the teachers who get results, so they teach the kids who need results. But I like Mack's philosophy. He says that if you don't enjoy art then there's no point doing it. Art is for artists, and it shouldn't be forced upon anyone. Artists don't do art because it's part of their timetable, they do it because it comes from within and it simply cannot be contained.

It was a fine day today, still very warm and bright, but in England at this time of year you get that very real feeling that summer is waning. I think it's to do with the position of the sun in the sky, but whatever it is it changes everything. In those long summer days in June and July you feel that the light is endless, and so are the possibilities. Everything comes out of its shell and blooms gorgeously in the light of the salubrious sun. But then, so quickly and so sadly, the sun's light changes. It's still bright and it may still be warm, but it lacks that quality... it seems less optimistic somehow, like it knows it's dying. That summer that seemed so bountiful and generous a few weeks ago feels taut and withholding, so that you have to grab it while you still can, desperately and soullessly. You clutch at it, but the more you try to hold on to the summer the less of its spirit you capture. Summer is a breeze.

At lunchtime, Carla, Danny and I sat at our favourite bench on the field while we still could, eating our packed lunches and watching videos on Carla's phone. Last year we had a party at our house to celebrate Mum and Graham's partnership, both in business and in life. They told us to invite all our friends and that's how Carla's sister Rosie met Mum's friend's daughter Jessica. They've become good friends and they've started posting videos online. Jessica's mum runs a small makeup business and I guess she asked her to make some promotional videos, but the way she's done it is pretty funny. I always liked Jessica, even though we don't have much in common, but to tell you the truth, Carla's sister Rosie terrifies me. She goes to our school, she's in year ten and she's super popular. Carla's other sister is in the last year of sixth form now; she's much more chilled out, like Carla.

Anyway, in these videos Jessica starts by telling Rosie that she's going to give her a beautiful makeover, but she's not allowed to see it until the end. What she actually does is make Rosie look like a troll, or a witch, or a zombie, and in one video she even makes her look like an old man. She uses amazing makeup artist skills to make it look incredibly realistic. Then, without removing the makeup, she covers it all up with more makeup and makes Rosie look absolutely stunning (which she is anyway, to be honest). I think it's really clever because it demonstrates the quality and coverage of the makeup and shows how it can transform you from a troll to a beauty queen.

We were just about to watch their latest video 'Evil Clown to Fairy Princess: Makeup Transformation' when we felt eyes on us. Sitting just a few feet away on the grass by the lake was a small boy barely visible behind his enormous backpack, which he had placed on the ground beside him. When he saw us look over, he turned his head in the opposite direction with such ferocity I'm surprised he didn't give himself whiplash. It was a very unsubtle attempt to make it seem as though he hadn't been staring. We went back to the video we were watching and thought no more of it until suddenly a great disturbance caught our attention. The small boy had been set upon by a gaggle of geese which must have approached when he wasn't looking.

We had been too absorbed in the video to notice, and the boy must have been trying so hard not to stare at us again that he hadn't seen them coming either. But on the other side of the lake four girls were watching maliciously, and we knew them all too well: Charlotte Henderson, Beth Amory, Andrea Michael and Ruby Driscoll. They are the sort of girls who love laughing at the misfortune of others, the sort who think they're better than everyone else, who never seem to have anything embarrassing or unfortunate *ever* happen to them.

The poor boy was desperately trying to fight off the three geese as they stole the entire contents of his lunchbox one peck at a time, and at this sight Charlotte and her gaggle laughed raucously. The boy was fighting a losing battle and being laughed at all the while, and you could tell he was getting quite upset, so we decided to go and help him.

"Don't worry about those vicious fat-arses," Carla said to him.

"They came out of nowhere and just started pecking me! They've eaten everything!"

"No, not the geese," Carla said, "I was talking about those waddling beak-faces over there!" She gestured towards Charlotte's gang, making sure they were in earshot. They turned their noses up and walked away, pretending they didn't hear.

"Oh, hah!" The boy smiled and blushed. It soon became clear that Carla was his reason for staring in our direction.

"What's your name?" I asked.

"Jamal," he said shyly.

"Come and sit with us on the bench, Jamal, you can have some of our lunches."

He followed us over and we each gave him a part of our lunch.

"Thank you; you're really kind," he said.

"No problem," said Danny. "It's best not to sit so close to the lake next time, though, the geese had twenty-eight goslings this spring and they don't seem to be leaving home anytime soon."

"All the benches are always full," Jamal said, "I haven't made any friends yet so I can't find anyone to sit with."

"Don't worry, us three took ages to find each other," Carla said. "You're better off taking your time finding people you really get on with. There are plenty of nice people in this school but there are plenty of mean ones too, like those girls on the other side of the lake."

"Are you going on the Isle of Wight trip?" Danny asked, "I met loads of friends there."

"Yeah I'm going. I'm kind of nervous though. Staying in a dorm for a whole week with a bunch of strangers... I've heard people do pranks on each other... I don't want to get pranked!"

"You're not going to," I said, "because you're going to be the one doing the pranking!"

We spent the rest of our lunch break tutoring Jamal on the art of the prank. I told him some of the ones I masterminded on the trip last year, and Carla showed him some online videos by this guy called Eric Derek. He's incredibly annoying and I think it's really pathetic that a man of his age spends his entire life pranking unsuspecting strangers, but some of his early stuff is all right, and much more harmless than the sort of thing he gets up to nowadays. I hope we weren't being bad influences on little Jamal, he seems like a good kid, but pranks are a tradition on the Isle of Wight trip, and as long as no one gets hurt I think it's OK. Hopefully it'll help Jamal make some friends, so he doesn't have to picnic with the geese any more.

Sunday 20th September 2020

Frogsplash has been acting weird all weekend. Well, I suppose it's not that weird for him, but I can tell something's off – even for a teenager he seems awfully indolent and introspective. Usually on the weekends when we're at home, Mum will do the big shop on Saturday morning to make sure there's enough food for the weekend as well as the upcoming week, and usually the minute she gets back Frogsplash comes stomping down the stairs at top speed and devours all of the best food before Mum's even had a chance to put it away.

"Oh, for goodness sake!" Mum says, "I've spent all morning buying all this food and then you just go and eat it!"

"Well, yeah," Froggo retorts, "that's what food's for, isn't it?"

"Well I'd like *some* of it to last longer than a day," says Mum.

"There's no point eating fresh bread the next day… the crust on the outside goes soft and the bread on the inside goes hard… saving fresh food 'til it's not fresh defeats the purpose of it."

"So, you're going to eat that entire French stick today?"

"If you want me to leave some to go stale then *fine,* I will. I'm just trying to make the most of it."

Then Mum rolls her eyes and Frogsplash slabs almost an entire block of butter onto his chunk of bread because it hasn't had time to soften so it won't spread. But today he didn't come down at all. I could hear his music playing so I knew he was awake. I say *his* music, but it wasn't the normal stuff he listens to; it was definitely coming from his room, but it was different, it had a sort of *whining* quality to it. I didn't see him today, either, at least not until dinner, during which we all were stunned into silence at the prospect of the dreaded Family Talk Time.

I wouldn't exactly say that *Family Talk Time: Round Two* was a success, but it was a little less hostile than last week's pathetic attempt. I tried my hardest to uphold my resistance, but this week it was clear that Frogsplash had given up the fight. Last time he was on my side and we were both raging against the maternal machine, but today he seemed to have surrendered himself to the inevitable. "This is happening," Mum said last week, and her insistence must have worn down the other three. I resolved to sit there without complaint, but I would not volunteer any of my thoughts or feelings. It was all I could do. My silent protest.

Mum did most of the talking this time. She said that the sudden arrival of Stephanie had been difficult for her because she had always wanted more children (Graham, who is around ten years older than Mum and already has two children from two different marriages, looked rather alarmed at this revelation, but it wasn't news to me). Mum went on to say that she knows it's too late for her to have more children now, and that makes her feel a kind of grief for the babies she never had. I felt bad for resisting these talks so much, as excruciating as they are, because Mum obviously needs them.

Graham talked a bit about how he sometimes worries about when he and Billy should come over. As it is, Billy has to share a room with Froggo whenever they stay the night, which is all right every now and then because they were mates before Mum and Graham got together, but obviously everyone needs their privacy sometimes. And that's what drove the conversation towards the idea of us all getting a bigger house together. Graham really wants to move in, and sooner rather than later. I must admit it took me by surprise. Graham and Billy have been spending a lot of time here, and we even went on holiday as a family last month, but I suppose I didn't really consider it to be a permanent thing.

Mum always seems so interested in what Dad's up to, I always thought she still cared about him too much. Maybe she does and that's why she's reacting to the Stephanie thing so dramatically. Or maybe she's just worried for us, her children, because she's never really trusted Dad to be responsible with us, and that's why she always asks what we get up to when we're with him. However, she feels about Dad, I'm not sure Graham is the answer. Don't get me wrong, he's all right, but he's just so... *plain.* He's like Mr Everyman. I know he keeps up with the football just so he can have conversations with other men about the football, rather than because he's passionate about it. He does the same with theatre, so he can talk to his classier associates about something they normally talk about. He asks us about school, and he talks to Mum about her interests, but it's like he's on autocue. The more I get to know him the less personality I see. I mean, even his name is dull. Graham. Gray-ham. *Grey ham.*

I suppose he is the opposite of Dad and maybe that's what drew Mum towards him. Graham is stolid whereas Dad was and is unreliable. But Graham is bland whereas Dad is fun. Graham is predictable; Dad is not. Sometimes I complain about Dad's lack of maturity, but Mum has that wild streak in her too. Every now and then she does something that you would never have expected her to do, something completely out of the ordinary. I think that either she will get bored of Graham or he won't be able to handle her spontaneity. I really like Billy. He's so easy to get along with and he has never treated me like Froggo's annoying little sister, even before Mum and Graham got together. I'd be happy to have him as a brother, definitely. I wouldn't really care about Graham being my stepdad either – not really – but I don't want us to get a house together and then suddenly Mum realises he's a crushing bore and then we have to all split up like before. He is a crushing bore.

There's something about Graham that bothers me. I've been sat here for some time trying to put my finger on it, and I think I've just worked out what it is. He talks to everybody the same, no matter who they are. He talks to me and Mum in the same sort of mild-mannered, pleasant exchange he would use to talk to the cashier at the supermarket or a stranger asking for directions. There's no depth or sense of familiarity to the way he communicates with us. The more I think about it the more unsettling it seems. It's like he's a robot and he only has one setting: **standard android mode (basic human replicon version A103)**. I'm trying to think now if he speaks to Billy any differently. Perhaps he does, but only when they're alone.

Wednesday 23rd September 2020

This morning we had a whole school assembly and our head teacher, Mr Wilcox, made an important announcement. I won't say it's the most exciting new I've ever heard, but it means we get a bit of time off from normal lessons, so there's a bonus.

"Good morning everyone," he said, "please be seated. Today I have the pleasure of announcing a very special whole school project. Every decade since 1960 Duke John Jameson School has buried a time capsule on its grounds, and this year will be no exception. The tradition goes that a suggestion box will be set up outside the main office and students will place their own suggestions of what to put in the capsule into the box. Two suggestions will be selected from each year group. In the past we have had a great many 'joke' submissions, none of which were particularly amusing. This year, to avoid this enormous waste of time, you must request a suggestion slip, which will be on a certain colour of paper, from your year head. They will give you one only if they approve your proposed idea.

"Any slips not of this particular colour will be immediately recycled without consideration. We do apologise for this inconvenience, but this is the price we must pay for the follies of former students. All serious suggestions are welcome – the more original the better! But please do take into consideration the size and the shelf-life of the item you have in mind – no giant pumpkins please! You will have two weeks to submit your ideas, and three weeks from today the winners will be announced. So, get thinking, and remember: the winning items will be dug up by future pupils one day – make it something that will marvel, amuse, astound or confuse!"

"You got any ideas for the time capsule?" Danny asked Carla and me today at lunch.

"Not really," said Carla, "I mean, it depends when they're going to dig it up, doesn't it?"

"How do you mean?" asked Danny.

"Well, you could do a photo album of all around the school, showing what the classrooms and the equipment looks like, maybe add in a textbook or something. But if they're only going to leave it for ten years the school won't have changed that much, will it? On the other hand, you could put a DVD recording down there for people to watch, but if they don't dig it up for another fifty years there probably won't be any DVD players left."

"That's a point," I said. "When do they get dug up? If they've been doing this since 1960 then there must be five time capsules buried here at the school, unless they've got dug up already. Why didn't Mr Wilcox say anything about excavating the old time capsules?"

"Maybe that bit comes later," said Danny, "they just want ideas for now."

"I guess," I said.

Friday 25th September 2020

Suddenly it all makes so much sense. Today we had our third Geography lesson with Mr Roberts, a.k.a. Richard. Richard Roberts. Rich Rob. Dick Bob. Dicky Bobby. Despite his outrageously embarrassing first impression, the other kids seem as though they're really starting to like him. He talks to us all like we're his mates, like we can share in-jokes and have a bit of a laugh. It feels *personal,* but not in a creepy way. It's almost the exact opposite of the way Graham talks to other people. Anyway, Richard's odd, slightly deluded personality kind of works in the classroom environment, because it doesn't seem to matter how much of a prat he makes of himself, he never gets embarrassed. He has no apparent weak spot, so it's impossible to wear him down.

He's gone off the survivalist phase much more suddenly than he does with most of the other ones, probably because it got him arrested. Usually he doesn't ditch one phase until he's got his eye on another one, so at the moment he hasn't really got a "thing" that he's trying to do. He's not trying to pretend to be something he's not, which means that for once he's not trying too hard. He's just being himself, and I think that's another reason the class is warming to him. He was in a particularly chipper mood this morning when he entered the classroom.

"Good morning, class! And what a very fine morning it is today! Are we all excited for the weekend? Anyone got any fun plans?"

"Depends how much homework you give us, sir!" said Sean Butler, trying to get Richard to not set any.

"Oh, Sean," Richard said. "Maybe you count homework as 'fun plans' but some of your classmates have actual social lives!"

Everybody laughed, except Sean.

"That's not what I meant, sir!" he said defensively.

"Well then, you might just be in luck today. I'm in a very good mood, so perhaps I'll give the homework a miss this week."

Cheers and wolf whistles erupted across the class.

"Why are you in such a good mood, sir?" asked Demetri.

"I'm glad you asked!" Richard said. "Today I am in such a fantastic mood because yesterday I found out that my oldest daughter has *finally* dumped that idiot boyfriend of hers!"

Here's where it gets interesting. I know who the idiot boyfriend is. Remember I mentioned the party we had at our house last year, the one where Jessica and Rosie met? Well they weren't the only people to hit it off that night. Jessica's mum Trudy brought one of her friends along, a recently divorced woman by the name of Fran. Fran is Richard's ex-wife, and she brought along her two daughters, Eloise and Gertie. The oldest one, Gertie, met my brother Frogsplash, and they've been dating ever since. The idiot boyfriend is Frogsplash!

I've known about this for ages, but Froggo never came clean to Richard because he always seemed so annoyed at this mystery boyfriend just simply because he had the cheek to date his precious Gertie. So of course, Richard is ecstatic that it's all over, but not everyone is going to come away from this in such good spirits. Now I know why Frogsplash has been moping about the house all week. He's heartbroken. Personally, I don't know what he saw in Gertie. She's a carbon copy of her mum, and her mum is an insufferable snob. They're nothing at all like Richard who, for all his faults, is an earnest, down-to-earth sort of bloke. I can't imagine them ever being a family unit, but I suppose opposites attract sometimes, just like Froggo and Gertie.

"Ooh," the class said when Richard announced this news. We love it when teachers reveal something about their personal lives. It's something they usually avoid doing, probably because it's a slippery slope towards revealing *too* much, which will always result in showing weakness. But such conventions don't apply to the likes of Richard. Like I say, he's an earnest man, and he's not afraid to appear human to his students, unlike most other teachers, who make a habit of keeping their personal lives separate from the classroom. I'm fully aware that this is likely to be a disadvantage to me, because Richard's personal life happens to cross over into mine, but so far he hasn't made any slip-ups since he mentioned my knickers in our first lesson. But, alas, the year is young, and he still has plenty of time.

For now, though, I was as keen as everyone else to hear the messy details of the breakup, purely out of concern for my dear brother, of course.

"So, what happened, then?" asked a girl in the front row. "Why did she dump him? Did she let him down gently or did she rip his heart out?"

"Well, I don't know the full details. To be perfectly honest with you, I've never even met the guy…"

Oh, how wrong you are, Richard!

"… but she was always going on about him… Frederick this and Frederick that! I was getting so sick of it, let me tell you…"

Of course! Richard doesn't even know Froggo's real name!

"…from what I could tell, he was your typical, scruffy teenage boy – at least until she came along! She sorted out his sense of style, but I guess she couldn't change his personality! Sounds like he was a bit gormless to me, she was always complaining that he paid more attention to video games and televised wrestling than he did to her. And she *hated* going over to his house because she couldn't stand his annoying brat of a sister…"

HEY!

"Anyway, seems like good riddance to bad rubbish, and that's exactly what she said to him. She told him, 'It's not me, it's you,' and then proceeded to list all of his faults, flaws, weaknesses and every single mistake she'd ever known him to make."

"Seems a bit harsh!" Ross Rillington commented, and I had to agree.

"Well, he was punching well above his weight; he needed to be put back in his place," Richard said in defence.

"It does sound pretty mean, Richard," I said, "Aren't you worried that your daughter might be a little cold-hearted? What she did, or rather, the way she did it, sounds unequivocally callous."

I got the feeling that the rest of the class were a little shocked at my brazenness. Granted, Richard is not like other teachers, but you don't normally say something so frank about somebody's child, no matter if they're your teacher or not. Of course, they all know that Richard and I have a [cringe] *personal relationship,* but none of them know that I'm much closer to this so-called idiot boyfriend than I am to Richard. Maybe he is an idiot, but he's not a bad person and he doesn't deserve to be treated the way Gertie treated him, nor does he deserve for his heartache to be made a spectacle of in the classroom!

Tuesday 29th September 2020

DJ JAMESON FEAT. THE BIG W MAKE SURPRISE APPEARANCE AT SMALL VENUE FOR IMPROPTU GIG!

Fans were stunned when niche rap artist "The Big W" turned up at an intimate venue for an unannounced, off-the-cuff performance of some of his freshest material. The performer, who is best known for his collaborations with DJ Jameson (AKA Duke John Jammin') charged no fee for the electrifying live gig and insisted that no other publicity was to be released. The result was a truly personal touch which will forever remain in the memories of those who attended.

It was a rainy day today, and quite astonishingly (for England) it was the first one of the school year. Last year on bad weather days, Carla, Danny and I had our own secret hideout, so we went there today at lunch time to take shelter (without having to ingratiate ourselves with the mass of canteen diners). It's the perfect little den because it's a completely soundproof room within the music department where we can chat and listen to music freely without being heard from outside. Students aren't allowed to go in classrooms alone during break times, but we can't be detected there. It's the only room in the school like it; it's used for music exams and all kinds of auditions, and Carla's eldest sister Louisa used to hang out there with her mates before she got to sixth form, when you're old enough to leave school grounds at break times. It's a tiny portion of solace amidst the crowded school day.

We ate our lunches and talked. Usually it's me with the family dramas, and although Frogsplash is still moping, there wasn't all that much for me to talk about. But Danny seems a bit stressed. Her twin brothers turn three in November, which means they won't start school for another two years, and it sounds like Danny's mum is really struggling. I know the twins, and they're extremely hyper-active – they would be a handful even if they were separated. Danny says she's heard her parents arguing, because her dad's always working late, and her mum never gets a break from the kids. She asked me how I felt when my parents started arguing, but I had to be honest with her, they didn't. They never, ever argued, they just broke up one day. So, I told her that maybe it's good that they're arguing, because it means they haven't given up. I don't know.

Danny is usually the most energetic one out of us three, but today she was more placid, and she wanted to sit at the piano and play. She has a piano at home and her dad has always tried to teach her and her brothers to play, but he always said they couldn't sit still long enough. She may not have any grades, but she's way better than her dad made out. She sat and tinkled at the keys while Carla and I sat on the bench either side of her, showing our support without needing to say anything. She was obviously feeling down, but there was very little we could do or say to help. Luckily, something truly extraordinary was about to happen, something which would have cheered even the dampest of spirits.

There we were, tucked away in the corner of the room behind the huge grand piano, when we heard someone enter. Danny stopped playing the piano and we all held our breath and crouched down so that we couldn't be seen. We knew we weren't supposed to be in a classroom, and the last time Carla and I got caught hiding out in there we ended up getting roped into taking part in the school play! So, I took a brief, furtive glance around the side of the piano just to check whether or not it was a teacher, and it could not have been any worse – it was Mr Wilcox, the *head* teacher! The good news was he clearly hadn't seen us, and he was wearing huge headphones and bopping his head to whatever music was playing through them, so he wouldn't be able to hear us either.

"It's Mr Wilcox!" I whispered to the girls. "He's wearing headphones – I don't think he can hear us... what should we do?!"

"Just sit tight," Carla whispered back, "he's probably just looking for some paperwork or something... I'm sure he won't take long..."

But he did.

Hiding behind the piano, we weren't able to watch his every move, but Carla and I, who were sitting on either end of the piano bench, were able to catch the occasional glimpse and describe it to Danny, who was almost exploding with the excitement and riskiness of it all. Fortunately, Mr Wilcox had his back to us most of the time so he couldn't see us, but that also meant that we couldn't see much of what he was doing. He was fiddling with some music equipment at the front of the room and he still had his headphones on, bopping away in a manner which didn't suit his head teacher image.

Mr Wilcox is, I would say, a very typical head teacher. He is stern and serious, and he never forms particularly close bonds with any of the children. He keeps a sensible distance, and never reveals anything about his personal life. He seems to know every single student by name, which I find very disconcerting, because I don't think it's possible to remember that many names without attaching some memorable information to each person. For example, I wouldn't have remembered Beth Amory's name if I hadn't also made a mental note that she is a compulsive liar. And I wouldn't be able to recall Ross Rillington if I hadn't had him down as an obnoxious snob. I would have never known Jake Atkinson if he hadn't thrown orange peel at me on the school bus. So, I'm wondering, what information does Mr Wilcox have that triggers his memory of me? Probably when I made the front page of the school newspaper, but I don't want to drag that up again.

Back to Mr Wilcox, I would say he's a very plain, ordinary man, but not like Graham, who tries to be everyone's casual mate in an insincere way. Mr Wilcox is a sincere man, and he doesn't try to be anyone's friend. He commands respect. He doesn't need your approval. But as I'm growing older I'm beginning to notice that adults are very complicated creatures. When we are young we always assume that adults have perfected this whole "life" business, because they always seem to have the answers. But I've seen my parents make mistakes, and I've seen them doubt themselves. Just because they survived their formative years that doesn't mean they're fully formed. I think Richard has had a lot to do with this realisation as well, because nothing could be a plainer example of an adult muddling through life directionless and capriciously than poor, confused Richard.

On further inspection I was able to see that the equipment Mr Wilcox was fiddling with was some recording equipment, and he was clearly trying to set it up. I got the impression that he had never used it before, and I wondered why he wouldn't just ask a music teacher to do it for him if he needed it for some school business. It was getting tense, because us three were beginning to realise that Mr Wilcox was not just popping in to grab some paperwork, but we had already been there for several minutes so we couldn't just burst out from behind the piano and reveal ourselves. There were still twenty minutes until the end of lunch bell rang, and as long as Mr Wilcox left before then we could get out of the situation without getting into trouble.

The problem was, he didn't seem to be going anywhere. In fact, it looked as though he was just getting started. After struggling with the recording equipment for some time, he eventually seemed satisfied that it had all been set up correctly. He retrieved a microphone from a box on a shelf near the front desk and plugged it into the recording device. Carla and I were whispering regular updates to Danny, safe in the knowledge that Mr Wilcox wouldn't be able to hear us over his music, which was so loud we could hear the beat pulsing from the headphones. He stopped for a moment, cleared his throat, took a deep breath and straightened himself out, as though composing himself before an important meeting with the school governor. Then he began to rap.

"I'm the Big W, double true, double who?
I'm a master of maths, double one makes two
I can drop English, you just watch me
I before E, yeah, except after C

They call me the professor 'cause I'm mad like a scientist
If you ain't met me you don't know what science is
I'm chemically, biologically, physically top
When it comes to education I'm the cream of the crop

What goes up comes down, that's gravitational pull
True say I got an inspirational school
This rap is sick, it's my motivational tool
To make the kids follow my educational rules

I can lay down history so fast it's a mystery
My textiles design is better than Calvin Klein
My brain's like a textbook, so insane you would be shook

And yeah I know music, just check out this sick hook!

My Geography knowledge is beyond compare
All around the globe, North and South hemisphere
Throughout this whole school I am the top learner
And check out my skills with a Bunsen burner

In ICT I run the programmes
And I spot the hackers and the online scams
They say I'm the boss and I have to agree
Ain't no Trojan virus gonna outsmart me

In Religious Studies I'm a demi-god
In PE I'm winning despite my dad bod
In French I'm the boss, je suis le meilleur
Je suis le roi du monde, oui, oui, monsieur

I think I've made my point, yeah, you catch my drift
So, I'm gonna rap this thing up now, finish it swift
I don't wanna drag it out; don't wanna trouble you
Just remember who's in charge – they call me Big W"

As you can imagine, the three of us were sat there listening in complete and utter incredulity. This was not the Mr Wilcox we knew. I'm quite certain no one knows that side of him. The shock quickly gave way to insurmountable hysteria as we were doubled over with barely contained laughter. We would definitely have got caught at that point if Mr Wilcox hadn't been wearing those headphones. You might be wondering how I was able to recall all of those lyrics so perfectly. Well, you'd probably have them memorised if you heard them *seven times!* It appeared Mr Wilcox was extremely keen to perfect his performance, because he went through it another six times before the end of lunch bell rang. That was when it stopped being funny and started being a really awkward situation.

Mr Wilcox was gearing up for round eight and we were still stuck behind the piano.

"What do we do?" whispered Danny. "We can't stay here all afternoon; we'll miss lessons!"

"He's showing no signs of stopping," I said, "and if we don't leave now, we'll definitely get in trouble."

"But if we do leave now there's a chance we won't get in trouble," said Carla. "Maybe we can slip out the door without him seeing our faces."

"No way; that's impossible," I said, "he's right at the front of the classroom!"

"What choice do we have?" said Carla. "Follow my lead…"

Before either Danny or I could protest, Carla got up off the bench and began walking towards the front of the classroom. She was right, we had no choice, so I grabbed Danny's arm and we stood up together, ready to face the music. Mr Wilcox was on the second verse, the bit about being a mad scientist. His back was to us, but he was facing the door. He was definitely going to see us leaving. And just like that, he sensed something. Maybe he could see Carla out of the corner of his eye, or maybe one of us blocked the light or he felt the vibrations of our footsteps through the floor, but whatever it was, it was game over.

He instantly stopped rapping and turned to look at us, first at Carla, then Danny and me. He locked eyes on all three of us and all we could do was stare right back at him. There was no point running because he had clearly seen our faces, and Mr Wilcox can put a name to every one of his students' faces. We carried on walking towards the exit, all the while holding eye contact with Mr Wilcox. There was a moment of mutual understanding: he realised we'd heard everything, and in that sense he was the one who got caught. So, he let us go without saying a single word. We slipped out of the door and rushed to our form rooms.

Sunday 4ᵗʰ October 2020

It was a very dull Saturday at home yesterday: Froggo is still hiding himself away in his room, Mum was busy working on her home-brewed wine, and Graham and Billy were working in the pub. So, I was delighted when Carla sent a message to Danny and me last night inviting us to go to her house today and stay for dinner. Carla's family is so different to mine, they're so much more fun and they just have a laugh with each other rather than worrying about imaginary problems like my mum does. No need for "Family Talk Time" at the Figueroa house! And no boring Graham or moody Frogsplash either!

The best part was that Carla's aunt, uncle, and cousins Sophia and Robbie were visiting from Puerto Rico, so there were even more fun and games. They were all incredibly welcoming, as Carla's family always are (with perhaps the exception of her sister Rosie) and we happily spent the entire afternoon in the living room with all of them, with Carla's dad playing the role of in-house DJ by putting on a selection of his old records for background music. He has an amazing record collection and really great taste in music, which was in such stark contrast to our experience of hearing "The Big W" rap that Carla felt compelled to tell her family the tale of our Tuesday lunchtime.

They all found it utterly hilarious and didn't seem to care a bit that we were breaking school rules by being in the classroom. Carla's sisters were especially entertained, because of course they know Mr Wilcox and couldn't believe there was this side to him. So strong was their disbelief, in fact, that when I said I could remember every single lyric they insisted on hearing my rendition of it in order to prove our claims. I might have been nervous performing a rap in front of my own family, because some of them seem to be distinctly lacking in any hint of a sense of humour, but I knew Carla's family would enjoy it, so I rapped the entire thing, word for word, only stumbling slightly when it got to the bit in French, and they absolutely loved it.

For dinner we had slow roasted lamb and mushrooms stuffed with rice and Mediterranean vegetables and it was incredible. The only thing more delicious than the food was the knowledge that I was missing out on the dreaded Family Talk Time back home! After such a warm reception of my rap recital earlier this afternoon I felt confident enough to talk to Rosie, Carla's extremely beautiful, popular sister from year ten.

"Carla's been showing us your makeup tutorial videos online," I said. "They're absolutely brilliant!"

"Oh, thanks!" she said. "Jessica does all the work really; I'm just the model. We're thinking of quitting now though."

"Oh no, why?" I asked.

"Internet trolls. They're vicious. They just criticise every little thing – it's *horrible*. It started with the one where she made me look like a troll, which is a bit ironic, don't you think? They said things like 'she looks like a troll *before* the makeover' and a lot of people have been making fun of Jessica's lisp... it's just stupid stuff really, but it gets to you after a while."

"You're kidding!" I said. "That's crazy! They must be jealous... or just really mean. But don't let them get to you!"

"I'm trying not to," she said, "but it's hard. I wish I knew who these people were and why they hate me so much. If they don't like our videos, they don't have to watch them!"

"Do you think it might be someone you know?" I asked. "You're pretty popular at school. Maybe it's someone who's jealous of you, someone who's too much of a coward to say something to your face..."

Rosie paused for a second, then she eyed me with suspicion for longer than a moment – longer than seemed appropriate.

"Hmm, yeah," she said in a much less friendly tone, "maybe it is," and then she turned away and began talking to her cousin Sophia.

What just happened? Does she think I'M the troll?! Oh Samantha, this is what happens when you try to be less socially awkward!

My confidence shattered and my anxiety ascending, I picked at the rest of my dinner and listened in on other conversations for the remainder of the evening. It was all so *natural,* not forced like at my house. If something is bothering someone in Carla's family they just come right out and say it. I'm not saying I enjoy confrontation, but it has to be better than all this unspoken, never-say-what-you-really-mean tension that my family are so good at. Everything's seething under the surface, especially with Mum, and it only seems to come out from its subterranean pit when she's had too much wine, and then she just apologises the next day as if to brush it under the carpet again! It makes no sense to me because I never feel the urge to say anything. I'm quite happy with my own thoughts and feelings. But Mum clearly needs to get things off her chest and yet she refrains. It must be so stressful having to talk things through all the time! Thinking things through is so much easier.

Saturday 10th October 2020

We're at Dad's this weekend and Richard is back on form, by which I mean, he's got a new obsession. The weird thing is, Frogsplash seems to be in on it too. It's this moody band called *Dolores's Dolorifuge* who like to whine about how unpopular and miserable they are in their songs even though they're really successful in real life. It's all so fake, but Richard and Froggo are all over it. Dad seems oblivious to it all, so I keep having to remind him that some of the lyrics aren't appropriate for Stephanie to hear.

"Oh, she won't pick up on it!" he said. "Look at her, she's miles away watching *Barry Bumble's Boat.*"

He had a point. Apparently, *The Animals of the Forever Forest* are old news. Barry Bumble is this extremely jolly older man with white hair and a beard who lives near a port in Cornwall. He takes his boat out on fishing trips with his incredibly naïve puppet friend, a city cat named Sampson. Sampson loves to eat fish, but he has no idea where they come from. Barry Bumble is keen to educate him in an extremely patronising manner, and Sampson asks some awfully obvious questions. There seems to be three songs that are sung in each episode: the question song, when Sampson decides he needs to investigate something, like how tuna gets from the sea to the tin, for example. Then there's the answer song, which is pretty self-explanatory. Then finally, there's the "goodbye, haven't we had such a fun time, we must do it again sometime" song, which is basically the musical equivalent of that awkward moment in the hallway when you're leaving someone's house and you have to say goodbye a million times as you're putting on your shoes and coat and they're asking if you're sure you haven't forgotten anything.

"I was thinking we ought to go shopping," Dad said after lunch. "I've convinced Sophie to lend me the car seat for this weekend, but I'm going to need supplies of my own. I'm sure you two could do with some new gear for the autumn, anyway, am I right?"

"Yeah, whatever," I said, "the coat you got me last year is getting a bit tight. I told you we should've gone for a 12-13!"

"And I told you the store only sold kid's clothes aged twelve and under! My goodness, I'm going to have to buy you adult sizes, aren't I? You're growing up too quickly, you two."

"At least you've got Stephanie to keep you young!" I said, smirking as Dad picked her up to take a whiff of the suspicious contents of her nappy.

"Well I'm up for it," said Froggo, and I'm pretty sure that was the longest sentence I've heard him utter since Gertie left him.

"I thought you hated shopping?" I said in genuine surprise.

"I do," he murmured in a deep monotone, his eyes glued to *Barry Bumble's Boat* so as not to communicate in a manner too friendly for the likes of me, his sister. "But I need new clothes."

I looked at him, wearing the delicate and dandy attire that Gertie had made him wear. Pastel blue chinos with scuffed knees and a once-smart, pale yellow polo shirt gone bad. He had neglected to iron it and there were greasy dribbles from takeaway meals eaten hastily and without implements. He looked like a bruised banana. Gertie had not only made him buy a whole new wardrobe; she had also made him throw away all the clothes he used to wear. He might have grown out of half of them by now anyway, but I bet he was regretting it, nonetheless. I felt sorry for my brother just then. He was right: he did need new clothes.

Dad drove us all to the big shopping precinct, including Richard, who no doubt needed to throw some money away on expressing his new phase in the most outward, obvious and skin-deep way possible: by buying paraphernalia and adorning himself in every recognisable symbol of his latest fad. When we arrived at the shopping centre we headed straight for the second floor, where there was a place to rent out these little pretend cars for toddlers so you can push them around while you shop and even put your shopping bags in the pretend boot! It's an amazing idea – Stephanie thought it was great fun and she normally has a full-on tantrum when you try to put her in a buggy.

We did the clothes shopping first because the baby stuff was going to be too much to carry. I fell in love with this shaggy, white and caramel faux fur coat that I'd seen in a shop window. I didn't even ask for it, but Dad caught me looking and he bought it straight away. He said it was a thank you for being so helpful and so loving towards Stephanie. I felt guilty at first because it was more expensive than usual, but then Richard went crazy in the rock music store buying *Dolores's Dolorifuge* t-shirts and hoodies for both him and Froggo. He actually *insisted* on paying for both! He doesn't get a lot of respect from his two daughters, and I wonder if maybe he's treating Frogsplash like the son he never had – if only he knew that this was the "idiot boyfriend" he was so keen to get rid of!

I don't even want to tell you how much we spent on baby stuff for Stephanie, and we didn't even get that much. We got the things we needed most urgently: a car seat and a buggy, and then we stocked up on nappies and some clothes for her to keep at Dad's flat. Froggo must have been in a good mood after Richard splurged on him, because he decided to give some helpful advice:

"Nobody chucks anything away any more, Dad," he said, "and babies grow out of things before they get worn out, so you can probably get most of the stuff you need second-hand. Look, on this app I've already found a gate to stop her getting in the kitchen and a toddler bed for when she grows out of the travel cot."

"Wow, thanks, Frogsplash," said Dad. "I'm so proud of you two, being such good older siblings."

Cringe. Dad's gone all cheesy since Stephanie came along.

It's late at night now. Stephanie went to sleep hours ago with Richard. There's a strange connection between those two now that they've both been dumped by Roberts women. It seems like a kind of rock bottom for Frogsplash. I like Richard, but he's not exactly role model material.

Wednesday 14th October 2020

THE RESULTS ARE IN! READ ON TO FIND OUT WHOSE IDEAS ARE TREASURES WAITING TO BE DUG UP AND WHOSE ARE HEADED FOR THE SCRAP HEAP!

In an entirely un-democratic selection process, an unknown cluster of potentially biased teachers has chosen two ideas from each year group which will, in just a week's time, be buried in a time capsule. The matter was not put up to a vote because, as we all know, all children are too stupid to be allowed to vote on events that will affect their futures.

Yes, Mr Wilcox announced the winning ideas for the time capsule. They weren't particularly inspired, but I suppose all of the truly original ideas weren't approved by the teachers because they didn't represent the school or put it in a good light or whatever. If you ask me, we should put the absolute worst stuff about our present-day school in the capsule so that future pupils can marvel at how comparatively primitive we are. I would put in photos of the girl's toilets in the science block, the one where not a single cubicle has both locking door and a toilet seat. If I could I'd also preserve a sample of the school cafeteria's shepherd's pie, because that is truly horrific.

So, here are the winning ideas:

Year Seven:

- A copy of the lunch menu (yawn).
- A packet of skImps. SkImps are this new craze that's going around with younger kids. They're these little plastic creatures, little imps I guess, and you fight your ones against your opponent's. Each one has different skills, powers and qualities, and each one comes from

one of twenty power categories. If you collect all nine from a power category you can attach them all together to build a sklUp. A sklUp is a built-up mega imp that basically defeats all skImps.

Year Eight (my year):

- A copy of the first ever year seven story to make the front page of the school newspaper. That was us, last year, and I'm in the picture that goes with the story. I'm sort of in the background but there's no pretending it's not me. Oh, and I look ridiculous and I've only just about got over it. I would be annoyed about this, but I quite like the idea of burying it. It will feel cathartic.
- A USB recording of last year's school play. I'm in this one, too! I played Puck in the end-of-year play last year. Hopefully I didn't look so ridiculous in that. This was Danny's suggestion, and she made the recording herself while she was in the audience watching me perform!

Year Nine:

- A complete homework diary. This was submitted by an incredibly neat, studious girl who appears to have filled out her homework diary perfectly. This is not representative of the school and for that reason I strongly object to its inclusion in the capsule. Everyone I know, including myself, defaces their homework diary with doodles, song lyrics and funny quotes. It's the number one distraction activity in lessons. Last year I wrote a poem in mine about a bee that fell in love with a park bench.
- A whole school photo (YAWN!).

Year Ten:

- A list of the top 40 music tracks.
- A list of the top 10 trending online articles. Both good ideas, I think. They're simple, but they will give an insight into what life is like right now.

Year Eleven:

- Example exam questions.
- A hair tiara. This is another craze. It's a hair accessory that's literally made out of hair. They're made from fake hair which has been stretched over a wire in the shape of a tiara. Usually people wear them in the same colour as their natural hair, so it looks like they've actually managed to style their own hair in the shape of a tiara. I can't decide if I like them or not, but I don't think me and my thin, mousy hair would be able to pull it off anyway.

Year Twelve:

You're not going to believe these ones. I'm 99 per cent certain that only two people from year twelve actually bothered to submit an idea, and I'm about 95 per cent sure that they were both entered as a joke.

- A local takeaway menu.
- An unclaimed item from the lost property box, selected at random. Truly uninspired.

Year Thirteen:

- Sociology students from across the year will conduct a research project asking everyone else in the year three questions: "What are you most looking forward to?", "What are you most worried about?" and "what are you most bored of?" The findings of the study will be placed in the capsule. I suspect this was actually a Sociology teacher's idea, although perhaps the kids came up with the questions.
- An anonymous poem about online bullying. Because it was submitted anonymously no one actually knows what year the person who wrote it is in, but the teachers decided it was so good it was probably a year thirteen.

So that's the end of that, I guess. And do you know what prize the winning entrants get? They "get to" dig the hole and bury the capsule out on the muddy field! Ha! They do get to skip lessons for it, and it will be on the front page of *The Daily Duke,* but that's hardly a holiday and a celebrity status!

Sunday 18th October 2020

We just had Family Talk Time and I am not happy. I'm so unhappy, in fact, that I can even feel myself relating to Frogsplash, who has kind of gone off at the deep end when it comes to emotional angst. Isn't it funny, the double standards parents put upon us? Like when Mum wanted to have Family Talk Time and insisted that we all talk and contribute to the discussion when we *really* didn't want to talk and really didn't have anything to say. And tonight, when she had a whole lot of stuff to say that we actually, genuinely had strong feelings about, and all of a sudden it "wasn't open for discussion". We were expected to just sit there and accept it, because we're children and our voices shouldn't be heard. Except when we'd rather not speak.

I suppose adults have to think about money as well as happiness. The two things are not the same, and that's why there are these things called "sacrifices". They aren't as bad as the sacrifices people did in the really olden days, but I don't think they're ever very good. The thing which Mum and Graham suggested (or, more accurately, *decided*) tonight is something I would definitely define as a sacrifice, but I suppose they were being careful not to use such negative words. They decided that Graham and Billy are going to move into our house very soon. They're going to rent out the flat above the pub and save up the rent money so that we can all get a bigger house together in the near future.

It's an intrusion, is what it is. It is going to affect me, but I can honestly say I'm more worried about Froggo. They're expecting him to share his room with Billy full-time, and although they have always been close friends, they're going through different phases and I can relate to that. It was hard enough when I drifted apart from my primary school friend Summer – imagine if we'd been forced to live together and share a bedroom! They say it's only temporary, but these things always take longer than planned. We can have all the family talks in the world, but when it comes to a decision the adults will always be on the winning side.

Wednesday 21st October 2020

Today was a weird day, but it was also a great day (for some of us). It was the day of the dig: the competition winners, including Danny, would be spending their afternoon digging a hole for the time capsule, but before that was this morning's full school assembly.

"Good morning, children, please be seated," said Mr Wilcox, in his oversized assembly blazer. We all sat down.

"As I'm sure you will all remember, today is a very exciting day. Today we will bury the time capsule that will represent our school at this moment in time. It will be unique to you, as a collective, and it will go down in history, hopefully to be dug up by future students decades from now!"

"Excuse me, sir," said Carla, and she stood up out of her seat and looked right at Mr Wilcox, who was at the front of the stage, a collection of senior staff sat behind him in a row. Children do not interrupt assembly. Not ever.

Mr Wilcox turned to face the impertinent speaker. Then there was this amazing moment, this beautiful, magical shift in tone which only Carla, Danny and I could have perceived, when he recognised Carla's face: the girl who boldly walked, right after his truly embarrassing, truly out-of-character rap in the music recording room. She was not going to be ignored.

Go, Carla, go!

"Yes, do you have a query?" asked Mr Wilcox, a.k.a. The Big W.

"Indeed, I do," she replied, amazing the onlookers with her cool irreverence, "I am finding it difficult to feel passionate about this school project. What is the point in burying a time capsule if it is never to be dug up? It's basically subterranean littering!"

"I don't understand…" stammered Mr Wilcox nervously, but Carla wasn't quite finished.

"If what you tell us is true, there must be six time capsules buried on this site, but nobody has ever dug them up! What's the point? All of this fuss, all of the time these people spent coming up with good ideas of what to bury, but what's it all for?!"

Mr Wilcox went bright red, and he was lost for words in a way which I don't think any head teacher has ever been. I think he'd have been less embarrassed if we'd shown a video of The Big W to the entire school.

"It's all right, Walter," came a booming voice from the row of senior staff behind him, "it's time I told the truth."

Mr Bellows, who was once a student at our school and has been a teacher ever since he graduated (which must have been a long time ago!) stepped forward solemnly.

"It's true, there are six time capsules buried on these school grounds," he spoke in elegiac tones, "but most of you will not know that they have, in fact, been dug up. Every ten years we have dug up each capsule, studied and compared their contents, and re-buried them in the exact same spot. But on the last occasion, in 2010, I made a grave mistake. As the school's longest serving member of staff, I was entrusted with the map which showed the burial point of each capsule, and I was also given the great honour of packing the fourteen chosen articles into the new capsule.

"Mr Wilcox, who was a newly appointed head at the time, asked me to back up a digital copy of the map on the school's computer system, but I was ashamed to admit that I did not know how to do this. I am befuddled by technology. I did not follow those orders, and for that I am truly sorry. But for this next confession I will never be relieved of guilt. There was a mix-up, and under my watch, the one and only map got buried in the most recent time capsule. It had been folded up inside an envelope containing Spot-Bot trading cards, which were popular at the time."

He hung his head in shame, as though confessing to a murder in a courtroom. None of us knew how to react. We didn't really care, but Mr Bellows clearly cared very deeply. There was some silence and then, quite remarkably, Mr Bellows began to sing a mournful song. It was the school song, which has always been a bit of a joke, but from Mr Bellows, without backing music or a chorus of several hundred children, it was a requiem.

"Behold the legend of the Duke – behold
We carry his great name with pride
For he was a man both virtuous and bold

May his spirit be our conscience and guide."

At this point his voice began to creak as he struggled to hold back tears.

"With great responsibility his great honour came
But in his wisdom he knew what to do
He took the title of Duke, fixed it to his name
And from thence his bravery grew.

The Duke took on fine and gracious pursuits
But nothing could be truer or finer
Than the lady he hoped would bear him his fruits
The charitable and kindly Carolina.

The lady so pure struck a chord in his heart
So, he told her his version of truth [WINK]
That he shared in her passion for books and for art
And had founded a school for poor youth.

His love for the girl grew deep and strong
And in him a great notion stirred
That he must build this school before too long
And so, make good his word.

But how to acquire the land and the bricks
To achieve such a selfless feat?
There was up his sleeve a great many tricks
For he was a wise master of deceit.

He met with a brewer and shook his hand
But the man was a weak, drunken fool
For he gambled away every inch of his land
So that Duke John could build his school!

The work was not done, though the bricks were all laid
For a school needs masters as well

John knew not how they all would get paid
But he had to act fast and not dwell.

Duke John used knowledge for his only tool
He sought teachers who had something to hide
He forced them to work for free at his school
Or he'd tell the church how they'd lied!

Meanwhile the brewer grew deeper in debt
John had taken his life and his pride
He grew mad with drink and bitter regret,
Jumped from the church roof and died.

The silly old man let us laugh at his shame!
So drunk that he took his own life!
But so, honoured now was the Jameson name
That Carolina agreed to be his wife.

Our history is written, we thank the Duke for his part
Our future is now ours to carve
He was strong in his spirit and true in his heart
Now thanks to him we shall not starve!"

Now he was basically sobbing.

"Behold the legend of the Duke, behold
We carry his great name with pride
For he was a man both virtuous and bold
May his spirit be our conscience and guide."

It was a strange spectacle, to say the least, especially when he still attempted to do the wink despite his eyes filling up with tears. At one stage Mr Wilcox tried to stop him, but Mr Bellows shooed him away quite dramatically. This poor man has spent near enough his entire life in this school, and he obviously feels as though he's betrayed us all.

"And now," he went on after the final verse, "I'm afraid to announce my resignation. I am not fit to serve you, Duke John Jameson."

"Alfred, can we at least talk about this? Come to my office, come on," Mr Wilcox pleaded, and he led the broken man off the stage and out of the assembly hall, leaving us all utterly bemused. The senior staff at the back of the stage sat there like lemons, looking to each other to do something to address the situation. Eventually my History teacher from last year, Mr Achilles, ran up from the seating area to take the stage.

"Well, I don't think any of us were expecting that!" he said, and we all laughed, so relieved that someone had broken the tension that it seemed like the funniest thing we'd ever heard.

"Let's hope that Mr Wilcox and Mr Bellows can resolve the situation in private. I'm sure this time around we will all be much more careful to remember where we buried the capsule, so let me assure you that this is not a futile project. Now, it looks like Mr Wilcox has left his notes here on the stand. It says here that the dig will commence this afternoon, right after lunch. The whole school will be permitted to watch the breaking of the soil and will then be given ten minutes to get back to their timetabled lessons, except the diggers themselves, of course, who are expected to miss a whole lesson. The dig will be supervised by PE staff, who will be on hand in case of any injury and ensure the safety of the pupils. You have all been advised to bring wellington boots and anoraks – if you have forgotten any of those you may use items from the lost property bin. Any questions?"

It was all a bit boring, especially considering the preceding drama, but I was excited to see Danny up there with the other competition winners. I was also a bit intrigued. How long does it take for fourteen children to dig a hole? Of course, it depends on the size and depth of the hole, but how deep do you need to bury it, knowing that people in the future mean to dig it back up again? It got me wondering about the other capsules and how far down they might be. I had to ask.

"Yes, sir, I was wondering, how deep do they have to dig the hole? Seems like fourteen people could dig quite a way down in one hour!"

"Well, there will be some taking it in turns, I suppose. Fourteen is a bit of a crowd! I have heard rumours of hot chocolate and biscuits for those who are waiting their turn to dig, though. It says here, that in past years the capsules have been buried four feet deep."

Four feet! It's not a bloody dead body!

The dig itself was a bit dull. It was drizzling with a constant light rain, and although Mr Wilcox did turn up to announce the official breaking of the soil, it was clear this morning's events had taken the wind out of his sails, and his lack of enthusiasm seemed to reverberate across the crowd of sodden children. I was amused to see that one of the year seven diggers had indeed forgotten his wellingtons and was wearing a pair of old trainers from the lost property bin which must have been at least three sizes too big. The fourteen chosen ones had a shovel each, although I noted that the year sevens' shovels were nothing more than the wood-handled spades you sometimes get at the beach.

We watched the lot of them plant their shovels/spades into the earth and then Mr Wilcox basically told us to all get lost. It wasn't really worth the whole ceremonial build-up. After school, Carla and I met up with Danny to ask her how it went.

"Oh, you know, as well as expected. The sixth formers and PE teachers ended up doing most of the legwork while the rest of us huddled around the refreshments table. The hot chocolate was like earthy water but at least it kept us warm!"

"Sounds like a bit of a dud competition prize!" I said.

"Yeah, especially as it'll probably never get dug up again!" said Carla.

"You've really got a bee in your bonnet about that, haven't you?" asked Danny.

"Well, yeah!" said Carla, "I mean, I don't think Mr Bellows should be beating himself up about it as much as he clearly is, but really, they should have had a better system in place for keeping track of it all rather than one copy of a stupid map! And Mr Wilcox should have known better than to trust an old fossil like Bellows to use a computer!"

"Funny you should say that," Danny replied, "I think Wilcox was a bit upset by it all. He stayed for most of the dig, but he seemed very distracted."

"Because he knows he's as much to blame as Bellows!" Carla said triumphantly.

"Maybe," said Danny, "I felt quite sorry for him to be honest. I even offered him my shovel and asked if he wanted a go at digging – it almost cheered him up until he looked up and recognised my face from the music recording room – then he looked even more mortified than he did in assembly this morning!"

"You know what, I think he's actually scared of us!" I said.

"Scared of us, or scared that we might reveal his secret?" Carla said in a 'cunning plan' sort of voice, "perhaps this could work in our favour..."

"How so?" Danny asked.

"I've got an idea," said Carla, her lips curling into a devious grin. "Tomorrow lunchtime the three of us are going to pay the Big W a little visit."

Thursday 22nd October 2020

We were gathered together in our usual spot, eating our packed lunches as we discussed our plans.

"It's perfect," Carla was saying, "we know his secret – we've got *leverage.*"

"He's still the head teacher," Danny said worriedly, "and this is practically blackmail. He might just say no, I'm not doing it, and if you tell everyone about The Big W then I'll put you in permanent detention – or worse!"

"He can't do that!"

"Of course, he can! He's the head – he answers to no one!"

"There's always someone higher up the ladder – a school governor or something. Look, if you don't want to do it, I'll go on my own!"

"No, no, I never said that!" said Danny, "I'm just making sure you know the risk."

"OK, OK, how about this: if he threatens us with some kind of punishment – permanent detention, exclusion, whatever, then we back down, no questions asked, even if it seems like an empty threat. Is that all right?"

"OK, I'm in," said Danny, "Sam?"

"Well, of course I'm in," I said, "but while we're on the subject of empty threats, don't you think he might call our bluff if we threaten to reveal his secret? I mean the idea of him trying to rap is so ludicrous I'm not sure anyone would believe it!"

"Maybe so," said Carla, smiling her shrewd smile once again, "but does he really want to bet against the odds of one of us having it all recorded on our phone?"

I have to admire Carla's determination, particularly for such a selfless cause. None of the past students who buried those capsules would ever know how hard she fought to preserve their memories.

"We need to dig it all up," she said when we were finally permitted to enter Mr Wilcox's office, "like an archaeological dig. We need to cover all ground until we've found them."

"Excuse me?" asked Wilcox, though he seemed more sheepish than reprimanding.

"She means the time capsules, sir," I added, also rather more sheepish than Carla, "we want to find all of them."

"It could be another project," Danny said optimistically, "but this time we could get the whole school involved. We could get each class to take it in turns digging. It would be like searching for buried treasure!"

"Sounds awfully disruptive to schedules," Wilcox said, but there was a certain tone in his voice, a certain look on his face which told us that he was scared to refuse us.

"It would be just like yesterday, only one missed lesson, one class at a time. We'd cover loads of ground."

"And we could plant trees and flowers – maybe some vegetable patches – it would be a great school project," I added, thinking out loud.

"But most importantly, we would find those missing capsules," Carla said conclusively, and we all fell silent, awaiting our answer. Mr Wilcox took a long, deep breath as he looked each one of us square in the eyes. He had the perfect poker face. We waited with bated breath, not knowing what The Big W was going to say.

"I arrived at school early this morning," he spoke, breaking the silence at last, "it was still dark outside, and the corridors were eerily empty. I was heading towards the music department to..." he paused, his cheeks reddening, "...to handle some paperwork, when I heard a mournful tune crying out through the hollow hallways. I went to investigate the disturbance, following the ghostly wails all the way to the History department, which was just dimly lit by the deep blue of first light coming in through the windows. A figure in white floated in the distance ahead of me like a spiritual apparition. Some people say Duke John Jameson died right here at the school; did you know that?"

What the hell is he going on about? Does he think the school is haunted?!

"I must admit I felt a chill run down my spine, but I am a sensible man, and it is my duty to apprehend any trespassers on school grounds, so I continued my pursuit, still in semi-darkness, the main light switch for the department being in the History teachers' lounge. Then, quite abruptly, the lights appeared to come on of their own accord. I was shaken, but I knew what I had to do. I went straight to the teachers' lounge, and that's where I found the ghostly, pale figure. It was Mr Bellows, pacing the room in his white nightgown, singing a slow tempo version of the school song. I had never seen a more broken man.

"My point is," he went on, "I have come to agree with you girls. We do need to find those lost time capsules. It has been an important tradition in this school for many years, and I believe it is the only way we will ever get the old Mr Bellows back. Of course, we will have to allow him some involvement in the process so that he feels relieved of the burden of guilt. I will make him coordinator. He will decide which class digs when and where. Does that suit you?"

"Yes!" said Carla, who was a little stunned that her plan had worked.

"Fantastic," said Mr Wilcox, "then everybody's happy!"

Sunday 24th October 2020

HALF TERM FURY AT CASA DEL DRURY!

Another Sunday, another Family Talk Time gone drastically wrong! Catastrophic clashes continue in the residential warzone occupied by the Drury clan which leave us all questioning how long Cassie Drury, the ruthless dictator behind this sustained unrest, will persist with her ill-advised attempts to reach a union with the other members. Surely it's time she realised that granting independence is the only route to a peaceful outcome?

Yes, it's the first half term of the school year. There's something about half term that's just so *boring*. A week isn't long enough to take up a new hobby or challenge yourself to reading the "Top Fifty Books to Read before You Die" (which I attempted one summer but didn't get past ten). We never go on holiday, or even make any plans, so we all end up just moping around the house. Mum's taken a couple of days off work but she's planning to spend them at The Mill on the Hill working on the wine she's brewing.

Anyway, it's probably a good thing she's not going to be around much, because she and Frogsplash are clashing like never before. She thought she was playing it safe at Family Talk Time this week. Instead of raising potentially emotive or divisive subjects she began by discussing Frogsplash's birthday next week. His birthday is on Halloween, so we always have a big party and Mum likes to invite as many kids as possible to keep them from roaming the streets egging houses.

"So, someone's turning sixteen next week," she began, "you know what that means? You'll be old enough to get married!"

Frogsplash remained silent.

"So, I was thinking the usual – put up a few cobwebs, skeletons, that sort of thing. I'll do a big shop on Friday, get drinks and snacks. I was looking at getting an entertainer in, but they all look a bit babyish…"

"I'm turning sixteen, Mum. I'm getting a bit too old."

"Yes, you're right. I'll stick to the basics, keep it casual, no entertainers!"

"No, I mean I'm getting too old for birthday parties."

"But it's tradition! We always have a party!"

It was becoming obvious that Graham, Billy and I were surplus to requirements, and yet we sat there, knowing that if we tried to get up to leave all attention would be transferred onto us. It was a vicious psychological game.

"It used to be tradition for us to put out a mince pie and a glass of brandy for Father Christmas, but we don't do that any more."

"No, but we still have Christmas, we still celebrate…"

"And we can still celebrate my birthday. Let's just not make such a big deal out of it."

"It's not just your birthday though, is it? It's Halloween, and I throw this party for all the kids in the neighbourhood and their parents, and all of your friends as well. It's not all about you, it's about everybody!"

"It's all right, Cassie," Graham cut in, "don't get all upset. He's just being selfish. He's a selfish boy."

Frogsplash looked at Graham for a moment, rage wrought across his face, but he didn't respond. I don't think he knew how to – we're still figuring out where we stand with him. Instead Froggo focussed even harder on Mum:

"Right. So, all these years it's not really been for my birthday. All this time you've been throwing these parties it's been for you and your little vendetta against trick-or-treating! Oh, and by the way, I know you made up that whole story about your Aunt Ruby! LIAR!"

Family Talk Time: making personal conversations public since 2020.

"That was for your own good! And these parties are for the good of the entire community, but of course you're only thinking about yourself…"

"Are you calling me selfish? That's a bit rich! Fine then, have your party, but don't pretend it has anything to do with my birthday, because I won't be here!"

And with that, he stormed out of the living room and up to his bedroom. I had only a split second to make a decision. If I stayed there long enough for Mum to start talking about the argument, trying to get support from the rest of us, then I'd be stuck there all night. I saw my chance and I took it. Seconds after Frogsplash left, I bolted for the door and escaped up to my room, which is where I'm taking refuge until Mum's left for work in the morning. I feel a bit sorry for Billy, being the only kid down there. I kind of threw him under the bus. But when it comes to avoiding open family discussions I'm afraid you have to be a little bit selfish sometimes.

Monday 25th October 2020

I waited until I'd heard both Mum and Graham leave for work this morning, then I went down to make a cup of tea.

"Hey," said Billy, who had obviously had the exact same idea, because he entered the kitchen only a few seconds after me.

"Oh, hey," I said, "want a brew?"

"Yes, please," he replied in a tired voice, and he sat down at the kitchen table, dragging a food magazine from the centre by the salt and pepper grinders, flicking slowly and mindlessly through its pages. Normally I would have taken my tea up to my room and drank it in bed while reading, but it didn't feel right leaving Billy there on his own.

"Bit awkward, isn't it?" I said as I laid our mugs down and pulled up a chair opposite Billy. "Is Froggo any better when it's just you and him?"

"Not really," he said, "he's got his headphones in most of the time, listening to that awful emo band."

"Yeah, I'm not much of a fan either. It must be hard for you having to share a room with him."

"At the moment it is. If you'd told me a year ago that I'd be living with my best mate I'd have thought I was the luckiest kid in England!"

"Be careful what you wish for."

"Exactly. You know what this is all about, don't you?"

"Gertie dumped him."

"Yeah. I think he's too embarrassed to tell your mum."

"You'd have thought she'd have figured it out for herself!"

"Your mum's not stupid; I'm sure she knows. But she also knows that if she tried to talk to him about it it'd only make things worse."

"True! Who wants to talk to their mum about stuff like that?!"

There was an awkward pause, and I felt bad because I should really be more sensitive around Billy. His mum left and never came back. He'd probably give anything to talk to his mum about stuff like that.

"Well they're going to have to talk eventually, even if it's not about Gertie," he said at last.

"And I plan to be well out of the way when that happens!" I replied.

"That gives me an idea," he said as he got up to refill the kettle, "how would you like to come work at the pub for a few evenings this week? It'd be a great excuse to steer clear of the drama, and you'll get paid a fiver an hour."

"Really? Aren't I too young?"

"Not if you're just collecting glasses and topping up ketchup sachets. I'll be there to make sure no one hassles you, not that you'd get any bother. They're all regulars who just want a quiet drink and sometimes a meal. It's almost empty on weekdays anyway, so when there's nothing to do you can just sit in a booth and do your homework like I used to."

"And your dad wouldn't mind?"

"He'd love to have you at the pub! I know he feels a bit out of place here, because of the way he and I just sort of popped up and invaded the space that belonged to you guys. But the pub's his domain, that's where he feels in control. I think that's why he wanted to get your mum working there, too. The pub's his territory and when we're there he's the boss. Anyway, I'll need you there to keep me company – I'd rather be earning money in the pub than sulking about the house all week with old moody chops upstairs!"

So, it's settled then – my first job! I hope I don't break anything.

Wednesday 27th October 2020

I'm never going back to that pub. It was horrible. You know I hate being the centre of attention, unless I'm in complete control of it and it's on my terms, like when I was in the school play. But this was different. It was way out of my control and even Billy, who's usually Mr Confident, struggled to handle the situation. I thought that I could just collect glasses, take them to the kitchen, load them in the dishwasher and that would be it, totally hassle-free. But there was this one table with three men who were drinking their beers so quickly I kept having to go over there to get their empty glasses. They were probably in their late twenties and they were those thick-necked, muscle-bound type that look like they spend too much time in the gym and would take just about any opportunity to take their shirt off and strut around in public like proud, bulky peacocks.

I overheard a lot of their conversations and they didn't even seem to be mates. All they did was berate each other or try to one-up the others in some way, like there's no such thing as friendship, only competition.

"What do you make of the new bar girl?" I heard one of them say as I walked away with their empty glasses. He had a tattoo of a spider's web on his neck. He spoke loudly, not making any attempt to hide the fact that he was talking about me.

"Not a bar girl," another said as he took a big gulp of the next pint he'd already got lined up, "too young – she just collects the glasses."

"Ah, too young, that's a shame," the first one said, "I like the look of her. Big lips."

"Yeah, you fancy a bit of that?" the third one asked, "not much going on in the chest area."

"Oh, they'll grow, she'll develop nicely that one. You know what you gotta do with them ones – get in there early, bide your time. Get in while they're young, just be friendly, let 'em know they can trust you, be a mate to 'em. And then you wait, just be patient and wait, all the while they're growing up, filling out in all the right places…"

"She already looks a bit full, that one – you see the thighs on it? Like two kebab cones rubbing together!"

"You know me – I like a bit of meat on the bone!"

They all laughed. I couldn't listen to another word of it. There were still glasses to collect from other tables, but I could feel the tears rising hotly behind my cheeks and up to my eyes. I went to the kitchen, my only refuge, and loaded the glasses into the dishwasher.

"How's it going? Enjoying it?" Billy popped up from nowhere.

"Yeah, fine thanks," I said, focussing really hard on the dishwasher. I couldn't look him in the eye; he'd see.

"Sam? Are you OK?"

"Yep."

"Sam, look at me."

I looked up.

"You're crying! What happened?"

"It's nothing, really. It's those men... the ones sat in the booth. They were saying things about me. It's OK. They didn't even say anything *to* me. It's not a big deal."

"Yes it is! If they made you upset then it's a big deal. Ugh, this is all my fault. This was a bad idea. I should have known working here wouldn't be the same for a girl. OK, here's what we'll do: I'll come out with you and stay behind the bar with Arnie. I'll be right there, and if they say anything else you let me know and I'll get rid of them."

"You don't have to do that! You'll lose customers..."

"We don't need customers like that. They make everyone feel uncomfortable and they drag down our reputation."

"They're really big, Billy. I mean, they look really strong..."

"You are saying I couldn't take them in a fight?!" joked Billy, who's fifteen years old and probably weighs less than me.

"I'm just saying, what if they get aggressive?"

"Then they get barred for life and I call the police."

There was no arguing with him – he was already marching out to the bar, so I followed. He eyed the three men coldly, but they weren't looking.

"Just ignore them. Don't go to their table, they can bring their own glasses back," he said to me in a hushed voice.

83

I collected the glasses from the other tables and took them to the back to be washed. Someone from the kitchen handed me a small wicker basket full of ketchup and mayonnaise sachets to take out for some customers who had ordered food. I did as I was told, but the table of diners was right next to the booth. Too close.

"Oi, oi – here she is!" said the man with the neck tattoo, "about bloody time! We've got loads of glasses piling up here, are you gonna come get them or what?"

I had no choice.

"What time do you finish, darling?" he asked as I began putting their glasses on my tray.

"Nine," I said stiffly.

"You want a lift home? You can't be old enough to drive."

"No," I said defiantly, "you can't be sober enough to drive."

"You what?!" He raised his voice and stood up from his seat. "Been counting my drinks, have you? How many have I had then? It's none of your business if I want to drive home! I'm a paying customer! Hasn't anyone ever told you you're a lot more attractive when you keep your gob shut?"

Billy must have heard when he raised his voice. He came to intervene.

"Is there a problem?" he asked calmly.

"Yeah – HER!"

"Has she done something wrong?"

"Yeah – she presumed to tell ME, a loyal customer, that I'm too drunk to drive home. She needs to learn some respect, let me tell you…"

"Actually, I think you need to learn some respect," Billy broke in. "That's no way to talk to a lady, especially a young one who's just trying to do her job. It's our duty as staff here not to allow customers to drive if they are over the limit."

"You think you can stop me? How old are you anyway? Aren't there any adults working here?"

"Yes," came Arnie's voice as he stormed over to us, "and as part-owner of this establishment I'm going to have to ask you three to leave. This is a family pub and we have other customers here trying to enjoy their dinner."

I won't repeat the words that came out of their three mouths after that, but it was clear they were becoming belligerent. At first they refused to leave, then they started getting angry at Arnie, then each other. Finally, they all stood up and it looked as though it was over, but then neck tattoo picked up his empty glass and smashed it on the table. Shards went flying everywhere and he and his cronies made a swift but noisy exit.

Billy and I swept up the broken glass while Arnie went round apologising to the other customers and offering them all a free drink. It was such a mess. Billy insisted on calling his dad to pick me up. He didn't want to risk keeping me there in case the men returned, and even though it was still light outside he said it was too dangerous for me to walk home alone.

"I'm so sorry this happened," he said as we waited for Graham to arrive.

"It's not your fault," I said, "I shouldn't have antagonised him, he was big and I'm small – what was I thinking? He just made me so angry!"

"Come on, now, don't go blaming yourself! I actually thought it was pretty funny what you said. Unfortunately, though, there are some people in this life who don't have a sense of humour. Always be wary of those ones."

What, like your dad?

"What did you tell your dad? About what happened, I mean."

"I just said a customer got angry, kicked off a bit. I didn't tell him they were bothering you or anything like that."

"Thanks," I said. "Thank you for everything."

Friday 29th October 2020

Carla and I went round Danny's house today to hang out. There were plenty of opportunities for me to tell them about what happened on Wednesday, but the words seemed to die in my mouth before they even came out. I suppose I didn't want a fuss, and I was a bit embarrassed about some of the nastier things those men said. It was a bit awkward when Danny's dad came back from work. He had obviously had a stressful week, but Danny's mum didn't want him to talk about it in front of us.

"It's been a long week," he said the moment he sat down, "sometimes I wonder if it's all worth it…"

"Well we've had a busy day, haven't we, girls?" she said far too cheerfully, "and the twins have been up to their usual tricks! Anyway, it's the weekend now so we can all relax, can't we?"

Danny's dad didn't look at all relaxed. He ate his dinner in a brooding silence which set the tone for the rest of us. Luckily the twins were oblivious, because their nonsense chatter and giggles were the only relief from an otherwise cold and clinical affair.

Sunday 31st October 2020

A COLD AND CLINICAL AFFAIR: SWEET SIXTEENTH IS A SALTY WASHOUT AS PLANS TO PARTY ARE DASHED!

A recent study has shown that sixteenth birthday parties are becoming increasingly embittered, often to the point of complete cessation, thanks to the cynicism and world-weariness of the teens involved: "Why are we expected to recognise our own obsolescence with such cheerful celebrations? Our childhood is fading. We are slowly dying. Let us wither in peace!"

I hope my sixteenth birthday isn't as miserable as Froggo's. Mum didn't throw a party. She bought a cake and did a "snacky dinner" but it was not well received. I suppose he went through the motions, but he barely tried to conceal his lack of enthusiasm. Even with Billy and Graham here, and Max and Trousers getting fed under the table, there was still more than half of the food left by the time Frogsplash had gone back up to his room and the rest of us decided to call it quits.

"What a waste," Graham said as he began clearing the plates.

"Oh, leave that, I'll do it," Mum said, "most of the leftovers can be saved for another day."

"Nobody will want these stale remnants of such a depressing party," Graham said, and he seemed almost angry, seething as though this whole thing was somehow an affront to him. "You should have gone ahead with the Halloween party," he continued talking to Mum. "You always do this. Your head's so wrapped up in your children you forget about everybody else. It's like you're not even thinking sometimes. You let your son dictate everything that goes on around here, then you wonder why everything you do turns out to be such a miserable failure!"

What was he implying?

I've been lying in bed trying to get to sleep, but Frogsplash's room is right next to mine and he's playing this song on repeat. It's called *Anodyne Annie,* and he's playing it far too loud, but it is his birthday and we'd all be wide awake right now if we'd gone ahead with the party anyway so I suppose I can't complain.

It's by that moody band he and Richard like. I know all the lyrics now:

Annie has a smile on her pretty face
Annie never has a hair out of place
She wears pink blouses and full-length skirts
She hates my ripped jeans and slogan t-shirts

CHORUS:
Annie doesn't like me; she thinks I'm dumb
Annie doesn't like me; she thinks I'm scum
But she'd never ever tell it to me straight to my face
'Cause she's inoffensive; she's so straight-laced

Annie goes to school, she never skips class
She'd never admit that the teacher's an ass
She's a straight-B student with a strict routine:
Speak when spoken to; keep your hands clean

[CHORUS]

Every day the same, it's time for a change
One day Annie wakes, she feels quite strange
She doesn't feel like smiling, those days are done
She goes to school that day with her daddy's gun

Now Annie likes me, she thinks I'm cool
But she's holding me hostage in our high school
Now Annie likes me, but it's too late
'Cause I'm starting to think that she's not so great.

I wonder why he keeps listening to it. Does he feel like the boy in the song, or like Anodyne Annie? Maybe Gertie is Annie. Or maybe he just likes the song. I went downstairs to get a glass of water, but I ended up cuddling with the dogs because I knew I wouldn't be able to get to sleep for a while anyway. Then I heard someone open the front door and I was worried it was Frogsplash about to do something stupid. I went to investigate, carrying Trousers in my arms, with Max by my feet.

"Billy? Where are you going?"

"Oh, I didn't realise you were up. You can't sleep either?"

"Not with that racket! Must be even worse for you, having to share a room with him."

"Yeah, I'm going to the flat above the pub. Arnie's there. I might not come back for a while."

"Oh…"

That made me feel sad. Billy's the one I count on to keep spirits high. Max could sense something was up because she suddenly stopped being tethered to my feet and went over to Billy, her rightful owner, and looked up at him sadly. I knew how she felt.

"Billy Wilson, you're not going to leave without your baby, are you?" I said, looking at Max.

"I thought you might be mad if I took her."

"I'd be madder if you left her here pining for you! Go on – take her. You could both do with the company." I got Max's lead from the hooks in the kitchen and gave it to Billy. "Night, then."

"Goodnight Sam."

Monday 1st November 2020

All of my faith in humanity has been restored! Not only was Mr Wilcox true to his word, but I've never seen Mr Bellows happier. He led this morning's assembly with an alacrity so refreshing after the moody half term I've just had. He announced to the entire school what Carla, Danny and I already knew, that he is the coordinator of the great time capsule dig. Being of a historical nature, and Mr Bellows being the Head of History, he decided that we should each take our turn to dig according to our History classes, so that I will be digging with the other children in my History class, and so will everyone else. It starts today with the year sevens and will continue up the year groups until all capsules have been found, even if it means repeating the process several times. Our school grounds are quite extensive, but a lot of that is covered by buildings and the lake. I'm sure we'll find them – how exciting would it be to discover one?!

He showed us a photo on the projector of what the capsules will look like. Quite large and bullet-shaped, made out of metal, but of course they will be covered in earth and the older ones will have rusted. It almost doesn't matter what banal anachronisms are inside them now – if they are anywhere near as dull as the items we buried in our one then I'll struggle to take an interest. But the thrill of the hunt is what's driving us. Is it silly to get so excited over something so inconsequential? It's creating quite a buzz around school. The only one who doesn't seem enthused is Mack, my Art teacher.

"We're supposed to be studying landscapes this term, and those barbarians are destroying every bit of landscape we've got!" he said in our lesson today. "Landscape is all about undisturbed nature... *undisturbed!*"

He was supposed to be teaching us how to use watercolours, but he was really just doing his own painting and ranting about the dig while we watched. At some point he wandered off "to get more brushes" and returned twenty minutes later smelling of cigarettes, which is fairly typical of Mack, to be honest.

Thursday 4th November 2020

DIGGING UP THE DIRT ON LIFE BEFORE WIFI: ENCAPSULATING THE MILLENNIUM TWENTY YEARS ON!

A trip down memory lane for some; for others a spooky insight into our dark and dreary history – we reveal the contents of the first time capsule to be found.

They did it! The year sevens found one! It was mid-morning during Maths, and it was around the sort of time my concentration was beginning to wane, when all of a sudden Mrs Wheeler from the office came running in to announce that they'd found a time capsule. We were all called into the assembly hall immediately for the big reveal. Some of the contents were pretty generic, like a DVD of an American film about cheerleading that was apparently very popular with girls at the time. Most of the stuff was about the millennium: there was a CD single of a song entitled "Millennium" and there was a newspaper from 1st January 2000 which had a photo of the New Year celebrations by the Thames. There was a gossip magazine which was kind of trashy because all that was in it were rumours of celebrity scandals and photos of celebrities not looking their best, usually on nights out getting in and out of cabs with not a lot of clothes on. There was a whole school photo, and it was pretty funny to see Mr Bellows twenty years younger. I recognised a few other teachers, too. Imagine staying in a school for that long!

Probably the most interesting thing in there was a compact disc offering "1000 hours of FREE internet access". I don't know how you get internet from a disc, but Mr Wilcox said these were free trials that were handed out to entice people to connect their home computers to the World Wide Web. He said the internet was a very different place back then, though. There was also a science textbook, a pack of these little hairclips which look like butterflies and were kind of basic compared to the hair tiaras we have now, and there was a photo of a vegetable patch the school had started growing, which is now a barren bit of pavement where the school's industrial sized refuse bins live, so that was kind of depressing.

Still, it was exciting for all of us, especially Carla, who pretty much made this whole thing happen!

"I can't believe they actually found one! The plan worked! And did you see the look on Bellows' face? Like a giddy child on Christmas morning!"

"I'll bet we find them all now," said Danny, "they must be buried close to each other!"

"I hope so," Carla said, looking as giddy as Mr Bellows, "I can't wait to see what's in the really old ones!"

Saturday 7th November 2020

We were at Dad's today. Stephanie kept playing the same episode of *Barry Bumble's Boat* for almost three hours before Dad finally realised that this was not mentally stimulating for his two oldest children, so he decided to take us to the park.

"Can't you just take her?" Frog said moodily, gesturing towards Stephanie.

"No! We could all do with some fresh air and you're supposed to be getting to know your little sister. We won't go to that dodgy playground over the road, I'll drive us to a nice park. We can go out for pizza afterwards."

"Fine," said Frogsplash.

"If only I'd known, I'd have brought some paints with me. I've got to paint a landscape for my Art homework."

"You can take mine," said Richard, who went through a brief arty phase earlier on this year.

"Oh really? Thanks!"

"No problem, as long as I can tag along – I've been getting into outdoor yoga and it would be nice to do it in a park instead of on the pavement outside our block."

Dad's flat is on a busy road with a row of shops at the end, so the image of Richard doing yoga amongst irritable pedestrians outside the flat brought a smirk to my face. I exchanged a look with Dad, who had obviously had to endure this new phase in silent frustration. I bet the wheelchair and buggy users in the area weren't too pleased either.

"Yeah, course you can," Dad said. "People will think you're Frogsplash's dad and not me!" he said, referring to the fact that both Richard and Froggo were wearing the exact same black *Dolores's Dolorifuge* hoodie.

It was a gloomy day, not exactly ideal for creating a masterpiece, but if Mack will insist on choosing the autumn/winter term to get us to paint outdoors then he's going to have to be prepared for a sea of grey. This is England, after all. My art skills aren't up to much anyway, especially with watercolours. Maybe if I'd been taught how to use them by someone *competent*... but no, that's not fair. Mack is a very good artist. As a teacher he is... well, I like his attitude. He has *flair*.

I chose to have the playground on the far right, only the edges of it in view of the painting, because I thought the focus of a landscape ought to be the wide, open fields rather than the busy detail. In the foreground was a big, black dog which was pressing itself low to the ground without resting, in a hunting stance while watching a squirrel foraging for acorns on the ground. Just outside of the playground looking in (at Stephanie and Dad, but they weren't in the frame) was Froggo, his black hood covering his head from the drizzling rain. In the centre but further back was Richard in his identical black hoodie, doing a grand yoga pose in the middle of the field. It didn't turn out much like a normal landscape painting, but how can I make Frogsplash and Richard look normal?

Afterwards we all went for pizza and Dad and I were left tending to Stephanie while Froggo and Richard seemed to be in an entirely separate dimension. Richard was telling him about some of the idiot kids he gets in his classes and some of the stupid things they say. Why didn't Richard want to talk to me about school stuff? We literally go to the same school! It was like some exclusive boys' club, not that I care. It's inappropriate anyway, to talk like that about your students, although I bet teachers do it all the time.

When we got back, I helped Dad get Stephanie ready for bed and I read her a bedtime story. I like reading to my sister. *My sister* – it still sounds so unreal! I like reading to Stephanie; her books are so sweet and actually pretty clever. By the time I'd finished, Dad, Richard and Frogsplash were all drinking beer and laughing raucously at this American TV show where these grown men do all these incredibly dangerous and clearly very painful stunts and try to trick each other into all sorts of disgusting behaviour. I left them to it, but I didn't really mind; I haven't seen Frogsplash that happy in months.

Sunday 8th November 2020

It was the Family Talk Time to end all family talk times. I mean literally, I don't think there will ever be another one. Why do parents always think they know best? Despite many failed attempts, Mum kept pushing and pushing this thing, and I think she genuinely believed that the problem was us not cooperating, us not taking it seriously, us not being willing to try. Well today one of us pushed back.

For the first time since Froggo's birthday we were all there: me, Frog, Billy, Graham and Mum. Billy's been staying at the pub all week and Graham's been flitting between here and there, checking in on Billy every so often.

"It's time we addressed the elephant in the room," Mum began.

Can't we just ignore the elephant in the room like everyone else does?

"Frogsplash, you've been in a foul mood for far too long now, and it's starting to affect other members of the household. You need to lighten up, or at least be a bit more considerate. You're projecting all of this negativity onto all of us; it's a very unpleasant environment. Can't you at least try to be more positive, for all our sake?"

Yeah, great advice from the woman who wants us all to be open about our feelings: stop moping about and pretend to be happy; dissemble your depression because it's really getting on our nerves!

"If, by 'other members of the household' you mean Billy, then may I remind you that he doesn't actually live here? He has his own bedroom in the pub and yet you adults, without consulting either of us, have decided to squash him into my room because the situation suits you. But of course, *I'm* the one who's not thinking about how their decisions affect others, not *you!*"

"That's only a temporary thing, just while we're saving up for the new house. It's just not fair on Billy to have to stay at the flat on his own while we're all together here."

"I really don't mind," Billy cut in quickly, "all my stuff's there, I work there most nights, and that way we all get our own space."

"Oh," Mum said, the wind out of her sails a little. All of this Family Talk Time, all of the decisions she's made, and I don't think she once asked Billy what was on his mind, and she's not really given the rest of us much of a chance to get a word in either. When you think about it, it's really been "Mum Talk Time". Until Graham decided he would get involved.

"Well that's settled then, at least until I can start renting out the flat over the pub," Graham said. "But that's not the only issue. You've been very difficult. You're very difficult to live with. You're not doing your chores, you barely speak – and when you do, it's something rude or sarcastic or dismissive. You're playing loud music all the time, you don't go out with your friends, you never walk Trousers. It's not fair. Frankly, I think you're being extremely selfish. Childish and selfish. I'm glad none of this nonsense has rubbed off on Billy. The way you're acting – I'd be ashamed to call you my son."

"Oh, is that what you all think?" Frogsplash got to his feet. "You've all been talking about me, have you? All saying what a miserable, lazy nuisance I am? How much you hate having me around? Well you can stop your whinging, and Billy can have my room – I'm moving in with Dad!"

And with that, he stormed up to his room. Mum got up to follow him, but Graham stopped her.

"Don't," he said, "he needs time to cool down."

Once again we were left hanging around in the wake of a Mum versus Frogsplash battle, and none of us knew what to say. After a few moments we were all reintroduced to the querulous tones of *Dolores's Dolorifuge,* this time a different song, called "Paroxysm of Failure":

"When I was a little boy I was told by my mom
Son you can be whatever it is that you want to become
So, I tried hard all my life to be what I could be
And finally, I became the total epitome

OF FAILUUUUUUUUUURE! Yeah!
I'm a FAILUUUUUUUUUURE! Yeah!
I'm no good at sports and I suck at video games

I know I'm a failure in every state though I can't remember their names
I'm a FAILURE, yeah
I'm a failure
And I'm never gonna change!

When I talk to girls my mouth begins to drool
My jaw seizes, my body freezes and I'm left there like a fool
I stay at home with Mom, but today she'd had enough
She said, 'you're so pathetic, I just don't get it!' and she threw out all
my stuff

'Cause I'm a FAILUUUUUUUUURE! Yeah!
A stinking FAILUUUUUUUUURE! Yeah!
I can't do anything right and I have no talent or wit
My mom's so angry, she just can't stand me, now I'm living in a pit
Of FAILUUUUUUUUURE, yeah!
I'm a FAILURE
And I'm living in ****!"

It's a short but sweet song, but I think we all got the message pretty
clearly. It seemed as though Frogsplash was once again spending his
Sunday evening sulking in his room, and I suppose we all resigned
ourselves to it and tried to forget about it by watching TV together in the
living room, as far away from Frog's music as possible. So, it came as some
surprise when, at half past nine, the doorbell rang. Mum went to answer it,
and when I heard Dad's voice I went to see what was going on.

"Duncan?" Mum said, surprised.

"Hi, Cassie," he said, "I'm here to pick up Frogsplash."

"You what?!"

"He called me, he said... Oh, hi, Sam!"

"Hi, Dad, what's going on?"

"I told you," said Frogsplash, coming down the stairs with the biggest
suitcase we have, "I'm moving in with Dad."

"We haven't discussed this!" Mum said to Dad. "You can't just take
him!"

"I'm not taking him, Cassie. This was his decision. Shall we just go with it, for the time being, and see how it goes?"

"Well it doesn't look like I've got much choice, does it?" she said as Frogsplash shoved past her, walked across the gravel driveway, put his suitcase in the boot of Dad's car and climbed in the passenger seat.

"I'm sure it won't be for long," Dad said reassuringly, "he's a teenager... he's just trying to exert a little independence."

"Well, make sure he eats well and goes to school on time. No junk food!" Mum said, and I could tell she was getting upset, "and make sure he's doing revision every day – you know his GCSEs are coming up."

"I will, don't worry," Dad said, and that was it.

Monday 9th November 2020

It's our year's turn to dig for time capsules. My History lesson isn't until Friday, but it's still exciting, especially after the success of the year sevens last week. It's a welcome distraction – something to focus on. Things at home have been tough, but I'm not the only one.

"My dad quit his job," Danny said when we met up for lunch. "Just like that, without anything else lined up. Mum is furious, of course, but Dad's angry too because he says she should be supportive if he wants to follow his dream. He says it's not fair that he has to go to work every day doing something he hates, because life is passing him by, and he doesn't want to retire thinking 'what have I done with my life?' Then Mum says that she's made loads of sacrifices too, that she gave up a fulfilling career in advertising because she couldn't do that and be a mother at the same time. I suppose they've both got a point."

"But still, your dad should have said something first," I said.

"That's the problem – he did. He said he wanted to quit, that he was miserable, and Mum just said no, like his happiness isn't as important as money."

"Are you worried they're going to split up?" asked Carla.

"I don't know," said Danny, "I think if they can just come to a compromise it'll be OK. Dad's just fed up and Mum's just worried. If money weren't an issue none of this would be a problem."

"My parents have never had a lot of money, but they've always been happy," Carla said. "I'm not saying your mum's in the wrong, but has she even asked him what his 'dream' is?"

"No," said Danny, and I guess that gave her something to think about.

Wednesday 11th November 2020

PREPARE TO RAISE THE FLAGS, HANG THE BANNERS AND BEAR THE ARMS: HOUSE DRURY MARKS ITS MADNESS WITH ITS VERY OWN SIGIL!

Troubled times for House Drury, though they seem to be wearing it with pride. The Drury dynasty, allied with House Wilson, and joint with the bloodline of House Darling, has shown signs of spiralling madness in recent times. Today they inspired fear in the hearts of their enemies when they officially marked themselves with a dark and troubling escutcheon: The Black Dog.

You probably think I really have gone mad, and you wouldn't be the only one. Well, maybe not mad, but "troubled". Today was our first Art lesson of the week, so I handed in my homework even though it wasn't due until Friday, because although Mack says a painting is never really finished, I was pretty sure I was done with it. Perhaps, in hindsight, I should have taken a closer look. It was the landscape I did at the weekend, remember, the one at the park? Anyway, I left it on Mack's desk, and we got on with the lesson.

Remember that boy with the anger issues I told you about – Elliot? Well, he had very clearly made an attempt to dye his hair green last night, and whilst it had been something of a success in the hair department, it had also stained a large portion of his forehead a mouldy green. Patrick O'Neill, who is probably the loudest one in our Art class, was quick to comment.

"Hey, look – a walking troll doll!" he said as Elliot walked to his seat. Quite a few people sniggered. The class went on, and so did Patrick, only now he was whispering so that Mack couldn't hear.

"Psst, Elliot, you've got something on your head, mate!"

"Hey, Elliot, you know you were supposed to paint a landscape on paper, not your face!"

He went on and on, whispering insults that I couldn't quite make out, and Elliot began breathing deeply, heavily, like he was filling up with steam. Then he leapt up out of his chair and threw it at Patrick.

"SHUT UPPPPP!!!" he shouted as the chair bounced off the desk in front of Patrick and landed in the middle of the classroom. Then he charged towards Patrick and tackled him to the ground. Patrick looked shocked, but he held his own. They were grappling on the floor for some time before Mack took any notice of the melee, and by the time he did, Elliot had his hands around Patrick's neck and his face was red with rage.

"Come on, boys, stop it now," Mack said far too casually. He walked over and pulled Elliot off Patrick. "We can't have scuffling in the classroom; please take your seats and try to channel that passion into your work. You can take that anger and that energy, and you can use it in your brushstrokes, see?" He demonstrated by dashing his brush across the canvas in a forceful sort of way, creating the effect of a harsh wind blowing across the sky of his landscape. And just like that, we were back onto art, and everything carried on as normal.

It was only afterwards, when I was in Chemistry, that things took an unusual turn. I was sat gazing bewildered at the periodic table, which as of yet means nothing to me, when Mr Donahue knocked and entered.

"Sorry to bother you, Miss Chiu, but might I borrow one of your students?"

"You may," said Miss Chiu, "as long as you bring them back in one piece."

"Samantha Drury?" Mr Donahue called my name, which took me completely by surprise. He led me to his room, just a little way down the hall from the main office. He opened the door, letting me walk ahead of him, and I saw three chairs: one for me, one for him, and one already filled by Mack, who was sat holding my painting with an expression of concern.

"Please, sit," said Donahue, so I did.

"Samantha, my dear," Mack began, "this is not the first time one of my students has reached out to me through their art."

"You what?" I said, already feeling that what was coming was going to be utter nonsense.

"Have you heard of a boy called Malcolm Fillingham?"

"No," I said.

Nor do I care, but I'm sure you're going to tell me anyway!

"Malcolm was a student at this school some years ago. A fine student, through and through. If anything, he took his too seriously, choosing textbooks over friends, spending hours on school projects in lieu of social activities. He was one of those rare artists who did not appear to have a natural talent, and yet with persistence and hard work, as opposed to passion and flair, he was able to develop an incredible skill for it, just as he had done with the more academic subjects. But one autumn term, he came back from the summer holidays quite changed, at least in appearance. His skin had cleared, his braces had been removed, he'd developed some muscle and he'd had a haircut which very much suited him – it was your classic ugly duckling scenario."

Is this really an appropriate way for a teacher to describe a student? I dread to think what Mack sees when he looks at me!

"I know, I know I shouldn't concern myself with the physical appearances of my students, but I'm an artist, I can't help but notice the beauty of the things around me."

Oh, get over yourself, Mack!

"Malcolm's sudden metamorphosis coincided with a change in the tides no longer was it considered attractive or cool to be over-confident, boisterous or unacademic. Suddenly, unwittingly, Malcolm became exceptionally popular. He didn't let it go to his head as much as others might have, at least not initially. But once he began to accept some of the social invitations that came his way he realised what he had been missing. At that age – he was fifteen, I believe – the parties are at their wildest, and the enjoyment is more intense than even an already popular child would have previously experienced. But, to Malcolm, it was even more extreme, and he was completely won over by this new way of life.

"Malcolm's currency had changed. His value was no longer in his schoolwork, and he no longer needed validation from his teachers because he was getting so much more of it from his peers. He stopped trying in every subject, except for Art. For Art you do not need to keep up with any curriculum, so he was free to paint whenever he wanted, or not, and still play truant whenever it suited him. But a boy of such intelligence needs an occupation of the mind, and so he clung to art, and only art. Not only did he become prolific, he also became impassioned.

"Whereas before he had only had artistic skill, he now had the flair and passion as well. The wild lifestyle and intense romantic affairs gave colour to his work, and the complicated relationship he had with his identity after undergoing such a drastic change gave it depth and meaning. But art alone is not enough, at least not to the school. He was expelled with very little warning, and I desperately wished that I had stepped in to prevent it while I had the chance. He was a complicated, expressive child with a cynicism regarding other people – just like you, I think. What happened to him would have greatly damaged his fragile soul."

"That's very sad," I said, "but it wasn't your fault, Mack. He must have had other people in his life who ought to have helped..."

"Perhaps, perhaps, but I will not let it happen again! You're trying to tell me something with this dramatic painting, please, talk to me about it."

"What? It's just a landscape, like you asked. That's my brother there, we went to the park this weekend..."

"I see a dark, hooded figure, outside of the play area, segregated from all the fun, looming over the happy children like an omen. I see oppressive clouds in the sky..."

"It was a cloudy day! It's November! And that's just my brother wearing a black hoodie."

"And then there's this other hooded figure in a very worrying pose... he looks as though... Is he being crucified?"

"He's doing yoga, for heaven's sake! That's Richard – the Geography teacher, ask him if you don't believe me!"

"Richard? You call him by his first name?" It was Mr Donahue who interrupted me this time. "Samantha, was Richard there? Did Richard take you to the park this weekend?"

"Yes, Richard, Mr Roberts, go and ask him if you don't believe me! What, do you think I imagined it or something?"

"No, no of course not. Samantha, do you have a relationship with this teacher outside of school?"

"Yeah, I know him really well. He sleeps in my bed!"

Why did I have to say that? Next I'll be telling them how he confronted some teenagers with his trousers down while camping, or how he pulled a knife on some kids in the playground!

"Mack, I think we may need to alert the authorities..."

103

"No, no, my old bed! He's my dad's flatmate! We do NOT share a bed."

They looked entirely unconvinced.

"No, really, he is. You can call my dad if you want, he was the one who took us to the park, Richard just tagged along to do some outdoor yoga."

"In this same black shroud – what's the significance of that, Samantha? Does it signify death, or some impending doom?" Mack asked.

"No, it's not a shroud, it's just a hoodie! It's this band they both like…"

"What really concerns me, Samantha, is this dog. This black dog, here in the foreground. It looks incredibly menacing, like it means to bring harm," Mack continued.

"It was hunting squirrels."

"Did you see the black dog, Samantha?"

"Yes, it was right there!"

"Have you heard of a Gytrash, Samantha?"

I know you're talking to me, MACK, you don't have to say my name at the end of every sentence, MACK.

"No, never heard of it."

"It's an omen… a black dog that haunts solitary paths and those that travel down them."

"You mean it's a metaphor?"

"You're a quiet girl, aren't you, Samantha?"

Am I quiet, or are you just deaf to every word that I'm saying?

"You choose to remain solitary during my lessons despite my relaxed attitude towards talking in class. I never see you in the canteen at lunchtime, or the playground at break. Where do you go? Where are you hiding?"

"I'm not hiding!"

"You don't seem to participate in any sporting activities…"

"Because I'm crap at sport!"

"Ah! Self-critical… low self-esteem… a lack of confidence…"

"No… a lack of hand-eye coordination!"

"You don't attend any clubs, you keep yourself out of view, hiding in the shadows, away from the spotlight…"

"I was one of the main parts in the school play!"

"Ah! Acting – wearing a mask to hide the self from an audience, pretending to be someone else entirely… a strange art form indeed. You see, I can read people, Samantha, it's what I do. I reach down into the soul and see it in all its glory. The soul is made up of colours, you see. Each soul is made up of a unique blend of all the colours in the spectrum, swirled together like the shadows of dancing flames. As an artist, I am better equipped to decipher those patterns and colours than most."

Jesus, I knew he was a bit eccentric, but I had no idea he was this deluded!

"I see your true colours, Samantha."

"Oh really? What colour am I?"

"Many colours, many colours… blue, green, purple, yellow… do I detect a shade of pink? Yes – magenta, no – fuchsia… not a lot of orange, though… that's very telling…"

Mr Donahue, who had quite frankly let this thing go on long enough, interrupted:

"People often refer to depression as a black dog, Samantha. Have you ever heard of that?"

"I don't know… I think I heard a song called 'Black Dog' at my friend's house once but I didn't really get what it meant. Honestly, I just did a painting for my homework. I painted what I saw, and there happened to be a black dog there. Surely I can't be the first person to ever see a black dog as just a black dog and not some metaphor!"

I could see I was starting to win Donahue over, but Mack seemed more convinced than ever.

"It's always the quiet ones," he said, "if you don't talk then how can we help you?"

"I don't need your help! This is ridiculous! Earlier today a boy in your class tried to strangle one of the other students. He was in a total rage and you barely did anything. You certainly didn't drag him out of a lesson to perform some sort of self-taught psychoanalysis on him!"

"Oh, boys will be boys. He was letting out his emotions, not bottling them up, that's *healthy!*"

"Hang on a minute, Mack. What's this about strangling?" Donahue asked.

"Oh, it's this new kid. Some of the others were winding him up, a bit of playful banter…"

"That resulted in a physical altercation?"

"Well, yes, but…"

"I'm sorry, Samantha. Really sorry to have wasted your time. Mack here said he was concerned about you and I had to follow it up. You're free to go. If you wouldn't mind closing the door behind you…"

Once again I did as I was told, and no sooner had I shut the door did I hear Mr Donahue's raised voice demanding to know why he hadn't been informed about the incident with Patrick and Elliot. I had no idea Mack was such a looney, and I was incredibly relieved to have him off my case, even if it did mean dropping Elliot and Patrick in it.

By the time that bizarre ordeal was over with it was almost the end of Chemistry. I was tempted not to go back so as to avoid the inevitable odd looks from other members of the class who were curious as to why I got called out by Donahue. The thing is most of them wouldn't have asked me outright anyway. They'd have just formed theories in their minds, maybe they'd have gossiped or started rumours. That is, if I'm interesting enough (or popular enough) to be talked about.

I thought about lingering around the corridors until the bell rang, but if Mack caught me floating about like the Spirit of Lost Souls he'd probably take me to get lobotomised without a moment's hesitation, so I went back to Chem. I opened the classroom door without knocking – I belonged in there, but at that moment in time it didn't feel like it – everyone stole a glance at me while I walked heavily back to my designated seat.

Friday 13th November 2020

Today I found just the thing I didn't know I was looking for: something to keep for myself. It wasn't stealing... not really. Nobody owned it before, so how can I have stolen it? I mean, somebody must have owned it once, but they clearly wanted to get rid of it. It's not profitable anyway, it's sentimental. Or at least it might be, if I can get it open.

Finally, it was my History class on the dig rota. Every other class has been digging near to where the first capsule was found, but we haven't had any luck, and as today was the last chance for our year group we decided to go quite literally in the opposite direction and dig up the outermost edges of the school grounds. We must have been a good fifty feet from the edge of the school lake, and it was a sloppy, muddy mess, but that was all part of the fun. It was the last period of the day, which they'd done on purpose so that we didn't carry mud back into the school building, but it ended up being a sort of divine coincidence, because if it hadn't been the last lesson I wouldn't have had my backpack on me, and then I'd never have been able to stash it away and take it home.

The dig was far more gruelling than I'd expected, and I must admit that at times I questioned Carla's wisdom in setting this whole thing off, but I had to remind myself that we had already had one success, so there was a good chance of another, even if it was our last chance. We were forty minutes in, which meant only twenty minutes left to make a discovery, lest we become the first year group to try and fail to dig up a capsule. I was growing frustrated because my spade kept clashing with other people's, and it seemed as though I was digging that which had already been dug. Nobody was strictly overseeing, so I took myself off-course and headed several metres to the right, if only for the gift of solitude. I dug and I dug, and it felt satisfying. It was raw and it had purpose, and gradually I came to want the treasure.

I didn't find the treasure. Well, I didn't find *their* treasure. I found *my* treasure. The thing I've always wanted: a secret. I almost didn't notice it at first. I dug it up, flung the contents of my spade to one side and carried on digging, then I flung another load of earth on top of it and heard the clumps of earth ping against the metal. The sound alerted me that there was something else within my pile of dug up soil, so I looked over and I saw it: a small, metal tin. I dug it back out with my hands, dusted it off and examined it. It was far too small to be a time capsule, but it did look very old. It was crudely made, not a perfect shape and it can't have been particularly attractive even before the rust set in. The most intriguing thing of all is that it was locked, and there was something inside.

It was nearly time to hang up our spades and head home, and as far as I knew nobody had found anything. Well, nobody apart from me. But it wasn't a time capsule, it was something else, a mystery. I had no duty to share it with the rest of the school, so I slipped it inside my backpack, making sure no one was watching, and I spent all the bus journey home wishing I could take it out and look at it, but it was not worth the risk: Demetri, Rob and Jake always sit at the back of the bus looking for fresh ways to bother me, and they would surely snap up this little curio as soon as it caught their eye. When I got home I spent a good half hour trying to pry it open with various tools, before eventually giving up and tucking it under my bed, which is where it is now, but it's calling me. I must get inside it.

Monday 16th November 2020

I tried prising it open with a crowbar, I tried throwing it against the wall (more out of frustration than in a genuine attempt to get it open). I tried a butter knife, but the knife only bent. I bashed at the lock with a hammer. I even tried holding a flame to it, which was stupid really because the melting point for any metal is ridiculously high, but I thought maybe it would expand so that the lock loosened. I was desperate. I still am.

Tuesday 17th November 2020

Yesterday's futile attempts confirmed what I had already feared: the lock is unbreakable. So today I tried picking it with hair pins and coat hangers. I don't really know if there's a skill to picking locks, or even if it's possible. You see it in films but in reality it seems to be a complete waste of time. But I thought maybe, with this lock that looks really, really old, the mechanism won't be as sophisticated as the ones we have nowadays. Maybe it's not as old as it looks, it's hard to tell when something's been buried.

Wednesday 18th November 2020

No luck. Still locked. Luck lock luck lock luck lock. Lock lock lock lock
lock. I think I'm becoming obsessed.

Thursday 19th November 2020

Today I just stared at it and hoped that, with enough concentration, I could develop the power of telekinesis. That would be handy for all sorts of things.

Friday 20th November 2020

I spent most of my evening online looking up how locks and keys work and trying to figure out how to fashion my own key. I even looked up some local locksmiths, but that was pure madness. Imagine calling in a tradesperson to open up a bashed up old tin! And anyway, it wouldn't be a secret then, wouldn't it? When I do open this box I will be alone, and whatever's inside it will be mine.

Saturday 21st November 2020

I have to admit I was excited to go to Dad's today. I can't believe it's been two weeks since I've seen Frogsplash! I have missed him, but I also just wanted to see how he's been getting on. I think Mum and Graham pushed it too far with him before, and I don't blame him for wanting to get out of there. When I arrived, I was surprised to see that Stephanie was already there.

"Hey, Steph!" I said as I hugged her, "you don't normally get here before me!"

"Oh, yeah," Dad said, "the childminder was sick yesterday and Sophie couldn't get out of work. It's so hard for single mums, you know. But I can work from home, so I said it was no bother. I think Sophie's really beginning to trust me with her!"

It was nice to see Dad so excited to spend time with Stephanie. I never know what's going on inside my dad's head – we're kind of different – but I think he's matured a lot since Stephanie came along.

Sorry – thought. I *thought* he'd matured a lot.

He made pizza for lunch, with a few carrot and cucumber sticks with dips on the side, and we all ate on the sofa watching a family film, the weather being too grim outside to do any out-and-about activities. Dad put all the food on big serving plates on the coffee table and gave us smaller plates so we could help ourselves, like when we do a picky bits dinner. He made a plate up for Stephanie, though, otherwise she'd probably have just had one slice of pizza, licked all the topping off and left the rest (toddlers are gross).

Richard was out at this beer yoga class he'd found on the internet, but the rest of us tucked in without much hesitation. Stephanie was the only one who seemed to take issue with the lunch that Dad presented.

"No!" she said simply. The word "no" is so powerful, and all humans seem to realise that at a remarkably young age.

"Not this again, Steph, I know you must be hungry, and you love pizza!"

She got off her booster seat and wandered off to the bathroom. Frogsplash was smirking. Shortly afterwards she re-entered, carrying her potty.

"Stephanie, no, not again," Dad said, but she looked him right in the eye and removed her booster seat from her spot at the table. I was surprised at her strength. She clearly meant business. She placed the potty where the booster seat had been and climbed up onto it. She pulled down her leggings and training nappy, placed her naked bottom firmly in the cradle of her potty and took a huge, hungry bite of her pizza.

"Dad, what is she doing? You can't let her use the potty at the table!"

"It's just a phase, Sam. It's the only way to get her to eat."

"You mean she's done this before?"

"A few times, yes. Look, this is my third child, I know how to handle these things. If you tell her she can't do it then she'll throw a huge tantrum which will ruin lunch for all of us and put her in a bad mood for the rest of the weekend until I give in. And then, when I do give in, she'll know that throwing a tantrum is the best way to get whatever she wants, and that sets a precedent. Then it'll be wall-to-wall tantrums every other weekend!"

"So, your method is just to let her do whatever she wants to avoid conflict?"

"No – give me *some* credit, Sam! What I'm saying is, you have to pick your battles."

"So, you're just letting her eat and go to the toilet at the same time?"

"Well, I mean… it's not like she wipes her own bum, so her hands aren't coming into contact with the germs."

"Oh! It's nice to know you've thought it all through! So, what happens, then, do you stop eating to wipe her bum while we're all sitting here trying to enjoy our dinner?"

"Usually I just wait 'til after the meal."

"Usually?! How long has this been going on?"

"I don't know… a day, two days…"

"So, since she's been in your care?"

"Leave it out, Sam, it's funny!" Frogsplash said, and he did seem to be highly amused.

"Don't you find it off-putting while you're trying to eat?"

"Meh." Froggo shrugged.

"Is she... is she actually... *going?*"

No sooner had I asked that question than I saw her face straining, turning red, not breathing, then I heard the unmistakable sound – and there was my answer.

"No! No, no, no!" I protested, and I took my plate and went to eat in the kitchen, although I didn't have much appetite left by then.

"It's only natural, Sam!" Froggo called from the living room. "In one end and out the other!"

"So, you're all just going to sit there eating, knowing what's in that potty, and you're not even bothered by it!"

"Only natural!" Frogsplash repeated through a mouthful of pizza. He really wasn't bothered. Well, at least *he's* enjoying himself.

She went through the exact same routine at dinner. There she was, leggings bunched at her ankles, hands greasy with chicken dippers, only stopping between triumphant, victorious mouthfuls for the occasional exertion of excretive effort.

"Sophie's not going to like this," I said as I watched my little sister straining unashamedly before us all.

"Oh, she'll grow out of it," Dad said. "If she's still doing this when she's eighteen then I'll have a word, OK?" he added sarcastically.

"You need to be strict with your children, Duncan," said Richard, who had enjoyed beer yoga so much he was now trying out beer TV-watching.

"It's not doing any harm, and Frogsplash seems to approve!"

I'm not sure that the Frogsplash Seal of Approval should ever be validation of anything, but it has been nice to see him finally taking an interest in his youngest sister. He seems so much happier here, but if I say that to Mum will she feel better, or worse?

Monday 23rd November 2020

"Good morning, everyone, please be seated." The Big W began the whole school assembly exactly as he always does. "I have a very special announcement to make this morning, but first I would just like to take a moment to thank you all for your efforts to find the missing time capsules. It is a gruelling, often unrewarding task which you have all taken on with excellent enthusiasm. Please do not be disheartened by our slow progress; every inch of ground we cover brings us closer to our goal.

"And now for the really exciting news. As some of you may know, celebrity chef and ethical eating campaigner Oliver Jameson is a direct descendent of our school's beloved founder, Duke John Jameson…"

Beloved by who, the hundreds of teachers he blackmailed, or the man he drove to suicide?

"… I am very pleased to announce that Oliver Jameson himself will be paying us a visit this Friday! He will be going around the classrooms meeting and greeting all of you, so please can you all wear full school uniform and ensure you are looking your smartest, and of course I expect you all to be on your best behaviour. I'm sure he will be very interested to hear about our time capsule project, so if we could find even just one more before then that would really boost this special occasion. You can do it, year ten! We will have a full school assembly on Friday morning, where we will sing the school song in honour of our guest and his noble ancestor, and of course Mr Jameson will join the teacher's table for lunch to sample our wonderful canteen menu, so remember your table manners!

"Now, Mr Jameson hasn't given us an awful lot of time to prepare for his visit because he was quite keen to see us as we are – no airs, graces or special treatment. But there will be members of the press with him and his team, and photographs will be taken for the local paper and for his own publicity, so please do take extra care to keep the school neat and tidy. Anybody caught littering, leaving bags lying around or defacing school property will be severely punished!"

Wednesday 25th November 2020

1970: A TIME OF BLISS FOR THE BIG-THIGHED MISS! ONE YOUNG LADY LOOKS BACK WITH FOND NOSTALGIA FOR THE GLORY DAYS BEFORE SKINNY JEANS AND PHOTOSHOPPED ROLE MODELS

The golden glow of the golden age gives off an alluring gleam for those looking back in wistful wonder. But on closer inspection, is it a prime picture of perfection, or is it an extreme example of expectation? Perhaps the glossy exterior is less pleasant underneath the surface…

They did it! I don't know if the prospect of a celebrity visit was what spurred them on, but the year tens found the second time capsule. It wasn't at all close to the first one, which has thrown out all theories of there being a designated site, but that doesn't matter because they found it and it's a good one: 1970! That's the second oldest one! They found it yesterday afternoon, but the contents were a lot more delicate than the one from 2000 so it had to be handled with care. We weren't allowed to pass around all the contents and get our grubby kiddie paws on them, instead Wilcox took photos of all the objects and scans of all the paperwork, which he showed in assembly today and uploaded onto the school website as well.

There was the standard whole school photo, which must be some sort of unwritten necessity, and is only really worth it for the fact that you get to see Bellows at various stages in his life. In fact, this is the first time capsule that Bellows would have been part of, and the only one in which he was a student and not a teacher. He was seventeen and barely recognisable, but for his proud stance at the side of the photograph, presumably as some kind of honorary pupil. I looked at that young man in the picture, and part of me wanted to scream at him: "GET OUT! Get out of there while you can! Go and see the world! Find somebody to love! LIVE!" But of course, that would have done no good, and anyway, he might be happy with the path he has chosen. Who am I to say what living is? I'm only twelve.

The next item hadn't aged well: the damp had overwhelmed it, but Bellows was able to describe what it had once been. It was a ball, a small one for playing catch or cricket or tennis, only you could use it indoors without fear of it smashing the furniture or whacking somebody in the face, because it was made of a spongey material that was soft and lightweight. Apparently it was revolutionary, although it seems kind of insignificant nowadays. Worse than that, I think nowadays if you advertised a ball, or any toy, as something that kids could enjoy without damaging anything, they'd see that as a direct challenge and probably go out of their way to cause some level of destruction with it. I know Frogsplash would have done – maybe not nowadays, but when he was younger and less morose.

There was another toy – a Malibu Mindy doll. Mindy was this tanned, peroxide blonde plastic doll with boobs so big she would topple over when you tried to stand her up, although that was also helped along by her tiny feet that were permanently on tip-toes because the only shoes she was allowed to wear were very high-heeled stilettos. She had a waist so small that if she had been real she would have been missing a few ribs and probably some vital organs, and her legs were so long that any skirt she wore became a mini skirt.

The next item was my favourite, and another running theme for the time capsules. Last time it was a CD single but this time it was on vinyl: a song called "Big Yellow Taxi". It still worked on Bellows' record player apparently, but so we could all hear it clearly Wilcox played it digitally over the speakers. It was kind of fitting, really, because a lot of it was about what the singer thought the future might be like if we keep replacing nature with man-made stuff. It made me think of the last time capsule, where they'd planted a vegetable patch but somewhere down the line it had got paved over and made into a rubbish site.

Again, there was a hair accessory, this time a hair bandana with colourful patterns on it that had been preserved remarkably well underground away from the sun. And again, there was a newspaper, which I think might be worth a bit of money, because it was from the day the Beatles announced they were splitting up, which must have been huge news. There were football trading cards, a packet of boiled sweets which didn't look too bad considering their age, a really boring maths textbook and a teenage girl's magazine called *Rainbow*.

At first glance the early 1970s seem like they would have been a good era for me. The sixties sounded like a lot of fun, but I have one word for you (or is it two?): *miniskirts.* But in the seventies it was all about flares – a far cry from the trend that won't end known as skinny jeans, which I still wear despite the fact that they give my bottom half the appearance of two upside down traffic cones coated in spray-on denim. Hair accessories these days don't suit me either, all they do is draw attention to my thin, flat, mousy hair that's plainer than plain paper, but in the seventies they wore these patterned headscarves that really brightened up the whole cranial area, and they'd have covered up a decent portion of my sizeable forehead as well.

I like seventies music, too. There was loads of out-of-this-world psychedelic stuff, and then there was the soul, the disco, the Motown, the glam rock and the punk as well. Carla has introduced me to loads of amazing artists like The Clash and Led Zeppelin, and it would have been amazing to see them play back in their day, but after school today I went online to check out the time capsule items in more detail, and on closer inspection, I think I'd rather stay here in 2020.

It was *Rainbow* magazine that really shocked me. Every single item was about how to lose weight and/or attract boys. There was nothing about friendship, wellbeing, school, family, nothing encouraging creativity or trying a new activity… it was just appalling. One article was all about a study they'd conducted on competitive dieting, the results of which proved that it was the most effective way for girls aged ten to eighteen to lose weight… *TEN!!!* And it went on to suggest that in order to get your friend to diet with you, you should passive-aggressively hint at her that she'd gained weight or that other people thought she was fat. So, I suppose I was wrong – there *was* something in the magazine about friendship!

There was this really strict diet regime detailed in the magazine, and it said that everyone should do it, no matter what, because whether you're a "Big Betty", a "Chubby Chelsea" or a "Tiny Tina" you could always stand to lose a few more pounds. The worst part was the "advice" the magazine gave to girls who wrote in. There was this one girl who wrote in to say that she was happy with her body and confident in her personality, but she knew she was bigger than most girls her age and she was worried this would keep her from finding a boyfriend. The magazine's response was this:

"Food is fun, but fat is lonely. Why not lose weight? You'll have plenty of time to be fat when you're married!"

Now I'm thoroughly confused. I did a project on women's rights last year and I'm pretty sure second wave feminism happened in the sixties, but you'd never have guessed it reading that magazine! I know things had still come a long way since women weren't allowed to vote or work certain jobs but it's amazing how acceptable it was to criticise even young girls' bodies back then. And we're not talking mean-spirited playground bullies, we're talking professional, adult magazine editors speaking with the air of knowing what's right and what's best! I thought we'd got it bad with social media and skinny jeans, but *Rainbow* magazine is just about as harmful to self-esteem as it can get!

Friday 27th November 2020

The day of the visit! In some ways it was what you might expect: everybody got over-excited and became so overwhelmed with the notion of celebrity that the event itself became amplified and most of us were unnecessarily giddy by the time of his arrival. He was precisely on time, which I thought was very polite, and he behaved so much like a normal school visitor – getting a visitor's badge from the office, speaking to every teacher in every classroom, and then to all of us in groups in our classes. He really seemed interested, and like he was there to hear about us and not talk about himself.

He was a lot quieter than he is on TV, but I suppose he has to be loud when he's on camera, otherwise it would be pretty boring to watch. He had some photographers with him, whom I was very careful to avoid, but when he came into our Geography classroom during Richard's lesson it was very difficult to stay out of the limelight. Richard seemed to think that he'd landed his own high-profile talk show: *"Real Talk with Richard Roberts: using Geography to navigate your way through life!"*

He was dressed in what he probably thought were trendy student clothes. He wore a trilby hat, presumably to cover up his baldness, a white shirt with the collar up and the first two buttons undone, tapered, pin-striped trousers with polka dot braces to hold them up, very visible argyle socks, pointed shoes with a bit of a heel on them and a salmon pink cardigan that had a distinct charity shop feel to it. I kind of liked the outfit, but it's a style that young people have appropriated from old people, so when an old person dresses that way it kind of just makes them look… old, but like they're not quite doing it right.

He was obviously keen to make a good impression, but Oliver Jameson was more interested in us kids. He asked us about what we'd been studying in Geography this year, what our favourite subjects were, whether we'd like to see any changes made to the canteen menu. When he actually spoke to me I didn't feel as nervous as I'd anticipated. I told him that I prefer to make my own packed lunch because that way I can choose what I have every day and cook it to my own taste. I guess I was showing off a bit, because the real main reason I eat packed lunch is, so I don't have to sit in the canteen with everyone else!

We were rather abruptly interrupted when Richard switched on a very loud electric coffee grinder at the window by his desk. He had set up his own coffee-making station on the windowsill. Obviously I wasn't the only one showing off to Oliver Jameson! He probably would have tried to cook a fancy meal if only he'd been able to get an oven installed in the classroom, but I suppose a kettle was stretching the health and safety regulations far enough as it was.

"Sorry about that," Richard said once he'd finished grinding the coffee beans, "I'm a bit tired. I was up late last night cooking this home-made tabbouleh salad with marinated corn-fed chicken breast." He fake-yawned, clutching a Tupperware full of a shop-bought salad I recognised from Dad's fridge. "Maybe a coffee will perk me up. Would you like one? It's locally sourced."

"Really?" Oliver Jameson said, surprised. "You mean the coffee beans were grown locally, here in England?"

"Er... no. I meant *responsibly* sourced," Richard corrected himself, "they were locally bought. Well, locally ordered. I ordered them online, from my flat... which is local," he sputtered, showing the packet to Oliver Jameson.

"Blimey, Kopi Luwak!" he said, reading the label. "How could I possibly refuse?"

Amazingly, Richard had succeeded in his efforts to impress.

"Oh yeah, it's the only coffee I drink," Richard said smugly, leaning against the windowsill while the coffee brewed in the cafetière.

"Blimey, how much are they paying you here? I might have to get into teaching!"

"Is it expensive then, Mr Jameson?" asked Tamara Sandy.

"Please, call me Oliver. And yes, it's expensive – the most expensive coffee in the world!"

"How much does it cost?" Tamara asked.

"Oh at least thirty quid a cup – probably more like fifty," Oliver said.

I saw Richard's eyes widen. He probably ordered the beans late at night after beer yoga! He had just made a hundred pounds worth of coffee, which he now poured very carefully.

"How do you have it? Milk, sugar, caramel syrup, hazelnut?" Richard had obviously spent a fair bit on coffee syrups, too.

Oliver Jameson laughed. "I think it would be a bit of a shame to mask the flavour with added extras, don't you?"

"Of course, of course," Richard said nervously, "I just wasn't sure if you were used to drinking coffee of this quality."

Richard took a gulp and swallowed. Oliver took a sip and held it in his mouth, savouring the flavour, his face melting into a countenance of contentment.

"Just exquisite," he said languorously.

"Why is it so expensive?" Tamara asked as we all watched them indulgently enjoying their beverages.

"Ah, I'm glad you asked. It's very interesting actually," Oliver began, "the Kopi Luwak bean has a very unique production process. The reason coffee beans contain caffeine is to protect themselves from being eaten by animals – quite remarkable, really, to think that even plants have evolved in such a way. But there is one species in Indonesia which enjoys eating the ripest of the beans: the civet cat. The civet cat eats the beans, which undergo a special fermentation process during digestion. The animal then excretes the beans and the faeces is collected by farmers and processed into the coffee we are drinking right now."

"Wait, what?" said Demetri Michael, "you mean the beans are cat poop?"

"Essentially, yes," Oliver replied at precisely the wrong moment, because Richard had just taken another huge swig, and upon hearing that he was drinking ground up faecal matter, he spat it out with such force that it projected away from him, blasting Oliver Jameson's face and shirt with steaming hot coffee that had not only been in the digestive system of an Indonesian forest animal, but also in the mouth of an English Geography teacher. Oliver Jameson was speechless. For a moment we were all speechless. We just sat there staring at the scene in front of us like a car crash. Then Oliver Jameson dropped his fifty quid's worth of cat poop and ran out of the classroom, closely followed by his team and the press, who had captured every single moment.

"Did that go how you'd hoped it would, sir?" asked Demetri Michael, grinning maliciously.

"Don't worry, I'm sure it won't end up in the paper!" added Ross Rillington sarcastically.

You had to feel sorry for Richard. I've known him to be a walking disaster for quite some time now, but it's never been made quite as public as this. People at school (well, the students, at least) had a certain respect for him. He had this air of being laid-back, funny, approachable. How he handled these next few moments was crucial.

"Let this be a lesson to you all," he said at last, "always read the product description when you buy online!"

Everybody laughed.

"I'm going to send it back, request a refund," he continued. "If they ask me why I'll say, 'because it tastes like crap!'"

Again, the class laughed, and Richard seemed to be back in everyone's good books. Well maybe not *everyone*.

Lunch break was directly after Geography, and although Danny, Carla and I would usually hide out in the music room, the entire school had been instructed to eat in the canteen in honour of Mr Jameson's visit. That was Mr Wilcox's idea, and I can't help but wonder if he now regrets inviting such an audience to witness the events that were about to take place.

Oliver Jameson made a late entrance to the canteen, swiftly followed by his crew and the press. On screen he appears to be a man of average build, but it became apparent that a lot of that was down to loose-fitting clothing and clever lighting, because this lunchtime, after his shirt was soiled by the world's most expensive coffee, he entered the lunch hall wearing a PE shirt from the lost property box which was probably for fourteen to fifteen year olds. Our PE shirts are light yellow in colour, not exactly ideal for covering up bumps, and this one was stretched so tightly across his corpulent frame that a section of doughy belly was poking out between the top of his trousers and the bottom of the shirt. He tried his best to cover it up with his blazer, but it only had one button which brought it in under the breast, only to make it part even wider across the fuzzy, pale abdomen.

I had, of course, already told Danny and Carla about the events of the preceding Geography lesson.

"Ooh, I bet that made him angry!" said Carla.

"I don't know," I said, "it was hard to tell, he just sort of…ran off. He seems pretty chill, though, I'm sure he'll get over it."

"No, no, this is what he does: he *broods,*" Carla said, "haven't you seen his show?"

"Yeah. It's just him in his kitchen talking to the camera while he cooks."

"No, not that one! The one he does over in America, in the restaurant kitchens. Rosie watches all these American reality channels… He goes to restaurants unannounced and bombards them with his camera crew demanding to see the kitchen. It's probably all staged because the restaurant always seems conveniently quiet, but anyway, he goes to the kitchen and criticises everything: their methods, their hygiene, their efficiency, their recipes, their ingredients – everything. Then he offers to help them, says he can turn the place around and double their profits, but they have to listen to him and make whatever changes he suggests. They kind of have to say yes, because he's just gone on TV and exposed all their terrible secrets, so if they don't go ahead with this magical transformation no one's going to want to eat there.

"So, they agree to work with him, and he comes into their kitchen on a busy night and shouts and swears at all the staff. Usually he ridicules them in some way, often he makes them cry – one time he puffed a bag of flour in someone's face because they were refusing to follow his orders and thought they knew better than him. In fact, I've never seen an episode where he doesn't smash something or throw food in someone's face. But he's probably not like that in real life; I'm sure it's just an act…"

Oliver Jameson was being guided by Mr Wilcox to the area where you pick up your tray and slide it along telling the dinner ladies what to put on your plate. There are always a few options, but the thing I saw on most people's plates was the exact same thing I had last time I ate school dinners: pizza and chips. I love pizza, but I prefer a thin crust and I like toppings that add a bit of texture and flavour. The school's pizza is literally an inch thick with barely-there tomato sauce and a congealed layer of cheese which has obviously been cooked and then warmed up again hours later. Chips are just chips: tasty but stodgy. There's no salad or roast veggies, only peas and carrots which have been boiled for so long they're ninety per cent water and they always smell of cabbage, even though I've never seen cabbage in any of the serving trays.

Usually the alternative option is a baked potato with a choice of cheese, beans or tuna mayo. Most people choose cheese, which isn't a particularly balanced meal. The baked potatoes were there today, but there was also a third option, which can only have been to impress Oliver Jameson. It was lasagne: pretty standard, really, but I suppose it's more time-consuming to make and a little more nutritious than pizza and chips.

Once you've chosen your main you get to choose your dessert, which is either a sad looking bowl of pale strawberry jelly or an even sadder square of plain, dry sponge pudding with no jam, cream, custard or anything. Of course, there's also a selection of all the popular chocolate bars and sweets, and of course they're what everyone goes for. Wilcox was probably relieved to see Oliver Jameson choose the lasagne and (not that he had much choice) a side of boiled peas and carrots. He walked along the dessert area, surveyed the selection in front of him while Wilcox chattered away in his ear, then walked away, allowing himself to be led to the teacher's table by The Big W.

The hum of chatter seemed to cease when Jameson took a seat – it was as though we had suddenly been graced with the presence of royalty and none of us knew how to proceed accordingly. Oliver Jameson broke the silence by muttering some small talk, not to Wilcox but to the teacher sat on his other side. Gradually the silence broke apart as conversations spread, and things had almost returned to normal, until they took an unexpected turn.

"I'm sorry," Oliver Jameson said loudly and like he wasn't sorry at all, "I'm sorry but this is unacceptable. This lasagne is a pile of slime with about two per cent meat – and a very low-grade meat at that. I dread to think what kind of lifestyle that poor cow had before it was slaughtered! There are no real tomatoes in the red sauce, and I can tell the white sauce has been made from powder – I doubt there's any real milk, butter *or* cheese in this recipe, but you've sure as hell tried to cover your tracks by masking the lack of flavour with buckets of salt!

"And as for these vegetables – can you even call them vegetables? I don't know what's happened to them since they were picked from the ground, but they seem like poor clones that have been produced in a lab by scientists who live in an age where real vegetables have been extinct for hundreds of years! They are an abomination! And even the water… I mean, how do you get *water* wrong? I'm not a snob, I grew up on tap water, but the smell of bleach coming from these jugs and cups is so overwhelming there is no way there isn't a trace of it in the water itself. YOU ARE MAKING CHILDREN DRINK BLEACH! IT'S DESPICABLE! I will definitely be taking a sample of this to be tested, and that lasagne – I'm not one hundred per cent sure that's cow meat, and I will be checking the salt and fat content, too."

He got up, carrying his plate with him, and walked over to the bin. He turned the plate sideways, allowing the vegetables to tumble chaotically into the bin while the lasagne slid sluggishly down the plate, leaving streaks of sauce and grease in its path. He put his plate with the other dirty crockery and began walking from table to table, picking up people's plates and holding up their contents for all to see: pizza, chips, pizza, soggy vegetables, chips, chocolate, fizzy drinks, sweets. You better believe I was glad to have packed lunch today! He went over to the "dessert" section, which is really a cover name for what it actually is: a sweet shop.

"Look at this!" He was shouting now. "What food group is THIS from?" He picked up a packet of fruit gummies. "*Contains real fruit juice* it says! Oh, well that's all right then, no need to have your five-a-day after all! And when did THIS become part of a balanced meal?" he said, this time holding up a chocolate bar containing peanuts. "Oh, I SEE – *packed with protein,* it says, *full of energy!* Forget your lean meats, forget your grains – have a bar of chocolate! I am appalled and I am ASHAMED to share my name with this school! I have spent too much time abroad, away from my roots. Well no more! I will personally see to it that this disgusting school drastically reforms its menu!"

"Hang on a minute," Wilcox rather bravely interrupted, "you have come into my school as a welcome guest. We have gone out of our way to accommodate you at short notice, and you come in and insult all of us! This is not a disgusting school. We take pride in ourselves and we do the best we can on a very tight budget."

"*This* is the best you can? THIS?!" Jameson said, holding up a bowl of jelly which wriggled with rage. "Perhaps this is the best YOU can do, mate, but if that's the case then I must surely question your competence as head teacher!"

Now it's getting personal…

"You what, bruv?!" Wilcox responded.

Oh no, he's turning! It's Jekyll and Hyde, Banner and Hulk, Wilcox and Big W!

"Come say that to my face! I am committed to this school and these children! You think I set the budget? You think I design the menu? You think I don't want these kids to be as healthy and well-nourished as they can be?"

"I think your priorities are all wrong! How much do you spend on textbooks, for example?"

"Very little. We're all online now."

"How about PE equipment, art supplies, computers?"

"We are a school, not a restaurant! If the children or their parents don't like the food we serve they are free to switch to packed lunch."

"Oh, I'm sure the children *love* the food. But I bet the parents don't have a clue what awful slop their kids are shoving down their gobs each day! Well they will, they'll know all about it when this gets out – *everyone* will know all about it!"

"You say that like it's a threat, Mr Jameson, but the truth is we're on the same side here. I am thrilled that you would report this to the local papers – perhaps that might give the council a kick up the backside and finally provoke some change around here. And I would be delighted if you were able to offer us any added support yourself, but I do appreciate you have an extraordinarily busy schedule…"

He walked closer to where Jameson was stood, until each man was stood at opposite sides of a table at which six terrified diners froze, eyeing the contents of their own plates in fear of dietary criticism from Jameson. But Wilcox was back on track. He'd let himself slip for a minute there – Jameson had made it personal and Wilcox had felt the heat of the attack, but he was back, professional as ever.

"Obviously there is a wider issue to be addressed here," said Jameson, humbled. "You're a passionate man, like myself. I respect that, and I'm going to do what I can to help this school."

They nodded at each other from across the table, then they leant forward and shook hands in a most noble manner. It had been a magnificent spectacle, and I couldn't wait to see how it was going to come out in the papers.

Monday 30th November 2020

CHARITY BEGINS AT HOME FOR TOP CELEBRITY CHEF: PHILANTHROPIST OLIVER JAMESON MAKES GENEROUS PLEDGE TO HELP LOCAL SCHOOL

On a recent visit to local school Duke John Jameson, Chef Oliver Jameson discovered that the school kitchens were in a much more dire state than any of the restaurants he has visited on his hit US show The SOS Chef. *Mr Jameson has vowed to return to the school once a month, along with his expertly trained team, to cook for the children. He has banned all sugary treats and salty snacks from the canteen, and he hopes to inspire the children to make healthier choices and get cooking!*

Underneath the headline was a surprisingly flattering photograph of Jameson and Wilcox shaking hands – not over the table, like they had done initially, but a staged shot which must have been taken at a later stage, because Oliver Jameson was no longer wearing the stretched and grubby PE shirt, and his hair had been coiffed to perfection so as to conceal his receding hairline. Wilcox looked just the same as he always does.

It was the main story in our local paper, because not much happens in our town and any kind of celebrity is a pretty big deal. Most of us don't get the local delivered until Monday evening, but a few kids who do paper rounds had brought it in this morning, and it didn't take long for the news to spread. Nobody was particularly bothered about Jameson's announcement that he would be returning on a monthly basis, a few people were amused to read about the dreadful state of our school, but by and large the biggest concern was the dreaded snack ban, which was confirmed at morning break when the only things on offer were a selection of fruits, yoghurts and cereals.

"It's ridiculous!" people were saying in Physics, right after break. "It's a violation of our basic human rights – if we want to eat chocolate then we should be allowed to!"

"I mean it's not like we don't know the risks," another kid chimed in, "it's written all over the packaging how many calories, how much sugar, what our recommended daily allowance is, we know, we *know!* But now that's not enough; they've taken away our right to *choose.* It's so patronising!"

"*Exactly!* Do they think we don't understand the health warnings, or do they think we've got no self-control and we're just going to eat ten chocolate bars in one sitting or something?"

"And *by the way,* it's actually OK to have a treat once in a while. If they thought we were eating too much why didn't they just put a limit on it, one bar per person, per day?"

"Too much like hard work trying to organise and monitor it, I suppose. Much easier for them to just ban it altogether."

"No, no, it's not that, I reckon it's that Oliver Jameson. He's making an example of us. He's cracking down on sugar, making out like it's the biggest evil in the world. If he said it was OK to have a bit every now and then there'd be some fools who take that as a green light to eat however much they want."

"It's not fair, is it? Just because some idiots don't know how to look after their health the rest of us have to suffer! If they're stupid enough not to understand the risks then I think they deserve to get fat and die of a heart condition!"

"Well, he's not stopping me! He can take away our canteen snacks, but as soon as I get out of here I'm going straight to the sweet shop and buying twice as much junk food as I normally would and dedicating it all to Oliver Jameson!"

"You know what, I think I might join you!"

"Hey, I've got an idea that'll really stick it to him. Let's buy more than twice as much. Let's stuff our faces like mad and get it all on video. We'll eat ten chocolate bars in one sitting and post it online. We'll say this is for Oliver Jameson – you drove us to this! We'll call it *The Jameson Junk Food Challenge!*"

"YES!!!"

God, people are stupid.

Wednesday 2ⁿᵈ December 2020

It's a conspiracy, I swear. At the very least it's preferential treatment. It can't be coincidence. I only have one class with my friends, and I only have *two* friends! Meanwhile, Charlotte Henderson and her mates seem to have every lesson together, and most of those lessons are with *me*. It used to be just Charlotte, Beth and Andrea, but over the summer they recruited another member – Ruby Driscoll, who just happens to be another nemesis of mine. Last year Beth made it very publicly clear that she thought I ought to be on a diet, Charlotte made fun of Carla for being a tomboy and Ruby humiliated me in PE. I don't think I've ever heard Andrea say a word, she just follows them around like flies on a warthog. Yes, I think that's how I'll think of them from now on: Andrea the fly and the three stinking warthogs.

Apparently, Charlotte found out that Ruby's family has their own tennis court at their house, because she managed to become best friends with her just in time for the summer holidays. I don't think that girl will ever have a true friend: only players in a game, and the controller is always in Charlotte's hands. I like being alone quite a lot of the time, but I never feel lonely. Charlotte, on the other hand, is always surrounded by her followers, but I bet she feels lonely all the time.

It was Life Studies class and sure enough Charlotte, Beth, Ruby and Andrea were all sat together in the back row. They appear to be bolder than ever now that there's four of them, and they have unfortunately gained the excessive confidence required to push the boundaries in class. The more I study the human condition the more I think that confidence, much like wealth, is never evenly distributed: some of us have far too much and most of us have too little. Very few have got just the right amount. Charlotte and co. have got far too much individually, but as a collective they are obscenely arrogant. I've seen them receive a few detentions when they've overstepped those boundaries, but none of those incidents were as satisfying as what happened today.

Miss Andrews was teaching us a very valuable lesson on budgeting, investing and borrowing money. We talked about financial responsibilities and priorities, such as a roof over one's head and food in the cupboards, paying bills and debts promptly, and making tough decisions, like if you didn't have enough money to buy Christmas presents for your children, would you take out a loan even if you weren't sure how you were going to pay it back? She showed us the figures for the number of people currently using food banks here in the UK, and it was pretty eye-opening.

Charlotte and the gang clearly thought the topic was above them, probably because they have tennis courts and never have to wear the same outfit twice, so the idea of budgeting or having to borrow money must seem like a laughing matter to them. They were whispering all through the lesson, but when they started talking loudly and giggling incessantly Miss Andrews intervened:

"Would you like to share the joke with the rest of the class?" she asked Ruby.

"You what, miss?" Ruby replied.

"Well, one of you must have said something pretty funny, because you don't seem to be able to stop laughing. So, go on, tell us what it is."

"Well if you must know, miss," Charlotte spoke this time, "Ruby was just admiring your outfit. She said she reckons it must be your favourite, because we've never seen you wear anything else!"

"And what's your favourite outfit, Charlotte?" asked Miss Andrews coolly.

"My black sequined playsuit, if I'm going out," Charlotte replied without hesitation, "denim high-rise shorts, a crop top and my Georgia Armada jacket for a casual day."

"And you, Ruby, what's your favourite outfit?"

Ruby eyed her with suspicion, proving herself slightly more astute than Charlotte. "Probably my yellow polo-neck tennis dress," she said shortly.

"And who paid for that dress, Ruby?"

"My dad," she replied.

"And you, Charlotte, who paid for all your clothes?"

"I did," she said defiantly.

"Oh, did you? And where did you get the money from?"

"My mum, I guess."

"I paid for this outfit myself, from money that I earned," Miss Andrews spoke sharply and with confidence. "It's not my favourite outfit, but it's appropriate for work and that's important to me because working allows me financial independence, which allows me many more freedoms. I work hard for my money, often having to endure criticism from much younger, inexperienced females who choose to gang up on other females rather than stand in solidarity against a patriarchal world in which many women are still financially dependent on men, in which women statistically earn less than men, in which women are, on a daily basis, reduced to the value of their physical appearance, such as the way they dress, as opposed to their real worth and their contributions to society.

"If you continue to disrupt lessons, not pay attention and not learn anything then, unlike me, you won't be able to pay for your own outfits, because you won't be able to get a job, and if your only value is in your appearance, you're going to feel pretty worthless when that day comes. Perhaps you could borrow money, but getting into debt is a risky business, as I have just explained. Of course your parents could continue to support you, if they're willing, and then one day you'll wake up and realise that you're thirty-five years old and living with Mum and Dad while all these other people – people that you mocked because they were more interested in getting an education than looking perfect – are buying their own homes, getting promotions, travelling all over the world and fulfilling their dreams while you're stuck in exactly the same place you've been all your life, wearing a sequined playsuit that does nothing to hide your cellulite."

BOOM!

Friday 4th December 2020

The *Jameson Junk Food Challenge* has gone viral. Everyone's stuffing their faces in an act of defiance and posting it online saying rude things directed at poor Oliver Jameson. Well, I say that like he's an innocent victim, but it is a bit of a taste of his own medicine, because he says really rude things to people on *The SOS Chef,* and he wasn't exactly polite to Mr Wilcox on the day of his visit. Still, he was only trying to do a positive thing. A lot of people are criticising his lack of influence over the actual school menu, which hasn't changed at all. He's taken away the yummy snacks, but the lunches are still greasy, re-heated slop, and everyone's saying that, as a chef, that should be his real concern.

I don't know if Oliver Jameson has seen the videos, but if you ask me, he's doing the right thing by not making any comment. It's only a craze, but if he starts paying attention to it it'll take longer to die out. Mr Wilcox announced in assembly this morning that he has warned all the local sweet shops and fast food places not to sell to any kids from our school and asked the shopkeepers to report back to him if any of us attempts to. It's just a scare tactic, and a very weak one at that, because everyone knows that a shopkeeper cares more about money and customers than some head teacher.

He also announced that this year there will be no Christmas play. Mrs Willis, the drama teacher, was close to tears when Wilcox broke this news, but he says the school's funding has been cut even further and we can't afford props, costumes or extra staff to help organise the play. Instead there's going to be a fund-raising Christmas fair, with bouncy castles, fairground games, cake sales and entertainment. Sounds a bit babyish to me, but I suppose it's better than nothing. I am disappointed about the play, though. I was sort of hoping I might get cast in it again.

Sunday 6th December 2020

WEEKS OF FRUSTRATION AND PICKING LOCKS SHOULD HAVE SOUGHT A SIMPLER WAY TO OPEN THE BOX!

A humble metal tin has been a source of great intrigue after it was found buried several feet beneath the ground. The ancient box was gently excavated, lightly dusted and carefully studied before being bashed, battered, sawn and burned in many vain attempts to unlock it. But now that the contents have been unveiled, has the mystery been solved?

I did it! I did it, and it was so simple! For weeks now I have been at a loss with this stupid little box and its stupid little lock. I've picked at it, hacked at it, stared at it and, well, you know the rest, but I was looking at it all wrong. On the one side there was the lock, but on the other were the two metal hinges, quite rusted and very crudely made, but they were screwed in with the most standard of flat-end screws. All along I was trying to open the lock when I should have been removing the hinges. We keep the toolbox in the utility area with the home brew – perhaps not the safest set-up for a household with children, but I'm almost a teenager and in my entire life I've only got drunk by accident *once,* so that's pretty good going.

I gathered up all the flat-end screwdrivers and took them up to my room. The screws were very stiff, but we also had a greasing spray in the toolbox. I *may* have spilled a bit on the carpet in my room, but I'll just move my patterned rug, and no one will ever know. I waited (impatiently) for the grease to sink in, then nearly took my own eye out when my greasy hands slipped on the handle of the screwdriver. But you don't want to hear about that. You want me to skip to the good bit.

Inside the box was something so wonderful, so fascinating and so bewildering, it might just be the best secret anyone has ever uncovered. I dug it up at a time when I really felt like I needed something for myself, and that felt like fate. Well now it *really* feels like fate, because, my dear diary, what I found in that box was a *diary.*

It looks to be very, very old. It looks genuinely old, which is reason enough to be intrigued by it, but what fascinated me more is that whoever last possessed it felt a need to lock it up and bury it, rather than destroy it or simply leave it be. The pages are quite faded, and the handwriting is beautiful but difficult to read, but the real difficulty is in the language the diarist uses. It's extremely old-fashioned, and some of the letters of the alphabet aren't even the same as they are now. I can barely understand a word of it, but it is the most precious thing I have ever held. I feel nervous just having it, in case I lose it, or someone takes it from me. I know there are secrets in those pages. They are my secrets now, and I will read them all, somehow.

Friday 11ᵗʰ December 2020

It would seem I'm not the only one with secrets. Carla has been acting strange all week. She's acting shifty, like she's hiding something, and she keeps disappearing off before the end of lunch.

"I'm going to find Rosie," she said on Monday, twenty minutes before the afternoon bell rang. "She's just sent me a message… she's really upset about these internet trolls, but she's embarrassed so she just wants to see me… in private."

"She's *still* getting trolled?" asked Danny. "Can't she block them or something?"

"They keep creating new accounts," Carla said, "they're really persistent."

"That's horrible," said Danny.

"She doesn't still think it's me, does she?" I asked.

"Don't be stupid!" she said, which wasn't technically a "no", but I could question her no further because she'd already left. She's used the same excuse every day this week, always at the same time. Maybe it's true; maybe Rosie just needs a little bit of sister time to get her through the day, maybe Carla gives her a pep talk to prepare her for the afternoon ahead. They are a very close family, not like mine. Mine's falling apart.

Sunday 13ᵗʰ December 2020

What a dreadful weekend. Maybe I should move in with Dad, too. I stayed in my room as much as I could, reading the diary, watching videos on my computer, doing homework, but I had to go down for dinner this evening. Billy had very wisely chosen to take a shift at the pub, so it was just me and the adults. He's so lucky he has somewhere to go, a place where no one will degrade him by talking about him like he's not even there. For him the pub is a place of refuge, but for me it's a threatening, intimidating space.

When I sat down at the table they were already talking about Frogsplash.

"I can't imagine spending Christmas without him. I'll be so disappointed if he doesn't come," Mum was saying.

"Well, he is a disappointment," Graham said, and I felt the urge to throw my steaming broccoli in his face.

"I don't know what to get him for a present… I don't know what he's into at the moment… I feel like I don't even know him anymore!"

"Don't get him anything, Cassie," Graham said, "you shouldn't reward him for disrespecting us."

A Christmas present isn't a reward, dummy! And what's all this "us"? He never said anything to you!

"You've been too soft on him, that's what's caused all this," Graham continued. "He's spent too long without a proper, respectable male role model, someone to keep him in check, someone to say no to him and stick to their guns no matter how stubborn he is."

You never once called him up on his behaviour! You never said no to him, you never kept him in check! You let Mum do all the hard work and now you're trying to blame her for the outcome!

"Perhaps you're right," Mum said bleakly, "I have good intentions, like making him do chores, but I get so sick of moaning at him when he hasn't done them. Trying to get Frogsplash to do something is like getting blood from a stone!"

"It's never easy, Cassie, especially when you've let them get away with it for so long. You *have* to take control, remind them that you're the authority. Don't give them too much freedom. Like with Samantha – you let her hide away in her room all weekend without communicating with the outside world. It's not healthy. If she carries on this way, she'll end up just like her brother."

OK, first of all, I'm sitting right here. Don't talk about me like I'm not. And secondly, there is nothing wrong with my brother!

"Trust me, Cassie," he continued sententiously, like he was some sort of parenting guru, "they all change. They hit those teen years, the hormones kick in and it's like a stranger living in your house! Her grades might be good now, her manners, her respect for her elders, but that'll go. That'll all go."

I'm going to go if this carries on. No wonder you're twice divorced, you miserable lump of grey matter!

I could have argued, I could have defended myself and my brother, but I've come to realise that certain people will always believe that they are right, and to argue with them is not only infuriating but futile. An argument is only good if it leads to resolution, but I knew there would be none. I don't like the way Graham has changed, not just because he's being so critical, but because I no longer trust him. Not one bit. He talks about us kids being like a stranger in the house when we become teens, but if you ask me, *he's* the stranger. He must have been faking it: being nice so that we'd all accept him, and now that he's in he's beginning to reveal his true self.

He used to seem interested in me and Frogsplash. He'd talk to him about football and ask me about school. Now it just seems like he doesn't care at all about what we want. He wants us all to conform to *his* ideal. I bet he loves that Frogsplash is gone – out of the way, no longer obstructing his regime of total, rigid mundanity. How on Earth did someone as fun as Billy come from someone so humdrum? I bet Billy's mum was a livewire and that's where he gets it from. But she must have been too much the opposite of Graham, too irresponsible, because she ran away and abandoned her son. I used to think she was a horrible person for that, but maybe it's not that simple. Maybe being married to Graham was driving her mad. Maybe he criticised her like he criticises Frogsplash.

Now I'm worried. He's been criticising Mum, hasn't he? Making her feel like a rubbish parent. And who knows what other things he says when it's just the two of them? Mum seemed so much happier before, and she used to do things. She used to have that makeup club with her female friends. Now she doesn't see any of her friends, she just stays at home worrying about things. What if Graham's driving her mad like he did with Billy's mum? What if, one day, she feels so trapped that she feels like her only option is to run away, never to return, leaving me here with Graham? Right now, for the first time in a very, *very* long time, I really miss the way things were when Mum and Dad were still together.

Monday 14th December 2020

I was being dramatic last night, I was tired. Graham's just trying to support Mum through this difficult time with Froggo. He's raised Arnie and Billy all right, hasn't he?

"Sorry if I was a bit hard on you yesterday," he said this morning as he made me a cup of tea while Mum was in the shower. "It's just – your mum's so upset at the moment; she's not thinking straight. I don't blame you for wanting to stay in your room all weekend, what with us two always worrying and fretting about things! It's just hard for her; kids grow up so fast, and then all of a sudden they don't want to spend any time with you! But it's not your fault – it's not like we've been a barrel of laughs lately. Maybe we should get away for a while, just a short break to help us all relax a bit – a long weekend with the dogs, perhaps."

"Would Billy come?"

"Of course! You don't think he'd let us take Max away from him, do you?"

"Ha-ha, I suppose not! Yeah, that sounds really fun, although it's not really the time of year for it."

"True. Well I'll have a word with your mum, maybe we can book something for the spring, that way we'll have something to look forward to. In the meantime, what about this Christmas fair, that looks fun?" he said, reading the letter from my school that was stuck on the fridge.

"Oh that. I'm going with my dad, actually," I said a little awkwardly, "But I don't think it's going to be that great anyway. Bouncy castles and raffles – primary school stuff, really."

Tuesday 15th December 2020

"OK, WHAT is going on with Carla?" I said to Danny when, once again, Carla left us twenty minutes before the end of lunch.

"I know, right? I mean, I want to give her the benefit of the doubt, but there has to be something she's not telling us!" Danny said, as though relieved to be able to air these thoughts at last.

"I understand if her sister needs a bit of support," I replied, "but Rosie's one of the most popular girls in year ten – she's got loads of mates she can talk to!"

"But don't forget," Danny said, the cogs turning in her brain as she spoke, "she's being trolled by an anonymous person, isn't she? She's probably driving herself crazy trying to guess who it is. She's probably starting to wonder who she can trust."

"That's a good point. I suppose in a situation like that you can only really trust your family."

"But I trust Carla completely," said Danny.

"So, do I!" I said, in something of a rush to affirm my dedication to the friendship group.

"But it doesn't make sense," Danny mused, "she can literally talk to Rosie any time at home, why all these secret meetings at school?"

"Something's definitely up," I agreed. "Should we go and try to find her?"

"Samantha Drury! Of all people, you should know that everyone has a right to privacy! Imagine how angry you'd be if Carla and I came to find you every time you needed some space."

"You're right. Of course, you're right. But Carla's always so honest and open with us. Why won't she tell us what's going on?"

"I'm sure she will, when she's ready," Danny said, but a shadow of doubt drifted over her face like a passing cloud.

Friday 18th December 2020

It's the end of the last full week of term before Christmas. This weekend will be the Christmas fair, and next week we're in only on Monday and half of Tuesday, but today was the date we'd all marked in our calendars. Today Oliver Jameson made good his promise to cook for us all, and it was set to be an astounding Christmas feast. He insisted on cooking enough for every pupil, free of charge, so that no child would be excluded from a decent meal. Of course, all of our parents had heard about this generous offering from Mr Jameson, and who would turn down a free meal, especially one cooked by a world-famous celebrity chef? So, every child in the entire school was in attendance at the lunch hall today. Not a single packed lunch was to be seen.

Despite the enormous turnout, the kitchen was running on steam and everybody got served in good time while the food was still hot – not re-heated, but freshly cooked. Even the dinner ladies themselves were given a free meal while Jameson's kitchen staff prepared and served the food. It was a treat for all, and I couldn't help but think that if every school dinner was as good as this I honestly would not care if I had to sit in the canteen with all the crowds of obnoxious, cackling hyenas I call my peers.

"I can't even stop to breathe!" Carla said as she shoved another forkful of roast veg and gravy into her mouth. "How are they taking photos?!" She nodded towards the year elevens, who were taking pictures of their untouched dinner plates before tucking in.

"It's 'cause he's famous," I mumbled through a mouthful of turkey and stuffing, "they post it on social media hoping that *they'll* get famous."

"Not worth it," Danny rushed her words between morsels of roast potato. "It's food; eat it!"

"If this is food then I don't know what to call the stuff they usually serve in the canteen!" I said.

"Garbage," said Carla.

"No wonder he kicked up such a fuss last time he was here!" Danny said, "there's just no comparison!"

"It is incredible, but what are the regular dinner ladies supposed to do now?" I said. "It's like giving a Victorian child a videogame for one day only and then telling them they have to go back to their wooden building blocks! People won't stand for the old stuff any more. You mark my words: there'll be an organised insurrection before the school year is out!"

We each finished every last crumb on our plates before going back for our desserts, which Oliver Jameson insisted on serving separately so that they would be hot and fresh when we came to eat them. We were all given a warm slice of traditional Christmas pudding with custard made from scratch. After such a wonderful cooked lunch, we were all a bit disappointed; hardly anyone in the entire school managed to finish theirs, excluding some of the staff.

"You don't think he's going to flip out again if no one eats the pudding?" Danny asked, nodding over in the direction of Oliver Jameson, who was sat at the teacher's table chatting away with Mrs McAlpine.

"He seems too distracted to notice," said Carla, "let's just scrape the leftovers in the bin before he sees."

But as she got up to do just that she came face to face with a rather eager-looking year seven boy.

"Not today, Darnell," she muttered in a low voice, but so abruptly that it was sharp enough to send daggers in every direction. Carla brushed him off and walked away before he could say a word to her, but Danny and I caught the sting of her tone and exchanged an inquiring glance before following her to the bin.

We had not even finished pushing the offending puddings into the undiscerning mouth of the school dinner bin when already Carla was approached by yet another small bother.

"What have you got today?" asked the tiny, dark-haired girl with an insect-like manner, as though she was seeking flies to harvest in her web.

"Nothing, Niamh!" Carla snubbed her. "Not here; not now!"

But she had scarcely rid herself of Niamh before she began attracting further unwanted attention at such a rapid rate that she was soon surrounded by a whole hive of irritating little creatures.

"Not today!" she said to all of them, and she stormed out of the dining hall. Danny and I looked at each other in mutual bewilderment. There was no point pretending that what had just happened had not happened, so we followed Carla out of the dinner hall and, once we were in the corridor, broke into a run to catch up with her. Before we'd even opened our mouths to begin questioning her, she spoke:

"OK, you guys want answers. Just please don't think I'm a terrible person! I've been doing something… immoral."

"It can't be that bad!" Danny said as Carla led the way to the year eight locker area. "You wouldn't do it if it was something terrible!"

"I'll let you be the judge of that," Carla continued, "I've been smuggling contraband onto the school grounds. I've been selling all sorts of products without giving a moment's thought to what sort of awful chemicals might be in them! And the worst part is I've been selling them to little year sevens, knowing full well that what I'm providing them with is going to be detrimental to their health."

She put her key in the door of her locker, checked to make sure no one else was around, and opened it. Inside it was stuffed from top to bottom with sweets, chocolate, cakes and pastries.

"The baked goods – pastries, cakes, cookies – are always sold out by mid-morning. I get here early and go to the year seven locker area before coming here. But today there were teachers everywhere, inspecting the place ready for Jameson's visit. The fresh stuff sells at the highest price, but then it costs more to begin with. The real profit is in the sweets. They cost nothing to buy in bulk from the supermarket on my way to school; they're full of sugar, and by lunchtime most of my customers will be craving the white stuff. It's become a status thing, too. Those who carry sweets are seen as bold, edgy, and of course it shows that they've got the financial independence to be able to buy their own, off the radar of the school canteen's monetary system."

"Carla, this is genius!" I said in amazement.

"You don't think it's wrong?" she asked worriedly.

"No! It's only sweets and it's probably better that they have a few during the day rather than bingeing on a whole load of them later and posting videos of it all online."

"But can't they just buy their own stuff on the way to school?" Danny asked.

"Some of them can, but the ones that come to me usually don't have the opportunity because they get taken to school by their parents. The ones that do make their own way to school don't pass by a supermarket, so if they want sweets they have to go to the sweet shop or come to me. A lot of them are scared to go to the sweet shop because of Wilcox's warning; they see me as a safer option."

"And is it worth it?" I asked, "I mean, is there profit in it?"

"Three hundred and eleven pounds, sixty-five pence so far."

"Blimey!" I said, gobsmacked.

"This is seriously impressive," Danny said. "How did you come up with the idea?"

"I don't know. There was a gap in the market, and I decided to fill it. It's not exactly a mastermind notion!"

"Maybe not, but how many other people would have thought to do this?" Danny asked.

"So, you don't think I'm a bad person?"

"Of course not!" Danny said. "You're making money fair and square and you're giving people the freedom to choose what to eat. They know what's in the food, they understand the health risks. It's not like you're being dishonest or scamming anybody."

"Exactly," I agreed, "although you might have to be dishonest to a teacher if they catch you. I mean, if Wilcox finds out you will definitely get in trouble."

"That's another reason why I tried to avoid telling you guys," said Carla. "If you knew what I was up to then you could get in trouble, too. If I'm going down, I don't want to bring you down with me."

"We'll be fine," I said. "But what about you? You're bound to get caught eventually."

"Oh, you know me – I've got a way with Wilcox. He's been scared of me ever since we caught him rapping and I looked him straight in the eye as we walked out of that music studio – his face was a picture! He knew what I was saying with that look: *I know your secret; I know who you really are.*"

"So, you mean to blackmail him?" asked Danny.

"No!" Carla said defensively, "I won't have to. He didn't argue when I wanted to dig up the old time capsules and he won't argue now."

"This is so different, Carla," I said. "The time capsule thing was mutually beneficial: you got your way and it solved Wilcox's problem with Bellows and no one had to know about it. But this – the year sevens all know about it. If you get caught he'll have to punish you – he can't be seen to let you get away with it!"

"I think I'll be all right," Carla said confidently, and it was clear that she could not be dissuaded.

Sunday 20th December 2020

It's a Dad weekend and he's taking us all to the Christmas fair at my school. I really wanted to go because Danny and Carla are going, and there'll be loads of fun things for Stephanie to do there. Even Frogsplash seemed to quite like the idea of it; he's never seen my school before, and Dad said he'd buy him a drink at the FRED bar (Friends and Relatives of the Duke). There was only one problem: as a faculty member Richard was coming too, and guess who he was bringing? To make matters worse he could only fit one of his two daughters in his stupid lime green sports car, so the other would have to come with us in Dad's car.

"You don't mind, do you, Duncan?" he asked over breakfast this morning while Frogsplash was still in bed.

"I don't see why not," Dad said cheerfully. Either he'd completely forgotten about Froggo's past relationship with Richard's oldest daughter Gertie or he was doing a very good job of keeping it secret. I hope they're not going to tag along with us for the entire day. Richard's all right but his daughters each have the face of someone who is perpetually sucking lemons, and a personality to match.

"Dad, we need to get there for one p.m. to hear them call the raffle; I've got six tickets!" I said when it got to half past eleven and Frogsplash was still in bed.

"Don't stress, Sam, you know Froggo, he'll roll out of bed and be ready to leave in five minutes."

"Yeah but we've got to get Steph strapped in, pick up one of Rich's daughters and then drive the forty-five minutes to school!"

Dad's not great at timing. He's almost always late picking us up. He prefers to cut it fine when it comes to catching trains, arriving for cinema screenings, getting to the hospital in time to see his first daughter being born, that sort of thing. I, on the other hand, like to allow extra time for the million unforeseen circumstances which I, being the way that I am, have foreseen in nightmarish, anxiety-inducing detail.

"He may get ready in five minutes," I said to Dad, "but he takes an hour to get out of bed! Go and wake him up, please, I don't want to walk in on him in his pants!"

So, Dad went to wake the dead while I came up with a much simpler way to get us all to the fair on time AND avoid an awkward situation with Frog and Gertie.

"Well, he's not out of bed, and he's not quite awake, but he's... vocal," Dad said, which means Frogsplash probably made a sound that went something like "mnnneuuuurgh" and then rolled over.

"Never mind about him," I said, "it makes no sense for both cars to go to Fran's house. How about we leave now, pick up both of Richard's daughters and Richard can take Froggo when he's up?"

So, Dad went scurrying around grabbing anything and everything we might need to bring with us for Stephanie and away we went. I had sacrificed myself for the greater good. I had volunteered myself for a forty-five-minute journey in close proximity to the sulky, sullen, sour sisters that are somehow the spawn of Richard Roberts.

When we arrived at their address, Dad sent me to knock on the door while he stayed in the car trying to placate Stephanie (she always cries when the car stops moving). I walked up to the house with trepidation, feeling like the kid in the horror movie who's been dared to go and knock on the creepy old lady's door despite knowing the horrifying legend behind her haunting reputation. They had no friendly doorbell, no light-hearted welcome mat, only dead plants which crept across the house's façade like woven bones. But to be fair it is winter, and most plants look like that right now.

I banged on the lion's head knocker three times and waited nervously until the ice queen herself answered. She towered over me and looked down without smiling.

"Hi, I'm Sam," I said after waiting several moments for her to greet me. "You came to my mum's party last year, do you remember?"

"You're here for the girls," she said in a way which was not so much a question as a statement of fact, perhaps even an accusation. She peered over my head to check that there was a car waiting.

"Yes," I said.

"Gertrude! Eloise!" she called out into the depths of her long, hollow hallway. Shortly after, the two girls appeared silently, as if from nowhere. They looked even thinner than I remember in their matching woollen dresses and knee-high socks. They put on some very neat, expensive-looking coats which had sharp collars instead of hoods, which is very impractical if you ask me. They said a solemn goodbye to their mother and followed me gloomily to the chaos of Dad's car. They insisted on sitting next to each other which meant they had to sit in the back with Stephanie. Usually she stops crying once the car gets going but something about the presence of those girls seemed to have unsettled her.

Eventually Stephanie drifted off and we were all left in awkward silence.

"So, Christmas is just around the corner!" Dad said, attempting to get us all in the festive spirit. "You two got any nice plans?"

"Mummy's taking us to a health spa," said Eloise, who is the same age as me.

"Oh, that's… nice," Dad said unconvincingly, "not very traditional, though. Most people do that sort of thing in the summer, or at least in January after they've made their resolutions! I suppose it must be cheaper to go over Christmas, though…"

"No!" said Eloise, extremely offended by the implication that they were going on some sort of budget holiday.

"It's actually very popular at this time of year," Gertie insisted. "We go every Christmas. Everyone else can stuff their faces with chocolate and carbs if they like, that will just make it all the more pleasurable when we go back to school looking gorgeously rejuvenated and they all look like bloated pigs in meaty blankets!"

I can picture it now: the three of them on Christmas Day with seaweed-slime face masks drinking kale smoothies in cold, dead, silence, not daring to crack a smile lest it line their porcelain faces. I feel awfully sorry for the spa staff who have to spend their Christmas being talked down to by those three witches.

"Not very festive though, is it?" Dad said, "I mean, does Father Christmas know where to leave your presents when you're at the spa?"

"Father Christmas doesn't exist," said Gertie plainly.

"How could you say such a thing?" I protested. "Of course, he does!" Fortunately, Stephanie was still fast asleep, her ears closed to such vicious rumours.

I had been looking forward to the fair: the jingling of bells, the smell of mulled wine, the familiarity of repeated Christmas hits. The essence of Christmas is, I think, in the tiny, clichéd details, but it doesn't seem to matter that they're the same every year, because they're pretty much banned from existence for the other eleven months. Nobody has tinsel in March or mince pies in June! Of course, it's a bit cheesy and incredibly childish, but that's all part of the fun. But Gertie and Eloise were giving off such a powerful Scrooge vibe that by the time we arrived I felt like a fool for even smiling. I needed my friends; I needed my brother… I even needed Richard.

The place was heaving, it seemed as though everyone had come and brought their extended family along with them. I met with Carla and Danny at the bouncy castle, where Stephanie and Danny's twin brothers Finn and Jim let off some of the energy they'd been forced to reserve whilst strapped in on the journey to the fair.

"Oh my god, she's adorable," said Danny, watching Stephanie wipe snot across her red, sweaty cheeks. Poor girl, she's got the red cheeks gene too – must be from Dad's side of the family. Dad got chatting with Danny's mum, Amelia, who seemed a little stressed trying to keep track of the twins in such a busy environment.

"We had to get the bus here," Danny informed us, "it was hell, what with the double buggy and all. The first bus that we tried to get on turned us away because there wasn't enough space! My parents had to sell the second car, so we've only got the one and Dad needed it today, he's gone to collect his parents, they're staying with us over Christmas. I'm not looking forward to it, to be honest. There's so much built-up tension between my parents right now, and with my grandparents staying over they won't be able to let it out even at night."

"That's awful," I said, "especially at Christmas. But hey, at least you still get presents and chocolate – you see those girls over there?" I said, nodding towards Eloise and Gertie. "Remember them from Mum's party? They're Richard's daughters. They're going to a spa for Christmas where they'll only get to eat health foods – can you imagine?"

"No way!" said Danny, and we all stole an extra-long glance at the sisters, who were sat on a P.E. bench on the very edge of the hall staring at their phone screens, which reflected white light back upon their already mealy faces to give them the illusion of being borderline translucent. It didn't look as though Richard was going to have much luck spending quality time with his children, unless you include his surrogate son, Frogsplash.

We perambulated the ground floor in a rough group with Dad, Amelia and the kids until they'd exhausted all options in terms of infant activities and had cost both parents a small fortune in the process. Dad had got talking to Amelia about parenting stuff and started asking advice about potty training and toddler-friendly recipes and the like. It was an incredibly mundane conversation, and I'm pretty sure Dad has no intention of cooking Amelia's organic swede and parsnip mash. It occurred to me that he was playing it safe because he felt nervous. Maybe just because she's my friend's mum and he wanted to make a good impression, but Dad's not usually that conscious of stuff like that.

It's hard not to be conscious of the fact that Danny's mum is very beautiful. Perhaps that's what was putting Dad off his game.

What is it with these parents? First Mum with Billy's dad and now Dad with Danny's mum? Can't they find relationships within their own friendship groups?!

Stephanie was getting grumpy, so I suggested we stop off at the FRED bar to get some drinks and snacks, and Dad was more than happy to oblige.

"I'll get some drinks in!" he said with far too much enthusiasm. "What are you having, Amelia?"

"Ooh, I'll have a glass of Sauvignon Blanc, thank you!"

"What about you, Carla, aren't your parents around?"

"Oh, they'll be with my oldest sister checking out her A Level work, don't worry about them."

"Yeah, don't worry about them, worry about us!" came Richard's voice, and he held up his empty beer glass like a beacon to guide Dad towards the table at which he and Frogsplash were sat.

"You were supposed to call when you arrived!" Dad said to Richard, although he hardly seemed bothered.

"Ah yes, I think there's something wrong with my phone, you see. I've been calling and texting my girls all day but neither of them have got back to me. Ah, well!"

"They probably left their phones at home or something," Dad said in an attempt to spare his friend's feelings.

"Ah yes, that'll be it! So, who's this then?" Richard said, smiling cheerfully at Amelia. After all the introductions were done, me, Danny, Carla, Amelia and the little ones sat down with Froggo and Richard while Dad went to the bar.

Stephanie was in a particularly chatty mood, which is always fun because she comes out with some pretty funny stuff, and it was really nice for Carla and Danny to get to know her.

"So, are you excited about Christmas?" Carla asked her.

"Yes! I want to get presents!" she replied.

"And what presents have you asked for?" Carla asked.

"No!" Steph replied, seeming a little frustrated, "I want to get presents for Jesus – it's his birthday!"

"Ah, I see," said Carla, "and what sort of thing do you think Jesus would like?"

"Gold, Fenkinsen and Mrrr," she said without hesitation. They must have attempted to teach the nativity at her nursery.

"Goodness, where are you going to get all that from?" Carla asked.

"Nowhere. I can't give Jesus a present because he died crossing the road."

"Did he?" Carla asked, surprised. "Who told you that?"

"Mummy," Stephanie replied. "She said Jesus died on the crossing. It's very sad."

Bless her heart, we couldn't let her see us laughing, so we changed the subject to something less serious. Danny started asking her which TV shows she likes, and of course she knew all of them after having been subjected to them far more frequently than me thanks to Finn and Jim. I noticed Frogsplash and Richard had attracted a small audience of sixth formers while discussing some fantasy TV series they must have gotten into while Frog's been living at the flat, and they all seemed to have very passionate opinions on the subject. Dad and Amelia carried on getting to know each other and discussing parenting stuff until Amelia had finished her wine and offered to get another round from the bar.

"Better not," Dad said, "I'm driving."

"I'm not driving," Amelia said when it was Richard's round and she asked for a third glass of wine. "My husband's got the car, so we had to take the bus."

"With three kids? What a nightmare!" Dad said. "I'd offer you a lift but we're full up as it is – Richard's teenage daughters are with our group – despite their best efforts not to been seen anywhere near us!"

"Oh, that's all right, I'd have needed car seats for the twins anyway. It won't be so bad on the return journey – they'll be passed out and I won't be far behind!" Amelia laughed as she took a slightly desperate gulp of her wine.

Dad raised his eyebrows when Frogsplash also said yes to another drink, but he didn't stop him. He waited for everyone to finish their drinks then suggested we all go upstairs to the Christmas marketplace.

"I don't mind, but it'll just be tacky, throw-away novelty stuff," I warned him.

"Perfect!" he said, "I've got the most miserable git for my secret Santa this year – I'll get him a giant stuffed reindeer! And the flat's looking a bit depressing, we could do with some tacky, throw-away, novelty decorations, don't you think?"

"OK, but you have to promise me you'll make Gertie and Eloise hold the reindeer on the way back!"

"Deal!" he laughed.

"Sounds like fun," Amelia said, "but I'll only end up spending more money on the boys. We'd better make tracks."

"Ah OK, well it was very nice meeting you," Dad said, and we all said our goodbyes to Danny and her family and headed upstairs.

There were stalls of pick 'n' mix sweets, Christmas stockings, stocking fillers, wrapping paper, cards, and even one where they had these chocolate sculptures of things that people might have an interest in – there was a chocolate beer glass, a chocolate rugby ball, a chocolate guitar – they were very realistic but SO expensive. There were plenty of tacky decorations and, true to his word, Dad bought loads of them. There were hand-made wreaths, which were a little crude and rough-looking, but I suppose if you're weaving real holly leaves it's probably quite difficult to keep it neat.

One slightly optimistic parent was selling copies of his own self-produced album: a selection of old Christmas songs all covered by him and his acoustic guitar. We weren't able to listen to it, so any potential buyers were literally left to judge the album by its cover, which was a photograph of this bloke lying down casually with his guitar cradled in his arms. I noticed Richard hovering by this particular stall for longer than the rest of us, and I had a sneaking suspicion that he was considering taking up the guitar.

Richard bought a bottle opener with a little figurine of a drunk-looking elf on the top and, seemingly out of nowhere, he produced another bottle of beer for he and Frogsplash to share. Once again, Dad rolled his eyes but let it slide, perhaps in the spirit of Christmas. Carla and I were walking either side of Stephanie holding her hands, but she was beginning to tire and the three of us were hanging back from the rest of the group. I was just about to offer to go and find Richard's daughters so that we could start heading back when Dad, Richard and Frogsplash approached a stall with a familiar sign hanging above it: *Cassie Darling's Proper English Wine.*

"Frogsplash?" Mum said at once, her voice a little broken.

"Mum?" He stood frozen to the spot, although I noticed he drew his beer-wielding arm downwards in a vain attempt to conceal the bottle.

"Oh, hello," Graham said calmly, his everyman smile switched on to greet us all. It was the first time either he or Mum had seen Frogsplash since the night he left.

"Cassie, I'm sorry, I had no idea you'd be here," Dad said earnestly. "I've got the kids, I just assumed you'd be off doing your own thing."

"I am! I'm selling my home-made wine. Look, it's OK, it's not a problem…"

"You might have tried a bit harder not to let the boy get so drunk at such a public event," Graham cut in, referring to Frogsplash.

"Oh, and where is your boy? At the pub, no doubt?"

Perhaps I tell Dad too much about Graham.

"Yes, at the pub, earning his keep! Funnily enough, my son doesn't seem to have a problem with being around alcohol and staying sober. My son isn't lazy or workshy, either."

157

"Hey!" said Frogsplash, who had every right to feel affronted.

"How dare you!" Dad said, but he seemed at a loss for words, and Graham just stood there smirking, winding him up without having to say anything. Dad was growing frustrated. He picked up a bottle of *Cassie Darling's Proper English Wine* and held it firmly, his hand shaking. I could have forgiven him for smashing it, but I'm glad he didn't.

"This is awful! Are you OK?" Carla whispered in my ear so as not to alert Stephanie.

"I'm OK," I assured her, "let's just try to keep Steph busy."

So, we sat down on some plastic school chairs a little further away from the incipient situation. I rummaged around in one of Dad's shopping bags and dug out a singing, dancing Santa to distract Stephanie. I showed her how to squeeze his hand to activate him. Carla sat down next to me and squeezed my hand. We listened.

"Who's this prat?" Richard said loudly, a little slurred and quite uninhibited, gesturing in Graham's direction.

"Don't start, Richard," Dad warned him. "This is your place of work, don't forget, and this is my family."

Sensibly, Richard guided Frogsplash away and out of view, possibly to collect the girls, or perhaps to return to the bar – I wouldn't have blamed them either way.

Now that Froggo was out of earshot, Dad was able to speak his mind. "I have no problem with Cassie being in a new relationship," he said in a low tone, staring intensely into Graham's eyes. "I don't even mind another man being part of my children's lives – spending more time with them than I do, influencing them in ways I can't control – but I will not have another man undermining and belittling my children. What kind of a man would do that?"

"Excuse me, I have been supporting your children! When was the last time you took them on holiday? When was the last parents' evening you attended? Where were you for his or her last birthday?"

"I was working!"

"Of course, you were! Always time for work; never time for your children."

"Do you hear me complaining about having Frogsplash at mine? No, because I love it. And I would love to take them on holiday, I would love to be invited to parents' evenings. I have always got time for my children."

Graham scoffed and rolled his eyes in an over-exaggerated performance of disbelief. He didn't say a word. Normally I like it when people just say nothing, but sometimes you need someone to express themselves with words so that you can argue back. Graham was deliberately withholding his words to frustrate Dad, and it was working.

"What do you want me to do?" Dad said in response to Graham's eye-roll, his voice raised in anger. "Should I quit my job and become a full-time parent to a sixteen-year-old who can look after himself and two daughters who don't even live with me? We didn't all inherit a pub from our parents! We can't all just work the odd shift when we feel like it!"

I definitely tell Dad too much about Graham.

Graham began to retaliate rather more coolly and quietly than Dad. I didn't catch what he said because Stephanie had begun to cry. The sound of Dad shouting had upset her, and the dancing Santa was no longer important enough to hold her attention. I picked her up and sat her on my lap, assuring her that everything was all right, but toddlers aren't as stupid as you think. She recognised Dad's voice and she knew that something was wrong. I felt sad for her – life was never that turbulent for me when I was her age. Things were consistent back then, and I never had to worry about my parents' emotions. I truly believed that adults had mastered every single aspect of life.

Dad and Graham showed no signs of stopping, and Stephanie was tuned into it now, so I stood up, rested her on my hip with her arms wrapped around me and I walked straight up to them, leaving poor Carla sat alone and completely at a loss for what to do. Graham was shouting at Dad now, and I felt a dim satisfaction in knowing that he hadn't been able to keep his cool, but I was suddenly so conscious of all the many sets of eyes flitting in the direction of me and my family, passing their judgement on us for creating such a violent disturbance at such a family event. But they were right to stare; none of this was right. It was not right at all. I had been so caught up in my family's drama and so focussed on keeping Stephanie innocent to all of it that I had completely forgotten that it was all happening at my school, in front of people that I knew.

"Stop it!" I said to Graham and Dad, who were talking at each other, criticising each other in a storm of negative language. "You're scaring her! She's only a baby! Stop shouting!"

They both did as they were told, and everything seemed to fall silent. Stephanie stopped crying loudly and muted her distress down to a feeble whimper, but her cheeks were still wet with tears. I held her close to my chest, resting my head gently on top of hers. I just wanted her to feel safe.

Mum, who I realised had not spoken in quite some time, suddenly let out a noise that I could not possibly describe. She was staring at Stephanie. She was watching Stephanie and me like there was nothing and nobody else in the entire world. She was looking at Stephanie like the third child she always wished she'd had. Then she began to cry – not Stephanie, but Mum.

It was a plaintive yelp that she let out involuntarily and tried to contain too abruptly, so that it came out quite inhuman. It sounded out across the hall, raw like a wounded animal. That was the sound of my mum in pain and out of control of herself emotionally. Graham took her by the arms and directed her away from me, as though shielding her from an enemy.

"Now look what you've done," he said to me with venom, and he, too, turned his back on me. They walked away together, abandoning their wares.

"Samantha, I'm sorry," Dad said to me as he began to snap out of that awful atmosphere.

"Don't be stupid" I replied quietly. "Don't be sorry."

Carla helped us to pick up the pieces, and gradually we gathered the remnants of our parties together until we were ready to leave. Carla's oldest sister, Louisa, who had recently passed her driving test but could not afford even the cheapest of cars, was thrilled to drive Richard home in his sports car (Richard was a bit over the limit!). I went with Carla, her parents and her middle sister Rosie, and dad took Froggo, Steph and Richard's miserable daughters, which can't have been much fun for any of them.

The worst part was that I had to go back home to Mum's house. It didn't seem fair that I should have to go back there alone while everyone else got to drive off to the safety of their own separate homes. I'm sure Dad would have let me stay at his if I'd wanted to, but none of my school stuff is there and I wouldn't have a clue how to travel to Duke John Jameson in the morning. Besides, if I didn't come home it would probably cause even more arguments between Mum and Dad. Or should I say, Graham and Dad.

When Carla's parents dropped me off I noticed the second lock was still on the front door, which meant that the house was empty. Mum and Graham were probably packing the unsold bottles of wine in the car – surely they can't have stayed at my school after the scene they'd just caused. I wonder how many other people saw what happened. It had been very noisy and very busy there – I'm just hoping it was noisy enough to drown out the horrible sound of my family at war. I went straight up to my room and tried to busy myself with the old diary, but it's hard enough to concentrate on the old language and slanted handwriting even at the best of times. All I could do was lie on my bed and listen for the sound of the car pulling up on the gravel driveway.

Billy arrived home first; I heard his footsteps, his keys in the door, and then his voice greeting our dogs, Max and Trousers. I was glad he was home – things are always less tense when Billy's around. I thought about going downstairs and telling him what had happened today, but I wasn't sure how I could possibly tell the story without speaking some truly nasty words against his father, so I thought I'd better hold my tongue. Instead I played it all out in my head, over and over, wondering how on Earth such an open conflict could have unravelled. Why were Mum and Graham there in the first place? To sell Mum's wine, I suppose. It makes sense; it was just a bad coincidence.

When Mum and Graham came home with enough Turkish grill takeaway to feed an army, they sent Billy up to call me down for dinner. It was their peace offering. All I'd eaten since breakfast was a mince pie and far too many sweets, so some proper food was tempting. Part of me wanted to hide in my room, but I couldn't stay there forever, and the longer I left it the more awkward it would be when I finally did emerge. Besides, it was better to face them when Billy was there, too. I followed him down, nearly tripping over Trousers on the stairs.

"So, how was the fair?" Billy asked as we were heading down. "Dad was a bit nervous about meeting up with your Dad and Frogsplash."

Meeting up? What?

"But he seems in a good mood so I'm guessing it went OK?"

"Um, well…"

"I told him not to be nervous. I said I thought it was a great idea, arranging to meet up with you all at a family event like that. Sort of like an ice-breaker; a peace offering."

Arranging to... what?!

"Hey, Sammy!" Mum said as I entered the kitchen. She was the only one who seemed a little uneasy. "What are you having – chicken, lamb? Or you can just help yourself. Yes, I'll lay it all out on the table; you can all help yourselves."

"How was work today?" Graham asked Billy cheerfully.

"Oh, you know, the usual Sunday crowd, plus a few families doing their annual Christmas pub lunch. But how about you guys, how did the wine stall get on?"

"Oh, it was great! We had a fabulous time, didn't we, Sam?" Graham smiled at me without any hint that he was being disingenuous.

"Oh, yeah, the fair was great," I said vaguely.

"It was really great," Graham said, "Frogsplash looked well, didn't he, Cassie?"

"Oh yeah. He seemed really... happy."

What is going on? What universe were they in?!

"Good, good," Billy said mindlessly while tearing into his lamb shish. "And your little sister, did she enjoy it?" he asked me.

"Yeah, I think so," I said, even more vaguely. I didn't want to catch a nerve with Mum; seeing Stephanie had made her so upset.

"Oh, she was a little angel, wasn't she, Cassie?" Graham said. "We bought everyone lunch at the café as a bit of a friendly, no hard feelings gesture, and she was ever so polite. She ate all her grapes and ham sandwiches and she said please and thank you every time! Such a sweet little child. Makes me wish I'd had a daughter!"

WHAT? Now he's just making stuff up! And that bit about having a daughter – isn't that a bit insensitive towards Mum?

"Me and Arnie not good enough for you, Dad?" Billy jested.

"Oh, you know what I mean!" Graham said. "You two are fantastic sons, you really are. Hard-working, honest, responsible. It's just that little boys are so... messy! But I'm kidding, of course. I'm definitely not thinking about having more children!"

"Good, you're far too old!" Billy said jokingly, but I'm not sure Mum found it that funny.

"The wine sold very well too, didn't it, Cass?" Graham said.

"Oh yes, it was very popular. It was such a great idea of yours, setting up a stall at Sam's school!"

"Well, I think we've earned a glass or two ourselves, to celebrate your success!" Graham said, and he went to the hallway where the unsold bottles had been unloaded out of the car. While he was out of the room I watched Mum's face, hoping for some eye contact. I wanted to communicate with her. I wanted her to acknowledge that Graham wasn't telling the truth, even if it was only to me, even just a glance or a shrug. But she busied herself squeezing lemon on her salad until Graham returned.

"Oh yes, it was a good day all round," Graham said, as if to summarise. "A warm and wonderful start to the holiday season."

Monday 21st December 2020

HERO CHEF JAMESON SINGLE-HANDEDLY SAVES AN ENTIRE GENERATION FROM DIABETES, HEART-DISEASE, HIGH BLOOD PRESSURE AND GOUT!

Christmas came early this year for the pupils of Duke John Jameson School when celebrity chef Oliver Jameson took over their kitchens to cook every single child a delicious, healthy meal completely free of charge. But this is not just a seasonal show of generosity: Jameson has promised to return to the school every four weeks to provide his services to the poor, malnourished children of the run-down school. "They were in desperate need of my help." Jameson spoke to us after the event on Friday. "The school menu was atrocious… the head of the school clearly has no regard for the wellbeing of his pupils – I simply had to intervene. I dread to think how widespread this level of incompetence may be in our country's education system."

"Charming!" Carla said after Danny had read the article out loud to us, "Wilcox is going to love this!"

"It wasn't even that healthy," Danny said, "I mean, I know it was a special Christmas menu, but if we ate that all the time, we probably *would* get gout!"

"The bit that gets me," I pointed out, "is where Jameson says *'the school menu was atrocious'* – he's implying that he's actually done something to change the school menu when in fact it's exactly the same as it always has been on the other twenty-seven days – stodgy, greasy, bland and heavily processed."

"Perhaps he didn't say it quite like that," Danny suggested. "You know how these reporters like to skew things. Maybe he said something like, *'the school menu was atrocious, but I couldn't change it on a permanent basis because of a lack of government funding. "*

Danny doesn't make assumptions or jump to conclusions – she's good like that.

Friday 25th December 2020

Today was so much fun. I started out feeling negative, perhaps even a little hostile, because it felt as though these new people had come along, invaded our family and changed everything. Graham shouldn't have been there and Frogsplash definitely should. But I got a video call from Dad and Froggo this morning and they both seemed so happy that I decided to try and be positive. And then, when I went down for breakfast, Graham broke the "tragic" news that he would have to go into work for the afternoon. The Mill on the Hill is a family pub and they've been taking Christmas bookings, so I don't know why Graham left it to the last minute to say something. Sometimes I think he gets some satisfaction out of withholding information and only dealing it out in small, controlled portions as and when he feels like it. It's like he doesn't want any of us to ever relax.

Mum was disappointed, I could tell. She might have been all right with it, but she'd already told her family that she'd be bringing her new partner. Her sister, my Aunt Lola, was hosting this year, and their parents were going to be there, too. They had all been expecting to meet Graham, and now Mum was going to have to make excuses for him. It was unfair. I felt angry for Mum, but it was hard to feel disappointed because I knew I couldn't enjoy my day with Graham around. I didn't realise until today, when I knew he was nowhere near, just how tense I'd been feeling all the time.

But even Graham isn't cruel enough to make his fifteen-year-old son work on Christmas Day. Arnie was off meeting his new girlfriend's parents, so Billy was to spend the day with us. Aunt Lola loves animals so she insisted that we bring the dogs along so they wouldn't be alone for Christmas (as if they'd have a clue what day it is!). As soon as we arrived Max went absolutely crazy for Aunt Lola, who is six months pregnant. She and mum surmised that Max must be able to sense the hormones and, remembering her own pregnancy, fell into sympathy with Aunt Lola.

Lola had done most of the food preparation herself, but she let her parents (my grandparents) take over once we'd arrived. She sat down with us in the living room and Max immediately jumped up on her lap and curled up next to her bump – it was so adorable I swear Aunt Lola was close to tears! Grandad was in charge of drinks, and by the looks of his rosy cheeks he had already had a few sherries himself.

"Can I get you a drink, Frederick?" he asked Billy.

"Er… I'm not Frederick," Billy replied politely.

"Oh, that's right – you prefer to be called Frogsplash!" Grandad said. "Silly nickname, but boys will be boys!"

"No, Dad, this is Billy, Graham's son. Frogsplash is at Duncan's this year," Mum reminded him.

"Ah yes, you did tell us, didn't you. Such a confusing business all these family games of musical chairs!"

Mum rolled her eyes with no subtlety whatsoever as Grandad forgot to take Billy's drink order and instead went mindlessly back to the kitchen. Aunt Lola called her husband, Rashid, in to take over. My other cousins, Anna and Roland, were with their other side of the family this year, so I had only Lola and Rashid's twin daughters to play with. Sita and Satya are nine now, and like me they're very quiet, so while we waited for dinner we just sat down in their bedroom colouring in these beautiful patterns with these special glitter pens they'd gotten for Christmas.

I was surprised at how willingly they shared their brand-new pens with me – I'm not a selfish person but pens are precious things and there are few people I trust not to ruin or lose them! I like to think that they knew they could trust me because I honour the sanctity of stationery. I did wonder, though, how well the pair would cope with a new little brother or sister rampaging around their home. I'm not sure how well I'd have dealt with Stephanie when I was nine.

Grandma, bless her, had been so busy keeping an eye on all the food and making sure it would all be ready to serve at precisely the same time that she didn't even properly say hello to all of us until it was time to sit down and eat.

"Ooh!" she said excitedly as she spooned some roast parsnips onto Billy's plate, "you must be Billy! So lovely of you to join us."

"So lovely of you to have me, really, you've all been wonderful. And this food looks incredible!"

"Oh, what a lovely boy!" Grandma smiled broadly, and I could have sworn I saw her blushing.

Trousers was doing his usual routine of scampering around the outskirts of the table looking up at people sadly until one of us gave in and offered him some of our food. Max is rather craftier, and whilst everyone thought she was still asleep on the sofa after Aunt Lola had carefully scooped her off her lap and laid her back down, she had in fact managed to sneak under the table and settled by Billy's feet. Billy has a naughty habit of feeding Max under the table at home, and with the many gorgeous smells coming from Aunt Lola's kitchen, there was no way she was going to miss out now.

"So, Billy, what do you do?" Grandma asked him, forgetting that this was a family Christmas dinner and not a dinner party for young singles.

"Well, I'm still at school," he said, "but I work some shifts at my Dad's pub."

"Oh wow, very good, already earning at your age! Here, have some more sprouts, I see you've finished yours…"

I have a feeling I know who really finished the sprouts for Billy.

"…surprisingly time-consuming, preparing sprouts," Grandma went on, "you have to score a cross in each and every one before you put them in the pan. And just look at that huge pile of sprouts in the serving dish – took me ages, that did! And you have to cook them for just the right amount of time. If you overcook sprouts they taste absolutely disgusting!"

I could tell from the look on Billy's face that he thought they already tasted absolutely disgusting, and he was waiting for Grandma to stop paying such close attention to him so that he could feed some more of them to Max without her noticing. I was just trying not to laugh! Eventually I decided to throw Billy a bone and asked Grandma if she could get me a glass of water. He scooped up a couple of sprouts, making sure not to take all of them in case Grandma tried to refill his plate yet again, and passed them to Max, along with a bit of turkey skin to sweeten the deal.

"So, how's school, Frogsplash?" Grandad asked Billy, but Mum was in some kind of deep conversation with Aunt Lola and Grandma was still in the kitchen, so there was no one to correct him.

"Oh, it's OK. I've got exams this year, actually."

"Oh yes, what are your subjects again?" Grandad asked.

"Well there's the usual Maths, English and Science," Billy replied more confidently this time, "and my chosen subjects are History, French, ICT and... Classical Ballet."

Clearly Billy had decided to take the opportunity to have a bit of fun and wind Grandad up, although if Grandad remembers this conversation this time next year then really the joke will be on Frogsplash. The meal went on slowly, all of us becoming too full to eat any more and yet none of us willing to let the food on our plates go to waste (much to Trousers' disappointment, who was still waiting patiently for scraps). Billy managed to successfully juggle Grandma's shameless flirting, feeding Max under the table and creating a completely revamped image of Frogsplash to baffle Grandad.

"Oh no, I'm not into wrestling at all any more," he told Grandad while Grandma was up getting the pudding ready, "in fact, I don't really want people to call me Frogsplash nowadays. I don't like to correct people but, since we're on the subject, I prefer to be called Fishdive. That's my favourite ballet move."

"Hmm, interesting," said Grandad with thinly veiled disapproval. "So, how are your other subjects going? Do you have a favourite besides the, er, the dancing one?"

"I love French – the language of love! It's so elegant, so refined. And how I wish I could visit Paris, it has so much style and culture! But, alas, French happens to be my weakest subject. I'm far better at English. We're studying poetry this term and I've really gotten into it. I wrote a poem just last week about the loveliness of horses. Did I mention that I adore horses? I'm not ashamed to say that their beauty makes me quite emotional. Would you like to hear the poem? My teacher thought it was superb!"

"Um, perhaps later... ah, look, the pudding's here now!" Grandad said with great relief. I'm not sure what Billy would have done if Grandad had wanted to listen to the equine verse that I'm pretty sure he was going to have to make up on the spot, but I would have loved to hear it.

After dinner we all went back to the living room to watch whatever Christmas specials happened to be on TV. Aunt Lola went back to her armchair and Max jumped straight back onto her lap and curled up next to her bump. It didn't take long before Aunt Lola, exhausted from cooking, eating and generally being pregnant, also fell asleep. Mum had spent most of the meal talking to Lola about her own problems (Frogsplash, mainly) so now she took the time to catch up with Uncle Rashid. Aunt Lola had given Trousers a clever dog toy in which you hide treats and the dog has to figure out how to get to them, so the twins and I sat on the floor and played with him while Billy continued to entertain both Grandma and Grandad. It was all very lovely, until an incredibly pungent smell began to waft from Aunt Lola's armchair.

Those of us who were still conscious began to exchange glances as the smell became impossible to ignore. Nobody wished to comment on such a vulgar occurrence, but to say nothing would have been tantamount to lying. It would have been a milder form of the kind of denial that I've been subjected to at home ever since the fight at the fair happened. Thankfully, Grandad wasn't too shy to broach the subject.

"Corr!" he said gruffly. "At least it's not me for a change!" He nodded in the direction of poor, oblivious Aunt Lola.

"Oh, don't make a fuss, Alan," Grandma said gently, "she's pregnant for goodness' sakes! Remember what I was like when I was expecting Cassandra? It's hard enough creating an entire human being inside of you, getting heartburn every bloody hour and having your ankles swell up to a painful extent without people taking the mickey out of all your bodily functions as well!"

Grandma was quite right to defend her daughter, but the guilty look on Billy's face told me that he was ninety-nine per cent sure that the sudden influx of flatulence that was encompassing the living room was coming straight from his dog, who slept contentedly on Aunt Lola's lap after eating at least two human portions of Brussel sprouts.

Monday 4th January 2021

I thought *my* Christmas holiday had been bad. Christmas Day was fun, but the fun stopped there. With Mum it was like it had taken all of her energy just to be normal and actually participate in Christmas, because as soon as it was over she became tired and withdrawn. Billy had been the best, but between working and studying I hardly got to see him again. The only person who seemed omnipresent was Graham, and I resented him more than ever for it.

I was grateful to be back at school today, and I couldn't wait to catch up with my friends. Everything at home is so weird at the moment, I really needed the normality of talking to Danny and Carla, and even more than that, I needed to hear their viewpoints on the matter of Graham, who I'm still trying to figure out.

"So how was your Christmas?" Carla asked us when we all congregated at our usual spot.

"It was the worst Christmas I've ever had, to be honest," Danny said. "I might as well tell you guys now, but I don't want a big fuss or anything. Basically, my Dad never came home after he left to pick up his parents. Apparently he and Mum had decided it was best to give each other some space, but they didn't want to tell us about it straight away because they wanted us to enjoy the fair and at least have a little bit of Christmas fun before they broke the news. They haven't split up, or so they keep saying, they just need some time apart to think things over. I don't know why they chose to do this at Christmas, but it was pretty miserable, what with Mum trying to force all the usual traditions."

"Oh no, I'm so sorry!" said Carla. "Sorry, I won't make a fuss, I promise. It's not a big deal, I'm sure. It's just really bad timing, isn't it?"

"Well yeah, it did seem a bit cruel," Danny said. "Couldn't they have just waited, if not for me then for the twins?"

"They won't have done it to be cruel," I said, "Christmas can be a stressful time for adults, especially if they're having money troubles, which you already know they are. Maybe they knew that they'd end up arguing or getting upset if they were together, and maybe they thought that would be worse for you and the twins."

"You're right. The twins know exactly what's going on when they argue, but they don't have a clue what's happening at the moment. They think Dad's on holiday at Nanny and Grandpa's house. I wonder how long it'll take for them to start getting suspicious. What if he's still living there six months from now? That's a bloody long holiday!"

"I'm sure it won't be that long," said Carla, "they love each other! They'll soon start to miss each other and realise why they got married in the first place."

"Yeah, no offence, Carla, but you're not exactly the authority on the subject – your picture-perfect parents are hardly an example of a troubled relationship! But I appreciate the positive thinking. Maybe you're right, maybe they will miss each other, but what if they don't? What if they enjoy the time apart too much?"

"Well, I guess that might be a sign that they are better off going their separate ways," I said, perhaps a little too bluntly, "but it sounds like they're trying hard to work things out and that's a really good sign."

"Exactly," Carla agreed, "and I know it's hard, but try not to worry. You have no idea how it's all going to turn out. Worst case scenario: they do get divorced. I know it might feel like it now, but it's really not the end of the world. Just look at Sam – her parents are divorced and she's happy!"

And then I knew I couldn't say a word about Graham. I have to pretend, for Danny's sake, that my home life is happy.

Thursday 7th January 2021

While we've been wrapped up in our own worlds and cocooned in our soundproof music room there has been a shift in the dynamics of the social hierarchy in our year. Beth, Charlotte, Andrea and Ruby had been at the top, but from behind books, out of the shadows and concealed by anonymity a new and potentially stronger group has arisen, and believe me they are no friends to Beth and co. These girls are a different class, and I mean literally. Their parents are very, very rich, and they definitely all went to private primary schools. I've got nothing against private school, or wealth in general, but there's something wrong about a bunch of twelve-year-olds with highlights in their hair and professionally manicured nails who go around school flaunting their designer shoes and handbags. Or am I the one who is wrong? If you've got it, flaunt it – that's a saying, isn't it?

It's not even the handbags that I've got a problem with, really. It's the assumed status that comes with them. It's as though this one possession can somehow define who you are. They've come together, formed an alliance based on these tokens of their identity, like some kind of superhero group who each own an enchanted talisman and have to put them all together to battle against society's greatest evil: the high street brand rucksack. But I wonder, if you stripped away all the shoes and hairstyles, would these girls even get on with each other?

It happened today during morning break, and surprise, surprise, it was about a boy. We were all in the locker area putting our books away, getting our morning snacks and, in Carla's case, gathering together the pastries and sweets she intended to sell to the greedy year sevens who had already put in their orders for prohibited confectionary. Suddenly Charlotte Henderson came storming past and walked right up to this girl from the new group, who we now know is named Rachel, and straight up slapped her in the face!

"What the hell do you think you're doing hanging around with Connor Blake-Hudson?!" she demanded of Rachel.

"He's my best friend, of course I'm going to hang around with him," Rachel replied coolly.

"Well he's *my* boyfriend, so stay away!"

"He is not your boyfriend. You may think he is, because that's what he's chosen to have you believe. He is a very close friend of mine, he comes from my neighbourhood, and I know he would never go near someone as cheap and tacky as you!"

"You're calling *me* tacky? Look at those nails! You look like an American pageant child!"

"Better than looking like an English street rat!"

"I must be one special street rat to tempt Connor away from the likes of you!"

"Please! He'll be done with you within a week. You know what you are to him? You're a novelty. You're a spectacle. He walks around with you on his arm and parades you around like a mongrel dog that he's trained to behave like a pedigree. 'Look at the common girl, isn't she fascinating? Look at her simple way of life, see how content she is with so little – isn't it funny? Watch how she tries to fit in with us – isn't it pathetic?' You're nothing but a game to him, a bit of cheap entertainment. He wanted to see how hard he could make you try to impress him. He bet his friends that he could make you change everything about yourself just to make him like you. He wanted to see if you would pretend to like the things that we like, if you would start talking like we talk and dressing like we dress. Only you wear cheap imitations. Because that's what you are – a cheap imitation."

OUCH.

As much as I dislike Charlotte, I had to feel a little sorry for her. I can hardly come up with a retaliation to even the simplest of insults, but that was some pretty eloquent verbal abuse. Last year I was scared of these year elevens who liked to intimidate other girls by ganging up on them, cornering them and threatening them, but Rachel is much smarter than that. Rachel can cut you down with words alone, and that is truly terrifying. But it's OK, I'm not even on Rachel's radar. She is part of the elite. She is one of the diamonds, Charlotte is one of the pearls, and I am a speck of dust on the jewellery shop floor. As long as I don't get ideas above my station or get in the way of something Rachel wants, I should be fine.

Monday 11th January 2020

January is such a long and bleak month. Things at home haven't improved at all. Mum seems downtrodden all of the time, Billy is always studying, and Graham lives such a bland and structured existence it makes me want to scream. I had intended to pass the time by getting stuck into the old diary that I dug up, and today was going to be the day that I really put my head down and tried to make some sense of it. But Graham had other ideas. When I got back from school I went straight to the kitchen to put my lunchbox in soak and my PE kit in the wash basket, but if I'd known Graham was going to be sat at the kitchen table I'd most certainly have waited.

"Oh, hello, Samantha," he said in his mild-mannered, dull-as-dishwater way.

"Hi," I said shortly.

"Actually, Sam, can I have a word? Sit down," he said, not in a demanding sort of way, but more like he was trying to be my friend. I couldn't really argue, he hadn't given me anything to argue against. I sat down at the table.

"Look, I know it's all been a bit wobbly lately, and for that I really am sorry. I can't imagine how this must all be affecting you. The thing is, I know it's been affecting your mum a lot. And I do mean a lot. She's not been herself, I'm sure you've noticed. It's no surprise, really. Frogsplash has been gone a while now and she really misses him. And all this business with your new little sister – it's an emotional time. It's perfectly understandable that she would feel a bit down, but I have to tell you I am worried about her. I need to ask you a favour, Samantha. I need you to tell me if your mum does or says anything out of the ordinary. It may be that she behaves a bit strangely or says something that doesn't sound true. Or if you think she might be hiding something, talking to people in secret, anything like that could be a sign that things aren't OK and that I need to get her some help. Is that OK, Sam? Can you do that?"

"Oh. Um – yes, yes of course."

"I don't mean to burden you with this. And I'm sure it won't come to it, I'm sure your mum will snap out of it soon, but it's best to take these precautions. If there is something more serious going on then it's best to catch it early. I only want what's best for your mum. And for you, of course. I hope I haven't worried you. Like I say, I'm sure it won't come to it, this is all just in case."

"No that's all right, I understand. She really hasn't been herself lately, has she?"

"Try not to let it worry you, all right? Just, if you see anything, you know… let me know, yes?"

"OK."

I hadn't realised quite how serious it was. Or might be. But Graham's totally right, she hasn't been like Mum at all recently. Even on Christmas Day she spent most of the time venting all of her worries to Aunt Lola. I realise now that Graham is only trying to protect her. At the fair he was angry with Dad for letting Frogsplash get so drunk because he knew it would upset her. She hates to be reminded of how fast her children are growing up. And he'd tried to protect her from seeing Stephanie, too, and I'd just waltzed right up to them with her crying on my hip! I need to be more sensitive towards Mum's feelings right now – we all do.

Saturday 16th January 2021

LOCAL PERFORMER TO GLOBAL SUPERSTAR? OVERNIGHT SENSATION RICK THE GLOBE-WANDERER STUNS HIS AUDIENCES WITH ORIGINAL MATERIAL!

Forget indie rock bands and underground grime artists, the UK scene is all about the humble singer-songwriter. Rick proves there's no need for heavy production or experimental new tricks when it comes to baring one's soul. A geographical inclination has led this globe-wanderer down a long, old road, and his life experience shines through in this stripped-back, laid-bare solo effort.

I knew it. I knew it when I saw Richard admiring that bloke's self-made album cover at the Christmas fair. He's decided to become a singer-songwriter. He dug out an old guitar that Dad informed me he'd had since their university days together.

"OK, confession time," Dad said in the car on the way to his flat. "You're going to find out anyway. Richard and I used to be in a band together. For the record, I was never that into it. I played bass guitar and I only knew a few chords."

"Amazing!" I laughed, "I can picture it now! Tell me you've got photos? What were you called?"

"All right, but don't laugh… we were called The Hormones."

"HA!"

"It was Richard's idea. He thought it would be cool – like The Ramones. He was all about the raw emotion stuff. I remember him being really into Radiohead at the time."

"What does Froggo make of all this?"

"He's loving it even more than you. Honestly, if I'd known how much it was going to cheer him up, I'd have brought it up months ago!"

"OK, but why are you telling me this? You're not getting back together are you?!"

"Ha-ha, no we're not, despite Richard's attempts to reunite! No, he's gone solo I'm afraid."

"Oh dear. So, just The Hormone, then?"

"Ha-ha, yeah, something like that!"

"So, I'm in for a treat this weekend, am I?"

"Oh yes, he's been working on some new material, apparently. I've heard him practising guitar since Christmas, but he's been waiting to debut the new song in full. I think he's been waiting for more of an audience, actually. That's where you come in."

When we got in, Frogsplash was slouched on the sofa with a cup of tea in his hand and Richard was sat at the other end, perched on the edge of his seat and holding the guitar in position. He cleared his throat and, without any kind of greeting at all, he introduced himself.

"I'm Rick the Globe-Wanderer, and this is 'The Throat of Eternity':

I once loved a maiden young and fair
With chestnut eyes and flaxen hair
Her skin was golden, kissed by the sun
Her breasts were perky; she was so much fun

Now her eyes are tired, and her skin is white
Her lips are thin, always pulled so tight
She used them to suck the soul right out of me
She locked it in a box and threw away the key

She is the spider and you are the fly
Get caught in her web and you slowly die
With dry lips she gives you the kiss of death
With cold hands she squeezes out your last breath

She is the black widow and that's the truth
She'll eat your soul and she'll steal your youth
Entices men then rips the hearts from their chests
But still she has such exquisite breasts

She's no fun now she's grown so old
Her hair is grey, and her heart is cold
Used to wear bikinis, now it's thermal vests
Why must you hide away those perfect breasts?

She is the spider and you are the fly
Get caught in her web and you slowly die
With dry lips she gives you the kiss of death
With cold hands she squeezes out your last breath

She's the devil who laid my soul to waste
But still I'd do anything for one more taste
Maybe I'm crazy or just obsessed
I need one more touch, just one breast

Maybe then at last my soul could rest
If I could have one last touch, just one breast."

I feel like maybe Richard got a little bit of tunnel-vision towards the end. I'm not quite sure it's going to make it into the mainstream charts, but at least now I know, should it ever come up, whether he's a leg or a breast man. We all clapped and told him how brilliant it was because I think we've all learned by now that it doesn't matter how much you encourage or discourage Richard with these fads, he's going to do them no matter what, and he's going to get bored of them in due time anyway.

"You couldn't tell it was about Fran, could you?" he asked us once the applause had died down. "I really wanted to play it to the girls, but I don't think they'd like it if they knew it was about their mum."

"Well, there is a chance they might figure it out. Have you got any others you could play them?" Dad said delicately.

"Well, I've been working on another one called 'The Wicked Witch of East London', I could play that. I really want to reconnect with them, their mother's had them all to herself all over Christmas and I feel like they're drifting away from me. I haven't had a full weekend with them in ages."

I felt sorry for Richard. From what I can gather, his daughters drifted far away from him a very long time ago. Perhaps they weren't even that close to begin with.

Tuesday 19th January 2021

This morning we had Biology, the one lesson that Carla, Danny and I all have together, and Danny had a lot of stuff to get off her chest.

"So, Mum and Dad have come to an agreement," she whispered as Mr Pinter was going on about the respiratory system. "Dad's going to spend two more weeks at Granny and Grandpa's, and to make it fair, me and the twins are going to spend the second week there, too, to give Mum a break. Then he's going to move back in and really try hard to get his acting career up and running. They're both going to take part-time jobs and Granny and Grandpa are going to help out with the twins. The bad news is they're going to sell the house and move somewhere smaller, and probably in a much worse neighbourhood. Oh, and there's no way the twins can go to private primary school now."

"Well, Sam and I never went to private school and we turned out all right," Carla said. "The move might not be much fun but in the long run they'll probably both be much happier."

"I guess," said Danny, "but it's a lot of change in a very short time. And how long will it take for them to find jobs? What if one of them finds work and the other doesn't? If that happens they're bound to start arguing again! And what if Dad's acting never takes off? He'll be devastated, and he might never be happy again. I couldn't bear it if we made all these sacrifices and then none of it works out."

"You can't think like that, though," Carla said, "you just don't know how things are going to work out."

"And the thing is," I added, "when you've got a dream like that you have to try, otherwise you'll never know if you could have made it come true. At least if your dad tries to become an actor then he won't have any regrets. And he won't be able to resent your mum or you or anyone for getting in his way."

We carried on talking throughout the lesson, Carla and I listening intently as a tirade of worries and "what ifs" came tumbling out of Danny's mouth. The only interruption came when Mr Pinter suddenly began shouting at Elliot, the rather angry, troubled boy from my Art class.

"Right! That's it! I won't have you interrupting my class any longer! GET OUT!"

"I hardly said a word, sir!"

"You've been muttering under your breath for the entire lesson. Get outside, stand in the hallway and BE QUIET. I'll deal with you after class."

Elliot did as he was told and sloped off sulkily, the rest of us trying not to stare too openly. Mr Pinter was just about to get on with the lesson when Danny stood up out of her chair in the name of justice.

"That's not fair, sir!" she said, to everyone's surprise, "Elliot hardly said a word! He just mumbled something about being bored, that's nothing new. I've been talking all lesson, why did you punish him and not me?"

"Are you asking to be punished, Danielle?"

"I'm asking for us all to be treated equally! Just because he's got a reputation, just because everyone knows he got chucked out of his last school, everyone always expects the worst from him. How is anyone supposed to get a second chance if everyone has already decided they're guilty? No wonder he's so angry. I'd be angry too if small-minded, judgemental idiots kept making assumptions about me all the time!"

"Well, since you're so keen on getting sent out of class, you can go and join him. And you can have two lunchtime detentions for calling me an idiot. Go on, out you go!"

There was a rumble of stifled giggles and whispers as people expressed their surprise at such an interesting turn of events. It's always exciting when someone talks back to a teacher, but when they actually make a valid point and make the teacher look like a bit of a fool it becomes a very special occasion: it's a little reminder that teachers are fallible and even though we can't argue against their rules, sometimes we can still prove them wrong.

"So, I won't be here Thursday or Friday," she told us this lunchtime, "My first ever detention!"

"You're a political prisoner!" I said.

"You know me, I can't stand injustice," she said, "and he's actually all right."

"Who?" Carla asked as she zipped up her bulging rucksack ready to go and sell the rest of the day's sweets to her young customers.

"Elliot! We got chatting while we were out in the hall. He heard me giving Pinter a dressing down and he wanted to thank me. He said it's been hard enough moving to a new school without people like him always making assumptions. He moved home recently and that's why he moved to our school, but someone started this rumour that he got expelled and it just stuck. Then I got talking about my family and the move – it turns out we've got way more in common than I would have thought!"

LONG TIME NO CAPSULE: SIXTH FORM SUCCEED IN SUBTERRANEAN SEARCH FOR SCHOOL'S SECRETS!

After several months of fruitless digging, and numerous interruptions thanks to school holidays and adverse weather conditions, a group of year thirteens have finally uncovered a third time capsule. But eager scholars were in for bitter disappointment, as the capsule's contents failed to live up to the expectations of some of the school's more disciplined historians. Nevertheless, the capsule has revealed some well-kept secrets, and in some ways this discovery may prove to be more valuable than it first appeared.

It was the capsule from 2010, which might have been slightly disappointing because all of the teachers and quite a few of the students can remember what life was like ten years ago without the need for visual aids. But as it happens, this capsule was not of the informative kind. It had clearly been intercepted by the year thirteens of the time, and they had filled it with completely unauthorised items of their choosing. The only traditional item that remained was the full school photo, but this had been removed from its cardboard frame and every single faculty member that was pictured had been decorated with some very crudely drawn body parts, with the exception of Mr Wilcox, who had been made to look like a rat.

Of course, the items were all quickly confiscated and none of them were documented on the school website, but the year thirteens who had found them had already taken close-up photos and they had spread on social media in no time at all.

There was a plastic folder containing dozens of photographs from a year thirteen school trip to Paris in which it was very clear that not only the students, but several members of staff had had too much to drink on a night out. The only two teachers I recognised from the photos were Mack and

Mrs Wellington, so I guessed it was an Art trip, and I wasn't at all surprised to see that Mack was drinking wine and smoking cigarettes on the streets of Paris. The collection also included a girl's bra, an empty vodka bottle and something that was once known as a "lad's mag". As the photos spread online a lot of people remarked how hideously sexist this magazine was, and someone said they had been banned a few years later. The year thirteens had taken photos of the pages, but most of them had been taken down by the administrators of the various sites they'd uploaded them to.

By far the most interesting item was a remarkably well-drawn comic strip which had clearly been created by a student at the school. I guessed it was one of the people in the Art trip photographs, because he was clearly very talented. It begins with a depiction of Mr Beardwell, the previous head teacher, retiring from the school and interviews being held for his replacement. In the waiting area are Wilcox, Bellows and a few unknown people. On Wilcox's shirt is written "incompetent rat" and on Bellows' it read "sixty-year-old schoolboy". The others all have the label "legitimate candidate".

The strip then shows the next stage of the selection process, in which the only two remaining hopefuls are Bellows and Wilcox, and they are depicted as political candidates at a televised debate. Wilcox, who has grown rat-like teeth, whiskers and a tail since the last box, is pointing to a poster with a picture of cheese and a green tick, and next to it is the word "plague" marked with a big red "X", presumably denoting his party promises. Bellows, on the other hand, has a picture of some old textbooks with the green tick, and next to it a picture of a laptop with the red "X", denoting his old-fashioned stance on pedagogy.

Then you see all these rats sitting at a panel marked "school board" all gazing greedily at the promised cheese. Wilcox gets voted in, looking even rattier than before, and Bellows looks forlorn. The next scene shows Bellows looking sadly at a painting of Duke John Jameson, and then at a class full of children dying of plague. Finally, Bellows is depicted throwing himself off a church roof, mirroring the actions of Alexander Bell, the poor old brewer who killed himself after Duke John Jameson tricked him out of all his estate.

The last thing in the capsule was a note from the rascals who intercepted it:

We stole the map of the buried capsules from Bellows' office!
HA!
Good luck finding them now, LOSERS!
This school is going to fall to pieces with the rat in charge!
Lucky for us we're leaving this summer
Class of 2010 rules!

It might not have been the most educational find, but it was certainly informative. The "lad's" magazine was, if anything, even less feminist than the awful *Rainbow* magazine that was put in the time capsule forty years earlier! But it was meant for men to read, not women – does that make it better, or worse? They were both dreadful in very different ways, but you can't find either of them on the shelves now, so I suppose that's a sign that things are improving. Of course, the other thing we all learnt from this particular capsule was that Mr Bellows was not to blame for burying the map of the old capsules. Yes, he was still responsible for transferring it onto the school's computer system, and yes, he did fail to do that, but he kept the original map in a safe place. Poor Bellows – ten years of bitter remorse at the hands of some teenage rebels!

Thursday 21ˢᵗ January 2021

Inspired by yesterday's successful dig, I decided to return to my own endeavours to dig up the ghosts of the past and get back to the old diary. I knew Danny would go straight to detention after she'd eaten, and Carla is now over-subscribed with sugar-addicted year sevens as well as many members of our own year group, so I was left in peace for the most part of this lunch time. Away from all of life's distractions: Mum, Dad, Graham, everything, I was at last able to connect with the ancient diarist, whose name I am still yet to learn.

The earlier pages are the most faded, perhaps simply because they are older, but I think not. After studying them intently I have been able to feel a sense of desperation, urgency and strife. The words "poverty" and "penury" are often used, and I wonder if the author was struggling to afford ink. But that was not his only concern. He seems rushed and often signs off in a hurry, as though he has some pressing matter to attend to, or perhaps he is afraid that someone might catch him writing.

There are so many words I can't read or understand, but I sense an inner struggle: this man is not at peace. I know it is a man, because quite early on he writes:

"Mine desire to remain an honourable gentleman is threatened by mine other gentlemanly desires."

I don't quite know what that means, but it makes more sense than a lot of the other words on the pages!

I am now at home and I'm using my Shakespeare books, the ones that Frogsplash got me for my birthday last year, to help me try to understand the diary and particularly to help me work out if words had a different meaning back in those days. I'm not having much luck in finding the exact same words in this diary as there are in Shakespeare's plays, but perhaps that's because Shakespeare died over a hundred years before this diary was written. Oh, did I forget to mention, this diary that I have found, this diary, which is all my own, my wonderful little secret, was written in 1723! How amazing is that?

Reading Shakespeare is helping me in other ways, though. The books I've got all come with modern-day translations as well as study notes which basically tell you exactly what the character means as opposed to just a literal translation. Often Shakespeare's characters say something without ever actually saying it, usually in a very long-winded and poetic way which would sound utterly absurd in real life. I don't know if people really spoke that way back then, but it has helped me to understand allusions. I get the feeling that my diarist is alluding to something too. It's like he doesn't want to put it there in writing, right there for the eye to see. Whether he's afraid to admit it to himself or afraid that someone else will read it I am not sure.

Friday 22nd January 2021

At last, a breakthrough! I have been reading through the diary, picking up bits and pieces, but it has mostly been a log of activities and complaints of hunger and poor working conditions. But now, at last, I have found the thing which the man has been hiding – he is in love! And by the sounds of it he is completely obsessed:

I doth bethink only of the lady. In the darkness, hither in the damp. At which hour methinks of her I cease to be cold. The lady is the fire that banishes the dark, destroys the damp and conquers the cold. The lady burns hence the rats that share mine home, she smokes out the stench of rot and she blazes through the emptiness with her bright, wild dance. She glows, she glows. I am but an ember in her path. I am ash. I am soot. I am nowt. She climbeth the walls and a smile dost flicker across her countenance. She shines her smile down upon me. She consumes me. She fills mine lungs and clouds mine mind. She rises, she rises.

It really is like Shakespeare! Well, I don't know how much Shakespeare talked about rats and damp and rot, but this man is clearly very deeply in love. I suppose back then there wasn't a lot of entertainment around, especially if you were poor, so if you fancied someone there wouldn't have been many ways to take your mind off it. I have to carry on reading now; I have to find out if she loves him back. This could be the greatest love story never told!

Saturday 23rd January 2021

Graham came home from his shift at the pub with a Chinese takeaway, and even suggested eating in the living room for a change. He laid it all out on the coffee table and we all sat on the sofa and helped ourselves while watching whatever cheesy Saturday night entertainment we could find on TV.

"Ooh, did I tell you I spoke to Trudy the other day?" Mum said to no one in particular. "She's given me a great idea for the business!"

"Oh right," I said, only half-listening as I was watching quite an intriguing magic act on a TV talent show.

"Yeah, it's been ages since I've seen her, so she gave me a call to see how things are going, just a little catch-up, you know?"

"Oh yeah, how is she?" I said, still with my eyes on the screen.

"She's great! She's completely gone off men after that last one – remember whatshisface, who she dumped at our party last year?"

"Oh yeah – Alex," I said vaguely.

"Well he's still pining after her, bless him, he's got no chance! She's still working from home, running her own business. Best decision she ever made, she says, although she has put on a bit of weight. It's hard to resist the biscuit cupboard at home when you're running to your own schedule, and when she goes on her makeup evenings there's always more snacks and booze as well! Still, sounds like an all right life to me…"

"Yeah, sounds like the dream!" Billy said.

"Trust me, Billy, she is living the dream" Mum said brightly. "She's her own woman, completely independent, earning money doing what she loves. So, I thought I'd ask her for a bit of business advice…"

"Pah! That old tart!" Graham interjected. "I'm sorry, Cassie, but I don't think you ought to take advice from the likes of Trudy Palmer. Her life is a mess. She flits from one man to the next having these pointless, casual flings. She's got absolutely no class and no control of her life. It sounds to me like she's been sitting at home eating biscuits, claiming to be running a business! I bet the only reason she's 'gone off men' is because she's become so fat that no man would want her."

"Alex still wants her," Mum said in defence of her friend.

"Yes, and when was the last time he saw her in the flesh? She's probably gained three stone since then! Look, I'm just trying to protect you. Trudy's a bad influence; you don't want to end up like her."

"Oh," Mum said, clearly disappointed but not entirely disheartened. "Well, it was more of her daughter Jessica's idea anyway. She's had a lot of success with it. I've been thinking about it a lot, actually, and I'm really excited!"

Mum did sound excited, and it seemed like she was back to her old self. Mum's always coming up with new ideas and trying new things – it's what makes her feel like she's really living her life instead of just ticking over the days going through the same old routine. But she hasn't done anything like that in a while. In fact, I think the last time she tried anything new was when she met Graham and decided to go into business with him.

"So, what is it then, Mum?" I asked, paying much more attention this time.

"Well, apparently Jessica's been doing these online videos to promote the makeup business, and they've brought in more new customers than all of the group evenings put together!"

"Yes, I've seen them!" I said excitedly. "She does them with Carla's sister – they're brilliant!"

"They are aren't they?" Mum said. "As soon as I got off the phone with Trudy I went online and searched for them. They're absolutely fantastic, and so cheap and easy to make! Obviously I would do mine my own way. You can't do a makeup tutorial to sell wine! But I love the idea of making it funny, rather than just doing a straight sales pitch. I think what really works for Jessica's videos is that she's not overly professional or business-like and she doesn't bore you with loads of facts about the products, she's just having a bit of fun and relaxing in front of the camera. I think people really connect with stuff like that."

"Yeah, totally," I agreed. "So, what's your angle going to be then, any ideas?"

"Well, yes, actually I've been rehearsing it in front of the camera. Obviously, it's just practise at the moment and I'll probably make a few changes, but I could go through it with you if you want?"

"Yeah, go on then," I said.

"Yes, tell us!" Billy said encouragingly.

"OK, well the first bit you're going to have to imagine, because it's going to be filmed on location with some actors. Not professional actors, obviously, but Alana and Vincent at work are well up for it – ooh it's going to be so much fun! OK, so picture the scene: a young couple – that's Alana and Vincent – are enjoying a picnic in front of a beautiful stately home. They're wearing really classy clothes like in those proper English period dramas, and they're drinking wine and laughing gaily – all very quaint and traditional, like they're straight out of a Jane Austen novel or something. They clink their glasses together and the camera zooms in so that it's clear you're supposed to be focussing on the wine.

"Then the camera pans out – way out. You realise that what you've been watching is on a TV screen and that it *is* one of those period dramas. Then you pan out all the way and see me sitting on the sofa watching the TV. I'm lounging here with my feet up and my joggers on, my hair undone and the room all messy. I've got a glass of wine in my hand and the dogs on my lap. I'm eating a big bag of crisps and the dogs are licking the crumbs off my lap. It's basically the opposite of classy. Then I say to the camera: "Cassie Darling's Proper English Wine – it's *proper* English.""

"That's brilliant!" said Billy.

"Yeah, that sounds really good, Mum," I agreed.

"It's like a complete antidote to all the wine adverts you see on TV," Billy commented. "They're always out in some nice French or Italian village with the sun setting, eating fresh food and laughing with each other, but let's face it, here in England that's not how most people drink."

"Exactly!" Mum said with great enthusiasm. "That's exactly what I'm getting at! Oh, this is brilliant; I was worried people might not get it, but you got it in one!"

"That's a really cool idea," I said honestly.

"Kids, I know you think you're being nice by encouraging her, but it's cruel to lead her to believe that this is a good idea," Graham said frankly. "If one of your mates was going to embarrass themselves like this, you'd stop them, wouldn't you?"

"What's the problem?" Mum asked worriedly.

"Well for a start you don't have a stately home! And who's doing all of this fancy camera work? You can't do all that on your phone. And the costumes, they won't come cheap. But that's not even the real issue here, Cassie. A waste of time and money is one thing, but you'll get over that. Embarrassing yourself online for millions to see is the sort of thing that will follow you and your family around for years."

"I don't mind; Mum's been embarrassing me my entire life!" I said jokingly.

"Exactly," Graham said, as though my input somehow supported his. "Let's face it, Cassie, you do tend to make a fool out of yourself. It's like you've got no filter for shame, so I'm afraid one of us has got to step in and keep you in check. Remember when you tried to do a Karaoke night at the pub? I told you it wasn't that sort of scene, but you had to find out the hard way, didn't you?"

"That's true." Mum hung her head. "Those men sat in the booth were heckling me pretty bad. It was horrible, actually. I definitely regretted trying that."

"Exactly," Graham said again. "And this new idea of yours is on a much bigger scale – you're opening yourself up to a much bigger audience than those three men in the booth! And what about your children? You might be all right with making a fool of yourself but imagine embarrassing your kids on a public platform. You're being selfish, Cassie, do you realise that? You haven't given a single thought to how this might affect your children – or me. Every time you try one of these mad ideas of yours, you're being selfish."

"My god, you're right," Mum said, crushed, "I'm not Jessica Palmer – I can't do an online promotion. I'm not young and beautiful like her, for a start, and I've got my children to think about! What on Earth am I thinking trying to copy a trendy teenager like Jessica and expecting the same results?!"

"Exactly," Graham said, and I was beginning to find the word quite irritating, "it would be a disaster. Nobody wants to see you trying to be funny, Cassie. Jesus, I don't know how you get these ideas into your head. You're a grown woman, start acting like it!"

Monday 25th January 2021

"Good morning, all," Wilcox began the full school assembly. "Please be seated. As I'm sure you are all aware, last week we found the time capsule that was buried here a decade ago. Sadly, this had been intercepted by a very selfish group of individuals who, with their reckless actions, robbed the rest of the school of the chance to leave behind their legacy. But there was a silver lining. We discovered that the map of the capsules had not been lost by Mr Bellows, as he himself had believed for these past ten years. I am pleased to say that he can now breathe a sigh of relief and have peace of mind knowing that he was never to blame for the missing map.

"Because of this, I have decided to put an end to the ongoing hunt for the capsules. There is no longer any need to relieve our dear Mr Bellows from the burden of guilt, and as the digging process has been extremely disruptive to class schedules, and rather damaging to the school grounds, I believe it is in your collective interest to put an end to the search."

"Yeah right," Danny said at lunch time. "He's just feeling sour because of that cartoon they drew of him! He hates the idea that those kids did all of that and got away with it. If you ask me, he's the one who's being selfish!"

"Ah well, it was fun while it lasted," said Carla. "I can't say I'm too disappointed that it's over, I think I've had my fill of hair accessories, school photos and sexist magazines."

Tuesday 26th January 2021

"Right, today is going to be a practical lesson," Mr Pinter said at the start of Biology this morning, "and before we begin, I must warn you that it requires a strong stomach and a sensible attitude. I understand that there may be some of you who object to this method of study, and you are, in this instance, perfectly within your rights to sit out of this lesson and take quiet study in a separate classroom. Continuing our study of the respiratory system, we are going to be dissecting pig hearts."

A few people made fake retching noises and some of the girls pretended to squeal as though they were dainty little princesses who couldn't possibly partake in or even observe such bloody activity (I've seen all of them buying sausage rolls and bacon paninis from Carla, so I don't know why they're pretending to be so offended). Lots of people shuffled around, and no one left without first asking their friends if they were going to do it, but eventually the six or seven who had genuine reason to object to the lesson vacated the room and the rest of us were left nervously waiting for that which was to come.

I've never seen a real life organ before. It's strangely daunting to think that this ugly, alien object was not just a moving part, but the centre of life for a living thing. It looked so dead, but I suppose that's because it was. It would be quite another thing to see a living heart. Before we got started, before we got all clinical about it, I found it hard to look at the heart without thinking of all the other parts that must have connected to it, and the body that those parts supported. The parts wouldn't have existed without the pig, and the pig wouldn't have existed without the parts.

"There aren't enough hearts for everyone," Mr Pinter said, "but after losing a few class members to quiet study I reckon we can have one for every two of you, so if you could quickly split into pairs so that we can get started as soon as possible."

This is an awkward moment for any class, because it's basically a declaration of who you like the most out of everyone in the room, and normally I don't like anyone and would do anything to work alone, even if it meant I did a rubbish job or lost marks for "not being a team player". But when you're a group of three close friends it's even harder. You can't choose between them, and even if you're forced to choose at random you feel bad for the one who gets left out. I was just thinking how we should probably set up some sort of rota so that we take it in turns to be the odd one out when I realised that Danny had already disappeared. I shouldn't have been surprised, she doesn't find it so difficult to talk to other people, but I was surprised to see that she had positioned herself right next to Elliot, and they were already chatting away. She didn't even look back at me and Carla.

"She should be careful," Carla said to me in a low tone as she hunched over the heart with scalpel in hand, "that boy is unstable. One wrong move and it'll be her heart on the table," and she sliced right through the pig's heart without even flinching.

Friday 29th January 2021

OILY OLIVER OFFERS NO OLIVE BRANCH AFTER DASTARDLY DEFAMATION LAST MONTH. WILY WILCOX WILFULLY DECEIVES THIS NEW NEMESIS IN SUGAR-FUELLED SHOWDOWN

Corruption: the abuse of power for personal gain. You find it in politics and in business, but every so often you find it in the most unusual places for the most unlikely reasons. Most people do it for money or for power, but occasionally there are those who do it out of sheer resentment.

It was to be Oliver Jameson's third visit and second time cooking for the school. However, he may come across, I think he is genuinely passionate about children's health, and he has been true to his word despite having a hectic schedule and plenty of overseas commitments. He does come across as a bit of a pompous twat though. Wilcox seemed apprehensive at this morning's assembly, which is hardly surprising when you remember that after Jameson's last visit he gave an interview with the local paper in which he called Wilcox incompetent and said that we were all malnourished and in desperate need of help.

But it was before Jameson and his camera crew had even arrived that the drama began, at least for our little gang. It was morning break, and Danny and I were helping Carla carry her barrel bags full of sweets and pastries. Her empire has expanded quite rapidly since the start of this term, and although she's still managing to bring in enough supply to meet demands, she is struggling to carry all of the supplies. We help her in the mornings, when the load is heaviest, and she deals with the rest during lunch. We've become so used to it now that we don't even feel like we're doing anything wrong. I guess that's how gangsters feel when they get so used to all the violence and the money and never getting caught that it becomes just like any other fruitful activity. You do this; you get that. Bada-bing; bada-boom.

Don't get me wrong, Danny and I don't do any of the dirty work – that's Carla's domain. We carry the goods, we don't ask questions, and we get a little something for our trouble. What happens if we get caught? We keep our mouths shut, that's what. It's not about money – it's about loyalty; it's about trust. Do you think we sell to just anyone? Do you think some fresh, apple-cheeked kid can come skipping along and ask to sample a taste of what we're selling? They can't be trusted. Only loyal customers can be trusted. But let's get this straight: none of us are friends. We trust them because they've got too much to lose if they get caught, and they trust us for the exact same reason.

Ah, don't get scared – I'm only pretending! We don't have a clue what we're doing, and that's how we ended up getting caught. Like I said, we were each carrying a barrel bag – the sort a grown man might take to the gym – and we had just finished selling to our own year group and were heading to the year seven area. It's true that Danny and I only help carry the sweets, not sell them, but in the eyes of the law that's pretty much the same thing. We were in the narrow passageway that connects our year eight block to the year sevens' common area when we spotted none other than head teacher Mr Wilcox stood right in our path, staring straight at us. That feeling of guiltlessness had vanished as soon as we saw him. No longer did it feel like we were doing nothing wrong, like what we were doing was perfectly natural. Now it felt all wrong, but it was then more than ever that we needed to appear natural. We had to play it cool.

"Hello, girls," he said pleasantly, no doubt recalling our faces from our previous encounters.

"Hi, sir," we said, equally as pleasantly, and attempted to carry on walking, as though we were taking a stroll through the year seven area for the sake of our health.

"You know, I don't usually patrol the corridors during break," he began, and even then I think we all knew we'd been sussed out. "Usually I trust you all to behave and clear up after yourselves. But our good friend Oliver Jameson will be joining us shortly, and apparently he has grown so offended by the state of this school that he has even begun criticising our basic hygiene and tidiness in a blog he likes to call "*My Return from the*

States to Improve the State of our State Schools". I think he thinks it sounds catchier than it actually is, but he has never claimed to be a master of language, so I suppose we can forgive him for that. But he does claim to be an ambassador for the health of today's children, and that is why I am carrying out thorough inspections throughout the school grounds. Do you three have PE after break?" he asked, eyeing our oversized luggage.

"Yes!" Carla replied for all three of us.

"Those are not regulation PE bags," he said, "unless you are going on a camping trip which has escaped my attention?"

"Sorry, sir, we didn't realise there were any regulations," Danny replied confidently. "It's just a new trend. Barrel bags – they're all the rage!"

"Did you know there was a shortcut through the classrooms that leads here from the year eight block? Of course, you're not allowed in classrooms without a teacher present, but I can go in them whenever I want."

He was reminding us of when he caught us in the music room. He was letting us know that he had not forgotten and that we were on thin ice.

"That's how I managed to get here before you – I took the shortcut. I've just been inspecting the year eight common area, and do you know what I found?"

"No, sir," Carla replied innocently.

"These!" Wilcox raised his voice and produced several sweet wrappers and a greasy, sugary paper pouch that must have contained doughnuts.

"Follow me to my office," he said, and this time none of us had anything to say back to him.

"Perhaps you're expecting me to interrogate you," he said once he'd closed the door behind us, "but I'm not going to insult you by carrying on with such a farce. I know as well as you do that you've been selling sweets. I haven't checked the security camera footage, but if you try to deny it then I will. You only have three minutes to get to this PE lesson of yours, so I suggest you leave the bags with me, go to your lessons, and collect your bags at the end of the day. It should go without saying that I will be keeping a close eye on you from now on, and if you are caught selling *anything* my first move will be to contact your parents. Understood?"

"Yes, sir."

"You may leave."

"Wait, sir, can I just say, Danny and Sam had nothing to do with this," Carla spoke out. "It was all me: it was my idea, and it's been me buying and selling the sweets, they just helped me carry the bags, that's all. It was all me, sir, I swear."

"Oh, I know, Carla. Now off you go; you've got French with Mr Dewbury in one minute."

Damn, that guy knows everything!

We had to run to our lockers to get our books, and Carla kept apologising along the way even though she had nothing to apologise for. Amazingly, we weren't actually in any trouble, unless Wilcox had something up his sleeve that he planned on dishing out later.

I was so distracted by the morning's events that come lunchtime I had almost forgotten about the impending Jameson visit. Carla, who seemed far more relaxed about the whole business, reminded me and Danny as we walked to the dining hall.

"Louisa just had a free period, so she went to check it out," she said. "He hadn't started serving yet but she said it smelled amazing! It's chicken, leek and mushroom risotto, or just leek and mushroom for the veggies. I can't wait – my morning snack was in my barrel bag; I'm starving!"

Sure enough, when we arrived, plates of creamy, aromatic risotto were being served up, still steaming from the pot on the stove, freshly cooked rather than just being kept warm like the usual canteen dishes. If it had been a school canteen dish it probably would have had tiny specs of dried mushroom, some kind of flavouring that tasted vaguely of leek, and one or two chunks of tough diced chicken per plate. But this had real, earthy mushrooms with just enough garlic, juicy, freshly cut rounds of leek and tender fillets of proper chicken. The rice was so moist, and the flavours were perfectly balanced, it was hard to imagine ever being interested in chocolate or crisps or ice cream or anything else that I once considered to be delicious. *Delicious* – I don't think I should have even had the right to use the word until I tried this dish!

Oliver Jameson is my favourite person in the universe. Marry me, Oliver!

I was so enraptured I had forgotten all about the morning's drama, and I probably couldn't have even told you who I was sitting with, because none of us were saying a word. In fact, although the dining hall was at full capacity, I think it was the quietest I've ever known it to be. Everybody was enjoying their meal with such intensity that nothing else seemed important enough to talk about. It was only when the man himself, Oliver Jameson, clinked a spoon against his plastic water cup as though announcing a wedding speech, that any of us raised our heads from the rims of our dishes.

"Good afternoon, all," he began, "I hope you are enjoying your lunch. Forgive my interruption, but I would like to say a few words. I have been visiting some of your classes this morning, and I have noticed a remarkable change since I first visited this school in November. For one thing, I can see that there are no longer any overweight children in this school, which is simply wonderful..."

Yes, and it's simply not true!

"... I can also see that there are fewer class disruptions and that the children are no longer struggling to concentrate during lessons. Test scores are on the up, and that is no coincidence. Clearly my influence in this place is the cause of these vast improvements. You have all made great strides in these past few months, and for that I am very proud. I can only imagine the mess you would all be in if had stayed in America enjoying my celebrity lifestyle instead of returning to my roots and dedicating my time to all of you who really need me. Unfortunately, nobody else has the same level of power as I do when it comes to making changes, so I knew that it was up to me to step in. If only I could do the same for every school in the world!

"I am happy to see that sugar has been completely banished from these premises, and what a difference it has made! Do you see now, how even the simplest of changes can produce the most incredible results? Well done. Well done to all of you. Please will you join me in saying three cheers to your astounding transformation? Hip, hip, hooray..."

Everybody joined in, even me, but Oliver Jameson was certainly not my favourite person any longer. The sheer arrogance of him! How can he possibly believe he's made that much difference? For one thing, there are still plenty of fat kids in this school, and anyway, most of us have still been eating loads of sugar, whether we've bought it from Carla or the sweet shop or been given huge tins of chocolates from our aunties at Christmas. And what does he mean "test scores are up"? As far as I know we haven't had any tests at all this year. Oh, and those three cheers were definitely for him, not us.

At the end of lunch, Jameson got up and posed for photos in front of his ever-present camera crew. He walked along the length of the teacher's table shaking hands with the staff to show how friendly he is with all of them. I noticed that, unlike last time, the ordinary dinner ladies were not sat down enjoying the meal cooked by Jameson's team, and when I looked over to the kitchens in search of them, I saw that they were at the back scrubbing the pans and implements that Jameson's chefs had used to cook our risotto. I wonder if they got to eat any of it later on. Finally, for one last glossy photo, Jameson walked up to Wilcox as if they were old friends and gave him a big, matey hug. Wilcox's smile was so forced I'm surprised he didn't break his own jaw.

After school, Danny, Carla and I went to Wilcox's office to collect our barrel bags. Carla said she wanted to go alone to face whatever else Wilcox might have up his sleeve, but Danny and I insisted on joining her for moral support, and to help carry the fully loaded bags. We knocked on the door, but there was no answer, so we waited nervously outside.

"He's probably keeping us waiting on purpose," Danny said, "teachers love doing that. Pinter did the same thing when I had detention with him. It's a power trip, I swear. I bet he's in there right now, just sitting there watching the clock and enjoying every minute."

So, we knocked again, but still no one came to let us in. Five minutes went by, and we were just beginning to discuss giving up, when Wilcox came hurrying along looking very impatient, like a commuter with a train to catch who's got no time for other people getting in his way.

"Sorry, girls," he said as he unlocked his door, "I was just saying my goodbyes to Oliver Jameson… that man is impossible to get rid of! Come in, come in, do sit down."

He seemed friendlier now, less authoritative and more like an ordinary bloke. We took the three chairs in front of his desk and he took a seat behind it. He poured himself some coffee from a flask, took a sip, and seemed instantly more relaxed.

"I'm not keeping you from anything am I? Are your parents waiting to pick you up?"

"No," we all said. I had already missed the school bus; there was no point in rushing.

"Good, good. You know, Oliver Jameson's visit today really made me think. That speech of his was so... inspiring. He seems so sure that the overall health and performance of our pupils has improved since his first visit, that I'm sure we must be doing something right. So, I thought: why fix that which is not broken? He was so adamant that things have got better that I think we have a duty to carry on doing what we have been doing. And tell me, Carla, how long have you been doing this?"

"You mean, selling the sweets and stuff? Um, quite a while. Since early December, I would say."

"I see. Well, Oliver Jameson is convinced that this school has undergone some sort of miraculous transformation since his first visit in late November, so I suppose we had better keep up the good work!"

"You mean, you want me to carry on selling?" Carla asked.

"If you still want to," Wilcox said. "I'm just saying, I'm not going to stop you. And let's face it, even if I did stop you, someone else would soon take your place. It was a very good idea of yours, and I'm sure there are plenty out there who would like to steal it. But I don't want sloppy copycats, Carla, because sloppy copycats get caught. You're smart, Carla, you don't brag about your business and you make sure you can trust your customers to be discreet."

"They weren't very discreet this morning when you found all those packets!"

"Ah yes – Johnny Acapulci. He hid the packets well enough, but I had heard on the grapevine that he was planning to let off some stink bombs upon Oliver Jameson's arrival, so I searched his bag and requested that he turn out his pockets. I found no evidence of stink bombs, but the number of sweet wrappers was highly suspicious. When I asked him where he got them from he said he'd been to the shops on his way to school. I might have believed him, if I didn't know that he got a lift from his mother in the mornings. But I don't think you'll have any more trouble like that. All of your other teachers are far too preoccupied with the curriculum to have the sort of useless knowledge that I have of all my pupils. And like I said, your secret is safe with me."

"OK," said Carla, "I mean – if you're sure it's all right."

"Perfectly fine," Wilcox said, "only, I must ask you one thing."

"Yes?"

"If ever you do get caught, or if anyone starts asking questions, this conversation never happened. That goes for all three of you. Understood?"

"Yes, sir."

"Very good. This has been a lovely chat. You may take your bags and leave."

"What the HELL just happened?!" Carla said when we were far enough away from Wilcox's office that he wouldn't hear.

"I know, this is crazy!" I said.

"It's corruption is what it is!" Danny said.

"This is all because of Oliver Jameson," I said. "Wilcox hates the man! And who can blame him for wanting to get back at him for all the stuff he's said in the papers?"

"I'm sure you're right," Carla said, "but what does Wilcox get out of it? We can't let Jameson find out, otherwise he'll shut it down; so, what's the point? Jameson is still going to go around being smug, telling everyone how he's turned the school around, that it was a dump before he came along, and Wilcox is still going to have to just sit there and take it."

"But it won't matter to him any more," I said, "because he'll know that Jameson hasn't got the power that he thinks he has, and that he hasn't made the slightest bit of difference to this school. Wilcox will be happy in the knowledge that he has ultimate control here."

"Well, that's kind of messed up but I guess it's understandable," Carla said. "Jameson really is unbearably smug. What do you guys think?"

"I don't think you should do it," Danny said, "you're playing into his hands. You're giving Mr Wilcox too much power."

"That's not the way I see it," I said, "you've got all the power here, Carla. He wants you to do this and he's asked you to keep quiet. If he tries to back out at a later date then you can threaten to spill the beans."

"This was never meant to be about power," Carla said, "I just wanted to make a few quid!"

"Then make a few quid," I said, "you don't have to play their games. Just keep doing what you're doing, forget Wilcox and Jameson. Do it your way; if it gets too heavy or you're not enjoying it you can always stop. It's not like he's making you sign a contract!"

"True. And it's not like I'm going to eat all this lot myself!" she said, patting the side of her bulging bag. "I'll carry on, for now at least. You guys don't have to help me if you don't want to, though."

"Don't be daft!" I said, "we'll always be by your side." But Danny wasn't by our side, she was about ten feet back shifting her barrel bag from one shoulder to the other and looking rather fed up with it.

Sunday 31st January 2021

If you'd told me what was ahead of me before I went to Dad's this weekend I probably would have pretended to be sick. Not that staying home is much fun at the moment, but at least I could have stayed out of the way. In the end, though, I'm glad it happened. I arrived at midday, as always, and Stephanie arrived an hour later. It was bitterly cold outside, so we snuggled up on the sofa watching Steph's current favourite film – a Christmas film about a snowman and a frost fairy. I love Christmas, but it feels wrong to even acknowledge it from January to October. Kids don't get stuff like that though.

Stephanie was desperate for it to snow, so she whipped out her favourite Christmas present – the frost fairy's magic wand – and cast a spell to make her wish come true. I willed it with all my heart, because it would have been wonderful to see the magic in her eyes that you only get to have for a few short years before the cynicism kicks in and the weight of the world begins to press down.

"It's not working," she said mournfully.

"Here, I'll help," I said. "What's the spell?"

"Snowfall, snowfall, hurry, hurry, bring us all a frosty furry!"

"Are you sure?" I asked as I looked up the real words on my phone. "Oh, maybe this is why it wasn't working! It's a frosty *flurry* – a flurry is a little shower of snow. Maybe if we say it together and concentrate really hard we might be able to make it work. Shall we try?"

"Yes!"

"Snowfall, snowfall, hurry, hurry, bring us all a frosty flurry!"

We must have said it about twenty times, and I could tell Stephanie would have gladly said it another twenty thousand. I was close to giving up, but then it happened. They were only a few flakes and they melted when they hit the ground, but we definitely saw snow.

"Look!" I said. "It worked! Can you see it?"

"Yes, yes!" she said. "It's snowing! Daddy, it's snowing, look!"

"So, it is!" he said. "Well done!"

Obviously, he had no idea of the magic we had just performed. "Well done," just didn't cut it!

It was a light and brief flurry, not enough to settle and not nearly enough to build a snowman, but Stephanie was satisfied. Contented at last, she drifted off on the sofa next to me and Dad carried her to her cot for her afternoon nap. Frogsplash had been doing coursework in his room, or so he said, but he emerged at two-thirty ready for the football. He surrounded himself with snacks in a sort-of semi-circle so that whichever way he stretched his right arm it would reach a bowl of something, and he covered himself in Stephanie's snuggle blanket for ultimate game-viewing comfort.

"Sorry, mate, no football today." Richard came barging in. "This is ladies' weekend."

"You what?" said Frogsplash, baffled, but his question was swiftly answered when two gaunt figures emerged hesitantly from the porch.

"You remember my daughters, Gertie and Eloise. You met at the Christmas fair, remember? I've been meaning to have them round for ages! Their mum's just been... well there was... they've just been busy."

The girls made expressions which suggested that Dad's flat smelled of sewage. It kind of made me hope that Stephanie would do her potty-at-the-table trick at some point soon, just to see the look on their sour faces.

Frogsplash looked extremely uncomfortable with this surprise invasion. I was extremely uncomfortable myself, but I tried not to let it show. Richard is forever misjudging things, and I decided there was no point being angry with someone who is simply oblivious. Anyway, he has a right to see his daughters, and he lives in the flat too. It's just a shame that his daughters seemed to be expecting a palace.

"Take a seat, take a seat!" Richard said excitedly, clearly enthused to have his daughters to visit at long last. "We have so much to catch up on! How was your Christmas? Did you have fun at the spa?"

"I'm not sitting on that," Eloise said, nodding in the direction of the blanket which covered Frogsplash's lap and draped over the majority of the rest of the sofa. "It's covered in grease and crumbs and it smells." This may have been a fair description of both the blanket and the boy beneath it, but it was still rude.

Richard pulled the two chairs from our mini dining table over so that they were adjacent to the sofa. They were somewhat cleaner, at least visibly, so the girls sat down.

"The spa is not for fun," Gertie informed Richard, "it's for relaxation."

"Ah, well that's very important," said Richard. "You know how I like to relax? I play guitar…"

Gertie ignored him and carried on with her own preferred conversation topic, "The spa was very pleasant, Daddy. We feel fully rejuvenated, don't we, Eloise?"

"Yes. It was a cleansing experience," Eloise agreed. "We were planning to remain cleansed for as long as we possibly can. We are only eating raw food at the moment."

"There's some raw chicken in the fridge that you can have," Frogsplash said irritably.

"Oh, no!" said Eloise, "that could kill us!"

I think that was the point, judging by Froggo's expression!

"Rich, you didn't tell us your daughters would be joining us this weekend!" Dad said. "If you had done I would have prepared a bit better."

"But then it wouldn't have been a surprise!" Richard said. "And anyway, you don't need to prepare. We're not the sort to be fussy – we're happy with whatever, we don't care!"

"When you're ready, Daddy, we'll have our carrots and cucumber washed, peeled and cut into batons. But if they're not organic don't bother," said the ever happy, ever carefree Gertie.

"Um, I hadn't really thought about food," Richard said, "you got here at three; I sort of thought you'd have had lunch before you arrived."

"We're on a six meal a day plan," Gertie explained, "we're due our three p.m. vegetables."

"Sorry, I didn't know," Richard said, "I could go and see what we've got in the fridge…"

"No, that's all right, we'll go," said Gertie. "We need to make sure it's prepared on a clean surface anyway. We've brought our own disinfectant."

The sanitation sisters wandered off to the kitchen leaving Richard with me, Dad and Froggo.

"Aren't they fun?" Richard said sincerely. "It's so wonderful having them here! You know, I've been hoping that you guys would get to spend some proper time together. Samantha, you know Eloise is the same age as you? I thought you might become friends! And Froggo, did you know Gertie is your age? I had hoped that perhaps the two of you might become… well, more than friends."

Oh Richard, you are so far wrong you are almost right! But Froggo's been there, done that, and got the yellow polo shirt!

"But I don't want to put the pressure on," he continued, "it's not like that's the only reason I brought them over here. I've been wanting to reconnect with them, and I thought that I might have more luck if I do so using music as a medium. Music transcends all social barriers, that's a fact…"

Is it, though?

"I've been saving a song just for them. I'm going to play it when they come back in," he said, and I think that was the first time I caught a hint of nerves on Richard. Normally he's careless, if not totally oblivious, but this time he was trying his absolute hardest to connect. He disappeared off to grab his guitar then came rushing back to his seat, ready to perform at any given opportunity.

"So, I've been working on some new tunes," he said when at last his daughters re-entered with their sanitised plate of uniform-sliced raw vegetables. "This one is called 'Her Ship Sails On'."

"The day we welcomed you
Pink clouds on sky blue
Frost glistened that winter morn
When you were born

You blossomed in spring
A happy little thing
It seems such a shame
That summer came

In summer she sailed away
I miss her every day
Now my baby's gone
Her ship sails on

The sky was yellow and warm
Heavy with the coming storm
An autumn evening, I won't forget
When first we met

By springtime you could stand
But still you held my hand
By summer you were strong
Didn't need me for long

In summer she sailed away
I miss her every day
Now my baby's gone
Her ship sails on

In summer they sailed away
I miss them every day
Now my babies are gone
Their ships sail on"

You should have heard it. The melody was bitter-sweet, the chords were all in minor and his voice was raw and true. I never knew he had it in him. Even Frogsplash looked impressed. Sadly, though, his intended audience looked on blankly as the rest of us showered him in praise.

"Richard, that was brilliant!" I said.

"Well done, mate, I'm impressed," said Dad.

"Yeah, nice work," agreed Frogsplash.

Eloise and Gertie remained silent, idly gnawing on their carrot sticks like cows chewing cud.

"So, what did you think, girls?" Richard asked.

"Of what?" asked Gertie as though she'd not been in the room throughout the performance.

"Of the song!"

"I didn't get it," she said. "Why are you writing songs, anyway? It's not like you're going to get a record contract at your age."

"I know," said Richard, visibly hurt, "I do it because I enjoy it, that's all."

"Maybe you should do it in your own time, then," Gertie said. "You're supposed to be doing things with us that *we* enjoy – that's what Mummy said."

Wow, that was cold.

"How about swimming?" asked Richard, choking down the harsh words his eldest daughter just dished up, "that'll be a good way to keep up your health kick!"

"Oh, I didn't know you were a health club member?" Gertie said. "But Eloise is only twelve – will they let her in?"

"Um... no, they won't, I hadn't thought of that," said Richard, who is definitely not a health club member. "How about the public pool?"

"Hmph!" Gertie scoffed. "We're trying to maintain our health, Daddy, not jeopardise it! Those places are breeding grounds for all common infections and you might as well automatically sign up for verrucas as soon as you step inside!"

"I used to take you to the public pool all the time!" Richard said. "That's where you learnt to swim in the first place!"

"No Daddy, it's not happening," Eloise confirmed. "We've just come back from a five-star spa – can you imagine what the pool was like there? We're not going to one of those places now. You're going to have to try a little harder to impress us."

Eventually Richard managed to find a restaurant sufficient to please the girls, who jumped at the chance to get out of the flat and maybe eat something that hadn't been battered and frozen in a factory somewhere. He asked us if we would like to join them and, thankfully, Dad declined.

"Bloody hell, those two are the *worst!*" Frogsplash said when at last they'd left. "What the hell was I thinking going out with her? They're the rudest, most miserable people on the planet!"

"Well, yeah, that's kind of what I'd been thinking this whole time..." I said. "But, you know, you live and learn!"

And it was like a fog had lifted with Frogsplash. Clearly he was over Gertie, and it was almost as though the three of us now had this sort of connection: confronting Gertie and Eloise in the comfort of our own home had been a sort of shared negative experience that brought us closer together. Maybe it seems a bit extreme to liken it to trauma, but it had a similar effect.

"The thing that really got me," Froggo continued, "the thing that had me almost ready to say something to them, was the way they reacted to Richard's song. I thought about telling them how horrible they were being, but I thought maybe if I said it out loud then that would only make it worse. At least if we all overlooked it then maybe Richard could pretend in his head that they hadn't really been as horrible as it seemed."

"Probably a good decision," Dad said. "We all know Richard is good at deluding himself!"

"They were horrible, though," I said. "The song was supposed to be about them, wasn't it? It wasn't about a woman sailing away, it was about his daughters growing up and drifting away from him."

"Yeah, that's what I thought," Frogsplash said, "and they must have got that, unless they really weren't listening at all!"

"It wouldn't surprise me," I said, "they looked like they were trying their absolute hardest to ignore him."

"It's a shame," said Frogsplash, "it was actually a decent song. He clearly misses them a lot, but it's like even when he's with them he still misses them, because they're not the way they were. It makes me feel a bit guilty about Mum, to be honest. She probably misses me…"

"Of course, she does!" I said. "But you're not like those two – you haven't grown into a total snob! You haven't changed, not deep down, and if you saw Mum you'd never be as horrible as Gertie and Eloise are to Richard…"

"No, of course not!" Froggo said, "I should text her, shouldn't I?"

"Definitely," I said. "I know it probably feels awkward, but don't overthink it. You could send her a load of gobbledegook and she'd be thrilled!"

"OK", he said, "I just don't want to end up like them."

"What, eating raw vegetables? I don't think so!" I said.

"Sounds like a good idea to me," Dad said. "Not the raw vegetables! But yes, text your mum. You can carry on staying here, don't think I'm trying to get rid of you! We absolutely love having you here, me and Richard, but at least talk to your mum, maybe visit, and if you do want to move back in with her that's totally up to you. But no pressure! Just do what feels comfortable for you."

"All right, all right, point taken," said Froggo, "I have been dragging my heels a bit. Has she been OK?" He looked at me.

"Yeah," I lied. "Yeah, she's been fine. But I know she'd love to hear from you."

Monday 1st February 2021

"It's not the sugar," Danny was saying, "it's not a matter of health or lifestyle; it's a matter of right and wrong."

"So, what's changed?" Carla asked. "Why was it right before and why is it wrong now?"

"I suppose I wasn't sure if it was right before, but now I know it's wrong because you got caught and you've been asked to lie about it. Wilcox caught you and he decided to support you, but it's for all the wrong reasons."

"So, you're saying that the only barometer for conscience is Mr Wilcox? Just because he's an authority figure doesn't make him the measure of all things!" Carla said defensively.

"It's not about who he is, it's about how he's dealing with this whole situation. It's dishonest!"

"But Oliver Jameson has been dishonest, too," Carla said. "He's made our school look like a dump and made himself out to be a hero!"

"All the more reason to stay out of it," said Danny. "It's become a battle of stubborn men."

"It's a battle which affects our lives," said Carla, "and what happens when we let stubborn men fight those battles without us?"

Danny took a deep, pensive breath. "Not all battles are worth fighting, Carla. Let them have their sweets, or not. What does it even matter? Save your breath for something more worthwhile."

"It wouldn't matter to you," Carla responded, "because you've never had to worry about money. I've never worn anything that hasn't already been worn by my sisters. Look how scruffy my shoes are! See how the buckles of my school skirt have worn out and been replaced four times already? And your parents are moaning because they might not be able to send the twins to private school!"

"That's irrelevant!" said Danny, "I still wouldn't involve myself in corruption and dishonesty!"

"Psh! You're claiming to have moral superiority but that's only because you can afford to say no to opportunities like this. Being in the position you're in, you don't even have to be dishonest. The system favours the rich. The poor have to find other ways to survive."

"Excuses!" said Danny. "Self-pity! Rubbish!"

"Run out of articulate arguments?" Carla asked. "Fine!" and she walked off to sell her sweets alone.

"Don't even think about asking me to take sides," I said when Danny and I were left a duo. "I will never choose between you, so you're just going to have to make up."

"I understand," Danny replied, and she walked away, but there was a stubbornness about her which made me sure she wasn't hurrying off to make up with Carla.

And now they are at a stalemate. I'm left in the middle, just like I am in every other aspect of my life. *Ugh.*

Tuesday 2nd February 2021

This morning in Biology, Danny sat with Elliot, leaving me alone with Carla.

"I don't want you to help me carry the sweets any more," she said to me, "I don't know why Danny's getting so uppity about this whole Wilcox thing, but I should never have involved you two."

"How will you carry it all on your own, though?" I asked.

"Louisa used to play the double bass," she said, "it was absolutely enormous! I've borrowed the case for it and filled it up with all the goods. Now I can carry it around in plain sight without anyone asking any questions."

"Apart from: 'Hey Carla, have you started playing the double bass?'"

"Oh, come off it, no one around here takes any interest in what I do! If I started wandering around in a giant sombrero I don't think anyone would bat an eyelid!"

"I think they might! But OK, if that's the way you want to operate, that's fine by me."

At lunchtime Danny was nowhere to be found, and we guessed that she was with Elliot again. Carla ate a quick lunch, apologised for leaving me on my own, then went to sell her goods. I don't like the fact that they're fighting, but I was happy to be left alone. I will let them work out their differences in their own time, and in the meantime, I'm going to read the old diary.

Thursday 4th February 2021

TALE AS OLD AS TIME: SECRETS, LIES AND FORBIDDEN LOVE FOR EIGHTEENTH CENTURY SCHOOL MASTER!

Time changes most things: technology, medicine, even society itself. But there are those other things that remain constant: birth, death, love, hate, crime and passion. We take a look back at life before the industrial revolution, in which one man's story brings to life these everlasting themes of the human condition.

I have established that my diarist was a school master for what he calls a "charity school". I suppose this shouldn't come as much of a shock because I found it right here at Duke John Jameson, which has been on these grounds for over three hundred years. But time has a way of moving things around, and I suppose I had it in my head that this man was some sort of factory worker because of the way he's always talking about hard graft and dreadful working conditions. It's nice to be able to picture him here in my school, treading the same ground that I tread every day, although it's hard to imagine what it looked like back then.

But that's not the interesting bit.

"Dark days art upon us. We art governed by an abusive and dishonest tyrant. Every minute of every day I curse his name. We – all of us – curse his name. He hath a crooked hold over us. Wherefore ought a man so wretched in spirit be so blessed with finery? He is but a walking embodiment of mendacity and cruelty, and yet he be so rewarded with pleasures and powers beyond even the wildest of mine dreams! The finest of all, though, be the lady. Other fine things could I liveth without, if't be true I hadst the lady.

But I must not walketh that road once more. In the past I didst become involved with another, 'tis true. Wherefore must I desire only those women who belong to rich and powerful gentlemen? Wherefore am I so cursed in affairs of the heart? Once I did playfully love Eliza, and Eliza loved me far more than she had ever loved her father Edgar, the apothecarist, although I daresay we were no more than friends. Eliza and I were not soul mates, but kindred spirits in the exciting art of rule-breaking. Though those passions hath hence grown old with time, and tis with relief that I do believe Edgar knows not of our secret meetings. But, alas, we didst get caught, and though Eliza walketh free, I didst taketh that punishment which curses me still. Each day I must payeth for loose lips to be silenced.

I am provided some rations, enough to keep me alive, and I am given sufficient clothing to provide the illusion of fair treatment. If I were dressed in rags then surely there would be questions asked. We liveth in shared quarters. I has't becometh fond of mine fellow captives, but I long for those days now passed when I was free to be alone. Hither we art all prisoners. The students may call us master, but we art not masters of our own fate."

Of course! It's just like it says in the school song! If this man was a teacher at Duke John Jameson in 1723 then he must have been one of those poor people that John blackmailed into working for him. It sounds like this Eliza was just a friend of his, but they led each other astray, and I suppose they must have got caught doing something they shouldn't have been doing. This is such an incredible discovery! But what would Mr Bellows say if he read these words? Of course, it's obvious from the school song that Duke John Jameson was crooked, but to have him described by one of his staff as "the walking embodiment of mendacity and cruelty" is surely a cause to change our school song, and probably rethink the name of our school altogether!

Saturday 6th February 2021

This morning I was pleasantly surprised to hear that Frogsplash had followed through with his idea to get in touch with Mum. I thought he might have chickened out, but while I was making my toast, Mum made the announcement.

"Fantastic news!" she came bursting into the kitchen, "your brother's coming over today!"

"Really?" I said. "Oh, Mum, that's great! You must be so excited to see him!"

"Oh, I am, of course I am! Thrilled! But I know not to make a fuss. The last thing he'll want is a fuss. But then what shall we do? What if he comes here expecting a big day full of fun activities and I've got nothing planned?"

"A big day full of fun activities? He's not three, Mum!"

"Oh, but you know what I mean – he's going to be a guest, maybe I should organise something. Nothing huge, but perhaps it might be less awkward if I have a few things prepared. Shall I make a cake? Just a little welcome home cake…"

"No cake, Mum!" I said. "Just treat it like any other day with Frogsplash."

"But it's not though, is it? He doesn't live here any more! All of the rules have changed! And wouldn't it be odd to just pretend like it's any other day? I should at least do something to mark the occasion. Perhaps some balloons…"

"No balloons, Mum!" I said. "How about a walk in the park with the dogs and maybe lunch or dinner somewhere?"

"How about the pub?" she asked.

No, not the pub!

"Yes, the pub will be perfect," she continued, "we could time it for the end of Graham and Billy's shift so we can all eat together. Ooh, I can't wait!"

And so, it was decided. Frogsplash arrived at midday, much like me arriving at Dad's for the weekend, only in reverse. He was so excited to see the dogs and vice versa that their loud and clumsy reunion at the front door went some way to defuse the nervous atmosphere. Usually on a Saturday at home I would be in my room, but I felt that my presence was needed, so I joined Frogsplash in the living room while Mum made the tea, and I put the TV on for background noise.

After a few initial awkward silences, things weren't so bad. Mum asked Froggo about school, he asked her about work and the wine business, and the rest was idle observations of whatever happened to be on the TV screen at the time. It was a little bit strange, but it was nice. It was horribly cold out, but Max and Trousers still needed their exercise, so we all wrapped up warm, and Frogsplash burst out laughing when he saw us putting coats on the dogs.

"What on Earth are those?" he asked as I buttoned up Max's polka dot raincoat while Mum was still struggling to get Trousers' front legs through his khaki parka.

"Aren't they adorable?" Mum said through frustrated, gritted teeth as Trousers managed to escape completed unclothed. "Christmas presents from Aunt Lola! She sent you a card, didn't she?"

"Yeah, she sent some cash, I sent a thank-you text. Do the dogs really need an extra layer?"

"Don't be daft, of course they do!" Mum said as Trousers managed to get one of his back legs stuck in the front leg holes and started yelping because he couldn't walk properly. "It's the snow boots they're not so keen on…"

And I showed Frogsplash the flexible, rubbery sock-type things that Aunt Lola had also kindly given to Max and Trousers, although we had not managed to put more than three boots on all eight paws before one or more of them had come off again.

"Ridiculous!" Frogsplash laughed again. "They're definitely not wearing those!"

Eventually we all got out of the house in various states of dress. Frogsplash insisted that he wasn't that cold despite having no gloves, hat or scarf to speak of, whereas Mum was dressed for an arctic expedition. The dogs seemed happy enough now that their coats were on and they were out in the cold February air, although I must admit that the little fleece-lined hoods were probably lost on their thick, shaggy ears. The walk went well – we talked about the dogs and, like most English people most of the time, we made frequent remarks regarding the weather.

The idea of a meal at the Mill on the Hill with Graham and Billy seemed like a good idea in my head because five people is less awkward than three, and a cosy pub and a hot meal was becoming more and more appealing as the bitter cold tore through us. But in my heart I felt very uneasy about the whole business. I hadn't asked Frogsplash how well he'd kept in touch with Billy, who had once been one of his best friends, but from what I can gather from the past few months at home, Billy has been utterly absorbed in work – both academic studies and shifts at the pub – so they have probably become estranged.

But let's not avoid the issue any longer. That's not my main concern. Let's face it, at the very least things have been odd where Graham is concerned. I try to stop myself from thinking about it, because I think that I must just be imagining it all. Nobody else seems to have a problem with him, and he's never actually done anything bad to me, so why do I feel so uncomfortable with him being around? Probably because he's a man who is not my dad who has suddenly moved into my house and started acting like he *is* my dad. It's the classic step-parent scenario: it just takes some getting used to. But there is something there with Frogsplash which makes me think that he's picking up the same vibes as me. There is something about him and Graham together that gets those thoughts ticking once again.

We arrived at the pub at four p.m. when Billy and Graham were just clocking out. They were all scruffy from their shifts and we had the dogs scrambling around by our feet, so it felt comfortably informal, at least to begin with. We took our seats in the booth, and I was reminded of my horrible encounter with those men who'd sat there before. We chatted idly about the menu and about how we'd spent the earlier hours of the day, and it wasn't until we were finished eating our meals that anything remotely unpleasant began to surface.

"So, how are you getting on with your exam studies?" Graham asked Frogsplash.

"Um, OK I think…"

"Have you got your revision timetable all sorted?"

"I was going to do that a bit closer to study leave."

"I see. Well you know what they say: fail to prepare, prepare to fail. You don't want to fail, do you? There are some people who can breeze through their exams without much effort, but I'm afraid you're going to have to try a lot harder than most if you want the sort of grades you can be proud of. Billy's been predicted all 7s and 8s, haven't you, Bill?"

"Well… yeah, but…" Billy looked horribly uncomfortable. I think it was the first time I'd ever seen him stutter.

"All right Graham, don't pile on the pressure – it's early days!" Mum dived in to save both Billy and Frog.

"I'm just trying to motivate the boy, Cassie. I can't imagine he's getting much academic support at home…"

"I'm quite self-motivated actually," Frogsplash retaliated. Graham scoffed, but he didn't say anything more.

Monday 8th February 2021

It's the last week before half term, and I'm hoping that Carla and Danny will hurry and make up because we have plans. The year eight Valentine's disco is this Saturday and we had agreed to all go together. You know I'm not that into makeup and clothes but getting ready for a party together is a rite of passage for people my age. And I love Carla to bits, but she's even less girly than me, so if it's just the two of us we'll probably turn up to the dance in hoodies and jeans.

They will make up eventually, won't they? I mean, it was just a difference of opinion. Although they do both take their ethics quite seriously. And they are both very strong-willed. I was the soft, gloopy glue that was holding them together. I was the middle ground in every debate; I was the one who sat on the fence between them. I knew this would happen. Well, not exactly this, but remember at the end of the summer holidays last year? Everything was just too happy and bright. A little bit of sunshine and the world seems perfect; but it's winter now and everything's gone wrong. My family is in pieces, my friends are fighting and I'm right back to where I started: hiding in my room, hiding behind books and keeping everything to myself.

Friday 12ᵗʰ February 2021

This is only my second year at Duke John Jameson, but I'm told that sending a red rose to one's Valentine via a sixth form courier has been tradition here for around twenty years. But this year someone somewhere down the line very wisely decided to complicate the issue with a rainbow of roses.

"Red roses for love", Wilcox announced in Monday morning's assembly, "white roses for friendship, blue roses to politely tell someone that you're not interested and yellow roses for the teachers to send to each other. Three pounds per rose, you may submit your message along with your payment and it will be sent with your rose in a small card. Any crude or inappropriate messages will be disallowed, and the recipient of your rose may not know who has sent it."

And so, thanks to the genius behind this new initiative, about a hundred yellow roses and twice as many blue ones were being anonymously delivered to the most hated teachers in the school by frustrated sixth formers who were no doubt hoping that this would count as an extra-curricular activity on their university application forms.

Logistically speaking it was a nightmare: a lot of lesson time was wasted, although none of the students and only about half of the teachers seemed bothered by that. The real issue was the lack of control over the blue roses. The powers that be were able to censor the rude, mean and downright bullying messages that were usually sent with them, but people had paid to send them, and so they were sent. Usually the recipient was some poor unfortunate who is already perfectly aware of how unpopular they are without the need for a rejection rose. And usually they were sent with a blank message because whatever the sender had chosen to be printed in the card had been deemed too rude. But a blank message is hardly reassuring, it leaves too much to the imagination! It's basically an open invitation to interpret one's rejection in the most horrible, cruel and emotionally crippling way the mind can conjure. Not ideal, really, in these, our formative years. And then there were the yellow roses.

"I only meant it to be a fun, light-hearted way for me to tell a couple of the female teachers that I fancy them," Richard confessed to the entire class in Geography this morning, "someone should have stopped it! I never knew it was going to get so out of hand!"

Oh, Richard.

"How many teachers do you fancy then, sir?" asked Demetri Michael.

"Well, I don't know if I necessarily *fancy* them all, but I sent fourteen yellow roses," Richard confessed.

"Fourteen! I can't even think of one that I'd go out with!" Demetri said.

"Well, I was trying to keep my options open… I need to get back in the dating game, so I thought I'd send the feelers out in a few different directions."

"Did *any* other teachers send yellow roses?" I asked, trying to gauge just how much Richard had embarrassed himself this time.

"Well it's hard to be sure," he said, "because the cards were all printed in the same font, you couldn't really tell if they'd been sent by a student pretending to be a teacher for a laugh. But that's good, in a way, because if any of the teachers I sent roses to rejects me I can just say that it wasn't me who sent it, must have been some kid taking the mickey."

"Very mature," I said, "and what was your thinking behind the blue roses? Talk us through that." Richard's classes are often like this – he's always trying to be a friend first and an educator second, so we end up having a class chat rather than doing any work.

"The blue roses were a bit of a disaster," he admitted, "but I had good intentions. It's just so awkward when you know someone likes you and you don't quite know how to tell them that you don't feel the same way, especially if that person is your friend or someone you have to work with in class. I just thought, rather than have to have that horrible conversation, it would be so much nicer to just send a simple token to let them down gently and show that there's no hard feelings, you know?"

"Well, I suppose that makes sense," I said consolingly, "it's not your fault people decided to use it to bully each other."

I mean, I could have foreseen it, but you know Richard, he rarely thinks things through. By the end of this week the school was blanketed in a mass of mulched rose petals and discarded message cards with dusty footprints trampled over the heartfelt words that the sender had written in vain. Imagine someone confessing their love to you and just casting the card away to get trodden on by hundreds of careless feet. Some people are so savage.

Still, not everyone was left heartbroken. All of Charlotte Henderson's gang got at least three roses each, and the same goes for their rivals, Rachel Levine's group. Some of them are in a few of my classes, and since the fight between Charlotte and Rachel, I've become more aware of them. Unlike Charlotte's gang, who try to assert their power through rebellion and a disregard for the rules, Rachel's crew seem to prove their superiority by being the best and brightest: they get the best grades and they seem to find schoolwork very easy and enjoyable; it's as though nothing is a struggle for them.

Saturday 13th February 2021

It was the night of the year eight disco, and since there was no sign of reconciliation between Carla and Danny, Carla and I got ready by ourselves at her house. Well, not completely by ourselves, because her entire family was in as well as Jessica, daughter of Mum's friend Trudy and new best friend to Carla's sister Rosie.

"Oh, Sam, it's so good to see you!" Jessica said. "It's been too long! How is your mum? Mum said she spoke to her on the phone not too long ago."

"Yeah, she's... all right," I said.

"Wrapped up in that new boyfriend of hers, I bet! I told you, didn't I, once they get a man they get too wrapped up to even notice whatever mischief you're getting up to! It's great, isn't it? Anyway, I hear you've got a Valentine's dance to go to – so exciting! Ooh – we should do makeovers!"

Jessica is one of those bubbly types of people.

"Yeah, Jess can do makeup and I'll do hair," Rosie said. "Lord knows what you two would look like if you tried to do it yourselves!"

She had a point, so we both nervously consented and followed them up to Rosie and Carla's room. For the first time, I was invited over to Rosie's side of the room, which was decorated the same, but had a distinctly different feel to it. Carla's side is covered in band posters and books, whereas Rosie's is full of clothes, shoes, mirrors and makeup. I also noticed that she had a vase with four red roses and two white, and I recognised the heart-patterned ribbon around them from the many that were flying around school this week.

"Did you get any?" Rosie asked, catching me eyeing them up.

"No, nothing. Not even a blue one, although I suppose that's a good thing."

"Carla got one," Rosie informed me with a smirk.

"Did you?" I asked, and I looked over to Carla's side of the bedroom, but I couldn't see any roses.

"I didn't keep it," she said. "It was just from that little year seven from by the lake, Jamal."

"Aw, so sweet!" I said. "And so mean of you to not even keep it!"

"Hey, it's not like I threw it to the ground and trampled on it right in front of him! It would have been weirder to keep it, don't you think?"

"Yeah, I guess you're right. Bless him, I could tell he fancied you from the moment he laid eyes on you!"

"Yeah, well I'm glad he won't be there tonight – I don't need eyes on me."

"Well tough," said Jessica as she finished off Carla's eyeshadow, "because you're going to have a lot of eyes on you once this makeover's finished!"

"Oh, god…"

"It's all right" I said. "Everyone's going to make an effort; we won't stand out." But even while keeping my head still for Rosie to work on my hair, I managed to get a side-glance of Carla and she already looked stunning.

"Do you think Danny will still go tonight?" she asked later when Rosie and Jessica had left us in peace.

"I'm not sure," I said, "she's not been replying to my texts."

"Oh no! Is she mad at you now as well?"

"I don't know. She's probably just busy; she's got all that stuff with her family going on, hasn't she?"

"I don't want to come between you two. Maybe she's mad at you because she thinks you're siding with me."

"Maybe," I said. "but if she is then that's her problem. I said I wasn't going to choose between you two and I meant it. Maybe you should try talking to her – you can still be friends with someone even if you believe in different things."

"I think, for her, it's not what I believe so much as what I'm doing. It's like I'm working on the side of evil just because Wilcox isn't punishing me for breaking the rules, but I'm hardly getting away with murder! It's not a crime, and they're not even school rules! Jameson came swanning in making all these changes, acting like he owns the place just because he's a celebrity…"

"…and because he's a descendent of the man who actually founded the school," I pointed out.

"We don't even know if that's true! And anyway, if you're going to go around claiming the rights of your ancestors you ought to be making amends for their crimes as well. John Jameson only got that school through cheating and fraud. The man conned everyone he ever met, including his own wife!"

"I suppose you're right," I said. "You shouldn't be allowed to pick and choose which bits of history you want to use for personal privilege."

"Exactly! I reckon Oliver Jameson is just as bad as his namesake – going around scheming, using his status to get other people to do his bidding, making himself out to be superior all the time – I think he deserves to be taken down a peg. And that's what I don't understand, because Danny hates all that stuff too: privilege, abuse of power…"

"And that's the problem," I said, "Wilcox is abusing his power, too."

"Yes, but for the right reasons. It's annoying, because I'm getting kind of bored with it anyway. The year sevens are doing my head in and it's taking up all my time, but if I stop now Danny will think she's won."

"So what?!"

"This is a battle of wills, Sam. If I give in, she'll think she was right all along."

"You two are as stubborn as each other! What's it going to take to end all this nonsense?"

"She's the one who chose to take the moral high ground. She could have just made her feelings known, accepted that I respectfully disagree, then let me get on with it. It didn't have to interfere with her life at all, but she decided to stop speaking to us and run straight to her boyfriend!"

"That's the other thing I was wondering – *is* he her boyfriend now?"

"I don't know. I hope not; he's far too angry."

"Well don't say that to her face!" I laughed. "It's one thing to fight about business but telling her that her boyfriend is no good is definitely going to drive her away."

"Don't I know it! Rosie's exactly the same; all the boys she likes are scumbags, but she won't hear it from me. Speaking of which, don't you think these eyelashes she lent us are a bit much?"

"Maybe on my invisible, blonde lashes, but on you they look amazing."

"Are they restricting your vision as much as they are mine? I can't tell if it's because everything's now got a fuzzy black frame or because they're so heavy I can't open my eyelids all the way!"

"You'll get used to it. You can't take them off now otherwise you'll have a gluey eyeline."

"Ugh, how ridiculous. I was always taught to keep glue well away from my eyes."

"Come on, Carla, get in the party spirit! You'll forget all about it when you're on the dance floor."

"I am NOT dancing."

"It's a disco, what else are you going to do?"

"Oh god, I don't know. I was only going because you and Danny wanted to go! It's going to be awful, isn't it? Why are we going, Sam? It's going to be full of people. We hate people! And they're all going to be dressed up and trying to show off and prove how much better they are than the rest of us, and we'll just be sat at the edges of the room staring at them. And they'll be loving it because they crave attention."

Carla made several very good points, but you have to drag friends out of their comfort zone sometimes, don't you? I had to pretend that everything she'd just said was completely unfounded.

"Don't be daft – we'll have a great time! We can watch all the boys make fools out of themselves by trying too hard to impress the girls, and I bet some of them will come wearing their dad's tuxedos or way too much hair product. And there'll be some girls trying to walk in heels, and don't forget the teachers – don't you want to see them letting their hair down? I guarantee you Richard will have a few drinks and try to chat up some of the female teachers – he's on the prowl!"

"That does sound fun. I never believed half the stories you told me about that man until I met him for myself!"

"He is certainly unique! And yes, it will be fun. We don't even have to dance – we can just observe."

"Won't people think we're boring?"

"Carla Figueroa! When have you ever cared what people think?"

"I don't! It's just – if Danny sees us skulking about in the shadows she'll realise what losers we really are."

"Oh, cheers! Never realised you thought of me as a loser!" I said, but I was only joking.

"No, of course I don't, but you know what I mean – Danny could be friends with anyone! She's easy to talk to and she doesn't mind being around other people. She has friends in all her classes and loads of friends outside of school. She doesn't need us."

"No, she doesn't need us," I said, "and we don't need her. Friends don't need each other; they choose to be with each other and to be there for each other. She knows who we are, she knows we're socially awkward shadow-dwellers who prefer books to boys! And if she chooses to move on from that, then that's probably best for all of us. We are who we are, and if that's too different for her, then it's better we end it here rather than pretend to be who she wants us to be."

"Do you think we're going to lose her?"

"No. Not at all. I think you two had a silly disagreement and you're both too proud to admit it. Now put some lip gloss on and make Rosie proud!"

It was almost time to go and we still needed to get changed into our dresses. I never get changed in front of people if I can help it, but there was no time for deliberation, and I didn't want Carla to think that I would care about undressing in front of her. It's not like I think she's going to fancy me or anything – far from it – it's just that my body is different from hers. She used to be shorter than me, but she must have grown because she's about my height, only much tinier. She's got a small frame, like a little doll, and she's already starting to get soft curves. My whole body is soft, but in a blubbery sort of way, and I probably wouldn't have any boobs at all if I was skinny like Carla. Danny is thin, too, but she has more of a lean, toned figure – probably because she's a dancer. She has the sort of body where she could wear a bikini and go running on the beach and nothing would jiggle or flap about or change shape in any way. If I did that my thighs would sound like a seal clapping.

If I could have a body like either one of them, I'd be happy. I would rather have the figure of almost any other girl in my year than have my own. I look at them and I wonder why I don't look like that. I wonder if I could look like that if I tried really, really hard. Surely if I exercised enough? You don't see Olympic athletes with flabby thighs. So, it's my fault, really, it's my fault I look this way because I don't exercise enough. I'm too young to go to the gym but maybe Mum would let me go out running or riding my bike, as long as it's not dark out. I hate running and it is dark out by the time I get home from school. I could ride my bike on the weekends and in the evenings when the days get longer. But I can only ride my bike on the pavement which you're not really supposed to do. But these are just excuses, aren't they? Lazy people like me always find excuses.

I got changed hurriedly, holding items of clothing in front of my fleshy parts like tiny screens to block Carla's view, not that she was looking. I could tell she wasn't worried about what her body looked like; she wasn't trying to hide anything – and why should she? She has nothing to be ashamed of. We zipped up our dresses, slipped on our shoes, stumbled down the stairs in our two-inch heels and grabbed our coats on our way out of the door. Carla's dad, James, drove us to school, and although he complimented us both on our appearance he didn't make an embarrassing fuss like my parents would have done, and instead just played some seventies music to get us in the party spirit.

There was a buzz about the place when we arrived – not as potent as when I went to see Free Parking live last year, but that was a once in a lifetime sort of thing. James dropped us off, told us to have a good night and assured us that Carla's mum, Maria, would be there at nine thirty p.m. to pick us up. Everyone else was arriving at the same time, and it seemed as though they had all made a real effort to look nice, so much so that I barely recognised some of the people from my classes, particularly the girls.

"See?" I said to Carla. "Aren't you glad of those eyelashes now?"

"As long as they don't start peeling off halfway through the evening!"

"Trust me, Jessica knows what she's doing. If anything, you'll struggle to get them off!"

"Oh great," she said, but I could tell she was in better spirits now.

We were getting a lot of looks as we walked up to the main entrance, but in this instance that was normal because everyone was getting a good look at each other, checking out what they looked like out of uniform and in their best clothes. There were some surprises: people who normally wear glasses coming without them, people who normally have frizzy hair having it straightened, and I have to admit there were a couple of boys wearing tight shirts who have, as it turns out, been hiding some impressive muscles underneath their school blazers. Other than that, most people just looked like slightly more glamourous versions of their regular selves.

Pop music and tacky lights filled the hall when we walked in. Not a single person was dancing, everybody was just stood around in clusters chatting to their mates, and the poor old DJ's pleas to "get on the dance floor" "show us your best moves" "get down to this vibing sound" "chase that bass" and other such nonsense were falling on selectively deaf ears. Both Carla and I looked around nervously for Danny, and although most people seemed to blend into one glittering mass under the coloured lights and disco balls, there was one face that stood out.

Danny was wearing a pastel blue mini dress with a high neck and long, fluted sleeves. She wore matching ballet slippers and a matching Alice band in her hair. Danny has pale skin and pure white hair, and usually her eyelashes are white, too, but she was wearing mascara now and it made her look so grown up. It reminded me of last summer when we all babysat her twin brothers while her parents went out. Her mum looked so beautiful and glamourous when she was all dressed up, and that's exactly how Danny looked now. I tried not to stare, I didn't want to be a creep, so I looked around a bit, but the more my eyes wandered the more I realised that everyone in the surrounding area was stealing glances at Danny, too. It was an eye-catching transformation that was hard to ignore.

"She looks amazing," said Carla, "she's not like anybody else."

"I know," I said, "but she's still our Danny. You're romanticising her. And look, she's with Elliot. She obviously likes him. Let her enjoy her night and let's enjoy ours. Forget it, let's have some fun!"

But everyone seemed so intent on finding anything at all that might give them an excuse to avoid dancing in public. The main hall is on the front face at the school building, which is mostly made up of glass panes so that we can see out and others can see in. Richard's bright green convertible pulling into the overlooking car park was more than enough to distract the nervous party-goers, so they all went rushing towards the glass-paned front of the hall to see what lucky kid was getting dropped off in such a fast, expensive (mid-life crisis) car. There was an audible groan when Richard the Geography teacher stepped out alone in his too-tight suit that he probably wore to his own school disco thirty years ago.

Richard said a brief hello to Carla and me and, much like Carla's dad, he was surprisingly gracious in complimenting our appearance and then taking his leave to be a responsible guardian of the dance. Once again Carla and I were alone and speaking quietly to each other. Everyone in the hall was a small person having a small conversation under big, uncomfortable lights. It was awkward, but it was less awkward because we were all in the same boat. What was much more awkward was what happened next. Two sets of headlights flashed through the front-facing windows of the hall, and everything after that happened in a sort of jaw-dropping, what-the-hell-is-happening sequence of cringe.

From those two cars, fashionably late (of course) flowed Charlotte Henderson, Ruby Driscoll, Beth Amory and Andrea Michael. None of them turned back to say goodbye, as though they had been dropped off by a taxi driver rather than a parent, and they stalked long-legged and confident through the entrance, into the hall and straight up to the DJ without ever laying an eye on anyone else in the room. Charlotte and Ruby were at the head of the gang, and they spoke to the DJ like they owned him, as well as the venue itself. They must have made a request and the DJ, probably desperate for anyone at all to display some sign of enjoyment, followed orders.

The song came on and the four girls formed a line across the middle of the hall while the rest of us looked on, bewildered. Almost immediately they broke into a perfectly coordinated, very bog-standard dance routine that they'd obviously spent so long choreographing and rehearsing that they'd become completely blind to how basic and dull it truly was. Don't get me wrong, it drew the attention of everyone in the hall, because who else would be so brazen, so immodest, so self-obsessed to think that the rest of us are audience members to them, the main event? Carla and I were laughing our heads off, and everyone else around us was either doing the same or stood in stunned silence while this bizarre turn of events unfolded. It might have even got to them, perhaps it would have prompted a bit of healthy, sobering self-critique within the group, if only there had been some time for it all to sink in.

All it would have taken was a few minutes to reflect on their performance and I'm sure they would have realised that the whole thing had been severely misjudged. But there was no time, because before their song had even ended a set of bright headlights curved into the drop-off bay at the front of the school, which was just visible through the dance hall windows. It was an unwelcome disturbance for the desperately dancing girls, and it really caught them off-guard. They were visibly annoyed, and when everyone else's attention was diverted, they seemed to scatter chaotically rather than conclude their routine in an organised fashion. I must say it was highly unprofessional.

"Oh my god, it's a limo!" screamed a voice from a head perched at the front-facing window. Before long, almost everybody in the hall had scuttled over to see the enormous spectacle for themselves. It was indeed a bright white, stretched limousine, and out of it climbed Rachel Levine and her four faithful friends, Jennifer Bexley, Agatha Price-Watson, Eleanor Biggs and Nikki Hills. They all looked gorgeous, but that was nothing new. In fact, with all their usual expensive hair styles, manicures and makeovers the only thing different about them was the clothes they were wearing. They were probably all designer dresses, just like their school shoes and bags, but in my opinion they didn't look any more glamourous than the rest of us.

But that hardly mattered, because the limo had done more than enough to impress the majority as well as raining very hard on Charlotte, Beth, Andrea and Ruby's parade. Their desperate attempt to make an entrance had been well and truly overshadowed, and they must have been absolutely fuming. Rachel and her retinue strutted down the main path as their driver struggled to drive out of the small, curved bay which was designed for parents' cars no bigger than a people carrier. The five girls entered the hall victoriously, knowing full well that they had achieved their goal of attracting maximum attention and envy, although they would no doubt be even more thrilled when they found out that they had also interrupted Charlotte Henderson's dance troupe.

The girls greeted a few of their more peripheral acquaintances, the "hangers on" who probably only covet their friendship because it makes them more superior by association. They took to the dance floor with confidence, dragging some of those acquaintances along to make up the numbers, and before long the party was in full swing and at least half of the year group were up dancing while the rest of us stood around chatting.

"Look at Danny, she's all on her own," Carla said.

"She seems to be having a good time, though," I said. She was dancing by herself completely unashamedly, and she was doing a pretty good job of it. Danny goes to dance class every week, and she's very talented. She's not the sort of show-off who would do backflips or fancy, choreographed moves at a school disco, but you could still tell she was a good mover.

"Maybe I should go and talk to her," Carla said.

"Yes! Definitely!" I said. "It's about time you two sorted this out. What are you going to say?"

"I don't know – don't make me nervous!"

"Just say you're sorry and be done with it!"

"But I'm not sorry! I'm not going to apologise when I don't believe I've done anything wrong."

"OK, OK, just say hey, tell her she looks nice or something."

"She does look good, doesn't she?"

"She looks amazing! Every time I look over in her direction I see people staring at her."

"Maybe she's out of our league," Carla said doubtfully. "Maybe this whole thing happened for a reason. People our age change friendship groups all the time. She'll find newer, cooler people to hang out with."

"No, she won't!" I said. "Now come on, let's go. I'll come with you, so you don't feel so awkward." I dragged Carla over to the front of the hall where Danny was dancing, but before we could reach her, Rachel Levine herself grabbed Danny by the arm. Danny spun around in surprise and greeted Rachel with a smile. She gestured for Danny to move into the circle of dancing girls in the centre of the hall and she happily accepted, joining Rachel, Jennifer, Agatha, Eleanor and Nikki. She didn't look at all out of place. Not in the slightest.

I spent the rest of the evening trying to convince Carla that this was not the end of the world. At one point Richard came over to ask us why we weren't dancing, but he soon got distracted by the sight of Miss Andrews in her party dress and walked off to follow her.

"Ha! He's got no chance," I said, but Carla wasn't listening.

Eventually I managed to persuade her to get up and dance with me, but only because Free Parking came on. She was a bit awkward in her little dress and her tights kept falling down so she wasn't particularly enjoying it, but I wasn't going to let her back out.

"Look at them with their tiny dresses, open-toe shoes and bare legs!" she said, referring to Rachel and her lot. "Don't they know it's February?"

"Well, the limo probably had heating," I pointed out.

"Yeah but when has the school hall ever been warm? Don't they feel the cold? What's their secret?"

"Actually, I read about this somewhere. Apparently rich people have personal insulation implants nowadays – they were invented for rough sleepers, but the upper classes decided it was too good for them. You probably didn't know about it because the government want to keep it a secret – it's a *conspiracy!*"

"Very funny, Sam. All right, I know I sound jealous, but I'm not. Well, I'm not jealous of their money anyway. It just annoys me when people pretend to be so perfect, like nothing could ever bother them. They're still human beings but they want everyone to think they're better than human, like the rules don't apply to them."

"I know, Carla, but you've just got to get over it. It'll eat you up if you start comparing yourself to other people because you're only seeing what they want you to see. It's not real, you know that. Come on, we're here so we might as well enjoy it. You're a good dancer! Let's stay here, on the dancefloor, at least for one more song."

But the music went quiet when the Free Parking song was nearly at its end, and the DJ spoke up for the first time since the beginning of the night.

"What a beautiful night," he said, "but it's time now to slow it down. This is, after all, a Valentine's dance, so it's only right that we should end it with a sweet, slow jam…"

Then he turned the music back up and it was this sickly, romantic love song that no one in their right mind could possibly dance to. It was the biggest mood-killer imaginable, and even the most enthusiastic dancers soon began to disperse outwards, pushed towards the side lines to stand there nervous and awkward. Displaced from their happy, energetic dance floor, they were now quietly hiding in the shadows, living on the edges of society like the rest of us. Even Charlotte Henderson, who had started the night so sure of herself, was now a shadow-dweller. Rachel Levine had become unsettled by the change in tone and was now huddled with her crew, her phone at her ear, presumably beckoning her limo driver to come back round.

There were only two people undeterred by the DJ's regrettable song choice, two people who remained on the dancefloor, oblivious to the fact that for the rest of us the night had ended. Stood tall in a sharp, pale blue shirt, all of the awful hair dye long gone from his hair, was Elliot, and cuddled up to him, barely moving to the music, was Danny, looking even more beautiful now, smiling blissfully, completely unaware that she was in the spotlight.

"Looks like she had a good night, anyway," I said as we put our coats on and watched our friend slip away right before our eyes.

"I don't know why I was so worried that she was all on her own," Carla said. "A girl like Danny was never going to be on her own for long."

"He's just a boy," I said. "Boys don't last long. And in the meantime, you've still got me. Come on, I can see your mum's car."

Monday 15th February 2021

February half term – is there anything drearier? The good news (I think) is that Frogsplash will be spending more time here because Dad has to work. Of course, Mum's excited about that, but there is a fair chance that it might all go wrong and an argument will explode all over the house, but there's no point worrying about something that might not happen.

I sent a text to Danny yesterday congratulating her on her relationship with Elliot, and she did reply to say that yes, it is "official" and sorry for not catching up during the dance. She seemed far too excited about Elliot to talk about Carla, so I didn't push the subject. Things will work themselves out in time, or so I keep telling Carla. She says she wants to stay in and write this song idea she's had for ages. I think she's just staying in and sulking, but that's fine by me, because I have a very old diary to read.

Tuesday 16th February 1723

Mine forbidden love groweth like the vine, strengthening its grip around mine heart, its roots embedding themselves deep below the surface. Oft I doth dream of speaking the truth of mine feelings to the lady I love, but such an act carries with it a risk unthinkable to a man of mine position. I be not a Duke, nor a man of wealth. Should I loseth what little freedom I yet has't, I could not scrape together enough coin to buy it back. What motley-minded man would sacrifice his freedom for a mistress? But what recreant would not risk it for love? I am in the bowels of the devil's turmoil, and I has't not a friend to counsel me. No man hither doth I trust.

The potions in mine cabinet doth tempt me. Oft I doth long for sweet oblivion. It all began with Eliza. She didst steal from her father, the apothecarist, a strong and bitter concoction which we shared one summer's afternoon. It didst give us the sweetest feeling of freedom and beauty and intense joy. 'Twas glorious indeed! 'Twas nothing on this foul earth that could have soured mine spirits that day. The sensation was euphoric and divine, but 'twas a sinful thing to waste such potent medicines on souls as young and healthy as mine and hers.

When mine mother fell ill some months later I didst implore Eliza to provide her with that same potion which might relieve her of the terrible pain she wast then suffering. Eliza didst oblige. After mine poor mother was deceased, Eliza and I didst continue to provide stolen medicines to sick and suffering unfortunates who had not the coin to afford the potions for themselves. But soon we didst becometh known, and rich folk didst seek our medicines for the purposes of pleasure. We didst refuse them, for we had too little to provide the poor and the sick as 'twas. 'Twas then that one of these dastardly men didst inform the Duke of our crimes, and he didst threaten to have us both imprisoned if I didst not consent to work for him thereafter.

Days were dark then, and I didst pray for hope. When none came I didst think only of the potions and wondered what combination might be potent enough to end mine wretched mortal coil. But then I didst see that lady and knew that mine prayers hadst been answered thence. There hath been times I has't felt her sweet eyes upon me, and oft I do believe that 'neath her smile is a favour much sweeter than common courtesy. The lady showeth signs of warmth toward me, 'tis true. We share a divine admiration for books, and so oft I doth linger in the library long after mine work is done in the desires of finding the lady thither. We doth not speaketh oft, but on those fine and rare times when her soft voice blesses mine tired ears, I hear in it an added kindness, reserved, I believe, especially for me.

To tell her wouldst be to risk mine life. The lady hath been wed by law to mine enemy, mine cruel master. To speaketh so openly of mine sinful devotion would be a crime unto itself. To tell Carolina the truth of mine heart would be to risk it all. But what, pray tell, is't that I doth risk? What has't I that I would lose? I liveth a life so wretched I would sooner die than stay another day in such a state, so wherefore doth I hesitate to take a risk such as this? Peradventure, I doth hesitate because I knoweth mine master to be cruel, and I knoweth that fates crueller than death might befall me. Be it so? Am I too afeared to confess mine obsession? Would I liveth a dreary, dearn life or would I taketh a chance on truest happiness?

What words ought I to speak? I am most afeared to confess those deepest thoughts. It would be so unwise. Speaketh now, they say, or forever hold thine truth. Confession leadeth to punishment, dost 't not? But what punishment on this most wretched Earth be worse than nev'r knowing what may has't been so? I must allow mine heart to be read by her, and her alone. I must findeth the lady hither, alone in the school. I wilt seek the company of the lady and I wilt tell her true. I must taketh mine chance soon and tell her all. The lady, mine lady, Carolina.

Oh my god. He's in love with Duke John Jameson's wife! And he's going to tell her! This is way better than TV.

Wednesday 17th February 2021

Frogsplash has been round all day today and things seem to be going well. He and Billy were getting along, and they spent most of the day at the kitchen table doing coursework. I'd say it was just like old times, but I don't think I've ever seen them doing schoolwork together. I'm no idiot, though, it was obviously for show otherwise they wouldn't have felt the need to do it in such a communal space, but they were doing some work, at least. Mum was thrilled to have Frogsplash back and to see how seriously he's taking his GCSEs. She's probably had Graham in her ear all the time saying stuff about Dad being a bad role model or Frogsplash not "bucking his ideas up" and all that negative nonsense.

"I hope you're not copying off each other," he said when he got home from work and saw them in the kitchen with their notes and their laptops.

"We're working on completely different assignments, Dad," Billy informed him. "We don't even take the same subjects!"

"Good. And I hope you're using the internet wisely – not just looking up the answers!"

"No, course not," Billy said a little less assertively, which made me think that they were probably doing exactly that. But isn't that what research is? Just looking up the answers and then putting them into your own words? In Graham's day they had textbooks with all the answers, now we have the internet. You still have to know what you're talking about. Mum made them clear up all of their study aids so we could eat dinner together at the table "as a family."

"Isn't this nice," she said once we'd all sat down and begun enjoying our tuna pasta bake, "I can't remember the last time we were all sat down at this table together!"

Really, Mum? You don't remember the night Frogsplash stormed out?

"Well it's nice to be back," said Froggo, "although, I couldn't help but notice you've put my games consoles somewhere! Where are they? If you've hidden them to help Billy concentrate on his schoolwork, I understand – he's so easily distracted!"

"You idiot, they're at your Dad's remember?" Billy said.

"Come on, Froggo, don't pretend you don't remember sneaking into the house to get them last month," Graham cut in. "You thought we were all out at work and school – you should have been at school yourself! But it was my day off and I heard you come in. I saw you walking off down the drive with all your consoles and all those cables dragging everywhere – I'm surprised you managed to carry them all!"

Frogsplash took a few moments to try and process that information before saying, "Oh yeah…"

"How could you forget that?" Mum asked him.

"Don't be a fool, Cassie, of course he didn't forget! He was probably going to try and make out that they'd been stolen by a burglar or something. He's trying to cover his tracks because he shouldn't have been sneaking around here during school hours."

"Oh, I see," Mum said with a little disappointment in her tone. "Well, I know how important those consoles are to you. I'm not going to get mad at you now, we're having such a nice time. Just so long as that was a one-off, not a regular thing. You can't afford to be skipping school at such an important time in your education. Now I won't hear another word about it! Anyone want some parmesan?"

Frogsplash looked a bit peeved, presumably because Graham had just snitched on him in front of everyone, but none of us wanted an argument, so that's where we left it.

Thursday 18th February 1723

I wast a brave man this day. Nev'r has't I seen battle, but on this day I acted knowing that I might cometh to behold the face of death. Duke John Jameson could have me hanged for making advances on his wife, whom he worked so hard to court. He didst put all of his efforts into stealing the land and coin to build this school for her, and with those means he didst payeth other, stronger men to lay down the bricks. And tirelessly he then strove to blackmail us poor unfortunate souls to be his school masters, thus completing his kind and charitable project!

Oft I doth wonder wherefore the lady didst consent to wed the Duke, and oft I doth bethink that, peradventure, she didst not consent at all. He is a man of tricks and deceit and she, too, may be a depress'd victim of one of his cruel traps. A lady hath little power in this world, too little. If a man of high standing should so desire to wed her, a lady would be wise not to refuse that man. I doth not bethink 'tis a joyous marriage, for they has't spent several years without child. The wife is young, too young to be barren, but the husband is oft drunk on wines he hath surely procured from some illicit source, and I doth not suppose that he is fit to produce offspring.

Wherefore is mine mind so occupied with unknowable and inconsequential queries such as these? It matters not! I am playing for time, for I am afraid to write mine confession here in ink. But I ought not burden myself with fear now, for the deed hath been done. This eve I didst seek the company of sweet, innocent Carolina, and the lady didst not disappoint. I awaited her arrival in the quietest corner of the library, although 'twas entirely empty anyhow. Carolina, sent from the heavens, drawn by the angels and kissed with the light of a thousand suns. She arrived at dusk, her cheeks aglow from the caress of the gentle breeze that didst blow across the field at day's end.

"Carolina." I spoketh swiftly, lest the words fail me in mine worried state, "I has't admired thee for too long, mine heart has't becometh heavy with the swelling of passion. I love thee, Carolina, I love thine kind soul,

thine great mind and thine sweet countenance. I will love thee always, and though I knoweth thou art wed to mine master, I am not afraid. The one and only thing I doth fear is a lifetime without thee."

"Oh Edmund!" she spoketh to me. "How long I hath waited to heareth those words. I... I..." But she spake no more; the words didst fail her pretty lips. She dared not speaketh, but her eyes held true their gaze upon mine own. She stared deeply, right into mine soul. I knew at once that everything I'd felt before hadst been real. We stood quite still, frozen in time, eyes as large as moons, latched to each other by some celestial force. Divine entities, close enough to share the same air at long last, each feeding the spirit of the other, pouring our two souls into one. She drew her small figure up close to mine own and I didst bow mine head to reach hers. I felt a tidal wave of deep blue sea rise from her chest up to mine own: the heavy rush of reciprocated passion! I belonged to her and she to me. She kissed me deeply by the ancient and precious scripts afforded by our library hither.

Then she didst draw away and she didst look at me sadly, her large, mournful eyes wet with tears. "I cannot!" said she. "We cannot!" and then she didst run. The lady ranneth far and fast, leaving me wanting so much more. And yet, what more could I desire? Mine feelings art reciprocated! But the obstacle is the same that it hath at each moment been. Our circumstances have altered none; the lady be still married to the beast! Only now tis us versus the Duke, us versus the world. Nowt can ever be the same, not now that the lady loveth me. The lady loveth me! Mine Carolina!

But what might befall mine lady now? She be afraid of her husband. She be afraid of what might befall her should the truth find him. I has't made mine lady afraid! Forget mine folly and forgo mine happiness! Tonight, she wilt be sleepless with woe, frightened of the wrath of her vicious bedfellow, the Duke. What has't I done? I would not have her suffer. Now she, too, taketh the risk, and now she too might taketh punishment. She didst kiss me, tis true! If her dreadful keeper didst know it he would surely make her suffer! I must save mine lady from this fate. But how?

Well that escalated quickly! What are they going to do? Are they going to have a full-blown affair? Duke John Jameson doesn't sound like the sort of man who would forgive something like that. I wonder if I'm the only living person who knows about this. How exciting! And at last, I know his name. Edmund. His name is Edmund!

Monday 22nd February 2021

TRUE ROMANCE AT VALENTINE'S DANCE: HOW ONE COUPLE STOLE THE SHOW AT THE YEAR EIGHT DISCO

"It was just an ordinary school dance. Everyone was having a good time, there were some curious moves on the dance floor and some even more questionable outfit choices, as well as plenty of awkward people standing on the side lines who appeared to have come to a social event by mistake. But there was at least one person who knew exactly what she was doing: Danielle Dankworth. She wore a pastel blue Brigitte Beaumont mini dress and a braided hairstyle which is rumoured to have been done professionally, especially for the occasion.

"But even more flawless than her style of dress was her style of dance. Some of you may remember Danielle's performance at last year's end of term talent show, in which she proved herself a skilled mover, despite the disastrous finale which resulted in a hospital trip for poor Danielle. But, never disheartened, she made a full recovery and has clearly not lost her touch when it comes to throwing shapes.

"But it was not until the end of the night that Danielle put on a true display of elegance and class. When all else had given up hope of finding that special someone on the most romantic night of the year, Danielle had no trouble bagging the man of her choice. Intensely brooding bad boy Elliot Moore remained a mystery to many of us after he joined the school at the beginning of this academic year. But his charms at the disco were hard to ignore. They made the perfect couple as they danced slowly to the last song of the night, and with Elliot wearing a pastel blue shirt which so perfectly matched Danielle's dress, one has to wonder whether the pair had planned to spend the evening together all along.

"Could it be that this new romance has been budding right under our noses for some time?"

-   Written by Charlotte Henderson, Year 8 correspondent for *The Daily Duke*

Carla finished reading out the article with her eyes rolled up so far inside her head it's a wonder how she managed to see the paper.

"Of course, it's been budding for some time," I said, "and Charlotte would know that if she'd bothered to take any notice of Danny before she realised she looks good on the dance floor!"

"She's talking about them like they're celebrities," Carla said. "She didn't know who they were a week ago! And even if she did, she would have treated them like dirt. Imagine if Elliot had tried to talk to Charlotte when he had green hair – she'd have laughed him out of the school!"

"I wonder what it is," I said. "What's the magic ingredient that somehow, suddenly makes someone popular? What's changed that makes Danny cool now?"

"She got rid of us, that's what! Obviously, we were holding her back," Carla said.

"Is it because she's got a boyfriend? Does that make her cool? Was it the designer dress, or the dancing?"

"It was us; I'm telling you!" Carla insisted.

"It's probably a combination of things," I said, but I couldn't help but wonder if one of those things was me.

For the entire day it seemed like all anyone could talk about was the article. It's not often that our year group gets the front page of the school paper, and when it is it's usually about something academic, like a school trip or maths club competing against a rival school or whatever. Rarely does anyone ever get made into a celebrity by an encomium written in *The Daily Duke,* but Danny, so it seems, is the exception to that rule. She and Elliot tried to keep a low profile, I saw them together during morning break sat on a bench in the playground, all wrapped up in coats and hats, but I was inside looking out of the window, so I didn't get a chance to speak to her.

Tuesday 23rd February 2021

It was Mr Pinter's Biology lesson this morning. Carla and I sat in our usual places, near the back of the classroom so it's easier for us to talk to each other without getting caught. Recently Danny has been sat at the front of the class next to Elliot, but this morning she was nowhere to be seen, and Elliot was sat alone.

"I hope she's OK," said Carla. "She must be ill."

"Maybe she's just running late," I said. "Her mum usually gives her a lift in winter, doesn't she? It's probably traffic or something with the twins."

"Maybe it's family trouble," Carla said worriedly. "They've only got one car now and last time I spoke to her she said her parents had been arguing over it."

"I'm sure she's fine," I said. "It's only the first lesson of the day."

"Ooh, maybe she's had a fight with Elliot and she's skiving off to avoid him!"

"You sound a little too pleased about that," I said. "She's our friend, we want her to be happy, *remember?*"

"Yeah, happy in the long term. I've said it before and I'll say it again, nothing good can come of spending time alone with a boy as angry as that. Oh god, what if they did have a fight, I mean a proper fight, and now she's scared of him? You've seen him lose his temper, imagine if that was aimed at you, and there was no one else around to help you. Maybe you should text her."

"You should text her if you're that worried about her."

"But it'll sound wrong coming from me! She'll think that I'm *implying* that he's done something bad."

"You don't have to say anything about *him,* just ask her if she's all right!"

Carla took a deep breath and then attempted to surreptitiously retrieve her phone from her rucksack without Pinter noticing. She sat for some time with her phone in her hand under the desk, trying to think of how to word her text carefully, so as not to sound accusatory, and probably (knowing Carla) trying to sound concerned without sounding like she's admitting defeat in this ongoing battle of wills. I was excited, because this might be just the ice-breaker the pair of them need to make up. But before Carla had finished composing her message, the classroom door swung open and Danny walked in, smiling a gorgeous, pearly white smile at Elliot.

"Sorry, sir, I was at the orthodontist. I've got a note from my mum."

"I can see that," he said, "you've had your braces removed! I bet that's a good feeling, no longer having a mouth full of metal."

"Yes, sir," she said, smiling coyly as she sat down next to Elliot.

"Well that explains that," I said to Carla.

"Oh god, what chance have we got now?" she said miserably. "She was too cool for us when she had braces, now she's got a Hollywood smile on top of everything else! We're never getting her back now. We're doomed."

We really are doomed.

Friday 26th February 2021

Today was Oliver Jameson's fourth visit to the school. Little did we know, it was also to be his last. Wilcox seemed to be making less of an effort to clean up prior to the arrival of Jameson and his entourage, and I guessed it was because his visits are becoming less of an event, like how you want the house to be really tidy the first time you invite a friend over, but by the fourth or fifth time it doesn't seem to matter any more. He arrived some time during first lesson and went straight to the kitchens, although I don't really know how much of the cooking he actually gets involved with and how much he delegates to his team of chefs.

Carla was busy selling her sugary wares during morning break, and of course Danny was off somewhere with Elliot, so I wandered over to the canteen, partly to get a snack, but mostly to have a nose around to find out what was for lunch. Oliver Jameson was nowhere to be seen, presumably hard at work, so the reporter from the local paper, Trisha Tijani (according to her visitor's badge) was sat at one of the canteen tables drinking coffee and looking very busy on her tablet. Outside a dusty sprinkling of sleet made a bleak and uninviting scene, so I stayed indoors with my apple and cinnamon porridge pot, sitting at the table next to the one Trisha Tijani was sat at, hoping to catch a glimpse of the article she was working on.

I have been suppressing a deep passion for journalism ever since I started secondary school, mostly because my arch nemesis, Charlotte Henderson, is the head representative of our year group at the school paper. I don't know how she managed to get in there before I even knew that such opportunities existed, but girls like her always seem to have friends in high places who can get them where they want in life. She is a foul, arrogant bully and I refuse to work with her in any capacity, so my dreams of working for the paper and gaining journalistic experience have been put on hold. My life is far too busy and complicated at the moment, anyway.

When I saw the devil herself, Charlotte Henderson, walking towards me without her usual posse following behind, I had a horrible feeling she was going to say something nasty to me about eating. I could hear every single taunt before they had even come out of her mouth:

"You really shouldn't be eating carbs right now – you gained so much weight this winter."

"Oliver Jameson's doing his best to fight obesity in this school, but if you keep eating at every available opportunity, you're going to ruin it for all of us."

"Porridge – that's fuel food. What do you need energy for – sitting on your arse in History class until it's time for lunch?"

"I know your friend Danny is too cool for you now, and that other dark-haired one would rather hang out in the year seven common area than sit with you, but comfort eating will only make matters worse."

But that was all in my head. Charlotte walked straight past me and sat down opposite Trisha Tijani.

"Hi," she said with confidence, "Charlotte Henderson, Year Eight correspondent for the school newspaper."

Trisha Tijani looked annoyed at the disturbance, but she didn't turn Charlotte away.

"Hello. How can I help you?" Trisha said.

"Actually, this is more about how I can help you," Charlotte said deviously.

"You think you've got something interesting to tell me," Trisha said drily. "You want to get in the papers, is that it?"

"As a writer, yes, but not as a subject. I'm not an attention-seeker; I'm a truth-seeker."

"Oh really? And what truths have you got for me?"

"Well, I can't go giving away all of my secrets free of charge! I want something from you in return."

"I see. Well, Charlotte, I must say you do have the makings of a true journalist. You're not afraid to go out and get what you want! So, what exactly is it that you want?"

"Just some friendly advice, really. I want to know about defamation. I want you to teach me how to dig up dirt on someone, and I want to know how I can use it against them."

"Someone who has wronged you?" Trisha asked with growing intrigue.

"My reasons are not your concern," Charlotte said with astonishing confidence, and although she was being vague, I was pretty sure I knew that she was talking about Rachel Levine.

"This doesn't sound very ethical," Trisha said. "You do realise I'm just a small-time journalist? I usually run stories on charity bake sales and the tragedy of the closing-down family-run bookshop round the corner."

"Usually," said Charlotte, "but what if you had the chance to run a really big story? A scandal, something that goes all the way to the top."

I could not believe what I was hearing. This was vital information. And I couldn't believe they were having this conversation so close to where I was sitting! It confirmed that which I have long suspected: alone I am invisible; I am not on the human radar; I do not register as a sentient being. Good – this is good.

"The top?" asked Trisha. "You mean the government?"

"Well no, not the government, but he's still pretty high up."

"Who are you talking about?"

Charlotte looked at her with serious eyes. She meant business.

"The headmaster of this school," she said. "Mr Wilcox."

"Why, what's he been doing?"

"Well I'm not going to give it all away, not until you've helped me," Charlotte said. "But I will tell you this: he caught a student selling … things … to other students. They're running a business, making huge profits selling substances that are banned in this school. They're selling them to young children, even year sevens! Especially year sevens, in fact, because they're too young to get their hands on it any other way. This stuff is bad for them – it's ruining their health, but they've become addicted, they just can't help themselves, but as long as she keeps supplying it, they'll keep buying…"

She? She's talking about Carla!

"She? Who's she?" Trisha asked.

"I can't tell you who," said Charlotte cannily, "but the real story here is that Wilcox knows all about it, and not only is he turning a blind eye, he's actually helping her, possibly even condoning it! He's making excuses for her, covering for her when other teachers ask questions. And you've got to ask yourself: why would he do that? Why would he take that risk if he's not profiting from it? The answer? Corruption."

"Well, that does sound like a good scoop, if it's true," Trisha said. "Of course, I'll need more detail, to verify the facts. I wouldn't be much of a journalist if I simply took the word of a twelve-year-old and put it into print. I'll do some snooping around, and if I find even a shred of truth to your story I'll be in touch."

And just at that moment the bell rang for third lesson. I had just enough time to send a warning text to Carla as I hurried off to History, but even when I was sat in class, the lure of the vital conversation on my phone was too much to resist, so I clutched my phone in my hand and waited for it to vibrate while I pretended to listen to Mrs Michaelides talking about the Battle of the Somme (disrespectful, I know, but I will catch up. To think, none of that was even close to happening when Edmund was writing his diary!). Carla replied in almost no time:

Carla: "Charlotte, that sneaky cow! How did she know all that? Someone must have snitched!"

Me: "I have to warn you, she made it sound worse than it is. She didn't even say what you were selling – Trisha probably thought she meant drugs!"

Carla: "Well that can easily be disproved. I've got a double bass case full of chocolate! But who ratted me out? You don't think... Danny?"

Me: "Carla, no! She wouldn't..."

Carla: "But she was so against it. And she's the only one who knew about the whole thing with Wilcox. No one else knew that he knew..."

Me: "You didn't tell anyone else? Not even your loyal customers?"

Carla: "Of course not! I wouldn't trust them not to spill the beans if another teacher caught them! Look, I would never have dreamed that it was Danny. I swear, I don't want to accuse her; I really don't. But nobody else knew. Nobody..."

"Samantha Drury! What have you got there?!" Mrs Michaelides' voice nearly made me jump out of my skin. "Hand it over," she said, her hand outstretched.

Resignedly, I placed my phone in Mrs Michaelides' palm and said a feeble, "Sorry, miss."

"You can collect it from my office at the end of the day."

Straight after History was lunch time, and even amidst all of the drama, I was still very excited to find out what Oliver Jameson had got in store for us. I found Carla already in the queue and subtly slipped in beside her so we could chat (nothing to do with me wanting to jump the queue – nothing at all).

"I got caught with my phone," I explained to her, "it got confiscated. You haven't said anything to Danny, have you?"

"No, don't worry. I'm still trying to figure out who it could have been. Maybe Wilcox told someone else. But why would he do that? Who could he have told that would want to inform Charlotte? He's no friend to the students!"

"Maybe we shouldn't talk about it here," I said, "you never know who's listening."

"Good point," said Carla, changing the subject. "Do you know what we're having for lunch?"

It was king prawn, tomato and pesto tagliatelle and it was *divine*. It was almost enough to make me completely forget all of my many worries. I was worried about Danny and Carla, because before it seemed like a little petty falling-out, but what if Danny did tell Charlotte about the sugar business? I haven't ever seen the two of them together, but Charlotte just wrote an article about Danny in which she made her out to be some kind of queen, and you'd have to be pretty cool-headed not to let something like that affect your feelings about a person. So maybe Danny started to like Charlotte, maybe she thanked her – perhaps not in person, but on social media. Maybe they got talking, maybe Charlotte asked why she wasn't hanging out with us any more, maybe it all came spilling out…

Or not. Maybe Danny didn't do it. But if she didn't do it and Carla thinks she did then what's going to happen? The trust between us is fading fast, and all I can think now is that Danny was right. When you have to sneak around and deceive people, when you start colluding with the enemy (whether that's Wilcox or Charlotte Henderson), no good can come of it. I was mulling all of this over after I'd wolfed down my tagliatelle in record time and was feeling extremely disappointed that it was already gone, mourning the presence of food on my plate as though it wasn't me who had eaten it. I might have begun thinking about dessert if it weren't for the extraordinary turn of events that was about to unfold in front of me and everyone else in the dining hall.

Like every large communal space in the school, the dining hall has speakers in case any events need to be held there. But I guarantee you that hall had never seen an event like this before. The speakers began booming out a heavy bassline which shook every one of us into complete and utter bafflement, apart from Wilcox, who got out of his seat quite calmly and stood to face us. Seemingly out of nowhere, my good old Geography teacher/weekend flatmate Richard bounced into action with a backwards baseball cap on his bald head. He jogged over to Wilcox, who seemed to relax out of his usual stiffness and into a casual stance, replacing his textbook teacher demeanour with street attitude. I recognised this version of Wilcox; he had been trying to break free ever since his first confrontation with Jameson. Without any hint of compunction, The Big W began to rap to the beat in front of Jameson and the entire school:

"You come around here acting like the big cheese
But you ain't got a clue; you're just chattin' breeze
You come to my school thinkin' you're so hot
But you're the leftover grease in this cooking pot
So, don't step to me with your flashy frying pan
In this school there's only room for one big man."

Richard, who had been bopping his head supportively throughout the first verse, now took centre stage and continued the song:

"You said our kids were obese and our water's smelly
But you spilt coffee down your shirt and we saw your fat belly
You say our school's a mess and that you're our saviour
But you're rude, you're arrogant – it's disgraceful behaviour!
Our own dinner ladies are much more highly respected
We'd rather eat their food than risk getting infected

With your posh nosh, stuck-up, pretentious food
And your snobby, self-important, celebrity attitude.
You come here with your cameras and news reporters
Claiming you've come to rescue our sons and daughters

255

You tell the papers we're some kind of charity
I read those words with utmost hilarity!"

Back to Wilcox for the denouement:

"My school is outstanding, just ask OFSTED
We never asked for you to show your ugly head
We were doing just fine, we were just exquisite
'Til you took it upon yourself to start to come visit
So, do us a favour and do yourself one, too
Don't bother coming back, mate, we don't need you."

Needless to say, the entire school and Oliver Jameson were left utterly stunned. Even now I am struggling to comprehend the events of this afternoon. At some point down the line, Wilcox and Richard must have had some exchange about Jameson, discovered that they had both been humiliated by the man and bonded over their mutual resentment of him. In a way I'm not all that surprised that they chose to express it in the way they did – I was already aware of Wilcox's "extra-curricular" interests, and Richard is an impressionable man prone to brief and ill-advised phases which have usually been inspired by youth culture. I suppose the only surprise was the utterly, shamelessly public way in which they communicated their passion to the unsuspecting school and all its staff and guests.

All we could do now was watch and wait for Jameson to respond. At that moment in time I felt rather sorry for him. He isn't a bad man. He has got a bit of an ego, but that's kind of justified when you're talented and successful and you do a lot of work to help others. It was a classic case of jealousy (on Wilcox's part) and idiocy (on Richard's). Jameson stared long and hard at the rap duo, letting the silence hang in the air like the smell of grease that lingers there every other day of the month when the only available meals consist of chips and deep-fried something or chips and cheesy something. Today the dining hall smelled of basil, garlic and the freshest seafood you can get. But all good things must come to an end.

Jameson took one last cold stare at Wilcox and walked over to the kitchen, where he had a quiet word with his head chef. They packed up the specialist utensils they'd brought themselves and left all the rest of the dirty pans and equipment behind, following Oliver Jameson as he left the dining hall, and our school, for the final time. Trisha Tijani and a few other media people followed them out, some taking photographs while others pressed Jameson for a statement, but he departed with a silent dignity which seemed only to cement the idea that although he had been ousted from the school, it was he, not Wilcox, who'd come out of it the better man.

There was never any hope of Richard being the better man.

The regular kitchen staff had stayed awkwardly immobile in the food preparation area while all around them Jameson's chefs were packing up their things and departing. Now that they were gone, Wilcox wasted no time in instructing them to clean up the mess that was left and try to salvage the desserts, which were mini, single-serve apple crumbles that had been in the oven since before the speakers had begun playing out that heavy beat. Only a small number of people got up to queue for dessert, and even fewer came back with one once they'd seen how overcooked they were. The rest of us sat chatting to our friends and to other people, too. Even Carla and I couldn't resist getting involved with a conversation Jan Saunders and Nefa Tariq were having nearby.

"What on *Earth* was that all about?"

"They've ruined it for all of us!"

"Surely he's going to lose his job…"

"…at least a disciplinary…"

"… must be out of his mind!"

Saturday 27th February 2021

"Are you out of your MIND?!" I said to Richard when I arrived at Dad's this weekend.

"What do you mean?" he said innocently.

"I mean you teaming up with the Big W…"

"He prefers Big Willy now…"

(Both Dad and Frogsplash sniggered.)

"What were you thinking?" I reprimanded again.

"We were thinking that we needed to do something to get rid of that arrogant show-off, and that's exactly what we did! Problem solved."

"What problem? The only problem was with you and Wilcox and your fragile egos! The rest of us were enjoying Jameson's visits – or at least his food. But you two just couldn't stand to have a better man in your midst. Pathetic."

"All right, Sam, you've said your piece," Dad said, taking pity on poor, misguided Richard.

"OK, I know it was Wilcox's idea," I said, looking at the crestfallen old coot in front of me. "I'm just saying maybe you should choose your heroes more carefully. Or better yet – don't follow anyone. You're much better as a solo act anyway."

"You think?" Richard said hopefully.

"Of course," I said, "always be your own man."

"You're right," Richard said decisively, "always be your own man!"

When he emerged from his room ten minutes later dressed almost exactly like David Bowie in his Ziggy Stardust years, Dad decided that the rest of us ought to leave him some space and get out of the flat.

"It's called *All Ages Activity Centre*" Dad said once he, Froggo, Stephanie and I were all strapped into the car and ready to go. "It's a bit further afield, but apparently it's got the biggest soft play area for kids Steph's age, plus a diving pool and a gym."

"Can I go to the gym?" Froggo asked eagerly.

"Ah, you're too young, I'm afraid. You'll stunt your growth if you start lifting weights at your age."

"It says here on the website age sixteen and up. And you get a free day pass if you register online."

"I don't know, Frogsplash. You might hurt yourself on one of the machines. I'm sure your mum would have something to say if you broke your neck or lost a limb."

"The free day pass comes with a full tutorial of all the equipment. I've already signed up! I might as well go, that way you don't even have to pay for me to use the pool."

"All right," Dad said, "but if you end up wanting a full membership, you'll have to find a way to pay for it yourself! Will you be all right in the pool on your own, Sam?"

"Of course!"

POOL TIMETABLE:
13:00 – 15:00 PRIVATE HIRE: LUCY'S 7TH BIRTHDAY PARTY
15:30 – 16:30 – OVER 60S AQUA AEROBICS
17:00 – 19:00 ADULT SWIM
19:00 – 21:00 SWIMMING GALA

I'm not sure I'm quite the right age to gate crash Lucy's party or aqua aerobics, and the half hour intervals in between were for the poor lifeguards to check in case anyone had puked up birthday cake or lost their dentures in the pool.

"Sorry, Sam, I checked the timetable last week and it was open to the public until aqua aerobics! You'll have to come to soft play with me and Steph."

"That's all right," I said.

How bad can it be?

We walked in and there was so much screaming that at first I thought someone was drowning in the ball pool. Stephanie was so excited when she looked up and beheld the full glory of the place that she went bounding head-first into the foam-clad jungle without so much as a second glance at the family who had brought her here. All was well, and as long as I could adapt to the constant din of infant voices, I would be able to spend the afternoon wisely, focussing on a school project I had saved on the tablet.

"EXCUSE ME!" came the voice of a woman with dyed, ink-black hair in a scraped back ponytail. "EXCUSE ME! YOU CAN'T LET HER GO IN THERE WITH SHOES ON!"

"She's talking to you, Dad!" I nudged him; his head already buried in the sports section of the paper.

"Oh, sorry!" he said, looking over at the enormous adventure play area in search of Stephanie.

"She's up there," I said, pointing to a short, clear, plastic tunnel with at least five children all bundled into it, some of them trying to climb over each other like a litter of new-born puppies searching for milk.

"Blimey – I can't get up there!" he said, "I'd get stuck and cause a pipe blockage!"

"Fine," I said, and I kicked off my shoes and went into the fray.

There was no clear path to the see-through tunnel, and the only entrance that I was sure I could squeeze through was a series of vertical, escalating rope-net canopies, each one with a hole in it which you had to climb through to get the next canopy, then another ascending climb to the next one, and so on until you'd reached the first level. Then there were these huge, padded rollers which appeared to have a gap of only a few inches between them, but I saw four or five children squeeze between them with ease, so I tried my luck. I entered the tiny gap, feeling like a ball of dough between two rolling pins, and was mightily relieved when I made it through to the other side without anyone having to call the fire brigade.

There was another net canopy, only this one was longer and to get across it you had to wrap your thighs around a red ball attached to a rope on a zip wire and glide across. There was a queue to use it, and I felt thoroughly foolish crouching behind a bunch of three and four-year-olds waiting my turn. I'm sure they were giving me funny looks, even though they must have been too young to care. Eventually I reached the entrance to the transparent tube, which was made of a solid plastic so hard on the knees that I felt bruises forming with every advancement. It was still crammed full of children, and when I looked down through the plastic to see the ground ten feet below me, I began to fear that my additional weight would be too much for the thing to take.

Desperately, I clambered over several children, possibly elbowing one of them in the ribs and definitely feeling one of their sticky hands grab my hair for balance when they got pushed over by one of the others. I made it all the way through, but there was no light at the end of that tunnel, because Stephanie wasn't there. I could hear her crying. I couldn't see her, but my only way forward was a narrow, padded pole that you had to balance on like a beam to get to the other side. Of course, there were safety nets all around, but they were already full of children who'd given up on the balancing act and were just rolling around aimlessly in the void area which the safety nets created. I teetered across as carefully as I could, but with tiny hands grabbing at my ankles from either side, I felt like fresh blood walking over a pit of zombies.

One more squeeze through another set of those kitchen roll-shaped things, only this time they were horizontal and so close together I felt like a thick blanket being squashed through a mangle, and when I made it half-way through I was just a breathless torso dangling out of the other side, my arms grabbing for the floor so that I could pull the rest of myself all the way out. Eventually I reached the source of that cry I recognised so well. She was another level up, but I only had to climb a few squidgy platform things to get to her. Her tears subsided into a generally woeful moan when she saw my face and realised she was not alone.

She was sat at the top of a very high, very steep slide that was wide enough for several children to slide down at once. I sat next to her, our legs dangling over the edge dangerously, and when I looked down I could see that it was not only steep, but a completely vertical drop. It had been decorated to look like a waterfall and looking down it felt almost as terrifying. But you must always put on a brave face for younger children, especially when the thing you're facing is of no real threat. I wondered if Stephanie was too young for this place, but she'd managed to overcome the same obstacles that I had, and the staff were more concerned about her shoes than her safety. There was only one thing for it. I took hold of her hand.

"When I say three we're going to go, OK?"

She nodded.

"One... Two... Three!"

We pushed off the edge together and went rocketing down. It was exhilarating – I loved it! With my extra weight we went down much faster than any of the other kids and I was worried it might have been too much for Stephanie. When we reached the bottom and slowed down I looked over at her. Her face was blank – stunned. She could easily have broken into tears or laughter; she hadn't decided yet.

"Again! Again!" she said gleefully, and she grabbed my hand and pulled me up to my feet before I'd had any time at all to rest. It looked like we were going again, and although the journey to the top had been treacherous, I had to admit I was really looking forward to it. This time we took a much easier route to the top, which explains how Steph managed to get up there on her own in the first place. It was a simple ramp with foamy steps protruding from it, and although it was quite slippery in just our socks, we managed to ascend without sliding all the way back down again. Gradually we tried many different routes to the waterfall slide, and then I convinced her to try some other slides, like the big curly wurly one and the one which landed straight in the ball pool. It was so much fun! I was so glad the pool was closed!

It was the biggest indoor adventure playground I'd ever seen, and what with Stephanie being so small and so much slower than me I did lose her a few times but she didn't cry, she just charged ahead and carried right on, and I like to think that was at least partly because I'd given her the confidence to take on the challenge. Perhaps I could have left her to it, but whenever we did find each other again, she was so excited to see me and show me something new that she'd discovered that it seemed a shame to miss out on such a good way to spend time with her. And anyway, I was enjoying myself too. There's no shame in that, is there? I was bonding with my sister, I was getting exercise, I was having a bit of innocent fun! This is my last year of childhood before I become a teenager, so if you think about it, it really is my last chance to do things like this without being classed as a weirdo.

It was during one of those intervals in which I had lost track of Stephanie that I suddenly heard a raucous, jeering display of semi-masculinity. I had just slid down the big tube slide and landed in the ball pool when I heard them. Boys, not men, were walking past the window of the soft play area towards the showers and changing rooms. They were caked in mud and wearing royal blue football kits. I had seen them through the back window of the room earlier playing out on the football pitch. This particular bunch were in great spirits; they had obviously won, and such were their celebrations that they seemed to travel very slowly through the corridor, patting each other on the back, scuffing up each other's hair, fake-tackling each other, that sort of thing. I was still lying down in the ball pool with my head craning up above the surface when one of them caught my eye.

Then another one.

Then another.

Rob Battley, Hassan Ahmed and Jake Atkinson were all on the winning team, but the only real loser in this situation was me. I tried to bury myself in the ball pool. I stopped craning my neck and let my head fall back, but balls are not liquid, so I had to force myself under, sinking down and letting the colourful plastic spheres flood over me until I was covered.

I think I'm getting away with it! They must have walked past by now. I'll just stay here a little longer, just to be on the safe side... OUCH!

A child of about five or six landed right on top of my face, and I clambered out from under them to save myself from suffocating under their weight, not to mention avoiding the very likely event that another child would soon come down the slide. I was struggling to get to my feet, and I was more than a little short of breath, not to mention stiflingly hot after being buried under all that plastic rubble. My hair was sticking to my sweaty forehead and my top had ridden up so that my flabby belly was on show. I was still partially pinned down by the six-year-old so that my legs weren't entirely my own and I was conscious that I had lost a sock. I was dangerously over-heated and horribly lobster-coloured. I desperately wished that I was in the real pool, with water in it; lovely, cooling, water. How I longed to be cool at that moment. But I was not cool – not in the slightest.

Then I saw them. They must have spotted me before I'd even gone under, because they were all staring in through the window, their faces pressed against the glass, expressions of intense amusement on their usually gormless faces. When they realised that I had noticed them they burst out laughing. They must have been loving it. There I was, apparently enjoying the soft play playground on my own, red-faced and sweaty, trying to bury myself in a ridiculous attempt to hide from them, only to have a child land on my head, and now I couldn't even stand up! I was flailing like a red balloon in the wind, and it was as entertaining to them as a red balloon in the wind would be, if you happened to be a simple-minded one-year-old.

The one small saving grace was that they must have left their phones in their lockers, otherwise they'd have been snapping evidence of this social suicide to share with everybody who knows my name. They were still guffawing at the window when I'd finally got firmly to my feet and began wading through the balls towards the narrow, netted exit. A certain amount of damage had been done (*significant – it was significant*) but I still had options. I could try to save some face. If I could at least prove that I was not there alone, that I was there with a younger sibling, I might at least be able to validate my presence.

I looked everywhere for Stephanie, calling her name as I went, but of course that was futile over the cacophony of cries and screams that filled the air. I scanned the room looking for a tiny blonde toddler, all the while the three donkeys in the window were watching and laughing. Eventually, I spotted her at the top of the waterfall slide, so up I went, up the rope canopies, through the rolling pins, across the zipwire, through the transparent tube, over the zombie bridge, through yet more rolling pins, the boys watching my struggle every excruciating step of the way. I was just climbing up the foamy steps when I saw her push off. She was sliding down without me. I had reached the top of the slide, but she was gone. She was supposed to be there! We were supposed to slide down together! Why did I give her the confidence to go it alone? I had no choice.

Down I went. Down the waterfall, alone. Plunging to my death. What had once been simple, yet ecstatic fun was now a tragic fall from the highest height to the pit of despair. I slid down awkwardly, somehow slower than before, almost smearing down the vertical drop like mayonnaise down the inside of the jar: graceless and sluggish; greasy and blob-like, that about sums me up. Rob Battley, Hassan Ahmed and Jake Atkinson stayed just long enough to watch me baste the slide with my goose-fat sweat before traipsing off, still laughing as they went.

Monday 1st March 2021

SUSPICIONS, BLOCKED NUMBERS AND MISTRUST: A ONCE SOLID FRIENDSHIP HAS BITTEN THE DUST

Communication breakdown has caused the very foundations of a friendship to collapse. One member who was caught in the middle believes that these events were out of her control and that there is little she can do, so she decides to let things run their course.

The taunts on the bus this morning were not particularly inspired:

"Hey, Samantha, will you go out with me? I'll take you to the park, they've got swings and slides and everything – you'll love it!"

"Oi, Sam, did you watch *Barry Bumble's Boat* yesterday, or is that show a bit too advanced for you?"

"I need to finish my Maths homework. Hey, Samantha – you got a crayon I can borrow?"

There was no point trying to defend myself. Arguing with people like that only proves that they got to you. It might have gotten to me more if I had thought for a moment that my soft play adventure would have been big news around the school, but what could be bigger than the head teacher spontaneously breaking into a derogatory rap about a celebrity chef in front of the entire school?

It was in this morning's whole school assembly that Wilcox made the official announcement:

"Oliver Jameson's reign of terror is over!" he declared triumphantly. "He will no longer pay visits to our school, he will not bombard us with his cameras, his paparazzi and his news journalists. He will not badmouth us to the papers, and he will not dictate what we can and can't eat. I hereby declare that the ban on sweets is OVER!"

I got the impression Wilcox was expecting a roar of applause at this peroration, but it was more of a gentle murmur of approval. However pleased people might be to have their sweets back, I'm pretty sure none of us considered any of the past few months a "reign of terror".

"I might as well pack it in," Carla said as we sat in the music room eating our packed lunches, "I could keep selling the sweets, my rates are still cheaper, but it's easier for people to just get them from the canteen rather than hunting me down."

"You can't get freshly baked croissants in the canteen!" I said encouragingly. "You can't get half the stuff you sell in the canteen!"

"I know," she said, "but I told you I was getting bored with it anyway. I had a good run, made a bit of cash, but at what cost? I've made too many sacrifices. For one thing I've not had any time for guitar practice. Art before money! Passion before profit! I love music, and what could be more important than the thing you love?"

"I don't know," I said, "the people you love?"

And just at that moment, Danny walked in.

"Hey," she said pleasantly, though her face was an open book of nerves. "Sorry it's been a while. I didn't know how to get talking to you guys again. There was so much going on – it's been crazy! Suddenly everyone knows who I am – I never wanted *that*. But all this madness with Wilcox and Jameson, I mean, what the hell was that rap battle on Friday?!"

"More like a rap ambush!" I said, "Jameson didn't have a clue what hit him!"

"It made the local paper and everything!" Danny said enthusiastically, "Here, I've got a copy…"

She put her designer handbag on the desk in front of her – a gift from her guilt-ridden dad, no doubt. My dad buys me coats when he feels he's got something to prove, and stationery when he just wants to make me happy. She pulled out the newspaper and read the article written by Trisha Tijani:

"When I was assigned to do a piece on celebrity chef Oliver Jameson's ongoing visits to local school, Duke John Jameson, I was expecting to write a brief and uplifting article about one man's efforts to improve the health of our children, with perhaps a chance to sample some of his world-famous grub and exercise my skills as a food critic. My visit began simply enough, and it was not until the nine hundred or so pupils and staff had finished their meals that there was any sign that this was not going to be a routine lunch break.

"After a simple but delectable seafood dish a heavy bass suddenly blasted out of the school dining hall speakers. In an incredibly bizarre turn of events, school head teacher Walter Wilcox rose from his seat, soon accompanied by the Geography teacher Richard Roberts, who was sporting a backwards baseball cap most unfitting for a man of his years. Then the pair began to rap. They took it in turns to recite several verses of a rap song which was undoubtedly an original penned by the two teachers, the lyrical content being far too esoteric for any rapper you might find in the pop charts.

"Initially, I was under the impression that this was all a bit of a joke, a set-up that Jameson had been in on from the start, presumably to attract more media attention. But the message which the rap was sending soon became crystal clear. It was essentially an attack on Oliver Jameson, accusing him of pretentiousness and hubris, and taking a rather low blow at his 'fat belly'. It was an effort to shun the man from the school for good, and as far as anybody knows, it was a success. Oliver Jameson ordered all of his staff to vacate the school immediately, and they left shortly after, choosing not to comment on the events of the afternoon."

Danny looked up at us both with an expression of glee, eagerly awaiting our excited responses. This was her ice-breaker.

"Yes, but that wasn't the story you expected from Trisha Tijani, was it?" Carla said coldly.

"What?" said Danny, apparently clueless. "Who's Trisha Tijani?"

"Maybe you don't know who she is," Carla spoke like a calculating detective. "Maybe you had no idea Charlotte would go to the papers! Did your friend Charlotte tell you she could keep a secret? And of course, you believed her, didn't you?"

"Carla, stop it!" I said. "Danny's apologised! She wants to make up."

"I wanted to make up too, until I realised what a traitor she is! How can I ever trust her again?" Carla addressed me, now not even acknowledging Danny's presence. It was getting heated and bitter. "And you should think twice, too, Sam! You really think she wouldn't tell Charlotte things you've told her in confidence?"

"What are you talking about?" said Danny. "Do you mean Charlotte Henderson? Just because she wrote that article about me and Elliot, doesn't mean I'm suddenly best friends with her!"

The power of writing. It's a dangerous force! Articles, songs, letters, even diaries…

"I'm not talking about *that* article," said Carla, "I'm talking about the one that would have been in the local paper if Wilcox and Richard hadn't performed that ridiculous stunt. The one about me and my sordid business – the one you so pointedly disapproved of."

"I don't understand," said Danny, "why would that end up in the proper news?"

"Charlotte knew about it," I explained. "It seemed as though she knew everything, including the fact that Wilcox was in on it. She tried to get Trisha Tijani to run a story on it."

"That sneaky cow!" Danny scowled. "That girl couldn't care less about anyone other than herself! You really think I would want to be friends with her? I thought you knew me better than that."

"I thought I knew you, too," said Carla, sounding hurt, "I thought, at the very least, you would be honest when I confronted you. I thought you were going to tell me that you were chatting to Charlotte and it just slipped out, that you made a mistake, that you had no idea she was going to tell anyone, let alone a professional journalist. But no, now you're just lying straight to my face."

"I'm not!" said Danny. "It wasn't me!"

"Charlotte must have found out from someone! What about that boyfriend of yours, how much did you tell him?"

"Nothing, I swear!"

"Carla, this is crazy" I intervened. "You have no evidence that it was Danny. Of *course,* it wasn't Danny!"

"But the only other person who knew was… you," Carla said, looking at me.

"Oh great, so you're going to start accusing me now! Look, we don't know who did it, nothing bad came of it in the end, so can't we just forget about it?"

"I wish I could," said Carla, "but what is friendship without trust?"

"I'm sorry you don't feel that you can trust me," said Danny resolutely, and she snatched up her handbag and walked out.

"So that's it, then?" I said to Carla. "The friendship is all over. That's the end of our group."

"I can't trust her, Sam. I'm sorry. If we carried on being friends it wouldn't be real. I'd always be wondering."

"She didn't do it, Carla!" I said.

"How can you be so sure... unless it was you?"

"Come on Carla, why would I do that?"

"Well, you've lied before..."

"Yes. Yes, I did. I lied once, to get out of going to a dance class with you two. I still regret it, but I would never have done anything like that if I'd thought it would get one of you in trouble! And anyway, as soon as I got caught out I told the truth. You really think, after all this, that I would still be lying?"

"Who knows how your brain works. You deliberately try to alienate yourself from people, maybe this is one of those things. I suppose it's not your fault; you obviously learnt it from your mum."

"What?" I asked, astonished. "What the hell is that supposed to mean?"

"Oh, come on, like you didn't know! Our mums were best mates last summer, don't you remember? They sat around chatting, having a laugh, having a great time with each other every night. And then suddenly – nothing. You must have wondered why!"

"Well, yes, actually I did wonder, but I suppose I thought it was a bit of a summer thing because we were all round Danny's house all the time. And then Danny's parents started having problems, so that must have got in the way..."

"It shouldn't have got in the way of my mum and your mum, though."

"Well, no. I guess it just fizzled out."

"No, it didn't. They carried on talking on the phone. They talked quite a bit actually, my mum told me. She said they talked about *everything* – all her problems with Graham and your brother, she was always asking for relationship advice. And then one day my mum called your mum, but the line was dead. You know what that means? She blocked her number."

"No way! My mum would never do that!"

"But she did. I didn't believe it at first either. I thought mum was just having problems with her phone, but then she called your mum's number right in front of me. It was blocked all right."

"There must have been a mistake. Why would my mum do that? She would never block anyone's number, not unless they were being horrible to her."

"Are you saying my mum's horrible?"

"Of course not! Jeez, Carla, you're getting so confrontational. It's like you're looking for an argument at every turn!"

"Well it's about time things were all out in the open. Better to argue than to just block someone!"

"I'm sure there's an explanation about our mums, and I'm sure there's one about how Charlotte found out about your business. But even if there isn't, neither of those things had anything to do with me!"

"I just don't know who to trust any more. Everything's been ruined."

"No, it hasn't," I said. "You have a choice in this. But it seems like you've already made it."

I walked out, leaving Carla in our music room, alone.

Friday 5th March 2021

And then there was one. Things have come full circle: I am alone again.

Things at school have been strangely normal. Wilcox is back to his old self, which is very odd after seeing him unleash his alter-ego on the school. You'd have thought he might have lost the respect of his pupils, but I suppose people respect power, and he did successfully banish Oliver Jameson and call an end to his sugar ban, and everyone seems to be happy about that. Don't they see that these are short-term benefits? We might not have to clean up our school and host an obnoxious celebrity, and we might have access to sweets, but we'll never see food like that in our canteen again, and some of us are going to get fatter.

I feel like I'm the only one who can see the big picture. Danny's mind is clogged up with petty grievances she's chosen not to overlook – she could have just let Carla get on with it. Carla's too preoccupied with paranoid suspicions and questionable allegations, allowing them to take over despite the unhappy outcome. Mum was too obsessed with family communication to see that, in the long run, it was only going to drive us apart. Graham was too focussed on respect and discipline to realise that sometimes it's best to let us get our own lives in order. Richard got caught up in Wilcox's hate campaign against Jameson and so failed to see how his actions would affect us, the children. The only one who seems to be operating at every level is, believe it or not, Dad.

The thing is, if you try to have too much control over things, you'll never be happy. Nothing ever goes exactly as planned, and you can't expect to control people's behaviour or beliefs. You just have to get on with it, and that's what Dad does. It might have taken him by surprise when Sophie turned up on his doorstep with Stephanie, but he didn't let it turn his life upside down. He just accepted it, welcomed Stephanie into his home and adapted his life to make sure she could fit in it. That's not a bad way to be, when you think about it. So, I'm just going to let them all get on with it. If they need me, I'll be in the library.

Friday 5th March 1723

The rain hath fallen heavy last night, hurtling toward mine window like hammers thrown by some fell god above. The glass didst threaten to shatter as it trembled under the duress of the relentless attack from the skies. I, too, was trembling, for the damp, 'twas trickling in from such an array of orifices, and I can scarcely find the coin for a fire during waking hours, let alone those in which I should be at rest. But I wast awake still. That thought of Carolina runneth through mine mind like the wind through a never-ending tunnel: constant and omnipotent, like God. I praise thee, Carolina, mine Goddess.

I didst force mine eyes to close and I didst try to block those other senses which doth distract me so from mine precious nightly rest. I didst clutch mine bedclothes so close to mine chest that mine sternum would be bruised by morn. 'Twas but a vain attempt at preserving the heat mine body didst sparingly produce. I didst make some measly attempt at ignoring the ever-intensifying sensation of icy, deathly cold. 'Twas growing on me, in me. 'Twas travelling through me, into me, but didst not ever seem to leave me. As the chill consumed me I didst feel fettered to death.

The cold didst fester inside mine mortal vessel like disease itself. Mine bones didst groweth damp with the cold, mine blood didst sloweth and mine flesh thicken into rock. If, peradventure, I could has't slept but only briefly, I might yet has't made it through the night, or at least gone to rest peaceful and without suffering. But the rain didst persist in pelting away at mine window most insufferably, harder and harder, louder and louder, 'til didst sound like knocking, like some beast 'pon mine door, waiting at the threshold like some ragged dog.

I could not catch a wink for the din, 'twas harassing me, tormenting me, battering those walls that didst armour mine soul. The banging didst persist, now clear enough that it could be nowt but that which presented a solid form. Yes, 'twas a solid form at mine door. 'Twas a visitor. What visitor, at this late hour? Still I didst tremble, as much from fear as from the chill. I didst clutch mine coarse covers close to mine heart and rose cautiously from the hard and unforgiving floor I has't the misfortune to calleth mine sleep chamber. Frightened though I surely wast, I didst pull mine door open to greet mine late-night guest.

"Oh, Edmund," she didst cry. 'Twas mine sweet Carolina, half-frozen in her night gown, her face wet with cold rain and hot tears. She didst wrap herself around me, and though I wish'd nothing more than to stayeth in that embrace for all eternity, I didst usher her inside hastily, checking that watching eyes were not lurking in the shadows beyond.

"Mine child, what hath happened?" said I when we were safely inside mine chamber. "Mine love, thou art frozen! Tell thine tale whilst I light the fire." I awoke the dead embers in the hearth, not caring one speck of ash that this might mean I shalt go without kindling during daylight hours. I didst wrap mine bedsheets around her icy, smooth skin as she spoketh.

"He was blind drunk... John... he hath a vast supply of strong ales, all of which he stole from Alexander Bell. He was so rotten, so awful, so entirely void of compassion and sensitivity. It may be that thou has't seen him displeased, and indeed thou might even has't seen him livid, but believe me this, thou hath not seen him at his worst. He is a menacing malt-worm, intent on cruelty and torment! But I wilt endure it no longer! I doth not accept the terms of this marriage! I shalt not stand by!"

"Mine love – thou art a sad, poor thing! How you has't suffered! But no, thou art not a poor thing, not a helpless thing deserving of pity, thou art a brave and wondrous thing that ought to be revered! Thou art marvellous in thine strength, for thou hath escaped his vicious grasp!"

"Ay, me. I didst escape because I was not brave. I was too afeared of his fist to stay a minute longer. 'Twas not brave, but foolish, for in the morrow I must face him once again and be assured he wilt question whither I didst take shelter this night."

"Be not afeared, mine lady. Thou didst say he wast blind drunk, yes?"

"Oh yes, indeed."

"Then perchance he wilt not remember the circumstances of thine departure. He shalt awake in the morrow with a rotten head, and thou shalt be at his side. Thou wilt tell him that the ales he didst drink hadst gone bad – tainted by some chemical the brewer used to clean his barrels. Tell him thou didst know the symptoms from some past experience – thine father, *perhaps. Say that thou didst leave thine home in a desperate attempt to find help, for this bad chemical is akin to poison when consumed by man. Tell him that thou didst come upon a well-lit house and judged that the inhabitant wast yet awake. Twas an apothecarist, up late mixing potions for his day's work. He wast a kind man, who heard thine plea and gave thee this antidote..."*

Here I didst reach into the highest shelf within mine cabinet, retrieving a small, blue bottle of liquid.

"This wilt relieve his aching head but leave him peacefully bedridden for several days. He shalt believeth that he is recovering from an accidental poisoning, and he wilt be grateful that thou didst come to his aid like a true and doting wife. With any luck he shalt treat thee kinder as a result; at the very least he shalt not be suspicious and shalt be too weak in bed to raise his hand to thee or take yet more drink."

Mine Carolina was filled with gratitude and relief for the solution I hadst provided and she didst kiss me tender all through the night. Twas a magical night, but morning came too soon. Oh, sad and dreaded morn! Be gone, sunrise! Give me the night once more!

The plot thickens! Now they are poisoning Duke John Jameson! What a fascinating tale. But I do wonder how well it can possibly end, especially as I have been taught enough of the school's history to know that Carolina and the Duke stayed together and had several children – and of course there's Oliver Jameson, whose family tree can be directly traced back to the Duke, or so they say.

Sunday 7th March 2021

Yesterday was Billy's sixteenth birthday, and after Mum found out the hard way that sixteen is too old for a boy to have a party at home (especially when that boy is sulking about being dumped by Gertie) she and Graham decided to have a more mature celebration and invite a few friends to join us for a meal at the pub.

The Mill on the Hill was the obvious choice, and Graham even gave Arnie the day off work so that he could join us, leaving the regular staff with the slightly daunting task of serving Graham, their boss, and his family. Frogsplash came along too, and I'm pleased to say that things between him and Mum, and him and Billy, are near enough back to normal now. He even seemed to be getting on well with Graham, who is much more of a laid-back sort of person when he's in his pub. You might even say he was on top form, telling anecdotes, talking sport and engaging in what the menfolk call "banter". Yes, it seemed everyone was being entertained by Graham's antics. Everyone except me.

It was Mum, Graham, Arnie, Billy, Frogsplash and me to begin with, and half an hour later we were joined by Hayden and Joshua, who I've known for many years as the other half of Froggo and Billy's friendship group. There was also Harriet (Joshua's girlfriend), Janine (Harriet's best friend) and two new additions to the clan: Ryan and Shirian. I got the impression that Ryan and Shirian are new friends that Billy has recently acquired at school, perhaps during Froggo's dark and dreary *Dolores's Dolorifuge* phase, which really wasn't Billy's cup of tea. Billy is much more into party music, like dance and pop – basically anything that gets people moving but rarely has any meaning to it, and I guess Ryan and Shirian are the same, because they were playing songs on their phones and talking about them a lot. Frogsplash looked a little uncomfortable at this, but he turned his attentions to Hayden, Joshua and the girls and all was well.

It was only when all the food had arrived that we all started talking as one big group rather than separate, slightly nervous sub-groups. Graham asked if everybody was happy with their meals, and then he began a sort of sit-down speech, taking the opportunity to pull focus onto himself while everyone's mouths were too busy masticating to converse.

"You know, it must be nearly ten years I've been running this pub," he began, feigning a wistful look, but I could tell it was all choreographed for his audience. "I remember, because it was an awfully difficult time, my father finally popping his clogs, dealing with the stress of the will and the inheritance, and all the while planning Billy's sixth birthday party. We'd decided to make it a big one, because he'd settled into school by then, and he'd made some friends that he really wanted to invite. So, we hired out a church hall, hired a bouncy castle, put on a magnificent spread of crisps and cakes and booked a pair of highly recommended entertainers.

"So, it's all running very smoothly, the kids are getting high on sugar, playing musical statues, jumping on the bouncy castle, when in come these two clowns, making a remarkable entrance, cartwheeling and tumbling their way into the hall, to the great amusement of the children. They all seemed to be having such a great time, and the clowns were so captivating that us adults were watching them almost as excitedly as the kids. So, between me, Billy's mother and a number of grandparents, aunts and uncles, somehow none of us noticed Billy's absence until it was time for him to blow out the candles of his birthday cake.

"The candles were lit, everyone was waiting, even the clowns! We had turned the lights down low and some people were already half-heartedly murmuring the birthday song when it became apparent that the birthday boy himself was nowhere to be seen! We checked all of the toilets, then the kitchen, and then we started to panic. None of us could remember seeing him for a considerable amount of time, and of all the photos and videos we'd taken of the clowns' performance, he was not in any of them. Eventually we found poor little Billy, tucked right into the corner folds of the bouncy castle, whimpering in fear of the horrifying clowns! Poor lad, all the other kids were laughing – couldn't understand what he was so upset about!"

Everyone laughed, including Billy, and the story triggered a memory for me, too.

"Ah-ha, it all makes sense now!" I said. "Last year on holiday we watched that horror movie with the evil clown... I could have sworn I saw all the colour drain from his face!"

His friends all laughed, and Billy blushed a little, but he didn't seem too embarrassed – boys wind each other up like that all the time, don't they? It was later, when Joshua was telling a funny story about Tiny, the puppy he'd adopted from Max's litter, that Graham asked me to help him carry another round of drinks from the bar. I was a bit nervous – my brief stint as a glass collector at the Mill on the Hill had been borderline traumatic, but Graham had never known how bad that had really been, so I couldn't blame him for this insensitivity. However, when we reached the bar, well out of earshot of the rest of our party, Graham said something which made me feel uncomfortable in an entirely different way. He spoke in low tones and made no eye contact as we walked back with the drinks:

"What were you thinking telling that story about Billy? Making a lad seem like a wimp in front of his mates like that! That was a stupid thing to say, Samantha. Do yourself a favour and don't try to make people laugh, OK? It just makes you sound ridiculous."

I was so stunned I didn't know what to say, not that he'd given me much chance – by the time he'd finished speaking we were already back at the table, where I had to pretend that everything was fine.

I probably wasn't doing a very good job of pretending, though, because I was deep in thought. Had Billy really been that embarrassed? Perhaps Graham had picked up on something that I hadn't. Had everybody else thought that it was an inappropriate story to tell? It was barely even a story – I'd just said that Billy looked scared during a scary movie. It was Graham who'd brought up Billy's clown phobia, although I suppose it's more acceptable to be scared of clowns when you're six rather than fifteen.

How could I be so sure that Billy was OK with me talking about him like that? I wouldn't have minded my mum or my brother saying something like that in front of my friends, but then it's different for boys, isn't it? Graham had said that I'd made Billy seem like a wimp, and that's a shameful thing for a boy. Billy and his friends are always doing these macho wrestling displays in front of each other, and there I was undermining it with a few simple words.

They were talking about football now, which made it a lot easier for me to keep my mouth shut, because I don't follow any of it. I know that Graham follows the football so that he can keep up with conversations with his regular customers, but I don't think he would bother if it weren't for that. He doesn't support a team and when he watches it on TV he never shouts at the screen or gets annoyed with the players and he doesn't even crack a smile when someone scores. They were talking about a premier league player, Liam Fenton, who had been at the top of his game this time last year, but after his wife caught him cheating on her while they were on holiday together she'd divorced him and he'd gone off the rails, partying all the time, missing training sessions and generally playing badly.

Graham seemed to know more about it than any of them, and he was enjoying being the one with all the juicy details. Apparently, Liam had paid for the other woman to travel to Barbados at the same time that he and his wife were going, and that he'd paid for her to stay in the same hotel as them as well, which seems a pretty stupid thing to do. Now he's running the risk of being dropped from the team, and I can't say I feel particularly sorry for him. Graham was entertaining everyone with some jokes he'd heard about Liam Fenton and his poor, unsuspecting wife, who had apparently only found out about the affair due to some incriminating photos in *The Daily View,* a tabloid newspaper that she herself has a weekly fashion segment in.

"How does Giselle Fenton know who the prime minister is?"

"She checks *The Daily View!*"

"How does Giselle Fenton know what year it is?"

"She checks *The Daily View!*"

"How does Giselle Fenton know how to spell her own name?"

You get the idea. They mused that, had the photos been leaked to a paper with a more "intellectual" readership, Giselle would probably still be none the wiser, despite the whole thing happening right under her nose. Graham seemed to be having a right old time with the Giselle jokes, some of which were undoubtedly inappropriate for my ears, but Mum was too busy clearing up. I ought to have reminded her that she was not on shift at the pub and that she shouldn't be lifting a finger, but she obviously felt the need to do her bit, and the backup staff that Graham had brought in for the day seemed very flustered whenever they had to wait on their boss's table, so I suppose she was doing them a favour.

It was only when Graham had gone to the bar again that the slightly offensive Giselle jokes died down and instead a conversation about a certain teacher at their school began. This teacher was widely regarded as a laughingstock because of his regular attempts to relate to his students by appearing to share in their interests and even using the same slang that they do. It all sounded very familiar to me, but I refrained from getting involved in the conversation in case I embarrassed myself, or Billy, any further. It was only when Frogsplash said what I had been thinking that I felt I was allowed to participate.

"That sounds just like Richard!" he said. "He's this bloke who lives with my dad, and he teaches in Sam's school, doesn't he?" he said, inviting me to speak.

"Yeah, he's an absolute nightmare," I said. "He tries way too hard and just ends up making things worse for himself."

"Have you still got the video?" Billy asked me, and I knew he was referring to Richard's rap with Wilcox.

"Well it was never really mine. If I'd have taken the video myself I'd have focussed more on Richard, but my phone had been confiscated that day," I said, secretly hoping that they'd have a bit more respect for me after hearing that I was the sort of rule-breaker who had things confiscated. "But it was such a spectacle pretty much everyone else in the school managed to get some footage, and they could hardly keep it from circulating. This is probably the best one," I said as I scrolled through a few weeks of messages until I found the right video.

They all laughed raucously when they saw it, and most of them asked me to forward it to them so that they could share it on their own social media. They were all keen to know the context – of course they all knew who Oliver Jameson is, and most were aware that he'd paid a few visits to a nearby secondary school, but they wanted to know what he had done to deserve such an unfair dismissal. I was just about to draw out my theories about power struggles and bruised egos when Graham returned, and he looked incredibly sour when he saw that I was now not only contributing to the conversation but very much the centre of it.

My words faltered as I felt his Medusa eyes fix themselves on me, turning my party spirit into stone. Instead of spinning my yarn like a good story-teller, I trailed off with something like "Oh I don't know… must have rubbed someone the wrong way…" while Graham leaned right over me to place the glasses down and, once again, requested my assistance in carrying the rest of them from the bar. He led me away from the safety of the crowd, and I knew I was really in for it this time.

"You're embarrassing yourself, for goodness sake, girl, this day is not about you! Do you really think Billy wanted you, a twelve-year-old girl at his party? The only reason you're here is because me and your mum didn't know what else to do with you. And now you're stealing focus from Billy instead of keeping quiet! I expect you to be quiet, Samantha, that's the only thing you're good at. They're all teenagers, drinking beer and having a good time. They all go to school together, they all know the same people – people you've never even heard of, so they don't need you weaselling your way into their conversation."

"I wasn't!" I said, "Billy asked me a question – he wanted me to get involved!"

"He probably felt sorry for you – sat there in silence, all alone and looking miserable *as usual.* You were probably bringing him down, killing the mood, ruining it for everybody else. Don't kid yourself that any of them care what you have to say. People might be nice to you to make you feel better, but in the long run it's better that you know the truth. You're boring to people like Billy. You're boring to most people. Face it, Samantha, you'll never be the life and soul of any party. It's actually embarrassing, you trying to entertain people like that. It's painfully obvious that you're out of your comfort zone and that you're just desperate for attention. Just stick to what you're good at – staying out of the way."

Monday 8th March 2021

I couldn't sleep at all last night, and I spent most of today in a sleep-like state, almost as though I was out of my own body. Never have I felt so strongly that I don't want to talk to anyone and that, at the same time, I desperately need to talk to someone. Graham's words keep playing back to me, over and over, the most brutal ones seeming to have imprinted themselves on my brain. He had me absolutely spot-on. It's as if somebody had conducted an exhaustive research project on all of the worst things I think about myself, all of my biggest insecurities, and then repeated them all back to me with evidence proving that they are real and that my feelings of insecurity are justified.

Of course, Billy didn't want me there. Of course, all those older kids weren't interested in me. Why do I allow myself to get comfortable in situations like that? I should know my boundaries. I used to know my boundaries, but I became too confident. I was a better person to be around when I wasn't like this. You can't be annoying if you don't say anything. The thing is, people don't really want to hear what you've got to say, they want to have their say. Maybe if I was funny, like Billy. But I could never be like that, I'm too nervous, I can't carry a joke or tell a story like Billy can. That's why he's so popular and I'm not. That's why he's got hundreds of friends to choose from and I've got none left. I'm glad me, Carla and Danny have gone our separate ways, I was kidding myself thinking that we belonged together. Carla belongs in some kind of cool, non-conformist sub-group, Danny belongs in the mainstream spotlight and I belong somewhere deep within the shadows.

Thursday 11th March 2021

I'm doing my best to stay out of the way. Obviously everyone's going to get frustrated with me – I'm the youngest one in the house and I probably don't know half the stuff they have to deal with: paying the bills, taking the dogs to the vets, remembering cousins' birthdays, parents' evenings, endless laundry, not to mention the million other things they must have to do at work! Even Billy has to juggle work and exams right now, whereas I've got nothing to worry about – or at least nothing that anyone could call serious.

And all that is nothing compared to the duties involved in keeping a house in order – I mean, what even is a mortgage? How do you pay the window cleaner? What do you do when the boiler breaks down? And for Graham the stress must be double – no, triple – because he's got this place, his flat above the pub, and the pub itself! There must be constant problems with distributors and brewers and employees and licences, and god knows what else! Who prints the menus? Who organises the quiz every Thursday? How do you know when the meat's gone off? Who do you call when the coffee machine breaks? My head is spinning just thinking about it, and I can't imagine how many other issues there must be!

Friday 12th March 2021

I've reached a really tricky bit in Edmund's diary, so this lunch time when I went to the school library, I attempted to do a bit of research. I was looking for books to help decipher ancient languages, but the only thing I found that was of any interest to me was a guide to deciphering symbolic codes. I had a flick through it just in case it could be of any help, and I stumbled across a beautiful, endearing code called *Lucidia,* which uses symbols inspired by nature and which was created as part of a fictional dystopian novel entitled *Productivity.*

I was so intrigued that I decided to look it up, which was a big mistake because now I want to read *Productivity* instead of Edmund's simple old diary! But I promised myself, and Edmund, that I would finish it, so instead I looked up the premise and made a mental note to read it some other time. It said that *Lucidia* is a code used to communicate anti-establishment ideas amongst a secret society trying to escape an oppressive regime. The code is, they say, remarkable in its complexity, considering that it has never been put to any real use and has only ever existed in this fictional world, which sounds like hell:

"Work and procreation are mandatory for all, apart from the wealthy elite who control the labour system, and there are no arts, only corporate, manual, service and community jobs. Children are cared for by government-run *"Performance Preparation Centres"* which they join at six months old – as soon as they are ready to leave the mother's breast. In these centres, education is directed towards employment and is standardised so that everyone learns exactly the same subjects and exactly the same curriculum. When they turn eighteen they are allocated a job according to their performance in these subjects; they cannot object to or appeal this decision.

"When they reach working age, they must work every day, only accruing time off when they exceed their expected productivity. Productivity is at the heart of all rewards, sanctions and liberties, and is calculated by computers using a seemingly arbitrary formula which fails to consider human factors such as noisy distractions, tiredness, sickness, human error or lack of motivation due to harsh conditions. If they go below ninety per cent productivity their pay will be docked, below seventy and their children will be banned from classes which are likely to gain them rewarding employment. If they go below fifty per cent, they will continue to receive these sanctions and will also be demoted to a lower-paid, lower-satisfaction job."

It sounds horrible and yet oddly possible. As I get older, I realise that freedom is always conditional and that oppression can come from anywhere and in many different forms, often without you even realising it.

Tuesday 16th March 2021

I feel like I can't breathe. Everywhere I go, I'm holding myself in, tucking myself into the smallest spaces, living in hallways waiting until it's safe to walk through doors. If I could, I would squeeze myself between the cracks in the floorboards and let people walk all over me rather than take up even an inch of space. At home, I wait until nobody's in the kitchen before I go to get a drink. If somebody's in the bathroom, I sit and I listen until I'm sure they've left and retreated to another section of the house before I make my move to go in there, even if I'm bursting for a wee. I take baths instead of showers so that I can hear if anybody is outside in the hall. I haven't watched the TV in weeks.

At school I am the ghost of the library. Other people go there in groups to work on projects or help each other finish their homework but I am always alone, only taking up one seat, but often that's one more than I am entitled to. They crowd me out, sometimes two of them squeezing onto one seat and giggling at the absurdity of it as though it's the funniest thing in the world. So, I end their fun by offering up my seat so that they no longer have any need to share. It stops their giggling, but then I have no chair and I must sit on the carpet between two rows of bookshelves, huddled and squished, but undisturbed.

But living in the cracks isn't so bad. There is freedom in anonymity. If only I could be anonymous at home, I might be able to relax. If I stay in my room too much Mum will start sending me messages asking if I'm OK. And then, when I do emerge, she will come straight to me, pretending to start up a casual conversation, but it's so obvious that she's scanning me for signs of upset – one of her children has already moved out so now she'd hyper-sensitive when it comes to any level of detachment. If you hide too much you end up drawing more attention to yourself – there is a fine art to staying in the shadows.

But leaving my room isn't easy. Everywhere in the house I am under the eye. Everything I do is wrong and stupid and irritating and inconsiderate, and I feel so bad about myself because of it. There is no way I could possibly feel any worse about myself, and I'm so scared that I'm going to break under the weight of it. If I make one more mistake, hear one more criticism, feel the shame of one more failure, I might stop being able to do anything at all. The more I fail the more I struggle to do anything other than fail. I mess up and I'm so worried that I'm going to do it again that I can't even think straight.

Yesterday I burnt my toast and Graham told me off because I'd wasted two slices of bread. This morning I accidentally poured orange juice instead of milk into my cereal and then he was really mad because it was such a stupid thing to do that he thought I must have done it on purpose. I can't seem to figure out a way to get things done that won't result in me screwing things up, and I'm so preoccupied worrying about the consequences, terrified of what will happen if I do make a mistake, that I don't pay attention to what I'm doing and then I end up screwing up, just like everyone expects me to. What was that song that Frogsplash liked, the one about being a failure? Well it's finally starting to make sense to me.

Things go through my mind that I used to drive out – things that I could fight off with logical answers, but those answers don't work any more. I thought I couldn't be boring because I had such interesting friends. I thought I couldn't be stupid because I had such clever friends. I thought I couldn't be irritating because I had such down-to-earth friends. I suppose I thought that, if people like that wanted to spend their time with me then I couldn't possibly be all of those things that I thought I was. But since I've been told to my face, since Graham told me to my face that I am everything I always suspected I was, now I know the real reason I've ended up alone again.

It didn't happen how you'd have thought. They didn't just get bored of me and move on. It didn't seem like the break-up was anything to do with me, but that's just it – it wasn't. I'm not interesting enough to cause that level of change. It was the other two that broke it up, because they're the ones that matter, the ones with value and meaning and passion. I was just the weak link. If I wasn't, then why aren't either of them here now? They were the only ones arguing. If they'd both wanted to stay friends with me wouldn't they have argued over me? Even if only one of them had wanted to stay friends with me then that person would be with me at lunchtimes, or at least be talking to me. But they're not.

Monday 22nd March 2021

I arrived home from school at four p.m. and the house was empty apart from the dogs, who greeted me enthusiastically as I entered the hall. I knew that Mum was at work and saw that Billy had left a note by the hooks where we keep our keys, saying that he was going to Hayden's house to revise. I took off my jacket, kicked off my shoes and went to put my lunchbox in the dishwasher. The kitchen was like a bomb site: no one had emptied the dishwasher after it was put on last night, so the leftover mugs and cereal bowls from breakfast were piled up on the worktop.

One of the plates must have had some leftover toast on it, because either Max or Trousers had jumped up and knocked the plate onto the floor, where it had smashed into several shards. The stench of stale garlic and cooked fat from last night's bolognaise made me wonder how bad an abattoir might smell. My stomach churned at the thought of it, and I felt guilty for having eaten it. I went back into the hall to put some shoes back on – my feet needed protection against the scattered chips of ceramic plate; even the tiniest flakes can be surprisingly sharp. I had just slid my feet into my pre-laced trainers when I heard a key in the door. Graham. I remembered he had an early shift today, which means he got up at four-thirty a.m. to bring in the drinks delivery at six.

I would have bolted up the stairs to my room, but my bag was still in the kitchen and I knew that if he saw it in there he would realise that I had gone in there and then left without clearing up the mess, and then he'd have a right to be angry with me. I'm starting to learn how his brain works, I'm actively trying to understand his thought processes, because if I can predict how he's going to react to something then I might just be able to stay one step ahead of him.

But all this forethought had caused me to hesitate, and I was still in the hall when he walked through the door.

"ER!" he said sternly. "I think you're forgetting something – shoes off before you go any further!"

"But there's a broken plate in the kitchen – I was just going to wear them while I clear it up."

"You broke a plate?" he accused as he hung up his jacket and followed me into the kitchen.

"No. It was one of the dogs, they must have jumped up and knocked it off the side. Don't worry, I'll clean it up."

"Bloody hell! The state of this place!" he said when he caught sight of the kitchen. "It's worse than when I left it! I knew it. I knew no one would clear it up. Maybe if you had emptied the dishwasher before you went to school this morning everybody else could have put their dishes in and the dogs wouldn't have broken anything."

"I was about to do it just now…"

"Well it's too late now! The damage is done – LOOK!"

Then he did something I never thought anyone, not even Graham, would do to me. He grabbed my head with both his hands and pushed it downwards so that I was forced to look at the broken plate. I could feel the strength of his grip, and I felt so conscious of my skull, I could picture it in my mind's eye: all white and hollow and grotesquely morbid without any flesh on it. I focussed on that idea, that my skull was right there in between Graham's hands. I felt that he could have crushed it if he had wanted to. It was like my head was in a vice – stuck still, rigidly in place while the rest of me was just left there, attached to it, unsure what to do. There was nothing I could do – I could never have pulled out of his grip. He loosened it, he let go and he continued ranting.

For a few moments I didn't hear any of the words coming out of his mouth, my ears were ringing, my brain felt like it might explode from the great pressure it was feeling. He had tried to squash me with his hands, but instead of feeling squashed, I felt like something was trying to push its way out of me. All the anger and hate had been building up inside my head while it had been stuck there between those hateful, unjust hands. I thought I might scream or attack him. I wanted to. I wanted to tell him that he could never squash me, but I knew that if I said that he would try even harder to prove me wrong.

"What's the rule?" he was saying after I had swallowed down my rage. "Last one to bed loads the dishwasher, first one up empties it!"

"But you were the first one up!" I said foolishly. I hadn't meant to accuse him; I had only wanted to defend myself.

"I was up at four-thirty, long before the dawn. You have no idea how tough that is! And do you know how many times I've emptied the dishwasher at work today? No, of course you don't, because you don't think. You don't think about anybody other than yourself, do you Samantha? You're a selfish girl."

"I'm sorry," I said, "I didn't have time this morning, I had to get the bus…" I thought of Billy, who doesn't have to get up as early as I do, who doesn't have a bus schedule to keep to, and who was almost definitely the one who left the unfinished toast in the first place. But I knew better than to say any of that. I went to get the dustpan and brush.

"I told you, it's TOO LATE," Graham said, and he snatched it out of my hand. "There's no point you doing it now!"

"What about the dishwasher?"

"I was the first one up," he said, seething, his jaw clenched and his mouth in a vicious snarl, "I'll empty the dishwasher."

I wished he'd have let me do it. I knew that him emptying the dishwasher gave him the right to be angry with me for days, perhaps even a week.

Tuesday 23rd March 2021

I knew that Graham would be coming home at five p.m. today – an hour before Mum but an hour after me, giving me just enough time to make the house, and especially the kitchen, as clean and tidy as possible. Graham works predominantly in a kitchen, and the glasses and dishes probably pile up pretty quickly, so the last thing he'd want to come home to is more of the same. And he must have been tired after that early start yesterday – we all get cranky when we haven't had enough sleep. So as soon as I got home, I took off my shoes, hung up my coat and got to work.

I emptied the dishwasher first thing this morning, not wanting to make the same mistake twice, but there were plenty of other chores that needed doing. There were old newspapers all over the kitchen table, the olive oil had been left on the side and beneath it a smear of grease stained the wooden worktop. A trickle of something sticky had dripped down the front of one of the cupboard doors and collected particles of dirt as it had dried. The dogs had splashed their water all around the bowl and there were three different chargers plugged into sockets that were a bit too close to the sink for safety. There was a mini mountain of dried-up, used teabags next to the kettle and three tea-stained spoons lay motionless at its base like fallen mountaineers.

The more I cleaned up the more I noticed other things that needed cleaning up. There was a tray of prawns in the fridge a week out of date. A pile of junk mail sat unopened next to the fruit bowl and a large, empty pickle jar sat rudely in the sink like a fat toad. I wondered if our house always looked like this, and whether our guests thought we were filthy scumbags. When you think about it, it's a strange thing to judge people based on the tidiness of their house. We all use things; they're going to get dirty – so what?

I remember going round my old friend Summer's house for dinner one time, and her mum was obsessed with the appearance of her house. It was full of these awful, tacky ornaments, all arranged in clusters despite the fact that their styles were horribly mismatched. She had china cherubs, swans made out of crystal glass, plastic pigs wearing an array of different outfits, creepy porcelain dolls, decorative plates with floral patterns, fake, fluffy kittens curled up in wicker baskets and giant horses made of polished wood. She was always dusting all of it, as if that was going to make it look any better. We had pizza and garlic bread for dinner, but we had to eat it with a knife and fork, which was very alien to me. If anything, it made more mess, because cutting crusts with a knife makes lots of crumbs.

Summer's mum would be wiping the table and sweeping the floor all around us while we were still eating. At the time, I just found it really off-putting but now, when I think about it, it's really sad. Imagine cleaning up before the mess has finished being made! It's basically putting cleaning before actual living. If you can't even enjoy your meal without worrying about the mess you're making then you're going to struggle to enjoy anything. Poor Summer, I bet her mum never let her do painting or play out in the rain or bake cakes or anything!

I think life is too short to obsess over tidiness – why make the bed when you could be sat in your bed reading a book? But there is a balance to be struck – the dishwasher has to be emptied, clothes have to be washed and dried, if you spill a drink you have to mop it up. And sometimes, for the sake of a peaceful home life, it's best to clean absolutely everything, because not everybody has the same standards of cleanliness as you. So, I put everything in its place, threw away the junk, disinfected everything and vacuumed the carpets and sofas, even though Max and Trousers barked ferociously at the hoover the entire time.

I retreated to the secluded tranquillity of my room just before five, safe in the knowledge that Graham couldn't possibly find fault with my afternoon's work. I should have thought it through more carefully. This is what I always do – I focus too much on one thing, and then I only consider one eventuality. Today I focussed too much on a clean, tidy house, and I became so consumed with the minor details of tidiness that my small little mind became closed to the much more major consequences of my actions.

I was in my room, sat at my desk pretending to focus on my homework, but really I was just listening. Whenever Graham comes home, but especially when I'm the only one he comes home to, I listen very carefully. I listen, hoping to sense his mood from the pace of his step, the way he closes – or slams – the door, any sighs or disgruntled mumbling, and his choice of words when he greets the barking dogs. I heard his rapid footsteps crunching on the gravel, heard his key in the door, heard him slam it shut behind him as the dogs went running into the hall. I heard short-tempered imprecations as he shooed them away, called them filthy, told them to leave him alone. He unzipped his jacket and huffed impatiently as the dogs jumped up at him, making it difficult to take the jacket off.

"Get DOWN!" he warned them.

He went straight to the kitchen, where the sounds of his movements became indistinct. I could tell he was moving around a lot, opening and closing the fridge, looking in cupboards – or maybe drawers. Had he noticed my cleaning effort? I had worked tirelessly this past hour to make him an offering, but was it good enough to appease the angry god? Then I heard slamming – definitely drawers, kitchen drawers opening, and slamming shut, louder and louder like thunder, raging like a storm orchestrated by some angry, omnipotent overseer.

"WHERE ARE THEY?" he roared. "WHERE IS IT?" I thought that I could hear him seething, but how do you hear a thing like that? Maybe I felt it vibrating through the ceiling up to my floorboards, or perhaps the heat of his rage was rising, prickling my sense of touch without me even having to press my fingertip to it. Perhaps I could smell it, sour and full of loathing, like the back of a bin lorry on a steaming hot day. I was so tense I felt my jaw clamp down hard on my tongue until it bled. I could taste my own blood now, metallic and raw: the taste of fear. All that was left to do was to see it, and I knew it wouldn't be long, because he was on a time limit: he would have to let this out before everyone else got home.

I heard him ascend the stairs rapidly, heavy-footed with determination. I swallowed the blood from my tongue.

"WHAT HAVE YOU DONE?" he shouted as he hammered his fists balefully against my door. I didn't let myself think about what was happening before I ran to open it, willing this all to be over as soon as possible.

"WHAT HAVE YOU DONE WITH ALL MY STUFF?" he was still shouting, even though the door was now wide open, and I was stood right in front of him.

"Nothing!" I said. "All I did was tidy up!"

"My charger. What have you done with it? You've hidden it."

"There were lots of chargers plugged in all over the kitchen. I put them all in the drawer."

"So, you admit it? You hid my charger!"

"No! I tidied it away! It will be in the top drawer beneath the microwave."

"And my post? I had a stack of letters next to the fruit bowl."

"Oh… I thought that was just junk…"

"JUNK? Those were important documents! I needed those! Who are you to decide what's junk? Did they have your name on them?!"

"No… I just thought, if they were important documents, they'd have been put in a safe place."

"Oh, so it's my fault, is it? You're saying it's my fault for not putting them somewhere safe!"

"No, I'm not, I just…"

"The newspapers on the table… what about them?"

"They were really old. You must have read them… I thought you must have read them, I…"

"I was saving them," he said gravely, coldly. "There was a special offer: buy the paper every day for two weeks and get thirty per cent off a holiday for a family of four. But now, nothing. No more holiday. No one's going, and that's all your fault. You can be the one to tell Billy and your mum. Imagine how disappointed they'll be. Your mum works full time and runs her own business on the side – do you have any idea how stressful that is? And Billy, he's sitting the most important, stressful exams of his life and studying really hard to pass them. They both deserve a holiday now more than ever, and thanks to you they're not getting one."

"They're in the recycling! The newspapers and your letters – they're all in the recycling, I'll get them back."

I hurried down the stairs and into the kitchen. In the black crate we use for recyclable waste was a stack of fourteen newspapers, a scattered pile of unopened post, and on top of them an empty pickle jar and an empty tray of prawns. Graham picked up the jar first.

"THIS was in the sink. I was saving it for my mother. She makes her own pickles."

It was hard to understand his anger. He was getting worked up over *pickles,* and the idea of his mum making them seemed so kindly and quaint that it made me unsure. If his mum was sweet enough to make pickles, then how could any of this be real?

"I'm sorry," I said, "I didn't know…"

"LIAR! We had them at Christmas! You said you liked them…"

"I forgot! That was ages ago!"

"And now look – there's pickle vinegar all over my letters, and the newspapers. I hardly think I'll be able to use those vouchers now! And what's this doing in here? Did you eat my prawns?"

He held the empty plastic tray of prawns up accusingly. I had thrown them in the bin and rinsed the tray for recycling. I thought I was doing a good thing, but I know now that I was wrong.

"I'm sorry, I chucked them away. But they were out of date. Look!"

I went to the main bin to retrieve the film lid that had sealed the top of the prawn packet. There it was, on top of our rotting garbage, including a pile of uneaten, shell-on, raw king prawns. They were starting to smell pretty bad.

"Look," I said again, "Use by 16th March 2021."

"They had been in the freezer for ten days," he said coldly. "I took them out to thaw this morning. I see how adept you are at reading food packaging, why don't you read that bit for me too?" he asked, pointing at the price printed on the film.

"Six pounds," I read out loud.

"And that's six pounds you owe me. As for this holiday… I'll have to find some other way for you to repay me for that."

"I can dry off the papers! I can!" I rummaged in the recycling crate, gathering up all of the old newspapers, but Graham snatched them out of my hands and ripped them all up with malign purposefulness.

"It was going to be a surprise for your birthday," he spoke to me in the same tone that a teacher talks to a student that they really don't like, a scholar forced to educate a spoilt little brat. "It was a treat for all of you, of course, but I was going to book it on your birthday. Ten days in sunny Spain. Your mum really needed it after the year she's had. And Billy – it was going to be his first time abroad! Every year for his mother's birthday we would go to the same boring little cottage in Cornwall. Most of the time it rained, and he'd go back to school white as a sheet while his friends all had glorious tans. And they knew what it meant: he was too poor to go on a proper holiday.

"He still is too poor, but when I saw this offer I thought maybe, just maybe, I could scrape together enough money to finally give him the holiday he deserves. He's worked so hard revising for his exams, and he's old enough to enjoy the sports bars and the cocktails and really let loose – it was going to be perfect. And Frogsplash – he'd have loved it! They'd have had a great time together, and your mum would have been so pleased to spend all that time with him. It might even have been the final nudge he needed to move back in here, and you know how much your mum wants that."

"Hang on a minute," I said, "how could Frogsplash come if it's only for a family of four?"

"Like I said, it was going to be a treat for all of you, not for me. Arnie's off travelling this summer, so he can't stay and watch the pub. And anyway, someone needs to stay here and look after the dogs. I've got too many responsibilities to be able to go off on holiday. I'm staying here, and so are all of you, now that you've ruined it all. How do you think they're going to feel when they find out what could have been? I think they'll be devastated."

I began to cry. Of course, they would be devastated. What had I done? An amazing holiday in a beautiful, hot country, a chance for Mum and Frogsplash to bury the hatchet, a chance for them *and* Billy to all let loose after a stressful year, and ten whole days without Graham looking over my shoulder! It would have been bliss, but I threw it all away.

"Maybe," I said through thick, snotty tears, "maybe it would be best if they don't find out. I mean, they'd all be happier if they had never known about it, wouldn't they?"

"Hmm… so you want to lie to them? Very well. It will have to be our little secret. Go on then, you'd better get back to your room. Your mother will be home soon, and if she sees you like that she'll wonder why you've been crying – you wouldn't want that, would you? I'll dispose of these," he said, scooping up the shreds of newspaper, still soggy from the pickle vinegar I'd stupidly spilled on them. I went upstairs, shut myself in my room and cried for a long, long time.

Wednesday 31st March 2021

FROM BAD TO WORSE: ISOLATION, INTIMIDATION, STARVATION AND DESPERATION

Girl, 12, is sentenced to two weeks of harrowing solitary confinement when she learns that she will be in the care of her irascible tormentor for the duration of the Easter holidays.

Mum broke the news on Sunday that she couldn't get any time off work for Easter. She's already used up too much of her holiday taking time off to make and sell her wine at the pub.

"I know it's tough at the moment," she said consolingly, "but this is what it's like starting up a business: you've got to put in the hours, make some sacrifices, do whatever you can to get it off the ground. If all goes according to plan, then in a few years' time we'll be on easy street and then it will all have been worth it! Anyway, you won't be on your own: Arnie's working all hours at the pub trying to save up for his trip to Thailand, so Graham's managed to book some time off. I'm sure he'll be busy helping Billy prepare for his exams, but he's always got time for you, Sammy."

But Billy has been out of the house as much as if it were term time. The school stays open over Easter so that GCSE and A Level students still have access to the library, art studios and other resources. So, Billy's meeting Froggo, Hayden and Joshua there every day, and I can't say I blame him. I would give anything to have somewhere to go. I know now that nothing I do is right. I leave things messy; Graham gets angry. I tidy things up, Graham gets angry. The best thing I can do is to show no signs of existing, that way he can't possibly blame me for anything.

I get up early and have breakfast while Mum and Billy are still here. When they're here everything is normal, and I feel safe. I fill up two big bottles of water and take them up to my room. I would bring snacks as well, but Graham says I'm not allowed to eat in my room. He says adults don't eat in their rooms so I shouldn't either. He doesn't even like it when we all eat together in the living room, although he lets us sometimes, when he's trying to be more reasonable. I stay in my room all day: reading, working on school projects, watching movies, organising my shelves, clearing out my wardrobe, trying on different outfits, even practising hair tutorials I've seen online.

I manage to pass the time, but it's slow and lonely, and it gets harder to distract myself when my stomach starts to rumble. I tell myself that I don't need to eat because I'm barely even moving and am therefore not burning any calories, but it doesn't help much. I spend a lot of time listening, although I'm not sure why. I listen to Graham's movements; I like to know when he's near because if he's going to knock on my door then I would rather be prepared. So far, thankfully, he hasn't, but every time I hear the floorboard creak outside my door, I stop concentrating on what I'm doing, and my heart begins to race. Sometimes I think he hovers on the landing just to intimidate me, but I know that's just stupid.

At dinner we all eat together. Mum talks about her day at work, Billy talks about his revision, Mum asks him how Frogsplash has been getting on and Graham and I pretend everything is normal. Graham will have to work the long bank holiday weekend as the pub will be busy, and as Mum plans to be there too (and for some reason she still gets nervous about leaving me on my own) I get to spend all four days at Dad's. I don't care if it's forty-eight hours of baby TV, cringe-watching American teen movies, self-important layman's football analyses and Richard's poetic guitar playing – I can't *wait!*

Tuesday 6th April 2021

It was a nice, normal weekend at Dad's, and it made me realise just how over-dramatic I've been lately. Yes, things are tense at home, but there's a lot going on. Mum's working and trying to start up her own business, Graham's running an entire pub on his own, and he's got the flat to think about, plus they're trying to save up for a bigger house. Not everybody can be as laid-back as Dad! It was Stephanie's birthday last weekend, so to make up for the fact that Dad had missed that, Sophie allowed him to have Steph for the whole of the bank holiday weekend. We did presents and cake even though it just confused her because in her mind her birthday was ages ago.

Richard was on the cusp of a new phase: cooking. There has to be some kind of irony in seeing him in the kitchen, following word for word an Oliver Jameson recipe, but I suppose it only confirmed what I had already suspected: that Richard's resentment towards Jameson was rooted in jealousy. Oliver Jameson was impressive to Richard, and, deep down, Richard wished he could have been more like him. I decided not to point this out directly, and instead approached the subject from a different angle.

"So, do you have any regrets about doing that rap with Wilcox?"

"I'll admit it wasn't my wisest move," he said earnestly, "especially now the school board are carrying out an investigation…"

"NOOO!" I said. "Really?!"

"Afraid so," he said, "but I think it's mostly about Wilcox. Whatever my involvement was, it was still his idea, and as the head teacher he's got to take more responsibility."

"So, you think it'll be OK?"

"For me it will. They asked me a couple of questions, I told them the truth and that was that. But Wilcox – they've been in and out of his office for weeks!"

"Oh wow. Well that'll teach him to act like he owns the place! He won't be so sure of himself now!"

Richard is undoubtedly a flawed human being, but I don't think he deserves to be punished for being led astray by Wilcox – he's the head, he should have known better! On Sunday, Richard found a recipe for chocolate nest cakes that was easy enough for me and Steph to make. He let us use all his new cooking equipment and he didn't do that annoying thing that most adults do – interfering when you're making something because they think they can do it better. He let us make a complete mess of the kitchen and it didn't stress him out at all.

It was a fun recipe: you coat a bowl of dry wheat cereal in melted chocolate and then you form it into a nest shape in the cake cases. Then you add some sugar-coated chocolate eggs and a little chick made out of fondant icing and you're done! They looked amazing (although Stephanie's were a bit haphazard) and they tasted great. Stephanie was hesitant to eat hers because she was worried about hurting the chick, but when she saw how much I was enjoying mine she was swiftly persuaded.

It was nice of Richard to plan an activity for me and Stephanie, and Dad and Frogsplash were grateful for a break from *The Pirates of Pickle Lane* so that they could watch the football and Dad could get some rest after two days in a row of getting woken up before six a.m. by Stephanie. I had a good Easter, but now I'm back at home, hiding in my room, and I need escapism. I think it's time to check in on my old friends Edmund and Carolina.

Wednesday 7th April 1723

Carolina and I art a pair of sinful lovers, but we doth care not. We art not designers of our own circumstances, so instead we doth doctor them. We art skilled and clever doctors, and we administer the most potent of medicines to those that doth require the severest of alterations to mind and body. The Duke is a most damaged patient, but we art endowed with the necessary tools to give him the treatment he is wanting. Oft he requires sedation, and tis of mere coincidence that this doth leave Carolina and I free to spend our days alone, together.

"But what," spoketh mine Carolina, "what if't be true that another school master hither spies us sharing in each other's company? What then wilt our observer telleth John?"

"Worry not," said I, "for John is no friend to the masters at his school. Those fellows spare no love for him. 'Tis true we art segregated, caged like feral beasts, but we art cousins bound by that shared misfortune of having crossed paths with the devil Duke, and alas, having been played by him so horribly. We art disallowed the joy of sharing our feelings with one another, for the Duke doth trust us not. He knoweth that which wilt cometh if the lot of us should join forces. We would collude against our evil master. We would find strength in our numbers and our hatred, and we would surely form an organised mutiny. The Duke separates us to weaken us: alone we art but weak and isolated links of a chain that would be strong.

"But worry not, mine sweet lady, for us school masters art united by the misery and the contempt which fill our hearts and make them disloyal to the Duke. We art all driven by the vicious treatment he hath offered us these past few years. Mine peers would nev'r inform upon us, for we art not the enemy hither."

"Thou doth not understand!" said she, "the Duke hath power ov'r those folk! A power which they would not square against! Thou knoweth too little of that man's capacity to inflict pain. He is a master of torture and

suffering, and he would use those skills to draw the truth from any suspect or witness. For as long as the Duke lives we art not safe!"

"I has't in mine possession all the medicines needed to suppress the Duke's interest in our affairs," said I.

"But wilt he not harbour suspicions?" said she. "Our meetings art frequent, and I doth adore them so. I must declare that I could not wend a day without them, just as I could not wend a day without the beating of mine heart! But that which mine heart desires is thee, and that which it needeth is life. I fear the former might impede the latter, for the Duke wilt sooner have us die than allow us to shame him with our lover's meetings."

"Thou liveth in fear of the man," said I. "And mine love, I censure thee not for this hither precautionary concern, but the Duke be not a murderer! Tis true the man is cruel and unfeeling, but he would not has't the pair of us killed. His punishment of choosing is labour, for there be profit in such a sentence. A man doth bring no financial yield if he is dead, and nor does woman. Should the Duke discover the truth of our romance, he would has't us work off our debt to him, I am sure."

"Matters of the heart cannot be bought nor compensated with cheap coin nor cheap labour!" said she desperately. "And anyhow, I wilt not serve that man. I must be free of him. We must be free of him. I long to be happy with thee, Edmund! But even lovers as perfect as us can nev'r be blissful when a man such as the Duke looketh so darkly ov'r our shoulders with the fullest malice of his heart. He wilt make us suffer 'til our passions for each other have long since expired, and then he wilt make us suffer for many years more."

"Thou art correct, mine sweet flower," said I, though gravely I didst speaketh hither. "Thou must be rid of him. We must be rid of him. We wilt rid ourselves of him forthwith."

Did I read that right? Did I misinterpret the old language? Or are my dear Edmund and his sweet Carolina plotting a murder?

Monday 12th April 2021

It has been a long and gruelling two weeks, and to top it all off they made today an INSET day, so I don't go back to school until tomorrow. But I have survived and being so confined and isolated I have been able to complete all my homework assignments as well as reading Edmund's diary. Of course, I am eager to find out what happens next, but it takes an incredibly long time to decipher his old, faded handwriting, and although I've read at least twenty pages ahead, he has made no further mention of his and Carolina's plans to rid themselves of the Duke. Part of me wants them to kill him – is that wrong? Something about the idea of a manipulative tormentor finally getting his comeuppance really appeals to me.

Graham has been relentless. Yesterday he had a go at me for leaving a little puff of foamy bubbles in the tub after I'd drained it. He made me go back and rinse the bathtub right in front him until he was satisfied that it was free of residual foam. I didn't even realise you were supposed to do that – bubbles are clean, aren't they? But I don't argue with him any more. I'm looking forward to going back to school, but only because I have more freedom there than I do at home. I suppose I'm looking forward to seeing Carla and Danny, even if I don't actually speak to them, it will just be nice to see their faces.

Tuesday 13th April 2021

Being a Tuesday, the first lesson of the day was Biology, the only lesson that me, Danny and Carla all have together. I was the first one to arrive out of the whole class, and I guessed that most people were hanging around by the lockers after morning registration, catching up with friends after two weeks apart, getting the latest gossip or, in the case of Rachel's gang, boasting about their holidays to New York, Costa Rica and the like. Even Mr Pinter hadn't arrived when, less than a minute after I'd unpacked my books, Carla walked through the entrance. For a brief moment I thought it was going to be hugely awkward: I imagined she was going to sit down right next to me in her usual spot and that we would just sit there in stubborn silence until the lesson began, but she broke the silence almost immediately.

"Sam?" she said as she approached our shared desk, "Sam, are you OK?"

"What do you mean?" I said, slightly panicked by her tone.

"You look so different! You're so much thinner!"

"Oh... oh really?" I said. I had wondered why my school skirt had felt so loose this morning, but I thought I must have just forgotten what it feels like to wear my uniform. I thought about all the days I'd spent in my room with my stomach rumbling, and I thought about telling Carla, but it was hard to explain. I didn't think she would understand why I would rather starve than sit in the kitchen and eat with Graham, because I have no reason to be scared of Graham – not really. He's never done anything to hurt me, he's never even threatened to do anything like that, so it all seemed a bit silly.

"I have been cutting down on the snacks," I explained. "Just trying to lose the winter weight, you know?"

"Well you've lost it very quickly!" she said.

"Maybe you just didn't notice before. Sometimes when you haven't seen someone for a while you suddenly notice a change."

"True," she said. "Well as long as you're not taking Oliver Jameson's war on snacks too seriously. You don't have to any more, remember what Wilcox said? *His reign of terror is over!*"

It didn't take long for the two of us to get completely back to normal. Even when Pinter arrived, we carried on chatting in whispers and, perhaps because I was so relieved to have Carla back, I giggled more than I have done in any lesson ever.

"So, you're sure everything's OK?" she asked me again at lunchtime. She could obviously sense something, even through all of the giggles, so I told her a small part of the truth.

"Well, it has been a bit stressful at home. Mum's trying to work two jobs and she's probably still upset about Froggo moving out, Billy's stressing about his exams and Graham's always stressed about the pub, and I don't think they've got very far saving up for a bigger house."

"Do they even need one? Give it a couple of years and Billy and Frogsplash will be off to university! I've been sharing a room with Rosie all my life, but next year Louisa's going to be living in student accommodation and I'll get her room!"

"Well of course Louisa's going to university! But Billy and Frogsplash might not. Graham doesn't think Froggo's even going to make it to A Level! And besides, a couple of years is a long time to live in such cramped conditions."

"But it's not cramped though, is it? Your brother's not living at home!"

"I know, but I think Mum's hoping that if we get a bigger place with a room for each of us then he might move back in. She really misses him."

"I can understand that. My mum's going to go crazy when Louisa leaves, and she wants to go to Manchester – that's hours away!"

"She'll probably move back in after uni though, won't she? I mean, how many twenty-one-year-olds can afford their own place?"

"Oh don't, Sam, you're ruining the dream! She'll move back home, and I'll have to move back in with Rosie!"

"Not if Rosie goes to university!"

"That's true! Although at the moment her only ambition is to be a reality TV star... have you been watching *The Geraldine Tuck Experience*? I can't believe that woman's got her own show. It's so dreadful, but Rosie's got me addicted!"

"Um... I haven't been keeping up with much TV lately," I said nervously, thinking about all those hours spent in silence in my room.

"God, you must have been so bored over Easter! I was bored, too, and it was all my fault. I was so stupid, Sam, I'm sorry. If it weren't for me being so stubborn, we could have spent those two weeks together! And maybe we would still have Danny, too."

"Don't be sorry!" I said. "We all made mistakes, but our biggest mistake was not resolving things sooner."

"Too true," she said, "but I wasn't just being stubborn, at least not with Danny. I thought about it long and hard. I went through it in my head over and over again, trying to figure out how Charlotte Henderson could have known. It doesn't even matter now – not really. But it does, because even though nothing ever came of it, it matters because somebody must have told her, and they must have had ill intentions when they did it. If it was anyone but Danny I wouldn't care... but what if it was?"

"And what if it wasn't?" I said. "If it wasn't her then look at what you've wasted!"

"I know, I know! But I just can't shake the feeling. As much as I do miss her, I know that if I made up with her now it wouldn't be the same. I would always have my suspicions, and I don't want to treat a friend that way. Total trust, total truth – that's what I want."

I felt guilty because I hadn't told her the whole truth about my home life, but that revelation would just have to wait.

"I understand," I said, "and I refuse to lose you again, so let's just leave it there, shall we? Whatever will be, will be. So come on, you must have been working on some songs since we last spoke, let me hear them! Don't tell me you've been wasting all this time watching reality TV!"

305

Friday 16ᵗʰ April 2021

As it happens, Carla has been working on some songs, and she's been anxiously deliberating over whether or not to audition for a rock band in the year above called *The Sylphs*. Apparently, their lead singer/guitarist quit last term and they're looking for a replacement, but Carla's worried she's not good enough because she's too young and she doesn't know any of their songs. Usually Carla is super confident, but she seems nervous now. It's hard to get back up on your feet when you don't have any friends for support, but I'm here now.

She told me about this song she's been working on. She wouldn't let me hear it because it's not quite finished yet, but she described it as a "fantasy ballad". I had to confess that, although I'd heard the word "ballad" before, I had always assumed it was just another word for "song".

"It's a type of song," Carla explained. "A ballad is not just any song – it's a song that tells a story."

"I can't think of many songs that do that," I said, "it must be pretty special!"

"I don't know," she said, "I think maybe it's trying *too hard* to be special. Who wants to hear a song that tells a story these days? It's self-indulgent is what it is…"

"*I* want to hear it!" I said. "The only self-indulgence in writing a ballad is not letting anyone else hear it!"

"OK, well like I say, it's not ready yet, but I suppose I could tell you the story. It's about a girl called Grace who is desperately in love with a boy called Glenn. As young children they were best friends and they had the happiest times of Grace's life, but adolescence treats them rather differently. Glenn develops into a remarkably good-looking teenager, whereas Grace turns from plain to ugly as she grows older. She looks on in pain as Glenn dates a string of attractive girlfriends, but even they aren't beautiful enough for Glenn, and he quickly becomes bored of each of them.

"Grace becomes mad with love and desperation, and she hears voices on the wind which tell of a powerful witch who will grant wishes to those who are in deep emotional turmoil. Grace seeks out the witch and begs her to make her appear beautiful to Glenn and to make him want her forever, unlike the short-lived girlfriends he has tired of so swiftly. The witch grants the wish, but there is a horrible twist. She turns Grace into a beautiful butterfly, and Glenn is instantly captivated by her remarkable appearance. He wants to have her forever, just as Grace wished, and he traps her in a jar to keep by his bed.

"Glenn continues to have meaningless flings with pretty women, and Grace is forced to watch as he takes a different girl to bed every night. But what's worse is when he finally falls in love, and Grace has no choice but to watch him settle down with this woman, Rose. When they move in together, Rose decides that this remarkable butterfly is too stunning to be wasted in a jar on the bedside and decides that it must be displayed more proudly. She pins Grace by the wings to the wall above the mantelpiece, where she lives forever, watching her only love have children and grow old with another woman.

"Flipping heck!" I said. "That's so dark! I've never heard anything like it! But how on Earth are you going to fit that all into a song?"

"Is it stupid?" she asked. "It's too *different* isn't it?"

"No!" I said. "No, it's brilliant! It's brilliant-different! Since when did you care about being different anyway?"

"Oh, I don't... not really. Rosie keeps calling me a weirdo whenever she hears me practising..."

"Don't listen to *her!* She thinks Geraldine Tuck is a decent role model! Anyway, that's just what siblings do – they wind each other up, but I bet if she heard you play it in front of an audience she'd be cheering louder than anyone else."

"I doubt that! I don't know why I mentioned the stupid song in the first place, even if I do get into The Sylphs, I'll be playing their songs, not mine."

"You should audition for them with your song. 'The Ballad of Grace and Glenn' – they'll be blown away! There's no way they would turn you down."

"But it's not ready!"

"When are the auditions?"

"Monday."

"Well then you'd better get ready! You made me audition for the Christmas play with less than a minute to prepare, so I'm afraid you haven't got a leg to stand on! If you don't want to practise in front of me that's fine, I'll leave you to it. In fact, I insist. I need to go to the library anyway," I lied. "I believe in you, Carla, you're amazing. Don't waste this opportunity!"

To make sure she followed through I went with her to the instruments room to collect her guitar. I made her promise to work on her song and then I departed for the library, even though I was well ahead on my assignments thanks to the Easter of solitude. Carla would have done the exact same thing for me, and even though I was on my own in the library once again, I was not alone.

Monday 19th April 2021

Today was the day of Carla's audition with The Sylphs, and it was held in the music room where she, Danny and I used to spend our lunchtimes. I guessed that she had suggested the location; it had been her who first introduced it to me as her secret hideout, and it was the perfect place to hold auditions: fully soundproofed and kitted out with the highest quality music equipment. I wondered then if Carla and The Sylphs would adopt it as their own spot, and I felt a twang of loss just thinking about it.

I could tell Carla didn't really want me there, but that was OK because if I was auditioning for something I know it would put me off having one of my friends watching. Nevertheless, I was keen to show some support (and to make sure she didn't try to back out at the last minute) so I escorted her to the room, wished her luck and waited patiently outside the door, unable to hear a single note from the vacuum of the room within.

I couldn't help but think selfish thoughts. I had only just got Carla back, if she got into this band, I might lose her all over again. I was so miserable and isolated without her, and having no social life gave me too much time to think about my home life, and that's pretty miserable, too. But I want her to succeed because I want her to be happy. I'm not one of those people who wants everyone else to be miserable whenever they are. I'm not like Graham. Graham always has to control the mood. Like at the pub on Billy's birthday, it had to be him telling stories and making people laugh. And when he's angry, he can't just be angry, he has to spread it around like some vicious virus. Graham *is* a vicious virus, and he's infected our entire house.

Ten minutes after Carla walked in she came back out looking extremely chuffed. "I did it!" she said, "I'm in! They loved the song and they want to learn it straight away. You were right, Sam, thank you so much for making me do it!"

"Don't thank me, you're the one who did it! Well done, Carla, I'm so happy for you!"

We walked along the corridor, away from the music room, and I wondered if I would ever step foot in it again.

Friday 23rd April 2021

Both Frogsplash and Billy came to dinner at home this evening, and there was only one topic of conversation on the menu: their upcoming GCSEs and the impact the results would have on their futures.

"I need all A to Cs to get into Brigley House," Frogsplash was saying.

"Brigley House? What's that?" Mum asked.

"It's a sixth-form college. Dad's been helping me research them."

"Sixth-form college!" Graham scoffed. "Sixth-form colleges are for second-rate students looking for an easy ride. Don't tell me you're thinking of applying for sixth-form college as well, Billy?"

"Well, no, I want to stay at Maplewood Academy," said Billy. "Ryan and Shirian are definitely going to stay and we want to do all the same subjects, so we'll get to be in class together."

"That's my boy, stay in school. Young lads like you need that kind of structure and discipline, otherwise they go off the rails," said Graham, looking pointedly at Frogsplash.

"I didn't know you were thinking of college," Mum said guiltily, as though it was her fault she hasn't spent much time with Froggo lately. "I don't know much about them actually."

"I'll fill you in," Graham said sententiously. "They're glorified detention centres for layabouts with bad attitudes. Too lazy for school, too lazy for work, they go to these colleges where nobody can tell them off for being late or not turning up at all, nobody cares how scruffy they look or how disrespectfully they behave, no one even cares if they pass their exams – and that's the problem. They turn up if they want to, pay attention if they want to, work if they want to. Do you really think your son is going to thrive in that environment? This one here? He won't even bother to roll out of bed – you mark my words!"

"It doesn't sound like a great idea, Froggo," Mum said worriedly. "School is supposed to prepare you for adult life. This sounds like a step in the wrong direction."

"No, it's not!" Frogsplash said defiantly. "Sixth-form college is all about self-discipline: getting out of bed in the morning because you want to succeed, not because you're scared that some teacher's going to shout at you. It's about taking responsibility for yourself."

"That's all well and good," said Graham, "but who's going to take responsibility when you fail? You'll lose interest, stop turning up, come out of it with zero qualifications, and it'll be up to me and your mum to carry on supporting you because you can't get a job."

"Hang on, Dad," Billy cut in, "you don't have any A Levels and you've always had a job!"

"Ah, but I've always had the pub. When I was your age, I already knew that I was going to inherit The Mill on the Hill. It would have been pointless to stay in school when my dad had a job ready and waiting for me. But times have changed. You need qualifications to stay ahead of the game. We get all these foreigners coming over here taking the low-paid jobs, so you guys need to have something more to offer. You need to prove that you're more valuable in the job market."

"I don't see why you should have a say in this anyway," Frogsplash said in a tone that evinced a renewed sense of defiance in him. "I live with my dad now, and if I drop out – which I *won't* – it'll be him who has to support me, not you. I should never have brought it up. It's not your decision, it's mine."

I could not have been prouder of my brother in that moment. Watching the smirk drop from Graham's face, seeing him struck into stunned silence, was absolutely glorious.

"We just want what's best for you," Mum said in an attempt to defuse the tension, "as long as you try your best. And as long as you're happy."

She and Graham really are very different people.

Tuesday 27th April 2021

FROM GOOD TO BETTER: FRUSTRATION, CONVERSATION, REVELATION AND RESOLUTION!

That last word didn't rhyme with the rest, and it's really bugging you, isn't it?

"I can't believe it!" Carla was saying yesterday lunchtime, "I've only just joined The Sylphs and they've already booked us a slot at an open mic night! Not a school talent show or a mate's party but a real, adult open mic night! I know it's not as grown-up as a paid gig, but I still wasn't expecting anything like this so early on."

"That's amazing! When is it? Is it OK if I come?"

"It's in half term and of course you can! Just don't be expecting anything too extraordinary…"

"Don't be daft, you'll be brilliant! Oh, I'm so excited for you! This is amazing! Oh, I really hope I can come; it's not an adult only venue, is it?"

"I think you have to have an adult with you because they serve alcohol there. And you'll have to bring some ID; they don't allow under twelves because they have some comedy acts that are a bit rude! Do you think your mum or Graham could take you?"

"Um, maybe," I said, my heart sinking. If Graham caught a whiff of this, he'd do anything to try and stop me going. He'd say it was inappropriate for someone my age to go there. No, this sounds like a job for Duncan Drury. Dad absolutely loves comedy, especially if it's rude, and if he can have a beer while doing something I enjoy then I'm sure he'll be interested!

"I'm just annoyed with myself for wasting so much time with this sweets business. I've been trying to sell off my supply and still make a profit, but now that everyone can get what they want from the canteen they don't bother coming to me, so I've got a locker full of sweets and I still keep getting texts asking for fresh cookies and doughnuts! I'm selling in dribs and drabs, one item at a time, and it takes ages meeting up with all these different people all over the school, it's so frustrating. I just want to wash my hands of the whole business."

"You'll have to drop your prices or try and sell it off as a job lot. Do you know anyone who would want to buy that many sweets?"

"Ugh. There is one person, but I really didn't want to have to resort to this. He thinks he's a real ladies' man, and every time I sell to him he tries to flutter his eyelashes to get him a better deal! He's an irritating, over-confident sleazebag and I can't stand him."

"Let me guess: Johnny Acapulci?"

"Spot on."

And so, begrudgingly, she made arrangements to meet Johnny this lunchtime to sell him all her supply at half price, and I offered to go with her for support, and to make sure he didn't try to charm his way to a sweeter deal.

"Well, hello," Johnny said when we met him in the year eight locker area. "Look what we have here, two for the price of one, aren't I a lucky boy?" and from the cocky way he held eye contact with me, then with Carla, it was clear he was referring to us and not the sweets.

"Yeah, yeah, we're not here for the conversation, so if we can just speed things along…" Carla began.

"Oh, come on, Carla, don't be like that. We've had a sweet thing going these past few months, don't let it end like this."

"Really, Johnny, I just want to get this done, I've got other things to do."

"Ooh you're all business, I like that in a woman."

"Have you got the cash?" I said, now fully understanding why Carla found Johnny so frustrating.

"Ooh, another businesswoman, check you out!" he said, eyeing me up and down slowly.

"Look, if you're not going to buy them then we're going to leave," Carla said resolutely.

"All right, all right, I've got the cash. Look," he said, showing us a twenty pound note.

"I said half price," Carla said, "and I told you I could have sold this lot for fifty."

"But we both know it's not worth fifty, don't we? You could have sold it for fifty, maybe, but you didn't want to. You wanted to sell it to me."

"Yes, and that's why I offered you half price."

"I could buy this many sweets from the supermarket myself for less than twenty-five quid."

"Then why don't you?" Carla said. "Why do you come to me if you could just get it from the shop yourself?"

"Because I love our little chats, Carla. I get to see your gorgeous face instead of some warty old checkout woman who hasn't cracked a smile in forty years."

"She said twenty-five," I said.

"This is all I've got I'm afraid." He smirked, insouciantly fanning himself with the twenty.

"Fine," said Carla, "it's a deal."

"I'm sorry it had to end like this," Johnny said, handing over the cash. "You were doing such good business, things between us were going great, and now look at us! I bet you're gutted Wilcox screwed you over like that."

"Like what?" Carla asked, handing over two shopping bags full of confectionary.

"Well he called off the ban, didn't he? He effectively ruined your business. That's not cool, man, you and him were partners in crime. You had his back; he should have had yours."

"What do you mean I had his back? What are you talking about? Wait... you *knew?!* You knew he was in on it?!"

"Yeah, he told me. Must've been the fourth time he caught me eating sweets in the corridor, and still he didn't punish me or ask me where I got them. He brought me into his office, told me to be more discreet, then he explained all about your rotten little partnership."

"YOU!" Carla admonished. "It was you who told Charlotte! How dare you? I thought you were loyal!"

"Hey, come on now, I am loyal! I never mentioned your name, didn't even say what year you were in. It was Wilcox I was snitching on – I've never been loyal to him!"

"So, Charlotte never knew it was me?"

314

"Well if she did, she didn't hear it from me."

"Come to think of it," I said guiltily, "she never did mention any names when she was talking to Trisha Tijani. But she said she knew who it was. She must have been bluffing!"

"She's not as dumb as she looks," Carla said.

"Oh no, she's not dumb at all," Johnny said, going slightly misty-eyed. "Not just a pretty face, that one…"

"You fancy her!" Carla accused. "That's why you turned informant!"

"I never turned! You know there's no love lost between me and Big Willy. If you're looking to blame anyone you should blame him – he slipped up. He told me what was going on, he put you right in it."

"He really is a rat," I said. "Remember that comic strip of him in the 2010 time capsule?"

"They obviously knew him better than I did," Carla said bitterly.

"Never trust a rat," Johnny said. "Anyway, what do you care? Nobody found out in the end."

"None of your business," Carla said disdainfully. "You have no idea the trouble you've caused me!"

"The trouble Wilcox caused you!" Johnny corrected her.

"Yeah," she replied thoughtfully, "I suppose you're right. He really is a rat, isn't he?"

"Never trust a rat," Johnny repeated with an air of wisdom, and he walked away, tearing open a packet of gummy bears as he went.

"I wonder what it would take to bring Wilcox down," Carla said, the cogs still turning in her brain.

"What do you mean?" I asked, a little worried.

"You know, I wonder how easy it would be to get him sacked."

"Don't be daft!" I said. "He'll lose his job soon enough. They're holding an investigation, Richard told me all about it. He'll be the master of his own downfall. He made a complete prat of himself in front of the school and the local journalists, and he lost us the free Oliver Jameson meals, didn't he?"

"That's not enough," said Carla. "That might get him a slap on the wrist, but that's all. He's corrupt, just like Danny said. He might even have friends in high places, friends on the school board who will make sure he doesn't get sacked! I wonder what other dodgy deals he had going on… or still *has* going on!"

"You're missing the point!" I said, frustrated. "You should be thinking about Danny, not Wilcox!"

"You're right… God, of course you're right! All this corruption, it's got my priorities all twisted. Danny was right, too: I should have never got involved with Wilcox. And I should never have accused her – she would never snitch on me! Oh, Sam, do you think she'll ever forgive me?"

There was only one way of finding out, and we wasted no time in doing so. We forgot our lunches, slowly rotting and getting shaken up in our bags as we ran to the benches on the fields where we had last seen Danny and Elliot dining together. It reminded me of the first time I ever met Carla: I had been running on those very same fields, albeit in the opposite direction, and I had been running away from some terrifying year elevens when I had bumped into Carla and she had helped me get back on my feet. We ran and we ran, and in our haste, we forgot everything else – nothing was as important as reaching Danny. Finally, all of the pieces had fallen back together.

Usually we would climb the concrete steps up to the fields and the lake, but the fastest way is a grassy hill which takes a much more direct route. It's a steep and muddy climb, and you're likely to slip in your school shoes, but we went at such pace that there was too much friction, or maybe it was sheer will that kept us climbing upwards. We scaled it eagerly, and I felt an amazing power in my thighs as I made the ascent. We found Danny and Elliot sat at the same bench where we had once sat all together, watching Jamal the year seven getting bombarded by lunch-hungry geese. It seemed like years had passed since then; I feel so much older now.

"Danny!" Carla called out, catching her breath as we walked the final few feet to the bench.

"Carla?" she turned, surprised.

"You were right!" Carla said somewhat dramatically. "You were right about everything! I'm so sorry…"

"What are you talking about? What's happened? Sit down and tell me everything."

The pair of us sat opposite her and Elliot, and Carla began to explain.

"I should have known all along that you would never snitch on me! And I did, you know, I never really believed it was you, but I just couldn't think of any other explanation, and I thought that if I trusted you again then it would always be there in the back of my mind, but that was stupid, I should have trusted you anyway, because we're friends and friends don't lie to each other..."

"So, did you find out who it was?"

"Ugh, it was Johnny bloody Acapulci! I don't know why it never occurred to me that that creep would have something to do with it! Wilcox told him all about our set-up. You were right all along, Danny, it was a bad idea getting involved with Wilcox. He's a corrupt man and I should never have trusted him."

"Is everything OK? You're not in any trouble, are you?"

"No, no, I'm fine. But I feel awful. I should have trusted you."

Danny looked at Carla reprovingly, grasping this final opportunity to teach her the importance of honesty and loyalty. Elliot looked very uncomfortable.

"Oh, come here!" she said at last, and she leaned forward and spread her arms wide, pulling us in for a group hug. "Of course, I forgive you," she said, her voice muffled as our heads were still bundled together in an awkward, over-the-table hug. "All I ever wanted was for you to believe that it wasn't me. I'm so glad this is all over and you're not in any trouble."

"I suppose I did get lucky there," Carla said as we were released from our embrace and sat back down in our seats. "Wilcox would have gladly thrown me under the bus to save his own skin. Little did he know his little stunt with Oliver Jameson would end up protecting me from exposure!"

"He is such a terrible head teacher," I said.

"I don't understand why he hasn't got the sack," said Danny. "It's like the whole thing's just been swept under the carpet."

"Oh, but it hasn't!" I said. "They're holding an investigation – Richard told me all about it..."

"Ooh – juicy!" said Danny excitedly. "We have so much to catch up on! Like what's going on with you, Sam? You've lost so much weight! I can't believe we fell out over something so stupid, but I'm so excited to make up for lost time! Ooh – and now you guys can get to know Elliot *at last*! Ooh, yay!"

Carla and I smiled at Elliot, attempting to show some enthusiasm for this idea. Elliot, who had not yet said a word, looked as though he'd just been invited to share an enclosure with a pair of hungry lions.

Wednesday 28th April 2021

After several weeks of lying dormant, our group chat got back up and running yesterday evening. Carla told Danny all about The Sylphs and how she needed to practise playing with them in the music room at lunch time. I knew she was telling the truth, and yet I felt as though she was glad of an excuse not to get to know Elliot. Our reunion should have been so pure and simple, but Elliot is proving to be a spanner in the works. He doesn't have any friends of his own, probably because of his reputation for violent outbursts, or perhaps because nobody wants to make friends with the new kid. Either way, Danny is all he has, and I get the impression that he liked it much better when he was all she had too. Luckily, she doesn't feel the same way.

"Ooh, we can all hang out in the music room while you practise!" she said.

"I don't think the band will be OK with that... too many distractions. And the song is supposed to be a surprise for the big night!"

"Ah I see... Well in that case we don't want to disturb you. That's OK, me, Sam and Elliot can hang out on the fields together instead!"

Oh great. Samantha Drury: Third Wheel.

So, there we were at lunch today: me, Danny and Elliot, and believe me I was dreading it. For all his faults, I don't think Elliot is unintelligent, so he must have been painfully aware that my view of him is shaped by the behaviours he has displayed in front of me, and they have not been good. But Danny is my friend, and after so wrongfully being ousted from our group, I could at the very least get to know her boyfriend a bit and, if possible, try to see the good in him.

He was shy, nervous, much more of a quiet type than Danny. Of course, I of all people know that there's nothing wrong with that, but it was going to take some effort on my part if I was to make any progress with him. We sat at the same bench as before eating our lunches when I made my first attempt at conversation with Elliot.

"It's a shame Carla can't hang out with us at the moment," I began. It was a well-thought-out conversation starter. "But you know, music is her passion, and the band sounds really cool. What sort of music are you into, Elliot?"

"Oh, um, Free Parking, obviously, Nirvana, Radiohead, Dolores's Dolorifuge, Opportunistic System…"

"Ooh, I've never heard of them! Are they any good?"

"Well I think so…"

Duh! Of course, he does, stupid question, Sam!

"What genre are they?"

"Hmm… it's a bit of a cross-genre style really. Kind of experimental digital melodies with a strong political message in most of their songs. They're basically an all-female feminist group with a punk ideal and a modern approach to sound."

"Blimey! You'd get on great with Carla's dad – he sounds like a music magazine too!"

"Ha," he said joylessly. Then there was a long pause, and that was the end of that conversation.

It was frustrating being the only one to make any effort and getting almost nothing back. I thought I had him when he started talking about Opportunistic System, but it was like he'd been trying not to talk me, accidentally revealed too much and then closed himself off again. I wondered if I had ever been this difficult to talk to. Probably. I bet this is exactly how people used to feel when they tried to talk to me. I might have come a long way since then, but I still am that person underneath, and I still remember how it feels. I hated one-on-one conversations because they're very demanding. So, I changed tack. I started a conversation with Danny, hoping that Elliot would feel comfortable enough to join in when he was ready.

"So how are things at home?" I asked her. "Are your parents still going ahead with the move?"

"It's all right. Slow progress," she said. "Mum's working a few mornings at the twins' nursery, Dad's doing nights in a warehouse, they share all the parenting duties and spend the rest of the time house-hunting. There's not much time for either of them to chase their dreams right now, but we've got a buyer for the house and we've found one we like so things are really moving forward."

"That's a lot of change in a short space of time!" I said. "It must be hard for you and the twins…"

Danny made an awkward glance at Elliot before saying. "No. No, it's fine… can't complain…"

It was yet another abrupt end to a conversation I had attempted to start, and I was beginning to wonder what was going on. They did want me there, didn't they? I certainly didn't invite myself into that situation! Maybe Danny just didn't want to talk about family stuff in front of Elliot, but I could have sworn that was how they got talking in the first place – Elliot had just moved house and Danny had just found out that her family was going to have to move, too. The old me might have given up just then. I'd have assumed no one wanted me around and I'd have left them to it. But I reminded myself of how excited Danny had been for us all to hang out together, and I knew that it couldn't have been that. I would just have to keep trying.

"So how are you settling into your new house?" I asked Elliot, believing it to be a banal and inoffensive question.

"It's a home, not a house," he replied sharply.

"Oh. Sorry. But… aren't they pretty much the same thing?"

"No. I mean I live in a care home. I didn't just move house, I moved into the home."

"OH! Oh god! I wish Danny would have told me…" I said, glaring at her.

"I didn't know if Elliot wanted people to know," she said. "It wasn't my place to go telling people. The way they gossip and start rumours in this place, I wouldn't want to give them the ammunition!"

"That makes sense. I'm sorry if I pushed you into telling me. I won't tell anyone else," I said to Elliot.

"That's OK. You might as well tell Carla. But no one else, OK? Like Danny said, the people here are vicious. I think some of them already know, although I've no idea how. They keep saying horrible things about my mum. That's why I lashed out in Art that time. Patrick O'Neill is always trying to wind me up about her."

"That's horrible," I said, "I had no idea. So, is she… um, OK?"

"She's not dead, if that's what you mean. But she's not OK, not really. She can't look after herself, let alone me and Ben. He's my little brother, he lives in the home with me."

"At least you got to stay together," I said, hoping I wasn't saying the wrong thing again.

"Yeah, I don't know what I would have done if they'd have separated us. The home would be a very different place without him."

"What's it like there?"

"The place itself is OK. We have TVs, consoles, internet access, toys and swing sets for Ben – way more than we ever had at Mum's. But some of the other kids are a nightmare. They're very, very angry, or else they're completely mute. One girl never eats, some seem to never sleep, and no one seems to trust each other. It's a real hostile situation: nobody wants anybody else to know anything about them, so they lie about everything. They lie because they don't trust each other, and they don't trust each other because they lie."

"That's so sad. They must feel so lonely."

"They're not all like that. There are a few who seem all right, but you can never really be sure. You always have to keep your guard up."

"That must be tough. I hate dealing with new people even when they're being nice to me! And your mum, she must really miss you. Do you at least get to see her?"

"Yeah, we're allowed to visit once a week, but Ben doesn't always want to, and that's hard. He doesn't understand why she wasn't looking after us the way the carers do. She would never do anything to hurt us, but she couldn't give us the attention we needed. It was even worse when Dad was around, but Ben won't remember that."

"Is he... your dad...?" I trailed off. I didn't want to overstep any boundaries.

"It's OK, you are allowed to ask questions! My dad's in prison. He's the reason Mum is the way she is. He's the reason everything is the way it is."

"That's horrible. I'm so sorry."

"It's OK. Things are better now, and Mum is getting better, slowly. I just have a really short fuse when people say stuff about her. And the teachers are even worse – they all know my situation and they all treat me differently because of it. They pretend to be sympathetic, but really they're just expecting me to cause trouble. They don't think I belong here."

"They can be as snobby as the kids sometimes," I said. "Either that or they're completely bonkers! I mean, Wilcox is severely lacking in judgement and he's the man in charge! Mack is another one, but he's always been eccentric so I suppose we shouldn't be too surprised."

"What about Mr Roberts, the Geography teacher? He's not exactly professional!" Elliot said.

"No, he's not. But he's an all right guy. I bet *he* doesn't treat you any differently."

"Well, no, now that you mention it. He's a bit weird, but I don't hate his lessons."

"Wow, that's high praise indeed coming from you!" Danny said, and I realised it was the first time she had spoken in at least ten minutes. I had been getting to know Elliot without even thinking about it, and he wasn't at all what I had expected.

Wednesday 12th May 2021

Lunchtimes with Danny and Elliot have been a lot nicer now that everything is out in the open. I told Carla all that Elliot had told me, and since then she's made the effort to join us on a few occasions so that she could get to know him, too. I'm glad Danny is going out with him, he's a nice guy and if she hadn't found that out then I would have carried on believing he was a thug. It seemed as though everything was settling down once again and we were getting into a new groove with Elliot joining our team and Carla splitting her time between us and the band. But just as we were getting comfortable, a strange and unwelcome interference came to upset the rhythm.

It was a particularly warm day. Our usual spot on the bench offers no shade and Danny's skin is extremely sensitive to the sun, so instead she, Elliot and I sat on the grass beneath a tree to eat our lunch. I stuck my legs out in the sun in a vain attempt to get some colour on them, and after we'd eaten we all laid down and enjoyed the warm tranquillity of the afternoon. Danny and Elliot were muttering carelessly about their Biology project in the same way a married couple might ponder whether or not to get new curtains for the second bedroom. I had my eyes closed and I was listening to the breeze rustling the branches overhead when I felt a shadow cast itself over me and an ominous chill pass through my body.

"Hey, Danny," came a treacle-sweet voice coated in false friendliness, "Why don't you come out in the sun with us? You'd look great with a tan." I opened my eyes, sat up and saw Charlotte Henderson, Ruby Driscoll, Beth Amory and Andrea Michael towering over us, their school shirts tied up beneath their bras to show off their midriffs.

"I don't tan," said Danny, "and I can't stay in the sun. I'm albino."

"Ooh – exotic!" said Beth, who is not especially bright.

"No. I mean, I have albinism," Danny said.

"Oh. Well, I hope you feel better soon," Beth said, looking confused.

Danny huffed in frustration. "What do you want anyway?"

"We just wanted to invite you to hang out," Charlotte said. "We're expanding."

"Oh yeah, I'd noticed you'd put on a few pounds," Danny said bitingly, looking at their exposed bellies to make them feel self-conscious. Charlotte's nostrils flared but she didn't rise to the bait.

"No, I mean our group is expanding. Ruby joined us last summer, now we'd like to recruit you."

"I'm just fine where I am, thank you."

"I'm sure you are," said Charlotte, "but wouldn't you rather be better than fine? Wouldn't you rather be at the top?"

"Like I said, I'm happy where I am. I'm not interested."

"What about your boyfriend? I've heard some of the nasty things people say about him. If you joined our crew it would elevate his status, too. We'd make sure no one bothered him again."

I saw a shadow of doubt flicker across Danny's face – Charlotte had touched a nerve, but Danny resisted. "We can fight our own battles, thank you. Now can you leave us alone. Your expanding group is blocking our light."

Charlotte scowled venomously and turned away, leading her retinue off towards the field where they were known to sunbathe, hoping to draw the attention of the boys playing football nearby.

"What the hell was all that about?" I asked Danny once they'd departed.

"I don't know," she said. "They've been acting weird ever since the Valentine's dance."

"Seems like they really want you in their group," Elliot said.

"I'm sure they do," said Danny, "but I know it's not me they really want. I know they don't care about who I am. There's obviously something they think I have to offer."

"Any idea what that might be?"

"Well, I know they're in competition with Rachel's gang, and I know they're all about wealth and designer fashion. I wonder if that dress I wore to the dance had something to do with it. My dad bought it in an outlet and even then it was done in desperation because he was worried about losing me back when he and Mum were arguing a lot. But Charlotte doesn't know that. To her it's a status symbol – a bit like Ruby and her tennis court."

"You think that's why they made friends with Ruby – because she has her own tennis court?"

"Probably."

"And now they're trying to get you because of a designer dress!"

"Well, it's about more than the dress now. You saw the article Charlotte wrote – she thinks I've got a 'brooding bad boy' for a boyfriend, and I bet she's heard all about me standing up to Mr Pinter. She thinks I'm a rebel in designer labels, and that's just what she wants."

Saturday 22nd May 2021

Something really weird happened this evening. I had just got out of the bath and I knew that Mum wanted to use the bathroom after me, so I went to knock on her door to let her know that it was free. As I approached her door, I heard her talking quietly, which was odd because Billy and Graham were both at work, making us two the only ones in the house. She might have been talking to the dogs, but she always talks to them loudly and in silly voices. Likewise, when she's on the phone she raises her voice because she seems to think that the person on the other end won't be able to hear her otherwise.

It was definitely odd. I was barefoot on the soft carpet, so it was likely that she hadn't heard me approaching. The door was half ajar, and I thought that surely if she had been doing something really private she'd have made certain to close it, so I peeked. I know I shouldn't have. I should have respected her privacy, but I was worried. This was bizarre behaviour, and hadn't Graham warned me that Mum might start acting strange? Maybe he knows something – maybe there's something wrong with her. Maybe she's not well. I thought of Elliot and his broken family, and I thought that if there was anything at all that I could do to keep that from happening to us then I have to do it, even if it means spying on my mum.

Through the crack in the door, I could see Mum sitting on her bed in her dressing gown holding something very small next to her mouth and talking into it very quietly. I couldn't hear what she was saying, but the way she was hunched over it with her head tucked into her chest made it all too clear that this was a hushed and secretive communication. But with whom was she communicating? The only thing I could think of – the only thing that she might possibly be talking into – was a microphone.

She stopped speaking into whatever the thing was, tucked it under her pillow and stood up from her seat on the edge of the bed. I panicked and shuffled back down the corridor as quickly as I possibly could without making any sound. I swooped into my room, but I didn't shut my door, thinking that it might make Mum suspicious if she heard my door close just seconds after she'd ended her secret communication. I heard her enter the bathroom, but I couldn't hear her running a bath or shower, all I heard was the sound of her electric toothbrush buzzing. I longed to run back to her room and see what was under her pillow, but tooth-brushing is too brief an activity to allow me sufficient snooping time.

So here I am, left with so many questions. What was she talking into? The only logical answer is either a microphone or a voice recorder. But what would she be doing with either of them? If she was speaking into a microphone, then who was listening? I really don't think my mum is a spy! But why would she be recording herself talking? Were there secrets she just couldn't keep bottled up? Perhaps I'm getting ahead of myself. Perhaps she was taking notes in audio form – ideas for work, to-do lists or reminders. But Mum never takes her work home with her, and why was it all so secretive? Who keeps work things under their pillow?

I want to go and see what it is, but I know that's wrong. On the other hand, I know Mum rummages around in my room, because she let it slip during Family Talk Time that she found my diary, and I keep it in a much better hiding place than under my pillow! But I have no reason to believe that she ever actually read my diary. So, here's what I'm thinking: I can rummage around in her room a little bit, but if I find a voice recorder I'm not allowed to listen to it, and if it's a microphone I'm not going to try and find out who's on the other end. That's fair, isn't it?

Monday 24th May 2021

There was no chance of getting into Mum's room yesterday. Not only was Graham in the house, but he spent most of the day in the bedroom he shares with Mum "helping her" to clear out her wardrobe to make room for his own clothes. He has a couple of drawers for his standard, casual clothes, but he's decided to move his smart suits in here because he suspects Arnie of borrowing them while staying at the flat above the pub. They say it's good to be ruthless when having a clear-out, but does that still apply when you're clearing out somebody else's belongings? Not that I'm upset to see Mum's see-through, fluorescent yellow leggings find their way to the bin, but it didn't seem right for Graham to be the one making that decision.

I was in my room down the hall and I had my door open to better track his movements. Mum must have been sat on the bed while he rifled through her wardrobe, as if she had any say in what would stay and what would go.

"You're never going to fit into this," I heard him say, "when was the last time you were a size ten?"

"Oh, I know. But it's so lovely, I thought maybe I could give it to Sam…"

"She's not going to want your hand-me-downs, Cassie, and let's be honest, she's not going to look much better in it than you would!"

Wow – rude!

"And this dress – it's a bit tarty isn't it? You might have gotten away with it when you were in your twenties, but now you'd just look like mutton dressed as lamb."

"It still fits me, and I quite like it…"

"Well I don't. I like a woman with class… and look at this! This top's completely see-through! Imagine what your children would think if they saw you in that."

"Well I wouldn't wear it on its own; I'd wear another top underneath."

"Then what's the point in it? It's just not practical having a top that you can only wear with another top. It's the fashion industry tricking you into buying more clothes, and you've fallen for it!"

And so, it went on. Graham criticised every item in Mum's wardrobe, she came up with a defence for why she owned these garments, but ultimately gave in to Graham's argument every time.

I arrived home after school today to a seemingly empty house. I checked every room to make absolutely sure that nobody, especially Graham, was in, then I crept up to Mum's room. I tried not to get my hopes up – there was a good chance that whatever she'd put under her pillow on Saturday was not there any more. If it truly was a secret then she wouldn't want Graham finding it and judging by the way he was rifling through her wardrobe yesterday he wouldn't think twice about going through her stuff. If I was her, I'd keep anything private or precious very close to me at all times.

And yet there it was, right there under her pillow, exactly where I had seen her leave it. It was a small drawstring pouch made out of fabric, the kind you might get cheap jewellery in if you bought it at a marketplace or in a tourist shop on holiday. It could perhaps have held a small microphone, but when I picked it up it was so light I wondered if anything was in it at all. Perhaps Mum had removed its contents for safe-keeping, and perhaps my curious investigation was about to meet a frustrating standstill. I pulled gently on the drawstrings, upturned the pouch onto the pillow, and out fell six tiny, woven dolls with a positively minute scroll of paper that would not have looked out of place in a corked glass bottle, albeit an incredibly diminutive one.

The dolls must have been less than two centimetres tall and very thin. When I picked them up to examine them, I could see that their bodies and heads were made of cardboard wrapped in different coloured cotton, with tightly wound cotton for arms and legs. They were quite crude in design, but you could still tell that two were meant to be women, two men and two slightly smaller ones must have been children. They were still remarkably detailed for something so tiny, and the simplicity of them was certainly endearing, but what on Earth is my mother doing keeping them under her pillow?

Carefully I unravelled the tiny scroll, hoping that it might provide me with some answers. In very fine print were the following words:

WORRY DOLLS

There is a legend amongst the villages of Guatemala. These dolls may be small in size, but they possess a powerful magic. If you are having problems, share them with your worry dolls. Tell only one worry to each doll at night, then place them beneath your pillow. In the morning your worries will be gone.

It certainly wasn't what I expected. It did answer some of my questions, but it also prompted several more. What was my mum worrying about, and why was she confiding in these "magic" dolls instead of her friends? She had once been friends with Danny and Carla's mums, and even before that she had Trudy, Alana and a whole host of others. And I don't mean to insult the beliefs of the Guatemalan villagers, but there is no way that these little figures had apotropaic qualities. They were clearly little bits of woven string and they were no more capable of solving anyone's problems than a handful of buttons.

I know my mum is an eccentric person, or at least she was before Graham ironed that out of her, but she has never believed in magic or anything supernatural. In fact, she doesn't believe in anything that can't be backed up by scientific evidence: she doesn't believe in ghosts or karma or good luck charms or superstition, and yet here she is talking to these little dolls which were crafted by human hands for the sole purpose of selling them for profit. How could she be fooled by something so basic?

OPEN MIC DELIGHT! UP-AND-COMING BAND *THE SYLPHS* DEBUT THEIR CHILLING SONG *THE BALLAD OF GRACE AND GLENN,* STUNNING THEIR AUDIENCE WITH THEIR UNIQUE STYLE, HAUNTING MELODIES AND ORIGINAL STORY. 10/10!

The young band brought a breath of fresh air to the usually stale atmosphere in the dingy bar located in the town centre, which normally has little more to offer than washed-up crooners playing bad Oasis covers and bitter divorcees making tired jokes about their exes. Let's hope this is the start of a glittering career for the fantastical four!

It was Carla's open mic night at long last! It's not my usual weekend with Dad, but as soon as I suggested it he was well up for it, and actually it works out better this way because he wouldn't have been able to take us if he'd had Stephanie. He picked me up this afternoon and then we went to collect Danny from her place. Her parents were busy packing for the new house and the twins were making it very difficult by trying to play with the toys that had already been boxed up, so she was very grateful for an excuse to escape.

Frogsplash was equally pleased to get out for the evening because he's been cooped up in his room at Dad's finishing some coursework and, to make matters worse, Richard is apparently going through a comedy phase in which he likes to wind people up non-stop. Thankfully, since the disastrous rap incident with Wilcox, Richard has behaved much more like a normal teacher at school. I can only imagine the kind of jokes he'd make about me in Geography if he was still seeking the approval of the class!

We arrived at six p.m. and found Carla and the band huddled in the corner with their instruments in their cases ready to perform. They weren't due on stage for another hour, so we sat with them and watched the other acts nervously while they waited for their big moment. It was a fairly uninspired bunch. Most of them were older men doing cover versions of their favourite songs. There were two comics – one male, one female, who were both all right, although some of their jokes made me cringe! The best was probably a group of brothers playing different string instruments together – I thought they were amazing, but it didn't go down so well with the audience – I guess a bar full of students and middle-aged men is just the wrong crowd for classical music.

It was nearly seven p.m. when we bid farewell to the band and watched Carla, the keyboard player Maurice, the bassist Yaz and the drummer Kayla walk onto the stage and take their positions. Danny and I held our breath as Carla walked up to the microphone nearest the front of the stage. Maurice ran offstage again and came back with a stool for her to sit on, which she did after she'd adjusted the microphone for her height. The music began with Maurice playing an eerie tune on the keyboard, then a slow beat from Kayla, a low, haunting strum from Yaz followed by the first soulful chord from Carla. And then she began to sing:

"Childhood sweethearts at the age of ten
Nothing came between kind Grace and sweet Glenn
They held hands in the gardens and on the swings
They shared with each other all innocent things

But rarely in childhood does romance last
Innocence ends; appetites grow fast
Glenn lost his love for kindness such as Grace's
And fixed himself on girls with fairer faces

They held hands in the gardens and on the swings
She cries and she cries; she sings, and she sings

Grace's love only grew deeper and stronger
But Glenn could bear to behold her face no longer
Each night a different beauty went with him to bed
It pained Grace so sharply she wished she was dead

But hope was not lost for the suffering child
She heard tales on the wind of things strange and wild
She followed the whispers carried by the night
Which led her to wisp and phantom and sprite

They held hands in the gardens and on the swings
She cries and she cries; she sings, and she sings

"There's a powerful witch," the voices told Grace
And through the wind's mist led her to the place
She knocked on the door and she was not afraid
The door opened slowly; there stood the old maid

"What business is this?" the old crone spoke
"From the sweetest of sleeps, you have me now woke!"
"Forgive me, I beg you," our Grace did implore
"But ruined and desperate do I come to your door!"

They held hands in the gardens and on the swings
She cries and she cries; she sings, and she sings

So, Grace told the witch of her sorrow and pain
Of Glenn and the beauties, he did entertain
"Please make me a beauty, at least in his eyes,
"Make him want me for always; forever his prize."

The witch cast the spell; she did her wretched duty
She turned sweet, plain Grace into a fine beauty
Then with horror and anguish the girl tried to cry
But you can't cry or speak when you're a butterfly

Her eyes shed no tears; her voice never sings
All she can do is flutter her wings

The witch looked upon her and declared her promise
"He will want you for always – I swear to you this"

Grace had no voice to question, no fists to fight
So, she fluttered her wings and to Glenn she made flight

She planted herself on his shoulder and then
To her joy, at last, she enchanted fine Glenn!
Her colours and patterns had him so captivated
It mattered not to Grace that his love was belated

Her eyes shed no tears; her voice never sings
All she can do is flutter her wings

So fixated with Grace was the boy she held dear
That he promised that always he would keep this thing near
She may have been merely an ephemeral creature
But she'd make such a stunning ornamental feature

In prime position atop his bedside chest
Glenn kept her in a jar to show to each guest
Nightly he took new lovers to his sordid place
And each pretty girl admired the beautiful Grace

Her eyes shed no tears; her voice never sings
All she can do is flutter her wings

Grace's sadness darkened as the years went on
Until, at last, the girls were all gone
Instead she watched as the love of her life
Took in a new woman, and made her his wife

"What a beautiful butterfly!" said the woman, named Rose
"She should spread her wings, don't you suppose?"
So, Rose freed from the jar the beautiful Grace
Spread her wings and pinned them to the mantel place

Her eyes shed no tears; her voice never sings
Now she cannot even flutter her wings

So proudly now Grace was on display
So proudly is she still there now, to this day
Grace will stay there for the rest of her life
Watching her true love grow old with his wife

She will see them have children and watch them grow, too
She will watch them all die and wish she could too."

The audience erupted! People were getting out of their seats and cheering (me and Danny may have started it but still, we weren't alone!). The old blokes who were just there for a drink weren't so enthusiastic but most of the students seemed really impressed and Danny, Dad, Frogsplash and I were blown away!

"That was amazing Carla!" I said as she and the others re-joined us. "Truly out of this world!"

"It really was incredible," Danny agreed.

"Did you really write that yourselves?" Dad asked the band.

"Actually, it was Carla who wrote it," said Yaz, "we were just playing to her tune."

"Wow – I'm very impressed," said Dad. "A million times better than anything The Hormones ever wrote!"

"Who?" said Carla.

"Oh, don't ask!" I said. "Come on, sit down, relax – you absolutely smashed it!"

We continued to congratulate the band profusely until the next act took the stage, at which point we felt obliged to settle down and give them a chance to perform. It was a woman with a guitar singing an angry song about a man who had left her. There were lots of swear words and a sort of shouty singing style and she kept saying things like "Screw you, Steve!" and "Look at me now, Steve!" so it really felt like we weren't her true audience and that she probably should have just written a strongly-worded email to Steve and got it out of her system. Also, she was a toneless singer and I got the distinct impression that she'd learnt a bit of basic guitar for the sole purpose of getting back at Steve.

As the designated driver, Dad had been nursing his beer all evening and, as his glass was nearly empty, we began to say goodbye to Carla and the others, who were getting picked up by Kayla's mum a bit later. I was just giving the band one final word of congratulation when we were interrupted by a familiar voice coming from the stage.

"It can't be..." said Frogsplash, a look of grave realisation dawning across his face.

"Richard!" said Dad, turning suddenly to face the stage.

"I hope he's just singing one of his songs," said Froggo.

"I don't see a guitar," I said ominously. "Did he know we were coming here tonight?"

"No!" said Dad, "I deliberately lied to him because I was sure he would try to tag along! I told him we were going to a college open evening for Frogsplash and he said he was going out, too, but I never in a million years would have guessed he was coming here!"

"Well, we have to stay," I said, apparently the only Drury not to be horrified by this turn of events. "We have to see what he's going to do!"

"I don't know," Dad said, looking for an escape. "Don't your parents want you home, Danny?"

"Oh, they won't mind at all," she said, "the more kids out of the way the better!" So, it was settled, and those of us who knew Richard as a teacher were very excited for the upcoming performance.

"All right," he said casually, "I'm Richard. So, I've been living with this teenage boy for a while now. Nothing inappropriate, he's my flatmate's son. Now, I don't know if you know what it's like living with boys that age, but for me it's been an eye-opening experience. So, I'm sure you've all noticed that we've been having a bit of an early heatwave these past couple of weeks... Well, teenage boy hasn't. Oh no. He adheres very vigilantly to his once-a-week shower regime and I swear to god he thinks he can successfully mask it with cheap body spray. In fact, he uses so much of the stuff I reckon he single-handedly tore the hole in the ozone layer that caused this unseasonable heat in the first place!"

At that point people actually laughed. It seemed to be going well for Richard. Not so much for Frogsplash, who was staring daggers at Richard the entire time, refusing to make eye contact with anyone else in case they made any kind of acknowledgement that he was the subject of this public ridicule.

"They always think they're more mature than they actually are, teenagers. The other day he was getting ready for school and he couldn't find his razor. He only started shaving about a month ago but all of a sudden it's a daily necessity! So, I said he could borrow mine. I handed it to him, and he had the cheek to say, "Urgh – I can't use that! That's the cheap supermarket brand, it's only got two blades, I need the five blade one!" I couldn't believe it. The lad could go months without shaving and it wouldn't show, but apparently he needs heavy duty, top-of-the-range razors now that he's hit sixteen! He's only got a bit of downy fuzz on his upper lip. I imagine kissing him would be like kissing a duckling's arse. Not that I imagine kissing him... well, not often anyway!"

By this point Froggo's face was bright red, and even I felt sorry for him, but Richard wasn't done yet.

"Have you ever been in the same room as a teenage boy when he's watching TV? Well, after a while they start to get comfortable. They put their feet up on the sofa, lean back on the arm, stretch out a bit. Then they get even more comfortable, maybe they even forget that you're there, because they seem to be completely shameless when it comes to shoving their hands down their pants and... fiddling. Not just a quick adjustment, but a long and protracted session of personal fondling. And then his dad, my flatmate, comes in with a big bowl of crisps to share, and he dives straight in there with that very same hand, all the while not taking his dopey eyes off the TV screen!"

That got another laugh. By this point Dad was looking at Froggo's mortified expression with such pity that I could tell he was making up his mind to get us out of there, but just then, thankfully, Richard decided to change the subject.

"I didn't always live with a teenage boy I'm not related to. As horrifying as my current living situation might be, it used to be a hell of a lot worse. I used to live with a woman... We were married for fourteen miserable years. There should be a clause in every marriage contract which states that she can't take half your money after a divorce if she turned into a mean-spirited, scowling witch as soon as the honeymoon was over. Seriously, no wonder she's had to spend so much on Botox, the amount of frowning she's done over the years! She spent our entire marriage complaining and criticising, complaining and criticising..."

"But you know what the worst part is. Now she's turned my two daughters into sour-faced misers as well! I realised too late that I should have spent more time with them, to soften them up, give them a sense of humour, you know? It's a *Catch 22* really: I should have spent more time with them to make sure they didn't turn out just like their mother, but I only realised that when I noticed how much they *had* turned out like their mother, and now I can't stand spending time with them *because* they're just like their mother!"

"But it wasn't all bad. We had some good memories. I remember the best day of my life like it was just yesterday, and it would never have happened if I hadn't married her. It was a gorgeous spring morning, birds were tweeting, the sun was shining, little fluffy clouds drifted by... and my divorce papers came through in the post!

"But seriously, marriage can be a blessing. We had some great family holidays, totally carefree, the kids were laughing and playing, even *she* was smiling. It was such a gorgeous smile, all the more stunning for how rarely she used it. She wore a nautical striped bikini – a halter-neck that really accentuated her breasts. It was a long time ago, before I lost my hair and she lost all respect for me. I wish I could go back to those times... why can't I? Why can't I just live in the past, jump into those memories and live there forever? Why can't I go back? Why, Fran, why?!"

And then he began to cry. He was sobbing like a baby, right there on the stage in front of everybody.

"Why, Fran, why did you leave me? I could have changed! I would have changed everything for you!"

Then he fell to his knees, a crumpled mess on the wooden boards. And at that the crowd went wild! They were laughing hysterically, much more than they had done at any of his actual jokes.

"Oh, that's just cruel," Dad said, "laughing at a man in the midst of a breakdown!" And he got up to escort Richard off the stage. When he reached Richard, he put his arm around him and helped him up, and the crowd began laughing and cheering all over again.

"I think they think it's all part of the act," Carla said to me, "I think he's actually doing well!" And when I looked around at all the faces creased with laughter I realised she was right. Dad brought Richard over to sit with us and went to get him a beer to lift his spirits.

"That was brilliant!" I said to Richard while Dad was at the bar, "Hilarious stuff! I'm not sure Froggo enjoyed the first act, but all that stuff about Fran, you pretending to want her back, that whole broken man act – priceless!"

"You what?" he said. "Well yeah, I mean… if I'd known you lot were going to be here, I wouldn't have done that whole teenage boy bit! But… you really think they found it funny?"

"It *was* funny! Just look at the people still laughing – it was comedy genius!"

Richard lifted his heavy head and looked all around at the laughter he had spread, and he was in a much better mood from then on. He even got a few people coming up to him saying how great he was, so Dad decided to leave him to soak up the glory while he took the rest of us home.

Monday 31ˢᵗ May 2021

Today, for the first time in months, Mum seemed really, truly happy about something, because today she got the phone call that she's been waiting for. It was Frogsplash, and he wants to move back home! Apparently he said something about "privacy" and "respect" and although Mum seemed mildly, pleasantly baffled by it ("I don't know what he was going on about but it's wonderful!") it was pretty obvious to me that Richard's stand-up material was the catalyst for this sudden change.

I'm very excited to have him back. Between work and revision, I've hardly seen Billy, and I've felt as though I've been carrying all the household tension all by myself. Maybe when Froggo moves back in, Billy will feel more inclined to spend time at home and then we'll have the adults outnumbered again. He's coming home tomorrow! After Gertie made him throw out all his old clothes, and then he threw out all the clothes she made him wear, he's only got a few *Dolores's Dolorifuge* t-shirts to pack!

Friday 4th June 2021

Mum took a few days off work for Frogsplash's return. I told her it was completely unnecessary as I'm sure he'd rather just get back to normal, but she seemed so anxious to make everything perfect and ensure it all ran smoothly, I'm not sure she would have been much use at work anyway. Dad dropped him off on Tuesday evening and I chatted to him while Mum helped Froggo unload the car.

"How do you feel about all this?" I asked him.

"Oh, it's fine, I totally understand. It's Richard I feel sorry for! Don't tell your brother this, but he feels horribly guilty about the jokes he made on Saturday. He thinks Frogsplash moving out is all his fault!"

"And is it?"

"Well, yes, more or less. He was already winding him up around the clock, and then Saturday's gig sealed the deal! But don't let Richard know that, he's got enough on his plate as it is."

"What do you mean?"

"Oh, this whole investigation thing at the school. I shouldn't be telling you really, but it's not going as smoothly as he'd hoped. They keep coming back to question him again, as though he didn't tell them the whole truth in the first place. It seems they don't believe everything he's saying."

"Oh no!" I said. "Poor Richard, he does seem to dig himself into some holes, doesn't he?"

"He really, really does," Dad said resignedly.

Since then it's been a very full house. It's half term so I haven't been at school, and Froggo and Billy are on study leave now so they'll be off for ages. Mum doesn't know how to handle it; she wants Frogsplash to study hard for his exams, but she doesn't want to nag him because she's worried he might leave again. She keeps fretting over little things like what to make him for dinner. She's got it in her head that Dad let him eat takeaway every night and now she's worried he won't like her cooking any more. She really needs to just relax, but I don't think she knows how.

Friday 11th June 2021

Today was dry but overcast, so we sat at our usual picnic bench to eat lunch, this time joined by Carla, who is taking a break from band practice after the success of the open mic performance. We listened to music, taking it in turns to choose our favourite songs. Carla is really impressed with Elliot's eclectic taste, and they often talk about bands neither Danny nor I have heard of. Elliot was gutted to have missed The Sylphs' live performance, but the carers at the home would never have approved an outing to a rough old bar and even if they had it would have been unlikely they'd have been able to spare a certified adult to accompany him. He's really settled into our group now and he seems a lot better in class. This is why you should always take a chance on people.

Apart from Charlotte Henderson. Danny's not taking a chance on her and I think that's very wise.

"Hey, Danny." Charlotte grinned, her thick, brown hair waving in the breeze and flicking the faces of Beth, Andrea and Ruby behind her. "You thought any more about our offer?"

"That wasn't an offer," Danny said. "It was an invitation. You have nothing to offer me and I have already declined your invitation."

"You don't know what you're missing," Charlotte said. "You should think carefully. The decisions you make can take you in all sorts of directions."

"As long as I'm not going in the same direction as you, I'm fine," Danny said defiantly.

"Why not just give it a try? You never know, you might like it," Charlotte teased. "In fact, I guarantee you'll have more fun than you've ever had with this lot."

"I said no!"

"Leave it, Charlotte," Carla said. "Desperation is so very ugly. And you should probably get used to people saying no to you, it's going to happen a lot if you're still planning on that modelling career."

"No one asked you, Carl," Charlotte said, but she walked away, nonetheless.

"God why is she so persistent?" said Carla once Charlotte et al. were out of sight.

"She must be up to something," said Danny.

"Nah, I know girls like her," Elliot said. "They think they're all that, they think they can get whatever they want, then when someone says no to them, they can't stand it."

"I bet it's driving her nuts!" I said.

"Good," said Carla, "she deserves it. Who does she think she is, trying to tear Danny away from her real friends just for some popularity power trip against Rachel's crew?"

Sunday 13th June 2021

Things at school may be weird, but things at home are much, much weirder. Mum is a walking sack of anxiety, and the more I think about her and those worry dolls the more I come to realise that she's not herself at all. She used to be quirky and vibrant – back when she was friends with Danny and Carla's mums, she was the funny one, the entertainer. But now it's like she's not even there; the lights are on but no one's home. I worry about her. I think about how Graham made me feel during Easter when I was left alone with him, and I think about the fact that she has to share a room with him, and a bed. And now it seems as though she doesn't have anyone else. All her friends have drifted away and all she's got left is Graham.

I was just thinking all of this, up in my room alone, when I heard Mum's phone ringing from her room, and because it only rang once before stopping, I knew that she must have picked it up. Maybe I was wrong, maybe she did have others to talk to. Hopeful that my fears were unfounded, I went to investigate. I know I shouldn't keep spying on her like this, but I wanted to know that she still had someone she could talk to – someone besides a half-dozen half-inch dolls made out of string. As I crept down the corridor, I made a promise in my head that I would only listen in to check whether it was a friendly call or business, see if I could tell who she was speaking to, and return to my room.

But when I reached Mum's bedroom, I heard none of Mum's loud phone voice. I peered through the gap in the open door and saw not Mum but Graham, sat on the bed holding Mum's phone and scrolling through it furiously, as though performing some function very urgently. I knew at once that I had seen something I shouldn't and could only imagine the ways in which Graham would make me suffer if he caught me bearing witness to it, so I shuffled swiftly but silently back down the carpeted hallway to my room.

He had been spying on Mum. But then, so had I. I could hardly tell her I'd caught him on her phone because I'd been peeking through her door unannounced! And anyway, sometimes it's best to withhold information until you are sure what you're dealing with. The phone had rung just once and he had intercepted it, and he must have cancelled the call or else he'd have been talking. Who was the caller? What was Graham doing when I saw him? He seemed to be scrolling, swiping through screens rapidly, browsing an inbox perhaps. Checking Mum's messages, reading through old ones.

Maybe not. Maybe he cancelled the call by accident, felt guilty about it and scrolled through the recent calls list to delete the evidence of his crime. Even if that wasn't what he was doing that might be the sort of excuse he'd come up with if I said anything to Mum, and you can bet she'll believe him. She never argues with anything he says any more.

Monday 14th June 2021

Graham must have been on another early shift today, because he came home only a few minutes after I did. I was in the kitchen staring blankly into the fridge as though the perfect after-school snack was going to jump right out at me, when I heard him come home and enter the living room, where Frogsplash was watching TV.

"Busy studying, I see," Graham said foully.

"Taking a break," Frogsplash said, "I had my first exam this morning, I think I deserve a rest."

"You know, now that you're back living under my roof, your studies have become my business again."

"It's not your roof, though, is it? This is my mum's house."

"I'm the man of the house. I'm the breadwinner."

"No, you're not. Mum works, she earns her own money."

"Yes, but you don't. So, get off the sofa and get out. I'm watching the TV now."

"No. You've got a TV in your room, and thanks to you I no longer have any consoles in mine. What did you do with them anyway? Did you sell them? Making money by stealing from kids doesn't make you the breadwinner. You know that, right?"

"I am your superior. GET OUT."

"Fine, I'll go and revise some more. Thank you so much for motivating me, Graham. At this rate I'll get better grades than Billy!"

"OUT!!!"

Frogsplash went up to his room, laughing to himself as he climbed the stairs. He's really come a long way when it comes to dealing with Graham. I thought he handled it brilliantly and I wished that I had the confidence to talk to Graham like that, but when people are horrible to me I always get lost for words and then I end up crying, unable to articulate anything witty or provocative. I waited in the kitchen and listened until I was sure that

Graham was settled in the living room – I didn't want to cross paths with him in the hall, not after Froggo had got him all worked up like that.

I'm up in my room now and it's just sinking in what Frogsplash said about his games' consoles. The first time he came to visit after moving out he'd asked about them, and Graham had made up some story about how he'd caught Froggo sneaking back into the house to collect them, and Frogsplash had gone along with it! But I understand why. It's the same reason I don't tell anyone about how Graham treats me when no one else is around. It would upset Mum and Billy, it would anger Graham, and there's a good chance no one would believe me. My poor brother. Those consoles were the most precious things in the world to him. The new ones were valuable and had loads of data saved on them and the old ones were retro and had nostalgic value. It would have devastated him to lose them. It would be like Graham destroying all of my books.

Thursday 17th June 2021

Froggo's taunt about him getting better grades than Billy obviously really got to Graham, because he's since refused to give Billy any more shifts at the pub until his exams are over. What's more, he's disallowed them from revising together for fear that they'd distract each other. Billy has to study in their shared bedroom and poor Frogsplash is spending his study leave at the dining table in the kitchen, where Graham can "keep an eye" on him. I would be surprised if he actually cared what grades Froggo got. In fact, I think he would probably be incensed at any academic success he achieves because it would diminish his reasons for belittling him.

Graham desires control above all else, and the importance of these GCSEs affords him a valid reason to be strict and overbearing. He's asked Arnie to cover extra shifts at the pub and he's even got some students working temporary contracts so that he has more time to police things at home. To top it all off, he's stopped writing his shifts on the family calendar and refuses to tell anyone his working hours so that none of us have any idea when he'll be home and so that we live permanently on edge, conscious that at any given moment he might emerge, ready to check up on us and find fault with whatever we are doing.

Monday 21st June 2021

Despite his attempts at tyrannical rule over the household, Graham has been unable to break Frogsplash as he did once before. Something has changed in him. Perhaps learning to deal with Richard's light-hearted, well-meaning taunts has afforded him a thicker skin which now works as armour against more vicious attacks. Or maybe simply knowing that he can escape to Dad's whenever he likes makes Graham's threats feel less potent. Either way, it has clearly been bothering Graham to the point of extreme agitation. The problem is that although Frogsplash feels protected against Graham's foul moods, Mum and I still feel vulnerable to them, and the more he gets riled up by Froggo the more we begin to fear him.

The tension has been rising for days, so it was perhaps a good thing that it finally reached breaking point this afternoon, although it certainly didn't go the way Graham had hoped. As soon as I walked through the door, I heard Graham's cold voice creeping down the hall from the kitchen at the back of the house, where Frogsplash must have been studying for his Maths exam tomorrow. I recognised Graham's tone instantly, it was the same imperious voice he'd used on me when he was telling me that I'd ruined the family's chances of going on holiday. That voice feels like hot pincers grabbing at you all over, pinching your skin everywhere at once, making you feel sick with anger and hate and defencelessness. I hovered in the hall, listening.

"I've been checking your practice papers," Graham was saying. "Terrible. Just terrible. If I were you I'd be very worried. At the rate you're going you'll be lucky to get a passing grade in any subject. Imagine that – failing every single one of your GCSEs. Think about how that would feel, to walk in on results day and see all of your peers overjoyed with their achievements, and then being handed a sheet full of 1s. Crippling. It would crush you. And of course, results day is only the beginning of the despair. You'll struggle for the rest of your life. No grades, no further education, no career and no hope! You'll have to get an unskilled job and you'll have to work very hard to earn enough to survive on those wages, and you'll never be able to afford your own home. You'll have long hours, no leisure time, gruelling work, and you'll be living in the same bedroom for the rest of your life. A spirit-crushing, soul-destroying existence.

"I know what you're thinking. You've been feeling very defiant lately, haven't you? You're thinking that you're going to prove me wrong, that you're going to pass, perhaps even do well! You've got a lot of work to do if you want that dream to come true, but I suppose it's possible. Not that it matters much. You can pass all your exams and still be a failure. You've got no social skills, and you won't get very far without them. Can't really teach that sort of thing, though, can you? Shame… shame.

"Billy's got them, of course, he can talk to anyone – even the old drunks at the pub! It just came naturally to him, and that's why he's moved on from you and those other lads you used to hang around with. He's chosen a new, more advanced crowd in Ryan and Shirian, and I must say I'm proud of him for making the move – very wise. He only talks to you now because he has to live with you, but you wouldn't want to hear what the three of them say about you when you're not around. Let's just say they don't think very highly of you!

"And your mother. Your poor, worried mother. That woman is consumed with doubt by her concerns over you, it keeps her up late at night, and I'm the one who has to try and console her! What on Earth can I possibly say to make her think that everything's going to be all right? She knows you're never going to get into university or get a decent job and she's absolutely devastated by it. She worries because she doesn't know how you're ever going to take care of yourself. Bless her, all she wants is for you to be happy. She doesn't even mention the fact that you're such a burden, all she wants is what's best for you. But she can't see a successful future for you, and that's what's destroying her spirit.

"You must have noticed the change in her lately; so miserable and withdrawn. It's the guilt that's destroying her. She blames herself for the way you've turned out. I keep telling her she's not a bad mother, but she can't help but look at you and wonder where she went wrong. She's not the woman she was when I met her. You've destroyed her, do you know that? She's so miserable to be around, I must admit I've considered leaving her. But then she'd have nothing left at all and I couldn't live with myself. So, it has become my sad duty to support her and hope that one day she'll stop blaming herself for the shortcomings of her children. It's not easy living with someone so hopeless and depressed. You're her burden and she's mine... and you wonder why I resent you!"

At this point I heard the scrape of a chair pulling out from under the table. I heard books closing, the zip of a backpack, some shuffling... I crept up the stairs and crouched on the landing, out of sight but still listening, peering down at the hallway through the bannister.

"Where do you think you're going!" I heard Graham shout, but Froggo gave no reply. He strode into the hall, slipped his trainers on and slipped out of the front door with his backpack slung over his shoulder. He was angry, no doubt about that, but he had not let Graham win.

I had thought that Frogsplash might have gone running back to Dad's, so when he came knocking at the front door just before six p.m. as though nothing at all had happened, I was delighted. I went to open the door with Mum following me close behind. Since her anxiety has increased she has developed a somewhat irrational fear that I'm going to open the door to an axe murderer if I'm not accompanied.

"Forgot my keys," Froggo explained as he wiped his feet on the mat. I'm not surprised he forgot them considering the circumstances that led to his departure. And yet, he had a look of pleasant serenity across his face.

"Oh, I thought you were in your room," said Mum, "I've been calling you and Billy down for dinner!"

"I'm not late, am I?" Frogsplash asked politely.

"No, no, I was just being premature, giving you a chance to finish whatever pages you were on in your study guides. You have been studying, haven't you?" she asked as we walked through to the kitchen and sat down at the places she had set for us at the dining table. Graham was already seated, pretending to read the sport section of the paper.

"Of course, I've been studying!" Frogsplash said proudly. "I don't know why I haven't tried revising in the park before! Such a lovely day out, and I was feeling a bit... *stifled,* shut up in here, so I thought I'd take a stroll, clear my head, then hit the books. And you know, it was the most rewarding, informative study session of my life! I learnt so much and I actually *enjoyed* it. Bring on the Maths exam – I am ready!"

I saw rage flash across Graham's face, brief and severe as lightning, before he composed himself and once again feigned interest in the newspaper he held before him. Seconds later, Billy emerged looking slightly bleary-eyed.

"Sorry, I just had to complete that level..." he said, then quickly checked himself and tried to cover his tracks "...I'm on the advanced level of study in my Maths textbook!"

"Impressive!" said Graham, setting down his newspaper at last. I smirked at Billy, who had clearly been playing *Zombie Slayer 4* on Froggo's PC for at least the past hour, judging by the dazed way in which he seemed to respond to the real world. Mum served up a fine dinner of barbecue chicken wings, potato wedges and four different sides – no doubt an attempt to surpass the standards of deliciousness she believed Dad to have set when Froggo was staying at his place. After that, the dinner went by as normally as it ever does for our house; only Frogsplash and I were tuned into the near-imperceptible tone of irritation whenever Graham spoke.

Friday 25th June 2021

Frogsplash and Billy have finished their exams and I've never seen either of them as happy or carefree as this. It's as if they've been allowed to resume their childhood after so many years of seriousness. Froggo's final exam was two days after Billy's, but Billy waited until Frogsplash was finished before going out celebrating because he didn't want to start the party without him. I hope that that's all the proof Frogsplash needs to assure him that everything Graham said the other day was pure lies. Billy may have some new friends, but he still likes and respects Frogsplash and he would never laugh at him behind his back.

And all that stuff about Mum being unhappy because of Froggo, that's nonsense! It's Graham who makes her feel that way. But then I try to imagine how I would feel if Graham had said all of that stuff to me instead of Frogsplash. I would have tried to fight it; I would have tried to assure myself that it wasn't true, but once the seed has been planted it's incredibly difficult to remove. Graham's nasty ideas are like stubborn weeds – every time you think you've gotten rid of one it resurfaces, strong as ever, ready to cause you trouble.

Speaking of weeds that won't go away, Charlotte, Beth, Andrea and Ruby came by again this lunchtime.

"Oh god, here we go," groaned Danny when she saw them approaching.

"Hey, Danny," came Charlotte's dangerous voice. "How's things? Bored of this lot yet?"

"No, Charlotte. Now go away, for god's sake, I'm sick of this!"

"We've been thinking," Charlotte continued, ignoring Danny's plea, "and we've decided that, if you join our crew, we'll let your boyfriend tag along too. We hang out with boys all the time; one more won't hurt."

"That's a good start," Danny said confidently, "let's say we compromise. How about Elliot can tag along, as well as Sam and Carla here, and then you four leave the group to make it complete. Yeah, that sounds like a good arrangement, what do you think?"

"That's not funny," Charlotte said irritably.

"If you don't like my sense of humour then I'm probably not a good fit for your group. Bye!" Danny dismissed her cheerfully.

"We're not leaving!" said Charlotte, now sounding slightly desperate. "Not until you come with us!"

Danny contemplated her for a moment, stared into her face quite coldly, searchingly, before responding:

"I said no. This is getting out of hand, Charlotte. I'm not joking, this really is starting to feel like harassment. I'm not going to change my mind. I don't know why you're so fixated on this idea but it's making me feel uncomfortable now. I have a right to choose who I spend my time with, and I have a right not to be poached like a pheasant! I don't snitch on people for breaking school rules, but harassment is a criminal offence and if you or any of your group approach me one more time with this absurd proposal I'm going to have to report it to Mr Wilcox!"

"Well, that's not going to work," chuckled Beth Amory in childish delight. "This was his idea in the first place!"

"Beth, shut UP *you idiot!*" Charlotte scolded. "She didn't mean…" She paused, turning to address Danny once again, "It was Wilcox's idea for friendship groups to mix, that's what she meant. He wants us all to mingle a bit more… he said that in assembly, remember?"

It was a feeble cover-up and she knew it. Highly frustrated, she clamped her hand around Beth's skinny upper arm and led her away hastily, the other two scurrying behind.

"What the *hell?*" Carla was the first to speak. "Wilcox's idea? Why would he want… Why would he care…?"

"This is getting weird," I said. "What kind of game is he playing?"

Danny was silent and she seemed to go very pale, although it's hard to be sure with her complexion. I could tell her head was spinning; either she was shocked, or she was too busy processing this information, trying to work out what it meant, to make any comment.

"Are you OK?" Elliot asked her kindly.

"Yeah… yeah. It's just… well, it's a bit scary, isn't it? If this really was Wilcox's idea then he's some kind of master puppeteer, pulling all the strings out of view. And Charlotte was so persistent – what did he do to her to make her do his bidding – bribes, threats, blackmail?"

"Never mind her," said Elliot, "I'm more worried about you. What could he possibly gain from teaming you up with that lot?"

"Well, let's not get carried away," I said, "maybe it's not that sinister."

"Well what could it be, then?" Carla asked.

"I don't know… maybe he's grouped us all into certain classes for next year and he wants those groups to be more cohesive or something… I don't know! But it makes more sense that it's something professional and academic rather than some crackpot conspiracy theory!"

"But that doesn't explain Charlotte's eagerness," Elliot pondered. "Maybe Wilcox did want Danny to join their group for some reason, but why would Charlotte bend over backwards to make it happen? The girl was desperate!"

"And when was the last time Wilcox did anything for moral reasons?" Carla added. "We already know he's a rat! Maybe if he was a normal teacher it might be reasonable to assume that he was doing this for purely professional reasons, but we know better than that, we know who he really is."

"OK, these are all really good points, but we can't go throwing these accusations around without any evidence. Remember what happened the last time we did that?" I said, looking sternly at Carla, who blushed and avoided eye contact with Danny.

"But you have to admit this is different," Carla responded. "I was wrong to accuse Danny because she'd never done anything to betray my trust. But Wilcox is known for being sneaky, self-serving and dubious."

"True," I admitted, "but we still need proof."

Friday 2nd July 2021

EMPOWERMENT STRUGGLE: "MAN OF THE HOUSE" FACES DIFFICULTIES IN HIS ATTEMPTS TO OPPRESS AND UNDERMINE STRONG YOUNG FEMALE

The would-be dictator, 55, has orchestrated a string of verbal and psychological attacks upon the girl, 12, over the past several months. However, the pre-teen has been inspired by the resilience of her brother, who has recently freed himself from the shackles of domestic oppression.

School's out for Frogsplash and Billy so they now spend most of their time out of the house, hanging out with mates in the park, only occasionally returning home for dinner before going back out again and staying out well past my bedtime. I envy their freedom. This house doesn't feel like my home any more and I wish I could escape it, too. The atmosphere is oppressive and without my brothers it feels like it's all on me.

I thought Mum might have cheered up once Frogsplash moved back in, but if anything it just makes her more anxious because she doesn't want anything to upset him for fear that he'll leave again, and whenever he's out (which, as I've mentioned, is most hours of the day) she worries that he's not safe or that he's going to do something stupid. She's begun cutting out newspaper articles and pinning them to the memo board, sticking them on the fridge or else leaving them on the table or the worktop where they might be seen. She's like a silent health and safety ambassador leaving tokens of doom all over the house, snippets of disaster bearing headlines such as:

"BOY, 13, LOSES HAND WHILE EXPLORING JUNKYARD."

"TOP STUDENT, 17, ELECTROCUTED WHILE WALKING ON TRAIN TRACK AFTER NIGHT OUT."

"SKATEBOARD STUNT LEAVES TWO IN CRITICAL CONDITION."

"LIFE-CHANGING INJURIES AFTER CHAINSAW PRANK GOES HORRIBLY WRONG."

"THREE TEENAGERS NARROWLY ESCAPE DEATH PLAYING DARE-DEVIL GAME ON LEVEL CROSSING."

It might be more effective if Frogsplash actually spent any time at home, but in reality, all it seems to do is irritate Graham, who is not fond of clutter. Aside from mid-to-moderate annoyances such as this, though, he seems to have lost his passion for losing his temper with Mum or finding innovative ways to criticise her on a daily basis. She's so distant and distracted it's like she's not even there, so I suppose it wouldn't be very satisfying for him to try and make her feel bad about herself. She doesn't appear to have the capacity for self-reflection at the moment, she just sort of drifts from one day to the next. It's very strange and very sad. I know my mum is in there somewhere, but she's closed herself off. It's like part of her brain has shut down completely, the only remaining parts being the one that causes worry and the one that sticks to routine.

With Frogsplash absent and Mum mentally so, it was only a matter of time before Graham returned his attentions to me. Mum was in the garden picking grapes from the vine and I was in the kitchen preparing my lunch for tomorrow. Graham came marching in after a shift at the pub and I instantly sensed his mood. Most people come home from work exhausted, physically drained and ready to slump on the sofa but Graham, at least when he's in these moods, is like an overcharged battery, unable to stay still or relax, looking for an outlet for whatever it is that's got him so wound up. I braced myself for potential conflict.

"At home again, I see," he said to me, as though being in my own home was some sort of deviant act. I didn't respond. I know now that he is capable of interpreting absolutely anything I say as fighting talk.

"HELLO, I just spoke to you!" he said, more aggressively now. "No wonder you don't have any friends to hang out with after school, you're practically a mute! How do you expect to get by in life if you don't even talk? What, do you think that if you get through school OK then employers are just going to look at your exam results and immediately offer you a job? Qualifications aren't half as important as the gift of the gab. You've got to be able to sell yourself, and you have to come across as a normal person who can work with other people. And you can forget finding a husband or even any friends. You've got a long, lonely life ahead of you."

A few months ago, this sort of talk might have got to me, but I'm much stronger now. I don't want to be broken like my mum; I want to break free like my brother. I could see exactly what Graham was trying to do; it was a weak and pathetic attempt to disarm me. He was doing the whole "you've got no social skills" routine, which I've already heard him use on Frogsplash, so I know it's not really personal. It's not even about me, none of this is, so why would I get hurt by it?

I decided to continue ignoring him, because that's the closest I can get to being absent, like Mum and Frogsplash. He doesn't seem to get much satisfaction out of it if he can't get a reaction out of you, so I said nothing. I sealed my lips tight and I told myself it was a game: your opponent is going to try everything they can to get you to talk, but if you open your mouth you lose. The best way to play is to concentrate on your mouth, to focus on it as a real and physical part of yourself rather than just an idea in your head. Hold your lips closed and keep them firmly together. Don't even think about what the other person is saying.

"It's not just that you're odd," he went on, "I mean, not talking to anyone *is* odd, but it's also just bloody boring. At least with most people who are odd it makes them eccentric or a little bit entertaining, but you've managed to make yourself utterly weird and mind-numbingly boring all with one stroke. You might as well buy the studio flat and half-dozen cats now and be done with it. Your brother may not be as book-smart as you but at least he's got a personality. I've known you for over a year now and you still come across as bland as a slice of dry bread."

I had just finished making my lunch: salmon and avocado salad with red pepper and spring onion garnished new potatoes – not a slice of dry bread in sight. It was a recipe I'd learnt from Richard a few weeks ago, and I couldn't help but think what a better man he is than Graham. I clicked shut each of the plastic seals on all four sides of my lunch box, slid it onto the middle shelf of the fridge and walked straight past Graham without saying a word, casually striding up the stairs to my room wearing a smug grin. I only wished I could have stayed down there to see the distorted look of fury that must surely have been etched across his face.

Monday 5th July 2021

This morning in assembly, Mr Wilcox took the podium, still standing tall despite his despicable lack of professionalism and suspiciously manipulative treatment of a select few of his students. When he stands up there in front of the entire school, commanding respect and behaving like an honourable gentleman, it's hard to remember that there are many questionable facets to his personality, and that all we really know about his true character is that it's highly untrustworthy.

"Good morning all, please be seated. Firstly, I would like to remind you that auditions for the end-of-year school play are now closed. The casting list will be posted on the school website by the end of the day. Likewise, the sign-up sheet for the end-of-year school talent show has now been filled and no new acts will be permitted to take part. The schedule for the talent show will also be up on the school website later today."

Last year, both Carla and Danny took part in the talent show: Carla sang and played guitar and Danny danced. This year, Carla will be playing with The Sylphs, but Danny didn't sign up, whether that's because she's too embarrassed to take to the stage after falling off it and breaking her ankle last year, or because she'd rather spend her time with Elliot, I'm not sure. Last year, I played a fairly prominent role in the school's production of *A Midsummer Night's Dream,* and although it went well, I couldn't imagine auditioning again this year.

The thought of being up there performing in front of the whole school is absolutely terrifying and performing in front of family and friends would be even worse. Last year, Mum, Dad, Billy and Graham all came. Graham pretended to be supportive at the time, back when he still had to pretend, but this year I know he would mock my performance, and I'm already sensitive enough about going out of my comfort zone in front of an entire audience of people. Whatever he were to say, it would get to me, I know it. At the end of assembly, we practised singing the school song with Mr Bellows on piano. This, too, is an end of term tradition for Duke John Jameson.

Friday 9th July 2021

Graham's efforts to diminish my self-worth continue to disappoint. Today he had such a sheer lack of inspiration that he resorted to comparing me to his ex-wife, Billy's mum.

"She was a faker, just like you. She'd pretend to be strong, pretend to be coping, doing everything for appearances. She put so much effort into pretending to have a perfect life she hardly noticed me or Billy. Underneath the calm exterior she was a wreck, a total headcase. She was so determined not to show any sign of weakness that eventually she stopped showing any emotion at all. She was a total blank, a nothing – just like you. Until one day she snapped. She went absolutely insane and she disappeared into the night, leaving me in charge of Billy."

I realise now what he was really getting at. This was never about me. He's warning me: if Mum carries on the way she's going then she'll end up fleeing, too, and then I'll be left alone with Graham. It's fight or flight, and she's not putting up a fight at all. I have to get her to *wake up*.

Sunday 11th July 2021

I took my chance yesterday morning after Graham had left for work.

"Mum, when was the last time you heard from Maria?"

"Who?" she said vacantly.

"Maria – my mate Carla's mum."

"Oh, didn't I tell you? I called her once and a man answered. He said I'd got the wrong number."

"But you can't have done, can you? Her number was saved in your phone so you wouldn't have typed it in to call her."

"Yes, so I guessed she must have got a new phone and sold the old one to that bloke who answered my call."

"Don't you think he would have said something? Surely, he wouldn't have just said, 'You've got the wrong number.' He would have mentioned it if he'd bought the phone off Maria and kept her number. Not that anyone does that. Who keeps somebody else's old number?"

"Well yes, I did think it was a bit odd, but it was the only explanation I could think of. I must have called her on that exact same number fifty times!"

"It is possible," I said delicately, "that somebody might have changed the number in your phone. It's very easy to update a contact, someone could have changed the digits but left the contact name the same."

"But why would anybody do that?"

"I don't know… perhaps you did it yourself, by accident."

"That doesn't seem very likely." She gave a hollow laugh.

"Or maybe it wasn't an accident," I said. "Maybe you just didn't want to speak to Maria any more. It's OK, you know, I don't mind."

"Of course, I still want to speak to Maria, she's lovely! Why would you think that?"

"Well, because Carla says that you blocked Maria's number. She tried calling you and the line was dead."

"What, me? I wouldn't even know how to do something like that, and I certainly wouldn't want to!"

"No, I didn't think you would. But the thing is, Mum, someone did block Maria's number from your phone."

"Oh dear! She must have thought I was incredibly rude! I suppose it was one of those network errors or something – that sort of technical fault probably happens all the time."

"I don't think they do, Mum, and the truth is, I've seen Graham on your phone a few times. I hate to say it, but I think he might be behind this."

"Oh, don't be daft!" she said, but her expression showed no sign of amusement. "What possible reason could he have for stopping me speaking to Maria? He thinks she's great! She did that bit of carpentry in the pub last year, remember?"

"Oh yeah," I said slowly, running out of ways to try and make her see.

"Must just be one of those things," she said vaguely, and she wandered upstairs to use the bathroom.

This morning I awoke at seven-thirty a.m. I went down to the kitchen in just my vest and knickers, expecting nobody else to be up for hours, so my heart nearly leapt out of my chest when I saw Graham sitting at the dining table. He was sat quite still, not reading the paper nor finishing the crossword he had started before work yesterday. He was not even drinking a cup of tea.

He had worked a late shift last night, as he does most Saturdays, and even when he doesn't, he still insists upon a lie-in on a Sunday. He is a man of tradition and clinging on to these pointless rituals seems to give him a sense of importance, as though society itself is his only dictator and properness his only law. He is not the sort of man to challenge norms or question the way things are generally done. He does not break from routine lightly, and so it was with great trepidation that I advanced further into the kitchen.

As I walked closer, he pulled his chair out suddenly and stood up out of his seat, blocking my path to the kettle. He stood over me, not especially tall or broad, but still a significant physical threat, as well as a menacing psychological one.

"What have you been saying to your mother?" he spoke at last.

"Only the truth," I said. "Somebody's been trying to isolate her, and I have reason to believe it was you!"

"Oh? And what reason might that be?"

"I've seen you on her phone!"

"Seems a bit hypocritical of you, accusing me of spying on Cassie when you were spying on me."

"I wasn't spying. I was looking for Mum and I saw you on her phone. And what I'm accusing you of is much worse. It's one thing to look on someone else's phone, it's quite another to go changing numbers and blocking contacts!"

"I did no such thing, Samantha. I was afraid this would happen. I warned you, didn't I? I told you: too much silence, too much pretending to be OK and eventually you'd snap. You're losing your mind, throwing wild and bizarre accusations around. This is what happens when you have no one to talk to: the brain becomes starved of activity – not enough stimulation, you see, so it begins inventing things. I'm not saying you're lying, Samantha, I think you do genuinely believe the things you are saying, but you must understand that they're simply not true. You're desperately in need of a social outlet. You're craving attention, perhaps even subconsciously, you're behaving absurdly so that you can get a reaction. It's not your fault, you just need some friends."

"I do have friends!" I said defensively.

"Oh? And what do they make of this theory of yours, this phone number business you've been talking about?"

"Well... I haven't told them."

"Oh. Why not?"

"I don't know, I thought it might sound a bit... crazy," I admitted and then immediately wished I hadn't, so I began to backtrack. "And one of them has a boyfriend and he's always hanging around; I didn't want to say anything in front of him."

"So, you admit that it does sound crazy? Sit down, Samantha," he said as he took a seat himself and drew a chair for me right next to his own. Warily, I complied.

"Secondary school can be difficult," he began. "Obviously, it's taken you a bit longer than most to find your place, but you'll get there. But you've got to stop all this madness; you're only making life harder for yourself. I know there's been a lot of change lately but the rest of us are finally in a really good place and all this silliness of yours is really getting us down. Your brother's never been happier and your mum's thrilled to have him back. Of course, Billy and I are fine, we always are, so you're the only problem here. And now you've got your mum worrying about you because of these mad stories you've been telling!

"To tell you the truth she's been thinking of calling the school, asking them if they've noticed any unusual behaviours or worrying signs in you, and seeing if she can get you on the waiting list to see the school counsellor, Mr Donahue, is it? She was looking him up on the laptop the other day. I told her you might appreciate it if we tried to speak to you first, and I offered to do it because, well, you know your mum can get a bit emotional, and I thought it would be awkward enough as it is! Obviously, if you wanted to speak to the school counsellor then we could arrange that for you. Do you think that that's something you could benefit from?"

"No, definitely not," I said firmly.

"OK. Well then, do you think you could cut down on the tale-telling, for your own sake and for ours?"

"Um, OK," I said, dumbstruck.

"Great, I'm glad we had this talk. Can I get you a cup of tea?"

"Er… no thanks, I think I'll go back to bed for a bit actually."

And here I am, lying in bed, that conversation whirring round and round in my head.

It was a tactic, that's all, a clever way of disarming me: being nice to me and at the same time making me think I'm losing the plot. So, what if I haven't told my friends about this? I didn't want them to worry, that's all. And it's true that having Elliot around makes me feel uncomfortable about discussing family problems. I mean, whatever problems I've got they can't be as bad as his. Oh, and threatening to call the school, that was a cheap trick! I wonder what his next move will be and what the end game is… whatever it is, I'm not falling for it.

Thursday 15th July 2021

All week, Carla has been rehearsing with the band at lunch, leaving me alone with Danny and Elliot once more. It wasn't so bad last time, but there's something about the hot temperatures and the impending freedom of the summer holidays that's got them all loved up and touchy-feely. They spend most of their time rolling around on the grass kissing, leaving me sat there right next to them desperately searching for something else to focus on while eating my packed lunch.

It's gross and extremely awkward, but what really unnerves me is the way they can be locking lips for minutes at a time and then, all of a sudden, they just stop and start talking to me like nothing at all was going on. Surely they should only be thinking about each other when they're engaged in such a passionate act, but when they stop and immediately start asking me how much of my Maths homework I've done, I get the impression that they were never really embroiled in the moment as much as they made it seem. My guess is it gets a bit boring after a while but neither one of them wants to be rude and put an end to it too soon.

Today I'd had enough and told them I was going for a walk. I wandered further out to the main field right on the edge of the school boundary, which is still recovering from being dug up in search of the time capsules which seemed so important at the beginning of the school year. We've had very little rain so the seeds that were planted there haven't taken well, and I decided that the sparse, dry grassland was a barren and unpleasant setting for a solo picnic. I walked around so that I was on the opposite side of the lake to Danny and Elliot and I took a seat closer to the bank where the grass was fresher and more inviting.

I had barely clicked my lunch box open when, seemingly out of nowhere, I was set upon by those same vicious geese that had attacked young Jamal, only this time they had their offspring to feed and protect and were significantly more aggressive as a result. The two adult geese were at the forefront of the attack with their six goslings, now almost adult-sized themselves, bringing up the rear. Not far behind them was a second goose family emerging from the water to take advantage of what they perceived to be my offering.

They honked rudely at those which had preceded them as though arguing over the pecking order which had fallen into place by chance. I stumbled to my feet, but the larger birds took this to be a threat and one of them raised its neck and spread its wings in a bid to make itself appear larger, while the other took the opportunity to snatch my Mediterranean vegetable wrap right out of my hand. Struck by sheer terror at the prospect of almost losing a finger to a snapping beak, I dropped my lunch box, and the younger geese wasted no time in finishing off my cheese and grapes.

I was too embarrassed to go crawling back to Danny and Elliot begging for scraps of their lunches and anyway, the amount of saliva those two have been sharing lately is bound to cross-contaminate anything else their lips have touched. So, I went to the lower school common area and got a sugary drink from the vending machine to keep me going. The sugar hit was short-lived, and before the last lesson of the day had even begun I was starving again. It was a tedious Chemistry lesson: all theory, no practical, and I spent most of it watching the clock and trying to remember what was left in the fridge when I opened it to get milk this morning.

But it didn't matter, because by the time school was finally over and I'd endured a frustrating, stomach-rumbling, traffic-filled bus journey home I would have happily eaten my way through the jar of dog biscuits we keep hidden in the utility room. Fortunately, there were more delectable items in the fridge, and after kicking off my shoes and shrugging off my school bag I got straight to it. The first thing that caught my eye was a pack of ham. It was already open, so I didn't have to feel guilty about breaking the seal and compromising its freshness. There was also no need for cutlery, which was a huge bonus.

I grabbed two slices in one and began munching hungrily, swiftly accompanied by Max and Trousers, who were begging at my feet. Their sweet, sad eyes were enough to win me over, so I began tearing up the meat and distributing it between them, telling myself that if anyone were to ask where all the ham went I could legitimately say that the dogs ate it, even if that was only half-true. The ham lasted no time at all and I was already eyeing up half a tin of cold baked beans, trying to recall how long it had been in there, when I spotted something far more enticing.

A trio of fresh tex-mex dips sat modestly in waiting, needing desperately to be eaten before its expiry date. This was something of quality, far too good to be shovelled in by the spoonful, so I went to the utility room, which has become our pantry since Mum stopped using it for her home-made wine and searched for a worthy accompaniment. Perhaps a tortilla chip might have been more appropriate, but when I saw my favourite bag of hand-cooked, sea-salted, ridge-cut crisps I was far from disappointed.

I was more than half-way through the "share size" bag of crisps, guacamole dripping down my chin and onto my chest when, out of nowhere, Graham appeared in front of me. The shock of his sudden arrival and the horror of getting caught in this inelegant, slob-like, greedy act was so intense my heart began to pound in my chest and a very real, profound panic set in. I felt light-headed and thought for a moment that I might faint. I had to remind myself to breathe, and then, my hand shaking, I wiped the bright green avocado sludge from my chin and rolled the crisp packet up gingerly, suddenly void of an appetite. Graham simply watched, not angrily but pensively, as though drawing conclusions from the evidence laid out before him.

"Oh, I'm not surprised," he said at last, gently prying the tray of dips and bag of crisps from my guilty, greasy hands. "Food is comforting. All your life you've known for a fact that food fills an emptiness within you. And then, all of a sudden, there's this new emptiness and you've got nothing else to fill it with. So, the snacks become your friends. At the end of the school day, the other girls meet up with their friends or boyfriends to pass the hours as pleasurably as they can, but you've got a date with the fridge instead. I don't blame you, Samantha, but it has to stop. It's a terrible habit and a slippery slope.

"It's not just your physical health – or your physical appearance for that matter. It's about your mental health. You're substituting food for real happiness. This is a short-term fix, a simple comfort that's not getting to the heart of the issue. You're treating the symptom not the cause, but when you comfort yourself with food you stop pushing yourself to achieve real happiness. Not only that, but it's a compulsive behaviour that can easily be a gateway to substance abuse. I've had many sad cases become regulars at the pub. You get the older men who just don't know what to do with themselves after retirement, but the women tend to be younger; they've replaced food with alcohol, and it's become a dangerous habit.

"It's nothing to be ashamed of, but it can't carry on. These salty snacks are no better than the sugary ones, and don't go thinking guacamole isn't a sin just because it's made from avocado – that's the fattiest fruit in the world! Do you want to see how many calories are in one serving of these crisps? And would you like to know how many servings you've had?" he asked, reading the back of the packet grimly.

"No!" I replied desperately, "I'd rather not know."

"Probably best." He nodded sympathetically. "Let's just say, I don't think you'll need dinner tonight. I'll tell your mother you already ate."

"Um… thanks," I said sheepishly, and I walked up to my room in shame, still rubbing the corners of my mouth for guacamole build-up.

I know I was excessively hungry after school today because the geese ate my lunch, but the truth is I'm always hungry after school, and I always have a snack soon after returning home without even thinking about how calorific it is. I've never calculated exactly how many calories I'm consuming, but I try to be conscious of what I'm eating, whether there's enough fruit, vegetables and protein in it, so I always feel like I've got it under control. But then when I snack, I tell myself that it doesn't count as long as I eat balanced meals the rest is OK.

But I've just been kidding myself. Of course, they count – there are probably more calories in snacks than in main meals! And Graham's right that most normal people meet up after school and hang out, or else go to clubs where they do sport or dance or other activities. And I wonder why other girls are thinner than me! Graham might not have known that I skipped lunch today, but the way I was eating those crisps was undoubtedly unhealthy, and not just for my diet. I still feel hungry but that's because all I've eaten are sugary, fatty, quick energy release foods that don't sustain you. It's like Graham said – it's only a short-term fix.

Friday 16th July 2021

After school today I went straight up to my room, not even stopping in the kitchen to put my lunch box in the dishwasher for fear that the temptation of snacks would be too great. I tried to get back into the ancient diary I had been so engrossed in, but the old language is so difficult to decipher, and it seemed as though Edmund wasn't doing much besides moaning about the harsh conditions of his employment. I don't mean to sound heartless, but wasn't work pretty gruelling for everyone back then? And weren't there five-year-olds losing hands in factories and suffocating up chimneys?! I'm being unfair to Edmund because I'm hungry and that makes me irritable, but I must stay strong.

Mum made dinner tonight, and to my great surprise, Graham delivered it to my room. It was a creamy chicken and bacon pasta bake, topped with breadcrumbs and served with buttered peas on the side. It smelled amazing. Graham put it on my dressing table in front of the mirror and he told me I could eat it there, but first he wanted to show me something. He brought me over to my computer and typed the name of a website into the browser. It was called *"Thinspiration for Teens"* and the homepage contained the tagline: *"Portion control. Self-control. Lifestyle control."* It had several articles, "how-to" guides, links to forums and video uploads, inspirational quotes and helpful tips. Directly beneath the title and tagline was the website's "philosophy":

"We teach positive application of the virtue of self-restraint. Exercising willpower is a rewarding, self-affirming practice which boosts self-worth and opens your eyes to the incredible potential you have within you. Set yourself healthy, achievable goals and feel the amazing sense of achievement when you succeed! Try some of our lifestyle management suggestions from the list below."

"I did a little research," Graham said as he scrolled through the site for me to view. "This looks like it's got some really insightful content. I think it could be just what you need. It's purely for motivation, you don't have to subscribe or talk to anyone or give out any personal details. It's just got some good advice that you can read through whenever you feel weak. It's a support network: there if you need it, whenever you need it. And it's got some really useful tools, check this out..."

He clicked on a section called "Calorie Calculator" which opened up a search bar. He typed in "chicken and bacon pasta bake". It then came up with a selection bar with different weight options. He selected "500g".

"I weighed it for you myself before I came up here," he informed me. The website calculated that my portion of pasta bake contained nine hundred calories. "Add the buttered peas and you're looking at about a thousand calories just for dinner! And do you know how many you should be consuming in a day?"

"Two thousand," I said confidently, having read it on the back of food packets many, many times.

"For a grown woman, yes," he said, "but you're not yet thirteen. Naturally children don't need to eat as much as adults – I bet your little half-sister doesn't eat nearly as much as you! The older you get the more food you need – until you're fully grown, that is. If you click on this section here it will explain everything..."

He clicked on the "Information" link below the Calorie Calculator, which showed a chart indicating the recommended intake for different age ranges. For age 13-14 under the column "Guidelines" was written:

"You are not yet at full height and therefore require less energy to perform everyday tasks as well as fitness activities. Your body is young and does not need to regenerate tissue, strengthen brittle bones or repair damage caused by the ageing of cells. Therefore, the calories you consume must be spent on physical activity, or else they will be stored as fat. However, this is not the case for males. A boy of this age may have a ferocious appetite, this is because he is developing muscles that his female counterpart is not. It is for this reason that there is such a disparity between the recommended daily intake depending on sex for this particular age group."

Under "Recommended Daily Intake: Boys" was written "1,900-2,100 calories". And under "Recommended Daily Intake: Girls" was "1,300-1,500 calories".

"I'm afraid I was rather shocked myself," Graham admitted, "but having only ever had boys I suppose I wouldn't have noticed. I don't expect your mother knew either, or else she wouldn't have been over-feeding you with that crap." He gestured towards the slop of salt, fat and carbs that was now thickening on the plate upon my dresser.

"I mean, it's fine, if you think you've had five hundred calories or less today. What did you have for lunch? We can type it in the calculator."

"Oh no, it's OK, I don't want to eat it."

"Very good."

"But what about Mum? She cooked that from scratch."

"Don't you worry about that," he said, "I'll make sure she doesn't find out." And he took the plate from my dresser and left, closing my door behind him.

Saturday 17th July 2021

I went to sleep last night with my stomach rumbling, but I found that quite comforting – if my stomach is rumbling then I must be doing something right. I can't satisfy every craving otherwise I wouldn't be making any progress at all! Dad picked me and Froggo up at midday, Stephanie was strapped into her car seat in the back.

"So, what do you fancy for lunch?" was the very first thing he asked us.

"I only just ate breakfast," I said, "more like brunch actually, I'm stuffed!"

Frogsplash, who always rolls out of bed five minutes before Dad is due to arrive, hadn't set foot in the kitchen this morning, and therefore had no way of knowing that I was lying.

"Oh, I didn't get any brunch! Don't tell me I missed out on bacon and eggs!"

"I can do bacon and eggs for lunch if you like?" Dad suggested.

"Nah, better not, Billy and I are having a competition – which one of us can get the best six-pack by the end of summer!"

"Ah, I see," Dad replied. "Chicken salad it is then – no dressing!"

I was a bit annoyed with myself then, I could have easily had that without feeling guilty. Oh well, no calories is better than healthy calories, that's what *Thinspiration for Teens* says. And I thought that, if Frogsplash is on a diet, too, then that would massively improve my chances of getting a healthy dinner. It turns out, however, that my brother isn't quite as serious about dieting as I am, because when we drove past a fried chicken place close to Dad's flat, he decided that that was the ideal cuisine for the development of his abs. The smell of it in the car was intoxicating, and the thought that I wasn't going to get any of it was pure torture. I wondered how long we had left until we reached Dad's place where I could hide in my room away from the deep-fried devil.

I have learnt, in these situations, that the only way to endure it is to make a game out of it. I tried to guess how long we had left in the car, estimating it at seven and a half minutes. I allowed myself to look at my watch every time I thought a minute had passed, but I was not allowed to count the seconds. It's all about discipline and restraint, focussing the mind on what you're allowed and when you're allowed to have it. It took nine relentless minutes and sixteen sickening seconds before we pulled up outside Dad's place.

I went straight to my room when we arrived, determined to distract myself while the others ate. Fully prepared for precisely this situation, I had packed Edmund's old diary in my bag. I flicked through several more pages of the mundane, day-to-day struggles of life in the eighteenth century before finally finding the point at which Edmund resumed the tale of forbidden love between himself and his beloved Carolina.

Saturday 17th July 1723

Many a moon didst pass since word hath cometh from mine lady, and I knoweth not wherefore she hath vanish'd. In earlier days I didst oft see her rambling the moors nearby, even in the coldest of times, but the sun doth shine warmest now, and yet hither she is devastatingly absent! Whither has she wander'd, and what purpose hath she away from these grounds?! I hadst begun to grow most bitter towards the lady, believing her promises empty and her intentions cruel, for she didst offer me her heart before so selfishly taking herself away! But those thoughts of cruelty and betrayal were borne purely from mine own selfishness, for time hath writ a far darker tale which keepeth mine spirit from rest.

Gladly I would has't mine lady run free rather than the fate I now fear she hath met! Happily, I would has't her make a fool of me and breaketh mine heart! For now, I doth fear the worst. 'Twas mine own idea to poison her cruel husband, the Duke, and what then if he didst catch her in the act? I didst instruct her to put it all in his drink, but perhaps she wast fearful that the dose would be too heavy, and perhaps she didst add only a few drops, or else he spilled his cup before 'twas empty! This hath been a grave mistake for which I must take full blame. I must find her, death be damned, I would die before allowing her to suffer.

"Sam! Sam, we're going in a minute!"

I didst resolve in the earliest hours to gain entry into the chambers of the Duke and his suffering wife, Carolina, located in the grand house adjacent to the school building. I has't seen that place daily for years gone by, and oft I didst desire to hear the stories the walls would telleth from within. It would not do to attempt entry unarmed and unprepared; mine weapons art crude and impotent, but mine passions doth drive me forth and equip me with all the force of a thousand armies. I shalt ruin him! He wilt be trampled 'neath mine righteous foot!

"Come on Sam, Stephanie's desperate to get out!"

Early this morn I didst venture far beyond mine bounds, into the home of the Duke, armed only with mine hunger for justice and the kit of potions and poisons I has't procured over recent years. Mine heart didst rattle heavily in mine chest when I cross'd the threshold 'tween the school grounds I knoweth so well and the Duke's personal estate, but I didst not shiver nor hesitate, for mine was a noble and worthy mission. Mine foremost effort was to seek out mine Carolina's hiding place, desperate as I was to ensure her safety. But fate doth ne'er favour the brave, and 'twas the Duke himself who didst obstruct mine path after entry, like the cruel and violent dragon guarding the gold he didst not rightfully own...

Dad had to come and get me from my room, because even though I'd long since distracted myself from the temptation of the fried chicken, it was impossible to tear myself away from the engrossing developments within Edmund's diary. But Stephanie was desperate to go to New Bush Park, which is only a ten-minute drive away and has an amazing water feature for younger kids to play in. When we arrived, she was so desperate to get in, Dad had to physically restrain her just so that he could get her to change into her swimsuit. Dad sat on the grassy slope overlooking the play fountain, I chose the shade of a nearby tree and Frogsplash decided to take his top off and do sit-ups in the blazing sun. He looked like an absolute prat.

Don't get me wrong, I'm glad to have my old brother back – being a pale, insular, mope-about was not his true personality – but having a confident, outgoing brother gives me the right to point out when he's being a total prat whenever I feel that it needs to be said. I might even have to start saying it to his face if he's going to become one of those muscle men who take their tops off in public at any given opportunity. At any rate, I was glad we had all distanced ourselves from each other to some degree, because I was desperate to get back into the diary.

Snoring heavy as a beast, 'twas some surprise I didst see no smoke emit from his inflated nostrils. Undoubtedly drunk, he lay across the entrance hallway, his head propped up against the candle-lit wall, mouth sagging wide open for air. Not a moment didst I spare in mine decision to pour a dose into that blackened void known only for its malice and greed, so swiftly I didst reach for mine pouch of potions and poisons, and hastily did I deploy the contents of mine favoured sleep-inducing liquid directly into the mouth of the beast. For one so drunk as he was, the drug would act as a temporary paralysis, making him unable to move even if he were to become sober enough to gain consciousness.

Onwards I didst traverse, deeper into the glorious dwelling of mine deepest enemy and mine truest love – but whither wast she hidden? No known chamber didst contain her! Had she truly fled? Perhaps 'twas true that the lady hadst run away, from both her husband and from me. Peradventure mine parting words dids't frighten the poor lady, for 'twas a wicked deed I dids't suggest. But I could not depart that grand house 'til 'twas certain that mine lady was safe from the wretched hands of the Duke. Assured that the potion would now be at work inside him, I dids't call out her name.

"Carolina!" I cried, "Carolina! Tell me thou art safe from harm, sweet Carolina!"

"Edmund?" I heard it distant, but clear enough through the silent night's air, "Edmund, I am hither!" she dids't beckon. I followed her voice down the hall 'til I reached a door. "'Tis locked!" cried she. "He keepeth the key in his breast pocket. Hurry, mine dearest love, he hath been starving me for many a week!"

I didst runneth down the corridor back from whence I arrived and I didst retrieve the key from that beastly man. He hadst not moved a muscle since I dosed him with the potion, but he breathed just as heavily – curse him! Time didst begin to pass unnaturally from thence. It seemed not a second later that I had freed mine lady from the closet in which she had so cruelly been immured, and wast carrying her towards the kitchens whither I fetched her milk and bread to restore her health as swiftly as 'twas possible. Mine poor lady wast indeed wasting away, the Duke hadst surely meant to kill her with this punishment.

"Mine sweet love, thou art so thin and frail! That man hath been most vicious and unjust!"

"Oh, Edmund, 'twas purest torture! He didst eat his own meals right before me, and then he didst eat mine own meals too, and he forced me to watch it all! He gave me nowt but water, and 'twas only for thee that I didst drink it. 'Twas thee that didst feedeth me all that I needed, for thee alone fed me the desire to live."

"Mine poor lady, wherefore didst he treat thee so cruelly?" I implored.

"He didst catch me with thine poison, Edmund! He didst waketh too soon and see me pouring a second dose into his drink!"

"So 'twas mine own fault! Oh, cruellest fate, what unkind twist of events is this! Forgive me, mine sweet, please may thee forgiveth me! Oh, but I doth not deserve it. I am responsible for this suffering thou has't undertaken!"

"No! The Duke be the monster! I doth forgiveth thee, Edmund, for thou hath rescued me! But wherefore didst thine poison not do the deed?"

"'Twas potent enough for sure," said I, "but I didst forget, oh mine guilty folly! I didst forget that the man you call monster is monstrous in size as well as spirit. A man as heavy as he would require double the dose, or yet more!"

"It matters not now," said she, "but we must rid ourselves of him for certain this time. Doth not leave me alone with him once more, I beg thee!"

"Never!" I replied. "I hast an arsenal of potions upon mine person, but only one be a poison potent enough to kill. There is but one problem..."

"What?" said she in fear.

"'Tis potent enough to kill a man. But wil't be sufficient to kill a monster?"

"Come on, Sam, time to go. If Stephanie misses her nap, she'll be up all night!"

Monday 19th July 2021

It's the last week of term and everyone else seems to be in good spirits, but I'm worried about spending all my summer at home. Last summer, Danny, Carla and I all hung out at Danny's house, but things have changed since then. Danny's family have only just moved into their new home and they're nowhere near settled in. They're having to convert the second reception room into a bedroom for the twins, and they're having to try and sell loads of their old furniture because they've downsized to a much smaller house.

Carla's house is always hectic but it's fun rather than stressful. The problem is, I'm not sure how welcome I'd be there since all that drama with the blocked phone numbers. Anyway, Carla is spending a lot of her time with the band and Danny is glued to Elliot's hip, so I don't suppose we'll be hanging out that much outside of school anyway. Mum is still working double, splitting her time between her day job and the wine brewing business in the pub, Billy and Frogsplash are out enjoying their freedom after completing their exams, and Graham seems to be taking on fewer shifts than ever, so he'll be my main carer over the holidays.

It's very intense having him check everything I eat and making me weigh it and put it into the *Thinspiration for Teens* Calorie Calculator before I'm allowed to eat it, but it is a sure-fire way to make sure I don't cheat on my diet. I feel hungry and sometimes weak and dizzy, but I know it's OK because I'm still eating the recommended intake of 1,300 calories. My body just needs to get used to it. It's the freedom to be alone that I miss. He's always there, even when I'm alone in my room, knowing he's downstairs guarding the kitchen makes me feel stressed and anxious. I wish I at least had a holiday to look forward to, but I screwed that up for myself and the rest of the family a long time ago.

Thursday 22nd July 2021

Today was the last day of term and a half day – just barely enough time for the end-of-year school assembly, in which we all sing the school song celebrating the legend of Duke John Jameson. Singing those lyrics that I've come to know so well and looking at the school crest so proudly emblazoned above the main stage where all the high-level staff were seated, I felt a huge thrill come over me. I am in possession of an enormous secret. I have an actual, hand-written account of what the Duke was really like, and of an incredible scandal within his life.

Admittedly, it is no secret that he was a scandalous man, but I might just be the only person ever to know this part of the story. The diary has become extremely precious to me. It has been there for me when all others have failed. It has been there when my friends have fallen out over some inconsequential disagreement. It has been there when my family has fallen to pieces and had the happiness, energy and strength entirely drained from everyone in it. It has been there when corruption and manipulation have suffocated the trust and hope within me, because even if I can no longer believe in anyone in my life, at least I can believe in Edmund.

But the diary is drawing to a close – only a few short pages remain. As keen as I am to learn the fates of Edmund, Carolina and Duke John Jameson, I am too afraid to end it. What if Edmund lets me down? What if he's not the hero I thought he was? Or what if there is no end? Perhaps the diary just stops, with no conclusion whatsoever. Perhaps there is no happily ever after and the Duke wins, taking the diary from Edmund, never to be written in again. But then who buried the diary in that rusty old metal tin? I have to believe it was Edmund, or Carolina – who else would want it preserved in that way?

Even if there is a happy ending, I am hesitant to read it. What will I have left once the diary is done? I will have nothing to turn to, no story to escape into. And what will I do with the information I've learnt? I'm sure some local historians would be fascinated to know this even darker side of the famously dishonest Duke John Jameson, and even some major museums might be interested in such a well-preserved first-hand account of eighteenth-century life. But then what? It wouldn't be mine any more. Edmund wouldn't be mine any more. I'm being selfish, but none of these people can miss what they never had. Only I will miss the diary when it's gone.

Friday 23rd July 2021

The first day of the summer holidays was about as bad as they come. I awoke much later than usual, which is odd because my body clock is normally very accurate, but I have been tired since starting this diet, and maybe my body is winding down for the long summer break. My stomach was screaming out for food before I'd even opened my eyes. I ate less than a thousand calories yesterday, so I knew I was allowed to have breakfast. I went straight down to the kitchen, where Graham was keeping vigil in his usual seat, the one closest to the fridge. I said nothing to him as I opened the top cupboard and reached for a box of cereal. He said nothing as I bent down to the bottom cupboard to get a bowl. I poured the cereal and went to the fridge to get milk. It was not until I'd unscrewed the cap that he spoke.

"What do you think you're doing?" his tone was accusatory, though he did not look up from his newspaper to glare at me. It was unnerving.

"Getting breakfast," I replied shortly, irritably.

"No, you're not. You ate last night."

"I did not!"

"Don't lie to me, Samantha. You've been eating in the middle of the night. Your disgusting habits are growing worse!" He looked at me this time, and his face was taut with rage.

"I have not! I've been asleep all night, I only just woke up!"

"At nine thirty? That's not like you. Anyone would think you'd got up in the night when everyone else was in bed!"

"I didn't, I swear!"

"So, what's this then?" he said, and he got up to retrieve a large, empty packet of pasta salad from the bin.

"I don't know; I didn't eat it."

"This belonged to your mother. She was going to take it into work for lunch today, but when she looked in the fridge this morning it was gone. Do you know how many calories were in this, Samantha?"

"I don't care because I didn't eat it!"

"Dirty, greedy liar! You're a fat girl and you're a disgrace!"

"How do you know it wasn't Frogsplash or Billy who ate it?"

"Because look!" he said, delving further into the contents of the bin. "Empty kebab wrappers, and chip paper, too. I was still awake when they got in last night and they were both eating large kebabs and chips."

"That doesn't mean they didn't eat the pasta, too!"

"Are you accusing them of greed, Samantha? Because we both know you're the only glutton around here…"

"I didn't eat it. I don't know who it was, but it wasn't me."

"Lies! You thought you could sneak down here and stuff your face when no one was watching, just like the first time I caught you. You're a typical woman – a liar and a sneak."

"I am not lying," I said one final time. I would not stand there and be repeatedly accused of a crime I did not commit. My stomach was rumbling, churning like a tornado, folding in on itself through lack of use. I poured the milk on my cereal and opened the drawer to get a spoon, but Graham grabbed me by the wrist to stop me.

"Don't you dare," he said coldly, squeezing my wrist with all of his strength, but I would not let him overpower me. With my free hand I scrambled around in the drawer for a spoon. His right hand continued to grip mine, but with his left he slammed the drawer shut, hoping to catch my hand. It would have been extremely painful if he had succeeded, but I was too quick. Growing ever more frustrated, he now reached over to the worktop and picked up my bowl of cereal. He lifted it above my head and poured the contents over me, milk and all. He let go of my wrist, leaving me standing, milk soaking through my pyjama top, turning it see-through and exposing my naked body underneath. I felt extremely vulnerable. Flakes of cereal covered my head and slid down the back of my neck. It dripped into my ears and eyes and my body reacted in the only way it knew how: I began to cry.

"Now clean it up," he said. "Do it quickly or I'll make you eat it off the floor instead."

He watched me clean it all and even shooed the dogs away when they came to help by licking up the dregs. I went upstairs to shower, and when the drain clogged with soggy cereal, I'm ashamed to say I ate a bit of it, shower suds and all. It was revolting, it was a moment of madness. I was just so hungry. I wanted desperately to escape but I knew he wouldn't let me go out on my own because he'd think I was going to buy food, so I sent messages to my friends asking if they'd like to meet up.

"Sorry, I'd love to but we're packing for Puerto Rico and Mum's getting in her usual panic! See you as soon as I get back, promise. Xx." Carla said.

"OMG would LOVE to but I'm helping Dad decorate my new room and I'd feel bad leaving him to do it on his own, he spent so much on my new double bed!" came Danny's response. I was utterly alone. Sadly, desperately, I turned to Edmund and Carolina to give me the strength and hope I needed.

"So, the dose might not kill the brute?" Carolina didst asketh.

"There be but a small chance that 'twill, but 'tis an old potion brewed many years ago, and 'twill only have lessened in potency over time."

"What might't do then, if't doth fail to extinguish him?"

"'Twill steal away his consciousness and he wilt plunge into deepest sleep – not a thousand battle-cries could rouse him. His heart wilt slow and his breathing wilt be strained and heavy for several days. He wilt awaketh drowsy and weary, his body shalt feeleth leaden and thick with sloth, but he wilt move again in time. If't doth not kill him his normal faculties wilt return to him within a week."

"A week is plenty," said she, "give 't to him now, before he waketh! Then thou must drag him out to the bottom of the poppy field and meet me there. He is a great, heavy beast, I warn thee, but 'tis downhill from here and you needn't be gentle with him. Drag him, push him, roll him, use whatever means necessary! Meet me at the bottom of the poppy field 'neath the willow, hurry!"

I didst carry out mine lady's bidding without question. I didst return to the Duke's collapsed body in the hall and pour mine bitterest poison down his throat. I watched in fascination for signs of death, but the man wast so heavily dosed with drink and sleeping potion that no change didst cometh o'er him. I listened to his chest; it gave a long, wheezing breath. I began to drag him, as mine Carolina instructed, out of his home and onto the o'erlooking field. He wast indeed a great weight, but mine hatred and determination wast greater still. I rolled him down the poppy field like a monstrous, drunken hay bale.

There I found her, shovel in her frail arms, digging furiously.

"Mine sweet, how didst one as weak from starvation as thee build so deep a trench in such brief time as this?!"

"Dearest Edmund, I am driven by a loathing far deeper than this trench! Mine is the strength of a hundred innocent victims, mine arms art those of the brewer from whom he stole this land, of the lady whom he tricked into funding his schooling, of the teachers whom he forces to work under strict rule, of the children he beats and all the women he hath e'er abused! I dig with the force of all whom he hath wronged!"

Her words didst moveth me, and grateful wast I to behold that she hadst provided an extra shovel for mine own hand's toiling. With the haste and fury of all the sufferers of injustice that has't e'er lived, we didst dig a cold, deep grave for the Duke. At what time we didst feel satisfied, we didst taketh one final look at the disgraceful man. I pressed mine ear to his chest, and once more did I hear that deep, wheezing breath. He lived, but he would liveth no more. Together we didst push him in and swiftly we didst shovel the earth back into the hole, covering him with a heap of dirt six foot deep. The man would breathe his last that night.

This is unbelievable! They buried him alive! There are still more pages left but now I'm even more terrified to read them. What if they get caught? How will they explain the sudden disappearance of the Duke who owned the school?

Friday 30th July 2021

FAMINE AND FEAST, FREEDOM AND FURY, FRIENDS AND FOES – FUN AND FRUSTRATION FOR FAMILY FAILING TO FUNCTION

What began as a mild emotional ghost train has accelerated into a full-speed, exceptionally volatile emotional roller-coaster, but will all of the passengers ride it out, or will some fly off the rails?

It's a confusing battle of wills. I don't want to show Graham any signs of weakness, and I know that giving into food makes me weak. But by not eating I'm doing exactly what he wants me to do, and that's weak too. Plus, there's all the stuff on the website that says self-control is a source of empowerment and that it's good for my confidence because I'm setting and achieving personal goals. And then there's that little voice in my head that says *"I do want to be thinner; I do want to look like the models and the actresses…"* It's so hard to know what's right. All I know is that I have to avoid conflict with Graham. I would do anything to not have him shout at me again.

I'm starving. We're going to Dad's tomorrow and I've never been more excited to go, not because we'll be celebrating my birthday a few days early, but simply because I'll be allowed to eat. How much longer can this continue before somebody takes notice? I've thought so many times about telling Mum, but I know I can't because Graham always has a clever way of twisting things. He'll say that it was all me, that I've got an eating disorder, and then he'll make me show Mum the browsing history on my computer and it'll look like I've been obsessively counting calories, but it was him all along. He must have planned it, right from the start, to do it all from my PC so it could never be traced back to him.

He'll make Mum think I've got a really bad problem and then she'll definitely make me see a counsellor or a psychiatrist and when I tell them what's going on, they won't believe me either. They'll say I'm desperate for attention or something patronising like that. It'll be just like Mack with the painting. Yesterday when Graham brought up my dinner, he fed it to the dogs right in front of me and made me watch. For a split second I actually felt angry at them. They were stealing my food and they didn't even care. When they were done Graham picked the plate up, called them to follow him out and rolled an apple on the floor towards me. I waited until he was long gone before I ate it.

Saturday 31st July 2021

There are chips and dips and sausage rolls and battered prawns and so much more, and we haven't even had cake yet! Dad went full kiddie party platter, probably for Stephanie's sake, but I have never felt more like a toddler at a birthday party than I did when we arrived today. There were mini pizzas and these swirly jam sandwich wheels that I haven't had in years, and jelly with sweets in and every shape, flavour and variety of crisps you can imagine! I still haven't really calmed down from the excitement of it even though I'm completely stuffed!

After the initial feeding frenzy, Dad put some music on the TV and we've just been laughing and joking and having a great time all day. At one point this pop song that's been everywhere lately called 'Shine on Superstar!' came on and Stephanie started jumping up and down wildly, screaming that it was her favourite song, and to my astonishment Frogsplash got up and started dancing with her. He must absolutely hate that song, but he didn't let it show, not even to me or Dad. Steph gave me a lovingly hand-made birthday card and I was amazed by my present from Dad. It was a set of professional quality curling tongs and a whole bundle of hair products.

"Dad this is amazing!" I said genuinely. "Thank you!"

"You haven't already got some, have you? I've kept the receipt in case you want to exchange them."

Why do grown-ups always do this?!

"No, this is brilliant, I can't wait to try them!"

"Well the lady in the shop said that thirteen is about the age girls start styling their hair properly, and she said these were good ones. She wasn't just tricking me into a sale, was she?"

"I don't know, Dad, I don't know what other girls do but I'm well happy with these, honest!"

"Oh good, good. I'd noticed you'd let your hair grow long so I thought I'd take a chance…"

The truth is I haven't, it's just that no one in my household has thought to take me to the hairdressers in a while, but perhaps that's not such a bad thing now.

"Can I try?" Stephanie asked when I opened the box to have a proper look. I almost said no, but then I had a better idea.

"OK, but you have to let me do it because it can be a bit dangerous. These things get very hot so you must never touch them, OK?"

"OK," she agreed, and I plugged the tongs into the socket but made sure they were switched off. I gently wrapped her soft wisps of hair, which are already perfectly curled, around the tongs and pretended to wait for it to set.

"There you go," I said. "Look how beautiful and curly it's made your hair!"

"Wow!" she said, amazed, and I thought how wonderful it is to have a sister to share these things with. I watched her happily dancing to the music clutching a handful of cheesy breadsticks and at that moment I made a silent promise that I would never, ever let her go on a diet.

Dad's been really amazing since Steph came on the scene. He's really stepped up, and not just for her, either. He's made a real effort with me and been a real support to Frogsplash, too. It couldn't have come at a better time really. If he hadn't remained so grounded through all these surprises life has thrown at him, I'm sure I'd have lost faith in adults altogether. Speaking of grown men facing tumultuous times, Richard arrived home just after eight p.m. and he was not alone. We heard him in the hall laughing wildly with several other, indistinguishable voices. It sounded as though they had all tumbled into the kitchen haphazardly, with muffled incantations of "oops!" "sorry!" "didn't see you there!" as they went.

Eventually Richard entered the living room alone, the owners of the unfamiliar voices still loitering in the kitchen. He was wearing the same baseball cap he had worn during the rap, as well as a huge grin on his face. I could tell he was a bit tipsy.

"Hey!" he said. "Happy birthday, Sam! Where's your Dad?"

"He's just putting Steph to bed. Actually, you might want to tell your mates to keep it down a bit... who are they anyway?"

"Oh, they'll come in soon, I told them to wait in the kitchen 'til after the big reveal."

"The big…?" and then I noticed a trickle of blood dripping slowly down the side of his head. "Richard, you're bleeding! Take your cap off, I think you've cut your head or something, let me take a look – you can't be too careful with a head injury."

"Oh, they said that might happen, but the hat's integral to the routine! It won't have the same effect without it."

"He must be drunker than he looks," Frogsplash said to me, "he's not making any sense."

"Does THIS make sense?" Richard said dramatically, and he whipped the cap off his head to reveal a thin layer of short, brown hair atop his bloodied scalp.

"Oh my god! You got the transplant, you *actually* did it!" I said, astonished.

"But you said they cost a fortune!" said Froggo. "Where did you get the cash?"

"Well I got a pretty decent redundancy package in the end; thought I deserved a bit of a treat after that whole debacle!"

"Redundancy?" I asked.

"Oh, didn't your dad tell you? The findings of the investigation were irrefutable – all my fault, apparently."

"But that's not true, it was Wilcox's idea!"

"I know it was, Sam, and I know it's unfair, but that's life. Some people lie to save their own skin and it works more often than you'd like to think. He threw me under the bus, no doubt about that, but I'm not foolish enough to challenge the likes of him. All things considered; I've come out of it all right. I mean, look at me!"

I allowed my eyes to wander over his once bald head and fully take in the transformation. He looked like a child's doll that's been given a buzz cut: the places where the hair had been implanted were too perfectly distanced from each other that it made a sort of pattern, little clusters of short brown hairs, spaced in perfectly aligned rows about half a centimetre apart. Add to that the rather unnatural, straight-across hairline and the overall look was rather artificial. The blood wasn't very attractive either.

"But what did Wilcox tell them?" I asked, deciding it was best to get back to the subject in hand.

"Oh, you know, he said I have a track record for trying to appear young and hip, and that the whole rap thing was just another example of my desperate attempts to be "down with the kids". He got staff and students to back him up and everything! And he said I had it in for Jameson ever since the Kopi Luwak incident, apparently Jameson humiliated me, but if I recall it was him who ended up with coffee down his shirt! Then he said I had an "inappropriate" relationship with a group of sixth formers just because we went to the pub a few times, but I only bought drinks for the over-eighteens, so I don't see what the problem was!

"Then came his final statement. It was such a pack of lies I almost found it funny! I remember it word for word, pretty much, let me see...

"I only went along with it because Mr Roberts assured me that Oliver Jameson was in on the whole thing. He said that he and Jameson had a playful relationship ever since their first meeting, and that the rap was intended as a bit of fun that would entertain the children. I thought it would be a great idea to get involved, that my students would be blown away seeing their headmaster in such a different context, and so I thought, 'what could go wrong?' Mr Roberts assured me that I was doing a good thing – that this would draw more publicity to the amazing charity work that Oliver Jameson has been doing, raising awareness about the health of our young people by performing a rap battle that would appeal to their generation. Never did I think that it could go so horribly wrong!"

"Ugh, what an immoral, perfidious man he is!" I said. "He's getting away with everything – it's so unfair!"

"That's just the way it goes, I'm afraid. But hey, we're wasting our breath talking about him – we should be celebrating! It's your birthday and I've got hair, waheeeeeeeeey!"

He extended his celebratory "wahey" all the way to the kitchen, where he rallied his guests and led them into the living room to join us. They appeared to have raided both the fridge and the cupboards for drinks, and a couple of them apparently found it funny to drink their cocktails out of Stephanie's sippy cups, which annoyed me so much I didn't even recognise who they were.

"Hey, you're in our school!" said a girl in denim hotpants, "I helped out on your Isle of Wight trip last year, remember me?"

"Oh hey!" I said, struggling to make the connection between the drunk girl drinking vodka out of my baby sister's beaker and the sensible older role model I had looked up to at the very beginning of my secondary school life. She sat down next to me, presumably finding it some kind of novelty that she was partying with a year eight, and Richard sat down next to her.

"So, you must be in year eight now," she said, "how are you finding it?"

"It's OK, I guess. It can get stressful, but I suppose it must get a lot worse as you get to sixth form! You're in year thirteen, right?"

"Not any more," she said, beaming. "Just finished my A Levels."

"See?" said Richard, his hand squeezing her bare thigh. "It's not inappropriate!"

"That's exactly what this is," Dad said, entering the room after finally getting Stephanie to sleep. "Who are all these people, Rich, and why have you brought them here?"

"We're here for the party!" said one of the boys. "When are people going to start arriving?"

"What party?" Dad said.

"Rich said there was a party back at his place!" the boy said, not picking up on Dad's tone at all.

"Yes, *my* party!" I said, "I'm thirteen! And this is it. This *is* the party."

"Oh, you're joking!" the boy said. "This isn't a party! This is rubbish!"

"Well then you won't mind leaving, will you? Come on, the lot of you, OUT!"

"Oh, come off it, Duncan, don't be like that! I could do with a good night out. I've lost my wife, my kids, my home and now my job!"

"I know, Rich, I know, but I've got my own kids to think about. Can't you lot just go down the pub or something?"

"We can't. Denise doesn't turn eighteen 'til the twenty-eighth of August!" The girl who had been sitting next to Richard blushed and got up, looking embarrassed. She shuffled off into the hall and disappeared. The rest soon followed suit, making their excuses and departing rather awkwardly, some still carrying the drinks they had pilfered from our kitchen.

They had, in their haste to leave, made it quite clear that Richard was not welcome to join them, and that made it obvious that they'd only wanted him because he'd promised them a place to get drunk, but he didn't seem disheartened. In fact, he was still in unprecedented high spirits. After all – who needs teenage friends when you've got hair?

Tuesday 3rd August 2021

As chaotic and unpredictable as a weekend at Dad's might be, I was absolutely devastated to come home on Sunday. The food was great, spending a happy time with family was better, but my favourite thing about Dad's place now is that I feel totally accepted, no matter how many mistakes I make, stupid things I say or guilty pleasures I indulge in. I used to feel uncomfortable with Dad, but things have done a complete U-turn. But I won't even allow myself to think about moving in with him, because I know Mum would fall to pieces if that happened.

It was of almost no surprise at all that my return home was met with disappointing news.

"I'm so sorry, Sammy, but I've taken too much of my annual leave to work at the pub for Graham. I didn't want to, but before he got all these temps in, he was short-staffed and so I booked some time off to help him out. I didn't realise I'd used up quite so much until my leave request for your birthday got rejected! But you're a teenager now, you probably don't even want to spend your birthday with your mum! I bet you'd rather hang out with your friends, wouldn't you?" she asked hopefully.

"Perhaps, but they're both on holiday. Such is the curse of an August birthday! But it's no big deal, honestly, Mum, you know I don't like a fuss."

"Well, we'll at least do a barbecue like last year! I'll get Graham to start it up – he's got the day off, so you won't be on your own. Billy's working an early so he'll be home by four and I'm sure your brother will be around. I'll get home as quick as I can, I promise."

It is my thirteenth birthday, and after such a fine banquet of cheesy puffs and iced biscuits at Dad's, I decided I deserved to eat today. I knew there was only a small chance that Graham would give me a free pass for such an occasion, but I felt I owed it to myself to try. I had woken up early, but it wasn't until ten a.m. that I plucked up the nerve to go down there. He was sat at his station by the fridge, forever on duty, and one stern look from him had me hanging my head in defeat and shame. Not wanting to appear as though I'd been tempted by food, I filled a glass of water and headed back to my room.

I told myself that I would eat later, when the barbecue had started, because I knew Graham couldn't use his tricks and lies in front of everyone, especially on my birthday. But I still deserved a treat, so I decided that it was time, at last, to read the final few pages of Edmund's beautiful diary. I retrieved it from my bag and climbed back into bed, sitting cross-legged with the book held closed and flat between my hands. I knew that it was the right time to read it, I knew that I should not delay it any longer, but before I could open it, I sat there and held it, crying. I did not want to say goodbye to Edmund, but stories are meant to be told, and I owed it to him to read what he had written.

Friday 1ˢᵗ October 1723

'Tis many moons since last I wrote, for writing be the occupation of those who art so filled with discontent that they must put their woes down in ink! But I must giveth thee some parting words from which thou might procure some comfort in these otherwise hard times. I wilt not bitter mine tale with talk of that which came before, but it be true that times has't changed most astonishingly! I has't taken the role of the man I slayed. I be the Duke; I be Duke John Jameson, founder and leader of the school hither. I liveth in his quarters, I sleepeth with his wife, and I perform those duties which he ought to have performed with greater fervour and morality than the true owner of that name e'er didst!

Proud am I to claim this position, for daily I am told that I suit it better and treat mine workmen fairer. Those that teacheth hither wil't ne'er confess to seeing another Duke with some other face. Those that worketh these grounds art happier than ever since I didst claim the Duke's post, and the questions asked have been nowt and none. We art happy, the lot of us. I wil't bury this diary and the secrets it doth keepeth to ensure that none should interfere with the contentedness that we has't found. None hither hath e'er been happier nor healthier. We groweth and flourish in the wake of the deservingly deceased.

This explains everything! Stories of the Duke in his youth were of greed, selfishness and manipulation, and yet we hail him as the hero who founded a brilliant school which has always valued hard work, fairness and equal opportunities for all. The legendary Duke we sing of every year at the end of term has been Edmund all along! And we know that he and Carolina had children, but truly they were Edmund's. This means that Oliver Jameson is not a descendent of John Jameson, but of Edmund! This is incredible. All these years we've been honouring the imposter, not the man. But he was so much more deserving of honour, wasn't he? I mean he did bury a man alive, but he did it for Carolina, and for all the other victims of the true Duke!

I sat for a long time reflecting on the story of Edmund and Carolina. In the eyes of the law they had certainly done a bad thing, yet it felt every bit the classic tale of good conquering evil, and the demise of Duke John Jameson was like a shadow lifted from everyone at the school and, I'm sure, the surrounding village: the end of a miserable era. Still unsure of what to do with the diary now that I had read every word, I put it back in my handbag, where I have become accustomed to keeping it so that it's with me wherever I go.

I thought I might go for a walk to think things over and hopefully come to a decision about whether or not to share my secret with the world. Normally Graham would keep me from going out, but he would be guarding the fridge in the kitchen at the back of the house, and I could easily slip out of the front door without him noticing. And then I could arrive home later, after Mum and Billy returned from work, so that Graham couldn't get me alone and shout at me for leaving or accuse me of going to a fast food restaurant or a sweet shop or something.

Usually our shoes are kept on the rack in the hall so that we don't tread dirt into the house, but I needed to make a quick escape, so I put on a pair of jelly shoes that had been relegated to my room after so much disuse. I grabbed my handbag and slipped down the carpeted stairs almost silently. I didn't stop to grab a jacket – a summer breeze is almost laughably unthreatening compared to the wrath of Graham. I went to make my escape, but the second lock had been turned, something we never do unless the house is empty, and there were no keys hanging on the hooks where they ought to have been.

In simpler times I might have guessed that Graham had gone out, forgotten that I was still inside the house and double-locked the front door for security. But these are not simple times. Graham was still home; I could feel his presence. Suspicious of my earlier attempt to gain entry to the kitchen and surmising, I'm sure, that I was feeling bolder today on my birthday, he must have locked me in. Not only that, but he had heard me rattling at the front door, and had come running into the hallway, a satisfied sneer on his face. I was caught in his trap.

Samantha Drury: prisoner; captive.

"Thought you'd do a runner, did you?" he said gleefully.

"I had planned to go for a walk, god knows I could do with the exercise!" I said in hateful jest.

"Popping out for a snack, were you?" he said predictably. "I've already lit the barbecue, but you couldn't wait 'til then, could you? Too greedy; too impatient. I expect you thought you could get a snack now and feast later as well. You really are a 'have your cake and eat it' sort of girl!"

"I really was just going for a walk," I said irritably. "Funnily enough, I don't enjoy sitting bitterly in the same seat every day, obsessing over routine and propriety, rotting from the inside out..."

"Show me your handbag!" he demanded.

"No!" I replied. "That's personal!"

"But why do you even have it? If you were only going for a walk, then why were you bringing it with you? What have you got in there? Food? Money to buy food. Something you couldn't carry in your pocket! Show me!"

The anger within him was bubbling close beneath the surface, in danger of erupting.

"No!" I protested again. "My handbag contains my things – teenage girl things! Those things are sacrosanct."

"Pssh! Words! Meaningless. The contents of your handbag are no more precious than the contents of our kitchen bin – and both are places that I am willing to go to prove your guilt!"

"Guilt? What guilt? What can you possibly say I've done wrong? What evidence do you think you will find that will make me look guiltier than you?"

His rage, I could see, was now becoming uncontrollable.

"Let's see, shall we?" he said villainously, and he snatched the bag I had slung over my shoulder. I clutched at it desperately as it was stripped from my body. There was only one thing in it I cared about, but Graham always knows how to make a caring person suffer. He tore through the contents of my bag and it felt like he was tearing bits of me apart, ripping and shredding at all the components of my very self, tossing them aside, discarding them like old receipts, empty wrappers and out-of-date travel cards. And then he found it, as I knew he would: Edmund's diary.

"What's this?" he said, realising that he had stumbled across some personal treasure of mine.

"That's mine, give it back!" I said, although I knew it was pointless to do so. He flicked through the hand-written pages without reading them.

"Aw, is it your secret diary? I bet you've written all your little teenage girl problems in here. Ooh, what have you written about me I wonder?"

"Nothing! It's nothing to do with you!"

"You really think I care? You think I give a toss about any of the insignificant thoughts that cross your dull, boring mind? You think I want to read one word of whatever innocuous drivel is written in here? Ha! Here's what I think of your pointless little diary…"

He marched down the hall and I ran after him, hoping that I might still be able to get Edmund's diary back once Graham was done with his speech. I followed him through the kitchen and into the back garden, where the barbecue had recently been filled with coals, firelighters and firelighter fluid and lit aflame. The fire was roaring, and the grill had not yet been put over the coals. It was the worst possible moment for Graham to have found something that meant so much to me. He threw the diary into the open flames and, in an instant, it was all over. The old, thin pages crisped up in seconds, blackening and then turning to ash as I watched, tears forming rapidly in my eyes, but he was not yet done.

"Perfect," he said. "The perfect kindling – just what it needed. We'll cook our food on the ashes of your diary… and on your birthday, too, how splendid. Of course, you won't be eating much. The meat I serve you will be raw in the middle – you'd be wise not to eat it."

I didn't care about the food any more, but the enjoyment he was getting out of making me suffer on my birthday was filling me with rage and desperation. If he was willing to go this far just to see me miserable then where would it end? I had to stop it. I had to put an end to it or else it would never stop. It would only get worse and worse until he breaks me, just like he broke Mum.

"I will eat it!" I said. "I'll get sick and you'll get arrested for poisoning a child!"

"What, for under-cooking some chicken? But that's a simple mistake – a mistake your mother herself has made. No one will believe a word you say, Samantha, I'll make sure of that."

"You're a small man, aren't you?" I said, changing tack and trying his own belittling technique against him. "You're a useless, pathetic old man who can find nothing more worthwhile in your stunted little brain than picking on a thirteen-year-old girl!"

"I AM NOT USELESS," he bellowed. "I AM THE ONLY USEFUL LIVING THING IN THIS ENTIRE HOUSE. I HOLD EVERYTHING TOGETHER. WITHOUT ME YOU WOULD ALL FALL APART!"

"We'd be better off without you," I said calmly. "You're the one that needs us. You need to bully us to make you feel powerful. But you aren't powerful. You're impotent."

That last word must have left an awfully bitter taste because he seemed to suck on the roof of his mouth like he'd just swallowed something nasty. He lurched towards me and grabbed me by my ponytail. He pulled my head down so I was bent backwards, then he leant over me and hissed in my ear:

"You don't get to talk to me like that. Don't you ever talk to me like that again. Apologise, NOW!"

"No!" I protested. "Pathetic little man! Pulling on my ponytail like a schoolgirl in a playground fight!"

"What did you say?"

"You heard me!" I said, although he was pulling my hair so hard I felt my scalp burning with pain. For one bizarre moment I was reminded of Richard and his ridiculous hair transplant. It was a funny thought, and in such contrast to what was happening there and then that it suddenly became wildly amusing and I let out a manic laugh. This was perhaps the most infuriating insult of all, and Graham certainly seemed to react badly to it. He was at the point of no return – no amount of reasoning or logic would have made him stop, the one and only thing on his mind was making me regret what I'd said and extinguishing that spark within me that had driven me to say them. It was time for him to fight fire with fire.

He wrenched me away from the patio where I stood and dragged me to the side of the garden where the barbecue continued to blaze, the flames licking at the final remnants of Edmund's diary: the leather cover which had bound those fine, delicate pages. I watched it turning blacker and blacker as he dragged my head so close to the flames that instantly I felt my cheeks turn scarlet. In no time at all my eyes filled with the smoke and I had to squeeze them shut as tightly as I could. I could hear his voice. He was saying something, ranting still, but I couldn't make sense of the words. My only sensations were pain and fear.

I was right that he would never stop, that it would just keep getting worse and worse, that he had lost control and would stop at nothing. He would burn me alive just so that he could feel that he had overpowered me. He held my face inches away from the flames, but he could have pushed me further in at any time, or the fire could rise suddenly, it might hit another firelighter and then it would swallow my head whole, engulfing it in flame. The heat was blasting my face as though my head was in an oven, and although tears were filling my eyes, they were dry before they had fallen down my cheeks. Then I heard a different voice shouting. Rescue.

"LET GO OF HER, YOU MONSTER!"

He let go at once, whether he was simply following instructions or whether he'd done it out of shock I do not know. I pulled myself away from the flames and opened my eyes. There was Mum running towards me and Billy standing in the doorway which opened out onto the garden, gaping in horror at the scene he had walked in on. I ran into Mum's arms and she clutched me close to her chest, but quickly felt the heat coming from my cheeks.

"My god, you're boiling! Billy, take her to wash her face and make sure she drinks some water!"

"You take her," he said, not unkindly. "She needs her mum, and I need a word with my dad."

Mum rushed me to the kitchen sink and ran the cold tap. She didn't need to tell me to splash my face, I was desperate for it. I let the sink fill up while I threw handfuls of water onto myself, then when it was full, I submerged my face in it, and it was the most wonderful, cooling relief I have ever felt. When I came back up for air Mum was waiting by my side with a cold glass of orange juice.

"Here," she said, "the sugar will ease the shock."

I drank it gratefully. I was weak enough from lack of food, but I wasn't sure if Mum knew any of that just yet. Still, there must have been some reason for her and Billy's sudden and dramatic entrance, for they weren't due home for several hours. I knew I ought to have felt shaky and faint, but instead I felt a surge of strength. I stormed back into the garden, clutching my orange juice, to watch this fresh scene unfold before me.

"... I found them in the "confidential" drawer in your office!" Billy was saying to his dad.

"And what were you doing in there?" Graham said viciously.

"I'm sick of those temps!" Billy said. "You've taken all this time off work just to lounge around at home... or so I thought! It turns out you were taking time off to terrorise Sam! But you haven't been at work and I've been left with all these temps who don't have a clue what they're doing, and they keep coming to me with their problems because there's no one else there they can call boss. You haven't been there and it's the busiest season of the year. So, I thought, if they're going to treat me like a manager and you're going to leave me there on my own to deal with all the problems a manager has to deal with, then I'm going to take a break like a manager. I can't sit and eat my lunch in peace with that lot bugging me, so I let myself into your office and ate my chicken burger alone.

"But an hour is a long time and I started to get bored, plus I was feeling guilty about having burger and chips when Frogsplash and I are supposed to be getting six-packs, so I went on your computer to search for protein shakes. I had only typed in three letters when your auto-fill kicked in and showed me a search term you'd typed in previously. Why, Dad, tell me why you would be searching for 'pro-anorexia websites'? It said you'd clicked on one called *'Thinspiration for Teens'* which is specifically aimed at teenage girls. But you're well in your fifties, Dad, and you're a bloke. You don't even have any daughters, unless you count Sam.

"And then it all started falling into place. It occurred to me how thin Sam's got lately. It's always difficult to notice when you see somebody every day, so I regret that I didn't pick up on it until now. But even then, Dad, I didn't really believe in what the evidence seemed to be pointing to. I thought I must have got it wrong, so I looked up this *Thinspiration* website and read some reviews. There were hundreds of parenting and healthcare pages, as well as the NHS website, condemning it as an extremely dangerous tool which over-calculates how many calories are in food, greatly under-calculates how many calories girls should consume, and encourages negative attitudes towards eating. Now why would you be interested in a site like that, Dad?

"But still I couldn't believe it. I thought I must have got the wrong end of the stick, but by this point I was suspicious, and I was running out of ways to dismiss the evidence that was piling up in front of me, so instead I looked for more. I upturned your entire office, not so much looking for evidence to incriminate you as for something to exonerate you, because you're my dad and you're all I've got left. I didn't want to believe the awful things that, when I think about it, I've been pushing to the back of my mind for a very long time. I should have been braver; I shouldn't have tried to hide from what my instincts were telling me was happening. My desperate need for a parent made me weak, made me selectively blind to your actions and your treatment of the people around you.

"But I never knew it had gone this far. If I'd known what you were doing to Sam, I would have torn you limb from limb. Pathetic little man, preying on the weak! Or at least you thought she was weak, but I bet she's been putting up a fight, hasn't she? And Frogsplash, it all makes sense now! We all thought he was falling apart, but it was you destroying him, it was you, it's always been you! And then he came back stronger than ever and you hated it! So, you sought your revenge. You didn't want him to find happiness pursuing a future you didn't approve of, so you withheld his post!"

Only then did I notice the envelopes in Billy's hand, flapping wildly as he gesticulated towards Graham.

"I thought they were nothing when I first found them – after all, I was looking for signs that you'd been bullying Sam. But when I found letters addressed to Frederick Andrew Drury in your 'confidential' file I didn't think twice about reading them...

Dear Mr Drury,

Thank you for your recent application to Brigley House sixth-form college. We were highly impressed by your application and are delighted to offer you a provisional place. Should you achieve your predicted GCSE grades or higher you will automatically be accepted into Brigley House. If you achieve lower than your predicted grades do not worry, there is still a good chance that you will be offered a place...

"You must have known how much this news meant to Froggo – he had his heart set on this college! And then there are these: five more letters, all with provisional offers that Frogsplash spent ages applying for! I called Cassie as soon as I found them, and she was just as confused as I was. You intercepted Froggo's mail and hid it, but why?"

Mum had come out to the patio and had sat down at the garden table. I followed her but stayed standing; I felt stronger standing. We watched together as Billy bravely confronted his father.

"For his own good!" Graham responded. "I told you what those colleges are like."

"Liar," said Billy coldly. "And what about Sam? How can you possibly defend the way you've been treating her?"

"Oh, come on! Chubby girl like her becoming a teenager, it clearly wasn't just puppy fat! She needed a firm hand, someone to force the issue before it got out of control. She'd have thanked me in a year's time when she was thin and popular!"

"She is not chubby. She never was!" Billy said. "And the only thing getting out of control was you. Control – that's what it's always been about with you. Face it, Dad, you've finally been caught out. I'm disgusted with myself for having taken so long to see it, but I'm much more disgusted with you. Get out. Get the hell out of here and never, ever come back."

And perhaps because it was coming from his son, or maybe just because he knew he'd been defeated, Graham didn't argue. His face was red with rage, but he didn't seem to be able to put it into words. He walked up to the garden table where Mum and I had been watching, picked up one of the chairs and hurled it aggressively at the back of the garden where it crashed, smashing a ceramic plant pot. And then he left.

Billy came to sit with me and Mum, and we all sat in silence.

"I hope you don't mind…" Billy said after a while. "I mean, me sending him out like that. You probably had a few things you wanted to say to him too."

"I couldn't have said it better than you," she replied. "Well done, Billy, that was incredibly brave. And I'm afraid I think I will still get the opportunity to speak my mind to him. He'll be back, even if it's just to collect his things. A man as stubborn as him won't be that easy to get rid of, unfortunately."

And just then we heard keys in the door, and we all froze. Billy looked furious, and stood up to confront his father yet again, but then he laughed when he saw Frogsplash strolling in from the kitchen, a simple smile on his face, carrying a huge birthday cake.

"Surprise!" he said and set it down on the garden table. "Your present's upstairs but I got this as a bit of an extra treat... I had it made specially! You two are home early – what's going on?"

"It's a long story," Mum said. "Sit down, we'll tell you everything."

"But first," Billy said, "let Sam eat cake."

We sat eating cake and told Frogsplash everything that had happened. Billy showed him all the acceptance letters from sixth-form colleges, but it was all so much to take in I don't think he really knew how to feel. He told us the truth about Graham chucking all his consoles away, confirming that the accusation that he'd bunked off school to get them was nothing but hateful calumny. Mum explained how he'd isolated her from her friends, stopping her from seeing Trudy and changing Carla's mum's number in her phone. Billy was appalled by what he was hearing – he'd been blissfully unaware of so many of his father's crimes until today. It must have been awful for him, coming to terms with the fact that he couldn't trust the only parent he had left.

"You don't have to see him any more if you don't want to," Mum told him. "And even if you do want a relationship with him, you're still welcome to stay living with us. It's completely up to you."

"I don't want anything to do with him," Billy said firmly. "But are you sure you don't mind me staying?"

"Of course! You're family, Billy, and you've suffered just as much as we have. It's not your fault your dad turned out like that. And you're sixteen now, that means you're legally old enough to choose not to live with your parents. He can't make you do anything you don't want to do."

That's exactly what Graham can do, I thought, it's his favourite trick.

"What about you, Froggo?" Billy asked. "Is it OK if I stay here, even if we have to share a room?"

"Mate, of course it is!"

"Well it seems silly for me to have the biggest bedroom now that I'm alone," Mum said. "You two should move into my room and I'll take yours – at least then you'll have a bit more space. And you never know, I might be able to afford to get the loft extended soon, especially now Graham's not around to take my profits."

"He was stealing your profits?" Billy asked, astonished.

"I suppose it was stealing, yes. The wine was selling really well at the pub, but he never paid me anything. He said he was doing me a favour giving me somewhere permanent I could sell it rather than just the odd Christmas fair, so he took everything. Of course, I'll have to find somewhere new to sell it from now on."

"You should sell it online," Billy said. "I'll help you set up a website."

"And you should do that online video promotion idea you had!" I said, "That was brilliant, and it was only Graham who was stopping you."

"Maybe I will." Mum smiled. "It seems Graham was stopping us all from doing a lot of the things we wanted to do. How do you guys feel about going away for a week? I bet I could find some good last-minute deals."

Tuesday 31st August 2021

We had the best time in Barcelona. We went to water parks and beaches and I made so many friends at the hotel where we were staying. One night, Billy got a bit too drunk on cocktails and became a little emotional about everything that's happened recently, which is understandable. He kept apologising to us for Graham's behaviour and he seemed particularly upset about what he'd put me through, but we just kept telling him that there was nothing to apologise for, then we took him up to bed and in the morning he didn't remember a thing.

We're back at home now and Mum wasted no time in reconnecting with her friends, including Carla's mum, Maria, and Danny's mum, Amelia. She explained everything that had happened with Graham and they kept saying how sorry they were that they hadn't made more of an effort to find out what was going on. I told Danny and Carla everything too, apart from the bit about Edmund's diary, and they apologised profusely for not recognising the signs. It's crazy that the only one to blame is the only one who doesn't feel the need to apologise. I wouldn't accept it even if he did, none of us would. It's not like he just made a mistake or messed up a bit, everything he did was calculated and malicious.

Graham's pernicious presence in this house could have had a severe and lasting effect, but we aren't going to let it. We haven't let it turn us bitter or untrusting; we haven't let it take away our self-esteem and it won't ever let our love for Billy turn to resentment: the cycle of acrimony ends here. With the help of her friends, Mum has returned almost entirely back to her old self, although she still goes white whenever she hears unexpected footsteps on the gravel of our front drive. She keeps double-locking the front door, too, even though she knows Graham still has both of his keys. But I understand. The longer we can delay his return the better, even if it's only for a few seconds.

Sunday 5th September 2021

THE DARK DAYS HAVE BEEN DEFEATED – NOW SAMANTHA DRURY COMES UP FIGHTING!

Samantha Drury is a nervous pre-teen no more! She is tougher than ever after facing the toughest of times. Now thirteen and feeling stronger and more righteous than ever before, she vows to take down the patriarchy one corrupt figure at a time!

Today was the last day of the summer holidays, and it was every bit as eventful as those which preceded it. Billy has been in contact with Arnie, his older half-brother, who is now travelling in Thailand. Arnie has been driven mad with phone calls from Graham since his dramatic dismissal from the household, and just when he thought he'd got him off his back, Graham called him with some alarming news: he was at the airport waiting for a flight to Thailand! Apparently, he's become obsessed with the idea of joining his eldest son on his gap year travels, which has got to be one of the worst things a parent could do – even Richard would know better than that!

Arnie has stayed strong and refused to inform his father of his exact location, but Graham found out through social media the name of the last hostel he was staying in, so he's got a good idea of where to start looking. It sounds like he's lost the plot! And now poor Arnie is looking over his shoulder wherever he goes just like we were. He was saving up for that trip for over a year! If I were him, I would re-route to somewhere completely different – America, India or Australia, perhaps.

But Arnie's strife was our relief – Graham won't come knocking any time soon. And we knew that he wasn't at the pub, which meant Billy could go and get his stuff from the flat and Mum could retrieve her wine-brewing equipment. Frogsplash offered to help and I said I'd help too, although I probably couldn't carry much of the heavy equipment. It was Billy who said that I probably shouldn't be there, that the pub had become a place for sleazy old drunks and that I might be better off elsewhere. He's become very protective of me after everything that's happened, but not in an oppressive sort of way.

So, Mum called Amelia and she was happy to have me. Danny decided to invite Carla, too, so we could all be together. We had missed out on so much precious time together in recent months. We sat in the shade in Danny's garden while her twin brothers played in the paddling pool. Every now and then they would misfire their water pistols and hit us instead of each other, but this was a small and welcome relief from the continuing summer heat. We were talking about going back to school and wondering what year nine was going to be all about when Amelia called out from inside the house:

"Danny, there's someone at the door for you!"

She looked confused at this. They've only just moved into their new house and we're normally the only people who visit her anyway. It might have been Elliot if he weren't absolutely terrified to meet Danny's parents. Danny went to see who it was, and I don't think any of us could have predicted that she would return, thirty seconds later, leading Ruby Driscoll behind her.

"Guys," Danny said uncertainly, "Ruby's got something important to tell us. She's really gone out of her way to find out where I live, so I think we should at least hear her out."

Ruby has not been especially friendly to any of us over the past two years at school, but I could tell straight away from her sheepish body language that she was not here to mock or criticise or put us down. Something had happened which had knocked the confidence out of her, and I know from recent experience exactly how that feels. We sat down at the garden table and, cautiously, she joined us.

"I've been expelled," she blurted out before we even had time to wonder what was going on.

"Oh no! Why?" Carla asked.

"Wilcox. He screwed me over. He set the whole thing up."

"What thing?" Carla asked encouragingly. She, of course, knows the bitter sting of Wilcox's corruption better than any of us.

"You know how Charlotte's gang have got a reputation for being rule-breakers? Well, apparently, they did some really bad stuff before I joined their group. I had no idea, but Wilcox decided to use this to his advantage. Instead of expelling them he got them to recruit me as part of their gang."

"But why?" I asked.

"Because he saw on my record that I went to a private primary school. He wanted them to find some way to get some dirt on me, do a bit of digging, you know, defamation of character."

"Trisha Tijani!" I said suddenly.

"You what?" asked Ruby.

"It was ages ago... I didn't know who she was talking about... Charlotte was talking to the local news journalist, Trisha Tijani, about trashing someone's reputation. I thought she'd meant Rachel Levine!"

"Believe it or not, Charlotte's not that petty," Ruby explained. "She hates Rachel, don't get me wrong, but a petty feud would never have been enough to provoke her into making deals with an actual journalist. Wilcox must have got her good, to make her go to those lengths. No, she was definitely going after me. She was looking for dirt, but there wasn't any. I've always behaved myself – I've got my sporting career to think about and I'm not stupid enough to tarnish that by doing something reckless. Well, I thought I wasn't..."

"When Charlotte couldn't find anything to damage my reputation, Wilcox ordered her to coax me into doing something bad – really bad – and then he was going to blackmail my parents. You know that prat Jamie in sixth form that everyone hates? The guy who cheated on pretty much every girl in his year. Well they persuaded me to slash the tyres of his car. Only it wasn't his car, it belonged to the school governor. He was visiting Wilcox about the investigation into that stupid rap battle. Of course, I got caught, it was all on CCTV, and no one believed me that the girls put me up to it.

"Then Wilcox called my parents. He said he was going to expel me and that I'd never get another chance at a decent education unless they paid for me to go private again. So, he said he'd let me stay on at Duke John Jameson if they paid him half the amount that a private school would charge in fees – he said it was a bargain, the scumbag. But my parents aren't stupid enough to play into the hands of someone like that, so they took the expulsion and now I'm going to a normal school. That's my punishment. Wilcox showed them the CCTV footage in front of me, it was awful. Wilcox ruined my life, and he's trying to do the same to you, Danny. You went to a private primary, didn't you?"

"Yes!"

"I knew it. He's got Charlotte and the other two trying to get you on side and then they're going to trick you into doing something awful. Don't fall for it, Danny. You can't let Wilcox win."

She looked devastated as she delivered these final words, and then she left rather hurriedly, perhaps because she didn't want us to see her cry.

"That man will stop at nothing," Carla said. "He nearly destroyed our friendship after the sweet business went sour."

"And he threw Richard under the bus during the rap investigation," I said.

"And now he's trying to blackmail my parents into paying for my education!" Danny added.

"Well, you know what year nine is all about now?" I said. "We are going to take Wilcox down."